A SINNER'S KISS

"Why is it, Miss Ellingham, that nearly every time I see you out of doors, you are with a different gentleman? Locked in an embrace."

"You exaggerate, my lord."

"Not really. First it was Pengrove, then Rosen, and now Roddington. Is this some sort of contest? Do you hope to kiss every unwed man in London this Season?"

"Do not presume to judge me, my lord," she said hotly. "You know nothing about me."

"I know that you have a fondness for kissing."

"Who I kiss and where I kiss them is none of your concern."

"What if I decided that it should be?"

"Ha!" She tossed her head, revealing the slender column of her throat. Lord, what he wouldn't do for the right to nibble at that delicate nape.

Carter reached out and placed his palm beneath her chin, bringing her face around so their eyes met. Then he slowly, gently brushed his thumb across her lips. As if reading his thoughts, she suddenly moistened her lips with the tip of her tongue. They glistened in the moonlight, so soft, so plump, so tempting.

"Ah, to hell with it," Carter muttered as he reached for her . . .

Books by Adrienne Basso

HIS WICKED EMBRACE

HIS NOBLE PROMISE

TO WED A VISCOUNT

TO PROTECT AN HEIRESS

TO TEMPT A ROGUE

THE WEDDING DECEPTION

THE CHRISTMAS HEIRESS

HIGHLAND VAMPIRE

HOW TO ENJOY A SCANDAL

NATURE OF THE BEAST

THE CHRISTMAS COUNTESS

HOW TO SEDUCE A SINNER

Published by Zebra Books

How To SEDUCE A SINNER

Adrienne Basso

ZEBRA BOOKS
KENSINGTON PUBLISHING CORP.
http://www.kensingtonbooks.com

ZEBRA BOOKS are published by

Kensington Publishing Corp.
119 West 40th Street
New York, NY 10018

All Kensington titles, imprints, and distributed lines are available at special quantity discounts for bulk purchases for sales promotion, premiums, fund-raising, educational, or institutional use.

Special book excerpts or customized printings can also be created to fit specific needs. For details, write or phone the office of the Kensington Special Sales Manager: Attn. Special Sales Department. Kensington Publishing Corp., 119 West 40th Street, New York, NY 10018. Phone: 1-800-221-2647.

Zebra and the Z logo Reg. U.S. Pat. & TM Off.

ISBN-13: 978-1-4201-0433-2
ISBN-10: 1-4201-0433-0

First Printing: January 2010
10 9 8 7 6 5 4 3 2 1

Printed in the United States of America

To Dad & Linda.
Your love, encouragement, and unending support
mean more to me than I can ever say.

Thank you—
for everything.

Chapter One

London, Spring, 1818

Dorothea's heart leapt with excitement as Mr. Arthur Pengrove shifted his position on the marble bench and moved close to her, perilously close. A gentle spring breeze blew the sweet scent of the exotic flowers from the garden into their secluded hideaway; the night sky glowed with dozens of twinkling stars; the muffled strains of music from the ballroom drifted near. It was a picture-perfect night, tailor-made for romance.

"Your eyes are the most enchanting shade of blue, Miss Ellingham. They remind me of a summer sky after dawn has struck, alight with the promise of a glorious day," he whispered as his eyes dropped to her mouth.

"Oh, Mr. Pengrove."

Dorothea's eyes fluttered shut as she leaned forward in subtle encouragement. Finally, he was going to kiss her! She had given Arthur Pengrove her exclusive attention for the past two weeks and now she was about to discover if he was the man she would marry, the partner with whom she would spend the rest of her life. It was a momentous, life-altering moment and her heart beat with excitement.

His breath wafted across her cheek. Valiantly, Dorothea tried to still her racing heart, tried to remain calm and in control. Hesitantly, timidly, Mr. Pengrove's lips at last touched hers. They felt soft, almost babyish, as they grazed her own. Her initial instinct was to recoil, but she squashed it, hoping the kiss would improve.

Alas, it did not.

How dreadfully disappointing! This was nothing at all like the tantalizing yearning she had longed to feel, the heady desire she so desperately sought.

Dorothea made a small, low sound in the back of her throat, thinking it would stimulate her reticent beau. But the noise succeeded only in startling him. Mr. Pengrove's limp, moist lips scuttled across hers a second time, then abruptly pulled away.

Dorothea's shoulders slumped. The stab of disappointment was a physical pain, deflating her body as well as her spirits. She honestly believed he could have been *the one.* He was the third man who had courted her this Season, the third man she had allowed to kiss her. Yet apparently her aunt Mildred's favorite adage of saying the third time was the charm was soundly flawed.

With effort, Dorothea resisted the strong need to lower her face into her palms and sigh heavily with frustration. It would be unforgivably rude to act so insensitively. Instead, she pressed her fingers hard against her temple, trying to ease the sudden pounding in her head.

Her despondency so overtook her awareness that she was barely conscious of Mr. Pengrove's actions until out of the corner of her eye she saw him sink down on one knee.

Oh, heavens! Now on top of her vast disappointment she was going to have to refuse his marriage proposal. The evening, which had started out with such promise and optimism, was fast turning into an unmitigated disaster.

Mr. Pengrove took her hand, placing it between his cold, damp palms. Dorothea's head snapped up, her mind racing to formulate a response that would firmly discourage him while at the same time spare his feelings.

"Miss Ellingham." His voice was a high-pitched squeak. He cleared his throat, then tried again. "Dearest Miss Ellingham. Dorothea. These past few weeks we have spent together have been a joy. More than anything, I wish to formalize our attachment, to make permanent our relationship and legalize our union. However, before I make a formal declaration to you, I must speak with your guardian. If you are agreeable?"

Dorothea stared down at him, unsure where to begin. He looked unfailingly earnest in the moonlight and terribly young. "My uncle, Mr. Fletcher Ellingham, is my legal guardian, but as you well know he has not journeyed to London for the Season," she replied.

"Then I suppose that role is now relegated to your sister," Mr. Pengrove said slowly. "Or rather her husband, Mr. Jason Barrington. I believe I must apply to him with my request."

Mr. Pengrove blanched slightly as he spoke, and Dorothea could not fault his reluctance. Her brother-in-law was something of a *ton* legend, known for his wild, scandalous behavior, his daring feats and dangerous exploits. He was hardly the sort of man Arthur Pengrove usually came in contact with, let alone knew.

"Actually, Gwendolyn and Jason are also not in Town. They are at home, awaiting the birth of their first child," Dorothea reported, seizing on what she thought would be the best way to extricate herself from this sticky situation. "As you no doubt remember, Jason's sister kindly agreed to be my sponsor for the Season. It therefore has fallen to her husband to act as my guardian."

Mr. Pengrove blinked. "The Marquess of Dardington?"

"Yes. And I do confess he has taken his role as my protector most seriously."

The remaining bit of color on Mr. Pengrove's earnest face drained away. Jason Barrington might be an intimidating presence, but the Marquess of Dardington was positively lethal. She did not blame Mr. Pengrove one iota for feeling ill at the prospect of facing that haughty, powerful aristocrat.

"I am certain he will require a formal request for a meeting." Mr. Pengrove removed his white linen handkerchief and wiped at the sweat forming on his brow. "It will take me several days to properly compose a letter that will adequately convey the seriousness of my intentions."

"Mr. Pengrove . . . Arthur." Dorothea gentled the tone of her voice. "I think it better for both of us if you do not rush to make an appointment to see the marquess. The household has been in an uproar lately as things have not been going as he wishes in the House of Lords. I daresay, he has been in the very blackest of tempers for the past week, far worse than usual."

"Egad!" Arthur's eyes widened.

Dorothea patted his arm solicitously. She genuinely liked Mr. Pengrove. He was but a few years older than her own age of twenty-one, possessed a pleasant face, a tall, lanky frame, and friendly, uncomplicated eyes. He had an agreeable temperament and a kind nature. Many in society labeled him dull, but Dorothea found his unsophisticated, straightforward manner soothing. He had a comfortable fortune and a lovely estate in Kent that he studiously and successfully managed.

She had been more than willing to overlook his close attachment to his overbearing mother, his somber style of dressing, and his enthusiastic passion for collecting insects. But the emotionless, soulless kiss they had just shared could not be overlooked. She shuddered, imagining herself spending the rest of her life trying to endure those kisses.

"I suppose it would be prudent to wait before approaching the marquess," Mr. Pengrove muttered, more to himself than to her. "So as to be sure I do everything correctly, properly, and most importantly in a manner that will not offend him."

Dorothea shook her head slowly. "I think 'tis even more prudent to reconsider our future."

"Reconsider?"

"Yes. I am honored beyond words to receive such marked attention from you, yet I must speak frankly. I think you are too young to wed, Mr. Pengrove. And I am certain that is what the marquess will say to you." She cleared her throat. "Among other things."

Mr. Pengrove shifted his weight off his bent knee, then slowly stood. He seated himself beside her, his expression thoughtful. "Perhaps a very long engagement would be best. If that is what you truly desire."

"Alas, I cannot afford that luxury." Dorothea stared at his profile. His chin was a tad weak, his hairline receding, his nose boasted a sharp hook. He was far from handsome, yet he truly was a nice young man. With time and maturity he would make some woman a good husband. She felt another stab of disappointment as she acknowledged that woman would most definitely not be her.

"As you well know, marriage is different for a woman," she continued. "My brother-in-law's family has been exceedingly generous in their support of me, but I cannot trespass on their hospitality for more than a Season. I therefore feel it is my duty to do everything possible to make a match this year. And since we both agree that you should wait several years before taking a wife, well . . ."

Dorothea's voice trailed away. She had given him a chance for a graceful, dignified exit. He pondered it for a moment, hesitated, then wisely took it.

"If that is what you truly wish, then I must of course honor your decision."

"I fear, 'tis our only option." Dorothea lowered her eyes, hoping she looked despondent. "However, I do expect us to remain the very best of friends," she said with a sincerity that was heartily felt.

"Nothing would please me more."

Dorothea smiled. She had not entirely misjudged him. His affections were not so deeply engaged if he could so quickly relent on his desire to make her his bride. And his intelligence had aided him admirably in making the correct choice. Though it was a bit troubling to see how easily he could be manipulated. Sighing, Dorothea admitted it was all for the best. Obviously, it was not just his inadequate kisses that made him a poor choice for her husband.

"Goodness, I have distressed you," Mr. Pengrove said, misunderstanding her sigh. "Please, forgive me."

"There is nothing to forgive," Dorothea replied firmly.

"Well, if you are certain." Mr. Pengrove's brow creased in a worried frown. He shook it off, then stood and held out his hand. "We must not stay out here alone any longer. I am worried that Mother will notice our absence and remark upon it to someone."

Dorothea hesitated. She was not ready to return. She needed a few moments alone to collect her thoughts and harness the remaining bits of her disappointment, for when she had left the ballroom earlier, she had firmly believed she would be reentering it as an engaged woman.

"You go ahead without me," Dorothea said. "I should like to enjoy a few more minutes in solitude, taking in the fresh air before returning to the crush of the party."

Mr. Pengrove's face darkened in distress. "I would never be so ungallant as to leave a lady unattended in such a secluded area of the garden. Who knows what might happen?"

"I'm sure it is perfectly safe," Dorothea countered, not believing any harm could possibly befall her. This was a private party, given by the Earl of Wessex. Only invited guests would dare to enter his garden.

Mr. Pengrove scuffed the toe of his shoe against the gravel path. "I really must insist, Miss Ellingham. Lord Dardington would have my head on a platter if anything happened to you. I am certain he would not approve of your being here alone."

"Ah, so you believe he would be happier if he discovered us here together?"

"Oh, gracious. We should leave at once!"

Dorothea opened her mouth to protest, then thought better of the idea. Mr. Pengrove's lips were set in a mulish frown. He was agitated, nervous, glancing over his shoulder repeatedly, almost as if he expected the marquess to jump out from behind the thick hedgerow and demand to know what they were doing.

She caught Mr. Pengrove's eye and gave him a hard stare. He sent her a fleeting look of apology, yet his stiff posture let her know he would not quickly abandon his position.

Dorothea knew if she pressed the matter she would eventually win the argument, but it would take more effort than it was worth, and do nothing but increase her already worsening headache. So instead she rose gracefully, automatically brushing away the few wrinkles that had formed on the skirt of her golden silk gown.

Dorothea placed her hand on his elbow. "Since you are

so very insistent, Mr. Pengrove, I find that I am forced to agree. For I must confess, your predictions concerning my guardian's reaction are correct. And I will admit, I much prefer seeing your head on your shoulders, than on a platter."

Carter Grayson, Marquess of Atwood, strolled along the garden path, enjoying the spring breeze, the twinkling stars, and the peace and quiet. He really ought to be used to attending society affairs where five hundred guests were invited to fill a ballroom that could accommodate half that number, but the truth was that it usually annoyed him.

Tonight was no exception. He had arrived late at the earl's ball and planned to leave early, but he could not yet make good his escape. He had promised his father, the Duke of Hansborough, that he would see him this evening, and his father had not yet arrived. Hence, Carter was trapped.

He turned a corner and followed the hedgerow down a gravel path. No lanterns had been lit in this section of the garden and the darkness seemed to creep in, erasing all sense of time and place. But Carter did not mind. The eerie stillness and inky blackness fit his solitary mood.

He paused beside a fountain, the tinkling sounds of running water soothing his spirit. Fifteen more minutes and he would return to the ballroom. Another hour and he would leave, his father be damned.

The merest trace of a smile broke the grim line of his lips as Carter speculated as to why his father was unaccustomedly late to the ball, knowing there had to be a specific reason. The Duke of Hansborough never did anything without calculated thought, and Carter had several theories about his father's behavior tonight. Each of them pertaining to marriage.

To Carter's great annoyance, marriage was very much

on his father's mind these days. And when his father got his mind wrapped around something, he was more tenacious than a dog with a bone, refusing to drop it until he was satisfied with the result.

Carter admired his father, respected his father, loved his father. Yet he often did not agree with the duke, and on this matter they were very much at odds. Carter did not oppose the idea of marriage. He knew it was his duty to take a wife and beget an heir, and he fully intended to do it. He had actually made up his mind to find himself a wife this Season, but this would be done on his own terms. A concept his father had a great difficulty understanding.

Carter resumed his walk about the garden, his footsteps echoing through the balmy spring air. As he rounded another corner, a muffled sound brought his head up. He spied a man and woman locked in an embrace, their lips fused together. He turned his head away, but a louder noise brought it back around.

He squinted a little, then arched an eyebrow as the couple ended the embrace and the man sank to one knee, prostrating himself before the woman perched so elegantly on the garden bench.

Bloody hell! He had stumbled upon a marriage proposal. The sight made Carter's gut clench. The night clouds shifted and a shaft of moonlight fell upon the pair, revealing the slight frame and somber profile of the gentleman. It was Arthur Pengrove.

Good Lord, what was the world coming to when a young, inexperienced pup like Pengrove took on the responsibilities of a wife? Carter continued to stare at the couple, suddenly feeling very old.

The future Mrs. Pengrove turned her head and he caught a glimpse of her features in the moonlight. She was very pretty. Delicate and refined. He thought he might have danced with her a few weeks ago, but was not entirely certain.

He believed she was somehow connected to the Marquess of Dardington, a fresh-faced, distant relation from the country who had come down to London for the Season. To find a husband, as was the custom with ladies of privilege. And apparently, she had been successful.

Not wanting to intrude on this private moment, Carter gingerly stepped off the gravel path onto the lawn and made his way soundlessly out of the garden.

The moment he reentered the ballroom, he began searching the crowd for his father. Instead, he located Viscount Benton, a handsome rake with a biting sense of humor. They had attended Eaton and later Oxford together, forging a friendship as boys that had deepened as they became men. They were alike in more ways than they were different, though Benton could be reckless in a way Carter admitted was almost frightening at times.

"Where the devil have you been hiding?" Viscount Benton asked.

"I was getting some air," Carter answered, bracing his feet so as not to be shuffled from his position. It really was a ridiculous crush of people on the ballroom floor. Heaven help them all if someone yelled *fire*.

Viscount Benton stopped a passing footman and pulled two crystal goblets brimming with champagne off a gleaming silver tray. "Champagne?"

Carter grimaced as his friend offered him the goblet.

"Yes, yes, I know," Benton intoned. "'Tis a drink for silly young girls, dotty old ladies, and swishing dandies, but the good whiskey is in the card room and it will take us at least twenty minutes to fight our way through this crowd. We shall expire from thirst before we reach the doorway."

"I suppose I shall have to make do with it," Carter grumbled, taking a long gulp. "At least it's properly chilled."

Benton nodded in agreement. "Lady Wessex might not have much sense when it comes to calculating the adequate numbers her ballroom can accommodate, but she certainly knows how to spend money on a ball."

"Not skimping on the ice hardly makes up for subjecting us all to this insanity," Carter insisted.

"If you hate it all so much, then why are you here?"

Carter felt his jaw harden. Benton was right, why did he come? To please his father? Yet he knew, and his father knew, that Carter would reject the woman the duke presented to him tonight. On principle alone, if nothing else. Still, father and son continued to play this game with each other. The duke made unrealistic demands and Carter complied halfheartedly, doing only enough to avoid the appearance of outright defiance.

"The Duke of Hansborough and Lady Audrey Parson."

The butler's booming voice drew everyone toward the doorway. An older gentleman and a very young woman glided into the ballroom. Back straight, eyes alert, mouth unsmiling, the Duke of Hansborough moved with the grace and energy of a far younger man. The dense crowd actually parted to make a path for him.

The female at his side clung to him like a vine on a garden trellis. She was tiny in stature, open eyed, and blatantly innocent. Carter's irritated mood deepened.

"Ah, now I understand why you are here tonight, Atwood," Viscount Benton said gleefully. "You were waiting for your father. And look, he has brought you a present! My, my, isn't she a pretty young thing? Not a day over seventeen, I'd wager."

"Shut up, Benton."

The viscount snickered. "Well, she isn't a cow, you must

allow him points for that at least. But those hips are almost indecently wide. Yet perfect for breeding plenty of little brats. How fortunate."

"Egad! It's Audrey."

Carter turned and faced the man who had just joined them. "Do you know her, Dawson?"

"Afraid so, Atwood. Her mother and my aunt are great friends. I've known her for years."

"And?" Carter prompted.

Mr. Peter Dawson tugged on his cravat, marring the perfect whiteness with a smudge of lint. He too had been a classmate at Eaton and later Oxford, though his personality and demeanor were nearly the opposite of the viscount and the marquess. "Audrey's a nice enough girl. Uncomplicated. Eager to please. She's been kept in the country nearly all of her life, which would account for her very quiet manner."

"In other words, she's a simpleton," Benton interjected sarcastically.

A flush of color bloomed on Dawson's cheekbones. He was a somber, self-contained man who seldom had a harsh word or criticism for anyone. "Not precisely."

"Why does your father delight in finding the most empty-headed females for you?" Benton asked before tipping his glass and swallowing the remainder of his champagne. "Even worse, why does he then insist you should marry them?"

Why indeed, Carter wondered. Did his father truly know his only son so poorly? How could he ever imagine such a young, sweet creature would hold his interest? The marquess sighed. "My father is an intelligent and observant man, but he has set his mind very firmly on the type of woman he believes will make me a proper duchess. Apparently my opinion of the matter bears little consequence."

"Hell, they are all the same." Benton sighed. "I am pestered no end by my grandmother on the importance of finding a woman with looks, breeding, and impeccable manners to make my viscountess."

"The last quality being an extreme necessity since you can be such an uncultured, uncouth fellow at times," Carter said with a grin.

"Possibly." Benton grinned back. "But at least my grandmother does not share your father's view and include cowering among the qualities that are diligently sought for a wife."

"Lady Audrey isn't cowering," Dawson protested. "Well, not much, anyway."

Damn, can this get any worse? Not only was he going to be forced to pay his respects to a female he had no earthly interest in meeting, his friends were being afforded a front-row seat to his humiliation.

Across the ballroom floor, Carter met the duke's gaze straight on. The older man narrowed his eyes. Carter braced himself. At times like this it was essential that he remember his father was descended from generations of ruthless, strong-willed men.

That blood ran through his veins also, yet somehow Carter had been spared the full intensity. Or perhaps it was not yet fully developed?

Carter calculated it would take several minutes for the duke and Lady Audrey to reach them. At that point introductions would be made, some inane conversation exchanged, and then he would ask Lady Audrey to dance.

Once that was done, he could leave. And in the morning he would tell the duke he was not interested in the lady.

"Good luck, my friend." Benton thumped him on the back. "As much as I would relish the fun of staying and watching you make an ass of yourself with the childlike Lady Audrey, the card room calls. Come along, Dawson."

Peter Dawson looked hastily from one man to the other. "Perhaps Atwood would appreciate some moral support?"

"Hell, no," Carter replied emphatically. "I counsel you both to save yourselves while you can."

The two men slipped away into the crowd, which had mercifully lessened, Dawson looking concerned and Benton appearing amused.

Carter glanced again in his father's direction and saw he and Lady Audrey were now engaged in conversation with the Earl of Wessex. It gave Carter a few moments to collect his thoughts, calm his emotions. Then suddenly the duke turned and caught his son's gaze. He lowered his chin slightly in greeting, then gestured with steely gray eyes.

The marquess bristled. Clearly, he was being summoned. It would be prudent to obey, yet Carter's feet stood firmly in place. The duke gestured a second time, the shade of his eyes darkening. Carter's eyes also darkened. But his feet never took a step.

From long habit, he kept a tight rein on his escalating temper. It would be rude and pointless to vent his frustration in so public a venue. No, this discussion needed to be held in private, for it was a matter to be settled between him and his father.

Though he was loath to acknowledge it, even at this distance Carter could see that Lady Audrey's hips were indeed unusually broad beneath the skirt of her silk gown. And her face, while passably pretty, had a most decidedly vacant look. Damn his father's interfering ways.

The pair ceased their conversation and once again started moving directly toward him. Suddenly, all of Carter's self-protective instincts kicked into high gear.

His father was being solicitous, almost conciliatory toward Lady Audrey. This was dangerous. Previously, the duke had allowed Carter to dismiss the women he presented after a single argument between the men, even as the duke balked at his son's attitude.

With the celebration of Carter's thirtieth birthday looming a few months away, the duke had become more adamant. The marquess worried that this time he would be unable to so easily dismiss his father's choice.

The subtle scent of lavender assaulted his senses. Carter turned. Marvelous! A young woman stood on his left, mere steps away. He wiped his annoyance from his face and offered her a smile. "Good evening." He bowed. "I am the Marquess of Atwood."

"Yes, I know." The young woman seemed taken aback by his forward manner, but she nodded cordially. "We met at Lord Willingford's ball a few weeks ago. How are you, my lord?"

"Longing to dance. Won't you please indulge me, fair lady?"

Without waiting for her to answer, Carter swept her into his arms. Mercifully, a section of the ballroom had been cleared for the dancing couples. He took immediate advantage and hastened toward the center, as far away from his father and Lady Audrey as he could get.

The woman in his arms let out a muffled sound of protest, but he ignored it, pulling her along with him. She was small in stature, barely reaching his shoulder. She was also very pretty, with delicate, fine-boned features, silky blond hair, and a slender, willowy figure that boasted high, firm breasts. There was something vaguely familiar about her . . .

Carter narrowed his eyes and studied her further, then nearly missed a step of the waltz when he realized her identity. Good Lord! It was the female from the garden, Arthur Pengrove's newly acquired fiancée. 'Twas no wonder she was glaring at him with obvious disapproval. No doubt this dance had been saved for her intended.

Oh, well. There would be other dances for her to share with Pengrove. A lifetime of them. For now his need was greater, and besides their dance had already begun. Actually, it was a good sign. His luck must be changing.

His even mood restored, Carter smiled down at his partner. "I have recently arrived at the ball. Tell me, has anything of great interest occurred?"

He expected her to blush and stammer and then gush about her very recent engagement to Arthur Pengrove. He would nod and smile and listen to her subsequent chatter, thus alleviating the burden of conversation. In fact, if he were very fortunate, he could lead her to the opposite side of the room and, at the end of the dance, slip quietly from the ballroom. Without seeing his father. Or meeting Lady Audrey.

But the very pretty future Mrs. Pengrove did not reveal the secret of her engagement, nor even hint that the momentous event had taken place. Instead, she gazed at him with a boldness that was nearly disconcerting.

Carter's eyes moved down her face, settling on her lips. She had an especially sensual mouth. His pulse quickened and he was suddenly assaulted with a fierce urge to kiss her. Pure lust, of course. Still, it seemed a pity that it would be Pengrove who enjoyed the taste of those lush, tempting lips.

"Why did you ask me to dance? Or rather, why did you pull me against my will onto the ballroom floor? Your haste was most extraordinary. Are you running from the law, perchance?"

Carter arched his brow. He could not possibly have heard her correctly. "Pardon?"

"I asked why you insisted that I dance with you," she replied calmly.

For a moment, Carter's mind went blank. Her forthright manner caught him very much unawares. Females generally blushed and stammered in his presence or else sent him sly, seductive glances. They never challenged him so directly.

"I was overcome by your beauty, fair lady," he said, deciding to disarm her with some harmless flattery. "It drove me to bold madness."

"What a bunch of rot. You barely glanced at my face before carting me away like a sack of grain."

Carter's brow raised as he feigned indignity. "I am the Marquess of Atwood, my good woman. I do not cart females away. I gracefully, elegantly sweep them away."

"Do you really? Even when they have promised the dance to another gentleman?"

Ah, it was as he suspected. She was piqued because he had stolen her away from her intended. "Your previous partner will have a lifetime to enjoy your dances. 'Tis only fair he give others a chance, dear lady."

She tipped her head to one side. "You don't know my name, do you?"

Caught! Carter bestowed his most charming, heart-melting smile on her, hoping to distract her question. But it didn't seem to work. Her gaze remained on him, solemn and intent. There was a long, drawn-out silence.

"Of course I know who you are," he blustered. "We met at the Willingfords' ball. You are Arthur Pengrove's future bride. And I should like to add that he is one very lucky fellow."

Her blue eyes filled with shock and regret, then quickly returned to a mischievous gleam. It was such a brief expression of emotion that Carter would have missed it had he not been observing her so closely.

"You do not find that to be a particularly odd name, my lord? Arthur Pengrove's future bride? Please, try again."

A stark challenge, plain as day, was written all over her lovely face. Damn. He wished he really did know her name, just so he could win this game. But alas, he had no earthly idea. Which was another surprise. How could he have forgotten such an enchanting woman?

He cleared his throat, stalling for time. "How amusing. This is rather like that fairy tale about the odd little man who helped the beautiful miller's daughter spin straw into gold. What was his name again?"

"Rumpelstiltskin."

"Yes, that's it."

"You are avoiding the question."

"Am I? I admit my thoughts are jumbled. Consumed by the events in the fairy tale. And fascinated at the similarities to our current situation. Truly, your hair puts spun gold to shame."

She muttered something under her breath. A word that no lady should know, let alone speak. Carter smiled. "Pardon?" he queried.

Though he highly doubted it was her intention, she had successfully entertained him as no woman ever had. Outside of the bedchamber, of course. Females often grew tongue-tied around him, no doubt because they were eager to make a favorable impression.

He knew that was not the case with his mysterious beauty. If anything, she seemed most eager to get away from him, which caused him to like her even more. Her wit was sharp, her attitude bold. Her voice had a warm pitch he found oddly sensual. The sound of it sent an unexpected potent spark of desire right through him.

Brought on, no doubt, by the knowledge that she was already claimed by another man. Truly, nothing added more to a female's allure than the knowledge that one could not have her.

"You have a devious mind, my lord," she finally said.

"Precisely. Therefore I understand how they work."

She laughed. It was a joyful, melodious sound and Carter found himself joining her in a wide smile. It took a few seconds for him to realize that the music had stopped and the dance was over. Regretfully, he released her from the circle of his arms, then almost immediately felt the presence of another person standing near.

Carter turned, fully expecting to see her newly acquired fiancé, Arthur Pengrove. Instead, his eyes clashed with the Marquess of Dardington.

A rather angry, visibly annoyed, Marquess of Dardington.

Chapter Two

"Atwood."

"Dardington."

The two men stood toe to toe, first staring, then glowering at each other, neither giving an inch. The scent of impending disaster swirled around them, permeating the air. Dorothea's breath hitched with panic. The last thing she needed was to be at the center of a very public disagreement between these two gentlemen.

Especially after she had faithfully promised her sister, Gwendolyn, that she would behave with the utmost propriety and decorum while in London. Instead, she appeared poised to become the unwitting star in a drama of Shakespearean proportions.

So, for the sake of all those guests who were regarding them with great curiosity, Dorothea kept a congenial smile plastered on her face. A smile she suspected fooled no one, yet hid some of the worry churning in her mind.

"Ah, so you gentlemen are acquainted with each other," she muttered. "How lovely."

She widened her smile, aware that their audience had grown in numbers. *Good heavens, they must all think I'm a simpleton. Yet better to be thought a half-witted female than a scandalous one.*

For an instant, the two men turned in her direction, each appearing slightly puzzled that she had spoken. She realized that their focus had been so exclusively on each other, both had temporarily forgotten she was standing there with them.

"I shall deal with this, Dorothea," Lord Dardington declared with quiet authority. "No need to trouble yourself."

"There really is nothing to deal with, my lord," she replied, striving to keep her tone neutral. "'Twas a simple misunderstanding."

"Hmm, perhaps. Or perhaps not, at least not on Atwood's part," the Marquess of Dardington said in a frigid, calm voice as his angry gaze returned to her dancing partner.

Reflexively, Dorothea took a step back. The growing alarm that had taken up residence in her chest heightened, even as she admired the steely nerve exhibited by Lord Atwood.

The Marquess of Dardington was a formidable man, in physical stature and in temperament. There were few who possessed the nerve to meet him so directly. Apparently the Marquess of Atwood was one of those few.

Easily half the *ton* feared Lord Dardington's volatile outbursts while the other half thrived on his antics and the endless gossip they produced. His wife, Lady Meredith, had assured Dorothea that Lord Dardington had mellowed with age, but she saw no evidence of that now. In truth, the most unsettling of all was the apparent calm Lord Dardington was currently demonstrating, despite his obvious displeasure.

The calm before the storm? Dorothea shivered, suddenly

feeling alarmingly light-headed. Topping the evening off by having her guardian make a public spectacle truly would make this the worst night of her life.

"Miss Ellingham had promised me that dance, Atwood. But you spirited her away," the Marquess of Dardington proclaimed. "Whatever were you thinking, man? Or rather, not thinking?"

The deep timbre of the Marquess of Dardington's voice vibrated along Dorothea's spine. She risked a small glance at the Marquess of Atwood. His face paled slightly; his jaw flexed. Her fear of an unpleasant scene increased.

"I was unaware of the circumstances, sir," Lord Atwood replied. There was a pause, a long silence, and then finally, "my apologies."

Lord Atwood rigidly inclined his head as he offered his apology. His voice held the proper amount of regret, his contrition appeared genuine. On the surface. Yet something in Lord Atwood's tone caught Dorothea's attention.

She would bet every shilling of her weekly allowance that the young nobleman would have done precisely the same thing even if he had known the entire circumstances.

Lord Dardington darkened his glare. Apparently he shared her view. The tension in the air escalated. The two men now locked eyes, much as two rams would lock horns. Dorothea supposed it was better than knocking heads, though that might come later, depending on how this conversation concluded. Wide-eyed, she licked her lips.

Fearful of her own safety if she dared to step between them, Dorothea tried to manage a disarming smile. But she need not have bothered. Both men were once again ignoring her, too intent on each other to be aware of much else.

She remembered suddenly the first time she had met the Marquess of Dardington. He had been cordial, pleasant, even charming. But then her temporary guardian had succinctly outlined his expectations of her conduct and the rules he expected to be obeyed without questions while she was a member of his London household.

He had also, rather graphically, described what would happen if she broke any of those rules. It had taken until the next morning for Dorothea's knees to stop shaking.

But the Marquess of Atwood did not appear to be having the same difficulties. Lord Dardington was casting him a stare that would cause any sane, mortal man to quake in his boots. But the Marquess of Atwood barely blinked.

Dorothea could not help but think of Arthur Pengrove. She was certain he would have fainted dead away if he were on the receiving end of such a stare from her guardian.

"I suppose I must accept your apology and thus excuse your deplorable manners," Lord Dardington grudgingly conceded. "Just see that it never happens again."

"Thank you for being so enlightened, sir." Atwood turned toward Dorothea and smiled. "Surely you can understand how I lost my head when I set eyes on the lovely Miss Ellingham earlier. I found her irresistible."

"Lost your head? Aye, along with any semblance of common sense," Dardington grumbled.

Lord Atwood grinned ruefully. "I am a gentleman, sir, not a saint."

Lord Dardington cracked a smile, but then his handsome face contorted into another grimace. "Be warned, Atwood. While she is under my roof, Miss Ellingham is under my protection. I take my responsibilities toward her with the same care and devotion I afford to my daughters, who thank God are still too young to be out in society."

"I understand." Lord Atwood's lips quirked into another thin smile.

"Good. Make certain you don't forget it." Lord Darding-ton shifted his footing and regarded the younger man steadily, his brooding concentration an unnerving scrutiny.

Lord Atwood's smile faded. Perhaps he was not as un-affected by Lord Dardington's manner as he tried to appear? Strangely, the notion that he took Lord Darding-ton seriously caused Dorothea's opinion of Lord Atwood to rise. Obviously he was intelligent to recognize a formi-dable opponent when presented to him. Yet he was clever enough, and levelheaded enough, to know when he was outmaneuvered.

"I will most definitely remember our conversation, sir." Lord Atwood turned and bowed over her gloved hand. "I bid you good evening, Miss Ellingham. Thank you for the delightful dance and the enjoyable company. It was the undisputed highlight of my night."

To her everlasting annoyance, Dorothea felt herself blushing. He was standing very close, close enough that she could feel the heat radiating off his solid body. She sternly told herself to calm down.

"I hardly know what to say," she replied.

His brow quirked. "A first for you, I imagine."

She smiled. She hadn't meant to; she wanted to be cool and dignified, even a tad dismissive. But he was simply too handsome, too charming. And Dorothea had always had a weakness for handsome, charming men.

"I am hopeful that when next we meet, you will handle yourself in a more proper manner, my lord," she said, re-gretting that he had released her hand. She liked his touch, had enjoyed feeling small and delicate.

"I assure you, when next we meet, you will not be dis-appointed." He leaned forward and whispered. "I vow that I shall even remember your name. Dorothea."

Then, with a conspiratorial smile, Lord Atwood took his leave.

"Woolgathering, Dorothea?"

"What? Oh?" Dorothea pulled her eyes away from the broad retreating shoulders of Lord Atwood and slanted a guilty look at her guardian. "I'm sorry."

"For ignoring me? Or for dancing with Atwood?"

"Both, I suppose."

The marquess offered his arm and she slipped her hand into the bend at his elbow. Heads held high, they crossed the ballroom and headed toward the room where the supper buffet was being served. The marquess ignored the curious gazes and the stage whispers of conversation several ladies indulged in behind their open, raised fans. Dorothea pretended to do the same.

"Atwood has always struck me as a somewhat impulsive man," Lord Dardington said. He glared at a young dandy dressed in the most appalling shade of puce, who was blocking the entrance to the supper room. The poor fellow gulped, reddened, then hastened out of the way. "I assume Atwood gave you no choice when it came to the dance? That is why you stood me up?"

Dorothea nodded. "He was very insistent."

Lord Dardington's face darkened. "Improper?"

"No, not exactly." Dorothea had fended off her share of unwanted advances through the years. This incident had been nothing like the others.

"I suppose you feel flattered that he singled you out for such attention," the marquess said.

Dorothea slowly shook her head as she ran through the events in her mind. "Actually, I don't believe he intended to select me. I was merely the closest female within his vicinity."

"Hmm, he might have been keen on avoiding someone else," the marquess allowed in such a tone that Dorothea surmised Lord Dardington had once done the very same thing himself. "Nevertheless, I must commend you on how well you conducted yourself, Dorothea. I imagine it wasn't easy for you to remain so calm and collected while Atwood and I squared off against each other."

"I believed sheer terror and a healthy dose of dread held me immobile, my lord," she answered wryly.

The marquess smiled. "I apologize if I upset you."

"I am just grateful that you each kept your fists by your sides and somehow managed not to say anything overtly insulting."

Lord Dardington nodded wisely. "Atwood probably would have taken a swing at me if I went too far."

"Fisticuffs at a formal ball?" Dorothea shuddered.

"No need to look so upset. If we did come to physical violence it would not have lasted very long. 'Tis far too crowded in here to land more than one or two solid punches."

"How comforting."

The sarcastic comment slipped beyond her lips before she could censure herself, but the marquess seemed unaffected by the tone of her remark. They entered the supper room where an army of their host's servants were scurrying about.

Dorothea paused a moment to take it all in, trying to commit each detail to memory so she could write to her younger sister, Emma, with descriptive accuracy.

The room was ablaze with candles that shimmered reflectively off the satin gowns and sparkling jewels worn by the ladies. The tables were studded with large vases of hothouse flowers; the buffet table groaned under the sheer quantity of so much lavishly prepared foods. Even after spending over two months in Town, Dorothea was still in awe of the spectacle and expenses involved in these parties. It was nothing like the quiet, simple affairs she had attended in Yorkshire.

For a split second she longed for the familiar, safe life that she was accustomed to, but then she ruthlessly threw the thought aside. What was wrong with her tonight? Apparently the proposal from Arthur Pengrove and the unexpected incident with the Marquess of Atwood were making a greater impact on her nerves than she realized.

When her older sister had invited her to come to Town, Dorothea had jumped at the chance, knowing this was the best opportunity she would ever have to make a good match, to establish a comfortable, happy life for herself. Being sponsored by the Marquess and Countess of Dardington had been an unexpected and very welcome boon.

Their social stature had afforded her the opportunity to mingle with the very cream of society, the most influential, aristocratic, and wealthy individuals. Yet somehow this extraordinary blessing was also a curse. The pressure Dorothea felt to find a husband grew with each passing week.

As she glanced at the well-dressed, well-heeled crowd, a weight settled in Dorothea's gut. What was she doing here? Was she reaching too far, hoping too much? Was it foolish to want to better herself through marriage?

Yet marriage was the only way she could separate herself from a life spent in Yorkshire, in the quiet, rather dull community where she had lived with her aunt and uncle for nearly ten years. To escape that fate, Dorothea was prepared to risk a great deal.

"We shall find my wife and then locate a quiet corner to enjoy our meal," Lord Dardington decided as he surveyed the supper room. Dorothea nodded rather meekly in agreement.

Her gaze too moved over the room, searching for Lady Meredith, yet idly watching for Lord Atwood also. Conversation and laughter flowed freely as the throng of guests began converging at the numerous banquet tables. Somehow Lord Dardington located his wife, Lady Meredith, among the crush. After securing a secluded table for the three of them, he hailed a footman to bring them a selection of delicacies from the buffet.

"Are you enjoying the ball, Dorothea?" Lady Meredith asked as they waited for the food to be brought. She was a pretty, levelheaded woman, whose face and form gave no hint that she was the mother of three girls, the eldest nearly ten years old.

Dorothea had been shy at their first meeting, but soon warmed to Lady Meredith's unpretentious spirit and kind demeanor. She admired the older woman's sophisticated attitude and optimistic outlook. She was also slightly in awe of how Lady Meredith managed her very stormy, volatile husband.

"The ball seems to be a great success," Dorothea replied, making a great show of interest in the china plate the footman placed before her and deliberately refraining from making any comments about her feelings on the events of the evening.

She swallowed her first bite of a delicate veal pastry, and had just filled her fork with another when she felt the marquess's gaze measuring her.

"Do you want to tell Meredith what happened or shall I?" Lord Dardington asked. "'Tis your decision."

"It was merely a dance," Dorothea answered slowly,

lowering her fork to her plate. "And a misunderstanding on Lord Atwood's part that the set had been promised to you."

"You cannot mean the supper dance?" Lady Meredith asked. "But you are here together. Did you not take to the floor as you planned, Trevor?"

Lady Meredith frowned and Dorothea understood her confusion. It was expected that those who partnered for the supper dance then partook of the meal together when the dance ended. Yet here she was with Lord Dardington; Lord Atwood was no where to be found.

"Atwood tried to steal her from me," Lord Dardington said. "He was successful with the dance, but I prevailed when it came to the meal."

Lady Meredith carefully examined Dorothea's face. "At whose request did you intervene? Dorothea's?" she asked her husband.

The marquess bristled at the question. "I am responsible for Dorothea's welfare. I would never forgive myself if I let any harm befall her while she was under my care."

Lady Meredith shot him a sharp glance. "Were you distressed, Dorothea? Did you need Lord Dardington to intervene?"

Dorothea slowly chewed on her veal, making certain to take a small bite so she wouldn't choke. Lady Meredith possessed an uncanny ability to see a situation more clearly than one might wish. It was a habit Dorothea found worrisome when it was directed at her.

"Lord Atwood took me by surprise, but there was no harm done by him." Dorothea knew what else she needed to say and she couldn't quite meet Lady Meredith's eyes as she strove to be tactful. "Though strictly speaking it might not have been necessary, I did appreciate Lord Dardington's assistance."

"As I said," the marquess crowed to his wife.

"It was actually the second time I danced with Lord Atwood," Dorothea interjected. "He partnered me at the Willingford ball several weeks ago." *Though clearly he did not remember me,* she thought wryly.

"Two dances? I was not aware." The marquess frowned as he poured them each some wine from the bottle the footman had left on the table. "'Tis no secret that his father wishes him to wed, but Atwood seems ill inclined to follow the duke's dictates. Plus his reputation hardly recommends him as a man I would consider a suitable husband, despite his wealth and title."

"Gentlemen with far worse reputations and reckless youthful behavior have managed to make solid matches and proven themselves to be good husbands," Lady Meredith said affectionately. "You included, my love."

The remark seemed to have a mellowing effect on Lord Dardington. "To be fair, I suppose Atwood isn't all that bad. Yet I still contend it won't be easy for any woman he takes as a wife. His father is a horror. Makes my own dear, autocratic sire seem like a tamed house cat in comparison."

"Heaven save us all from self-important aristocrats." Lady Meredith hoisted her wineglass and took a long sip. "Honestly, dukes can be the most dreadful snobs. Except for my father-in-law. He is a delightful man."

Lord Dardington regarded his wife with an easy grin. "I am certain you are the only woman on this earth who refers to my father as delightful."

She returned the smile. "It's true."

"Ah, how quickly you have forgotten the great struggle it took to make him your champion."

Lady Meredith waved her hand dismissively. "That was

ages ago. Besides, it was a challenge to bring him around. I like a challenge."

"I like a challenge, too," Dorothea said, internally scoffing at the notion that the handsome marquess was genuinely interested in her. She was a country lass, with an unimpressive dowry and very little family connections. "But I fear the Marquess of Atwood is a trifle too high in the instep to have any true interest in me. And I cannot even contemplate trying to impress his father, the Duke of Hansborough."

"Still, this was your second dance," Lady Meredith mused.

Dorothea shrugged. "Perhaps he was showing an interest in me merely to vex his father."

"Stranger things have been known to happen. We shall assess his sincerity when he comes to call," Lady Meredith decided.

Dorothea's eyes widened. "I do believe we are getting ahead of ourselves. Lord Atwood did not indicate that he would be calling upon me."

"That does not mean he won't present himself on my doorstep," the marquess grumbled. "Hat in one hand, flowers in the other. If he invites you on a carriage ride, I insist that you bring Meredith along as a chaperone."

"Dashing young men his age drive those sporty phaetons, Trevor," Lady Meredith said mildly. "There is only room for two. Where exactly am I to sit? On Lord Atwood's lap?"

"If you did, I would be forced to challenge him to a duel. 'Twould be a pity to end the life of one so young."

"Don't be ridiculous." Lady Meredith reached across the table and placed her hand over her husband's. He immediately turned his palm up and gripped Lady Meredith's hand tightly. "There will be no duels, Trevor," she said in a soft, yet insistent tone.

"I protect my own," the marquess said with exasperation, "and that includes Dorothea."

"Thank you," Dorothea hastily replied. Though it was rather appalling to think of the marquess fighting a duel for her, it also heartened her to know there was someone who would stand by and make sure she was safe, guarded from any man who would abuse her.

Her uncle Fletcher had not shown anything near the same level of concern for any of his three nieces, though he vowed to reform just before Dorothea came to London.

"Of course you must protect her," Lady Meredith said. "Using your intelligence and influence, not your sword or pistol." Lady Meredith pulled her hand away and brushed a stray wisp of hair off her cheek. "Now, there shall be no more talk of violence. The very idea utterly ruins my appetite."

After a moment's hesitation, the marquess nodded. He speared a delicate scallop with the tines of his fork and held it toward his wife. With an impish grin, she accepted the peace offering, her lips closing suggestively over the tasty morsel.

Good. That was very nicely settled. Though she was far too often the cause of it, family discord always made Dorothea nervous. She was pleased that Lady Meredith and the marquess had so amicably settled their difference.

Only one hurdle remained. Dorothea took a deep breath. "Arthur Pengrove proposed to me earlier this evening," she announced in a breathless rush.

Lord and Lady Dardington shared a cryptic glance before Lady Meredith's delicately arched brow lifted. "Really?"

"There is no cause for you to look so worried," Dorothea said with deliberate lightness. "I turned him down. Or rather, I convinced him he was far too young to take on the responsibility of a wife."

"Thank you," the marquess said sincerely. "Enduring a meeting with Pengrove would have been torture for me. I'm certain I would have felt as though I was kicking a rabbit when I forbade him to propose."

Dorothea's head swiveled in the marquess's direction. "You would have turned him away?"

"Of course."

The marquess nodded and returned to his meal, spearing a large piece of rare roast beef on his fork. Dorothea regarded him warily as he chewed his food with obvious relish.

"But what if I wanted to marry Mr. Pengrove?"

Lord Dardington paused, his fork halfway between his mouth and his plate. "Why in the world would you want to spend your life with Arthur Pengrove?"

"I don't. But if I did, would you prevent it? Can you prevent it?"

"My dear girl, I *can do* just about anything I please," the marquess answered in a firm tone. "And I want every gentleman within a ten-mile radius of London to be very aware of that fact."

Dorothea swallowed her panic. It was daunting to be faced with the reality of how much power the marquess had over her, even though this was only a temporary arrangement. The prospect of having to find a man that met with his approval was unsettling. Most unsettling, indeed.

Lady Meredith must have sensed Dorothea's distress, for she gave her husband a troubled look. "What Trevor means to say is that we have taken the responsibility for your future happiness very much to heart. We agreed to be your sponsor this Season so you would have the opportunity to meet and mingle with a variety of eligible men.

"Ultimately, however, it is your uncle Fletcher who will make the decision regarding the suitability of your future husband, since he is your blood relative. We only hope that you will at least listen to our advice before making your choice, since we are acquainted with most of these gentlemen and their families."

"Men can be idiots when it comes to finding a bride," the marquess said cheerfully. "In my case, it was sheer luck that brought Meredith into my life. I was too blind and pigheaded to at first see she was the very best thing that could have happened to me."

"Oh, Trevor."

Lord Dardington ran the tip of his finger lightly over his wife's bare hand. Dorothea glanced away. There was so much affection and regard in that simple gesture; it made her feel like a voyeur to witness it.

Was this what she wanted for herself? A husband who treated her as an equal, who considered her opinions, who on occasion deferred to her wishes, who obviously adored her?

Or did she want a husband who basically left her on her own? One who was an amiable companion, an elegant escort, a solid provider? It was a question she pondered daily, yet she had not reached a definitive conclusion.

The one thing she did know with certainty was that she would not marry a man whom she did not enjoy kissing. Hence any man she considered a reasonable candidate earned himself an uninhibited kiss from her. It was her final test. Alas, thus far no gentlemen had passed it.

Lord Dardington pulled his attention away from his

wife and once again regarded Dorothea. "It hardly takes a genius to see that Arthur Pengrove was not the man for you."

"He is a man of good character," Dorothea protested, feeling slightly annoyed that the marquess so clearly saw what she had not—that Arthur was very much the wrong man to be her husband.

"Yes, Pengrove is a fine man," Lord Dardington agreed. "A kind, affable fellow who would bore you to tears within a month of marriage. And then who knows what could happen? In my experience, an unhappy wife can make for all sorts of mischief."

Dorothea blushed to the roots of her hair. "Are you calling my honor into question, my lord?"

"No." He gave a great sigh. "Allow me to share with you the benefits of my age and experience, Dorothea. You are far too naïve and pretty for your own good. As a discontented wife, you would be easy prey for every rake and rogue in society. And believe me, we are in no short supply of them."

The marquess excused himself and went in search of some dessert for the three of them. Dorothea sat quietly, pondering his words.

"I hope Trevor has not caused you undue anguish," Lady Meredith said. "This whole marriage business can be rather nerve-racking for a female."

Dorothea nodded, her spirits lifting at Lady Meredith's kindness and sympathy. "I had no idea it would be so complicated, so confusing." She paused, then rushed ahead with her next question before she lost her nerve. "May I ask, were you in love with Lord Dardington when you married?"

Lady Meredith frowned. "Not at first." She thanked the

eager young footman who removed their dirty dinner plates and then turned back to Dorothea. "Is that what you want? To fall in love and then marry?"

Was it what she wanted? Dorothea felt a small shiver move through her. Slowly, she shook her head. "I suppose what I want most from the man I marry is the possibility of falling in love."

"Well, there are all sorts of marriages that are deemed very successful by society's standards," Lady Meredith said. "For the most part, being in love with one's spouse is considered rather bad form by many of the *ton*. Either before or during the marriage."

"Yet both you and your two brothers married for love."

Lady Meredith laughed. "Yes, the Barrington family is well known for its eccentricities. And I for one am very glad of it." The older woman's expression sobered. "I shall give you one piece of advice and ask you to consider it most carefully. Don't rush yourself, Dorothea. I can bear witness that the old adage, marry in haste, repent at leisure, is unfortunately true."

"Ladies, I come bearing gifts." The marquess's deep voice cut into the conversation. Lord Dardington appeared at their table with two footmen carrying large silver trays in tow. "'Twas too difficult to decide upon a single sweet, so I brought one of everything."

Both Dorothea and Lady Meredith let out a squeal of delight. With broad smiles they hastily made space on the small table for all the plates. The marquess resumed his seat and within minutes they were all busy tasting and then passing around the dishes, each exclaiming over their favorites and encouraging the others to have a sample.

As Dorothea chewed on a sinfully rich piece of cake, her thoughts turned to Lord Atwood. He had pulled her into a dance this evening without knowing her name. He had called her the future Mrs. Arthur Pengrove. How on earth did he know that Arthur had proposed? Dorothea believed she could say with a fair degree of certainty that the two men were not friends, making it impossible that Arthur would have confided his plans to the marquess.

Dorothea spooned a generous portion of raspberry trifle into her mouth. As the sweetness of the berries burst upon her tongue, she paused for a few seconds to relish the flavor. She took a second bite and decided this was most likely a puzzle that might never have a proper resolution.

Chapter Three

It was a pleasantly warm, cloudless afternoon. Carter rode cautiously through the clogged streets, as fast as the London traffic would allow, all the while thinking he should have brought his carriage. That vehicle most assuredly would have been moving at a snail's pace as his driver sought to negotiate around the other carriages, carts, riders, and pedestrians.

Carter was in no hurry to reach his destination. Far from it, really. His father would still be in a furious mood, no matter what time he called. The tersely worded message had arrived at Carter's bachelor rooms at the unfashionably early hour of nine a.m. His anxious valet had woken him the moment it was delivered, deciding a summons from the duke was sufficient reason to ignore his master's long-standing order never to disturb him when the bed curtains were drawn tightly shut.

Carter had thrown the unopened letter at his servant's head, rolled over, and pulled the covers to his chin. But his sleep had been effectively disrupted and he had been unable to restore it. Rousing himself two hours later, he bathed, allowed himself to be shaved and dressed, then ate a hearty meal. Deciding he could put it off no longer, the marquess reluctantly ordered his horse to be brought around.

The sunshine of the day had initially boosted his mood, but those good spirits diminished as he drew closer to his father's residence. Grimacing, Carter steered his mount around a tipped vegetable cart, secretly hoping his horse would stop to nibble on the greenery strewn about the street. But the animal kept his head lifted proudly in the air, disdaining the bounty beneath his hooves.

All too soon he reached the doors of his father's stately London mansion. It was the largest, and the oldest, residence in the square, a testament to his family's aristocratic ancestry, position, and wealth. Three reminders Carter did not need at the moment.

The same stoic butler who had never failed to intimidate Carter when he was a boy answered the door a split second after the brass knocker fell.

"Lord Atwood." The butler bowed respectfully. "May I take your hat and coat?"

Carter could not contain the smile that broke through as he divested himself of his outwear. His father's servants always managed to seem surprised when he appeared on the doorstep, as if he had journeyed from a great distance instead of from across Town.

Then again, most days he felt as though he lived a world away from this place and all it represented.

"Please inform my father that I have arrived," he said, brushing away an imaginary piece of lint from the sleeve of his blue superfine jacket.

"The duke asks that you await him in his private study," the butler replied.

Carter nodded, then held up his hand to refuse the footman's escort. Honestly, sometimes the formality of his father's home was not to be believed. He had grown up in this house, well, this house and several other estates. He certainly did not require assistance in finding his way to the duke's private study.

When he arrived, the room was predictably empty. And ominously quiet. Even the ormolu clock on the mantel barely made a sound as it ticked off the minutes. Restless, Carter remained on his feet, resisting the urge to pace.

Yet the longer he waited, the longer he was forced to review the events of last night in his mind. Dancing with Miss Dorothea Ellingham had been a mistake. She was a newly engaged female; he had no right to be flirting with her, no right to enjoy her company so very much; no right to use her as a way to avoid an introduction to the woman his father had expressly said he wanted Carter to meet.

And *not* dancing with Lady Audrey Parson last night had been an even graver error. It was that action that brought him to the predicament he faced this afternoon.

Finally, the duke entered the study. He spared a brief glance at his son, then perched himself regally on an ornate chair behind an enormous mahogany desk. Carter settled himself against the very uncomfortable straight-back chair opposite that desk.

"I thought to ask you for an explanation for your behavior last night, but have decided it would be a waste of your breath and an even greater waste of my time. There is simply no acceptable excuse."

Carter strove to elicit an appearance of calm. Yet all the while, his stomach churned and his jaw ached with the effort it took to keep it firmly shut. Arguments with the Duke of Hansborough were seldom won. Especially when the duke was in such a high temper.

"I was humiliated!" the duke roared at his son. "Made to look like a complete ass in front of half the *ton*. By my own son, no less."

"It was not my intention to insult you or show any disrespect, sir."

The duke's face darkened. "Intention or not, it was the result."

"True, I was aware that you wanted me to meet Lady Audrey. Yet there was a crush of people at the ball. It was easy to become lost in the crowd," Carter said.

"You did it deliberately," the duke accused, his voice dripping in irritation.

It was the truth and they both knew it. Carter had no ready reply, no adequate defense. He turned the conundrum over in his mind and wisely decided it would be foolish to try and talk his way around his father's ire. "I beg your pardon, Your Grace."

The duke hesitated and then apparently saw the sincere apology in his son's face. Nevertheless, a lecture ensued. Carter barely listened. It had all been said before, countless times. *He will run out of breath,* Carter told himself. *Eventually.* Carter waited, soundlessly adjusting the angle of his leg, trying to remain as serene as possible.

Finally, the duke paused. The color on his face was no longer a stark, bright red; it had dulled to a healthy-looking glow. "You shall marry by the end of the Season. I have made a list of females I find acceptable, women who will be able to admirably fill the role of future duchess. Certainly there must be at least one among them that will strike your fancy."

A list. *Hell.* Carter reluctantly reached for the piece of paper his father held out to him. With effort, he resisted the urge to crumple it and toss it in the unlit fireplace. Instead, he pretended to carefully study it, though his eyes blurred over the names.

"Is there a particular reason why you feel it necessary to

play the matchmaker for me, sir? Do you think me incapable of finding a woman on my own?"

"I am very aware that you have no difficulty finding women. All sorts of women. All sorts of improper women." His father's eyes narrowed. "I have left the task of finding a bride to you for several years and you are no closer to matrimony than you were when you first reached your maturity. You will be thirty years old in a few months. 'Tis time, Carter. Past time."

The marquess squirmed in his chair. It bothered him greatly to disappoint the duke. Far more than he would have liked to admit. Far more than his father would likely believe. He was tempted to reveal that he had reached the same conclusion and would indeed marry by the end of the Season, but that would be a grave tactical error and encourage even more of the duke's unwanted interference.

"These sorts of things cannot be rushed, sir. Surely you agree this is a most important decision?"

The duke sighed. "I am not a heartless monster. I understand your reluctance. Truly. But I would be a poor father indeed and an even worse aristocrat if I allowed you to become an idle, thoughtless man, one who will never do anything meaningful or important with his life."

The comment rankled. He wasn't all that bad. A bit of idleness, perhaps. A bit of gambling, a bit of drinking, a bit of whoring now and then. There were others, many others, far worse. "Forgive me, sir, but I fail to see how a wife will change anything."

"A proper wife, a family, will give you purpose, stability," the duke said.

Carter's brow lifted. He saw no logic in that argument. Some of the wildest, most hedonistic noblemen he knew were married men.

"Yes, yes, I know," the duke bristled, as though he read his son's mind. "There are far too many in society who marry for pedigree or fortune and then dally with others. But that is not our way. The Hansborough dukes are honorable men, faithful to their duty, their country, and their wives."

Carter leaned forward. "Precisely. Which is why I cannot rush the choice of a bride. I need to somehow discover a woman who values me for more than my title or fortune."

"Then you must seek her out! She isn't going to just fall into your lap like a ripe plum, my boy," the duke insisted.

A ripe plum, indeed. More like a rotten apple. Carter sighed. "With all due respect, sir, I have made an effort with the women you have thrust so unceremoniously at me for the last few years. It has all been for naught."

"Bah, you barely paid them any attention."

Carter's lungs strained for air as he struggled to hide his exasperation. "For most of these women, a limited acquaintance was all that was required. Several were mindnumbingly boring, or even worse, outright silly and giddy. A few spoke incessantly, while others sat so still and silent I worried if they were still drawing breath."

The duke glared at him. "You are exaggerating."

"Hardly. I am being kind. If the intent of marriage is to continue our illustrious, noble line, then you must allow it is imperative that I marry a woman I can impregnate."

The duke snorted with disdain. "Don't be vulgar."

"I'm being truthful, Father."

The duke rested his elbows on the top of his desk and covered his face with his hands for a moment. "I understand," he said quietly, his tone sympathetic. "Far more than you think. I know all too well what it feels like to be obligated to a title, responsible to a birthright, forced to follow the immutable rules of society. If you fight it, you will become an angry, bitter man. If you embrace it, you at least have a hope of finding happiness."

Carter tried to make allowances. He believed his father did indeed have his best interests at heart. But the duke was too much of an autocrat to completely understand. The need to control everything around him was strong and that included the actions and affairs of his son.

"I have always strived to be honorable, to do justice to our family name," Carter said grimly. "I do not shirk my duties, sir, yet I want to be allowed to choose the woman with whom I shall spend the rest of my life. Is that so very much to ask?"

The duke stood. He was silent for a long moment and then he smiled charitably at his son. Carter's intricately tied cravat suddenly felt much too tight.

"You present a compelling argument and I find I must agree. Perhaps I have been a bit too zealous. I'll own it must be lowering for a man to have his father interfering so obviously." The duke's smile widened. "Consult the list. I feel certain there is at least one woman among those delectable females you will be happy to *choose* as your bride."

"The thing is, old boy, you've never mastered the art of standing firm with the duke," Viscount Benton said, emphasizing his point with a swift slash of his steel rapier. "'Tis no wonder your father is at odds with your behavior. He wants you to do as he bids and cannot understand why you are refusing him."

Carter executed a swift parry of Lord Benton's thrust and lunged forward on his lead foot, questioning his initial opinion that an afternoon of vigorous swordplay with his friends might relieve some of the tension he was feeling. If Benton's mouth kept pace with his flashing foil, Carter would no doubt leave the fencing club with an even greater headache than when he arrived.

"This is not a simple dilemma," Carter insisted, his voice raised to be heard above the clang of their steel rapiers. "The duke is hell-bent on finding me a bride. By the end of the Season."

"This Season?" Benton visibly shuddered at the notion and Carter used the distraction to press his advantage. The viscount leapt back to evade the strong thrust and smiled. "God, that is a problem."

"Exactly." Carter's rapier moved in a shiny flurry, his sword chattering against Benton's. "He's made a list of women."

The viscount's left brow lifted higher than the right. "How positively medieval."

"I suppose that's one way to put it," Carter replied.

"There is, however, a very easy solution," the viscount said mildly as he advanced, his left hand curved in an elegant arc behind his head.

"Oh?"

They moved in a tight circle, sweat gleaming on their brows. "Find a bride yourself. One that is not on his infernal list."

"What?" Carter's shoulders dropped in shock. How did Benton know? He had deliberately kept this decision to himself. The very last thing he needed was for it to be known in society that he was seeking a bride.

The viscount's blade flashed up. Carter shouted, realizing Benton had made the comment to break his concentration. He countered the move and the sword suddenly flew from Benton's hand. It slid, clattering across the floor.

"I say, Benton, 'tis unwise to provoke a man when he's got a blade in his hand," Peter Dawson advised. "Especially one as skilled as Atwood."

Benton flashed an elegant grin, then offered his opponent

a salute. "I knew the suggestion of taking a wife would get to him. And I was right."

"Yes, but I still won," Carter said as he bent to retrieve the sword.

"That's only because you did not hear the rest of my plan."

"It was not necessary. Your plan is as daft as you are, Benton. I have no interest in finding a wife," Carter lied, shuddering to think of the consequences if the matchmaking females of the *ton* knew the truth.

"None of us do," Benton replied. "Well, except for Dawson. I suspect he will marry and have a parcel of brats clinging to his knees before you or I have a serious conversation about marriage."

"Hell, Benton, with that attitude, you'll wait so long to find a bride that you could very well end up marrying one of my daughters," Dawson quipped, then his expression sobered. "Strike that idea. I cannot imagine entrusting a child of mine into your care."

The viscount slapped him on the back. "I always knew you were an intelligent fellow, Dawson. Now come, you both must hear me out."

Benton poured them each a generous portion of ale and the three men settled into comfortable leather chairs that were set around the perimeter of the room. Against his better judgment, Carter found himself saying, "All right, out with it, Benton. I know we'll have no peace until you've had your say."

"My plan is brilliant in its simplicity." The viscount rubbed his hands together with obvious relish. "You must find a completely unsuitable female and present her to your father as your future duchess."

"Unsuitable?" Dawson questioned.

"Yes. The greater her unsuitability, the better."

Carter swallowed the rest of his drink. The ale had an

appealing, biting flavor as it slid down his throat. He reached for the pitcher and refilled his glass. "God knows, I shouldn't encourage you, Benton, but I find myself macabrely interested. What do I do next, after the duke has a fit of apoplexy from meeting this unworthy creature?"

"You present your ultimatum. Tell him you will marry this woman or you will marry no one." The viscount easily caught the towel Carter tossed at him. He held it up, then with a shrug, used it to wipe his damp brow.

"Are you not listening, Benton? I just said I have no wish to marry anyone, least of all an unsuitable female."

"Pray, let me finish," the viscount said indignantly. "When you present this female, a woman not personally selected by the duke to be your bride, a woman not on his exalted list, he will be appalled. Angry."

"Livid," Dawson interjected helpfully.

"Yes," Benton agreed. "Livid. And the duke will tell you that it is better to remain unwed than to tie yourself, and your illustrious family name, to an inappropriate female. You fight him on this, but are eventually brought around to reason and reluctantly agree with him." Benton leaned forward in his chair. "Now that is key. You must make a great show of being reluctantly brought around to the duke's point of view. If not, he will not believe you were serious about marrying the chit."

Dawson nodded his head in agreement. "Your character and convictions are strong, Atwood. It would be more believable if you initially stand firm against your father."

"In fact, it might even be better if you do not capitulate completely," Benton said, clearly warming to the plan. "Instead, tell him out of respect for his opinion, you will wait a full year and ponder all the implications of your choice before actually marrying the girl. And thus you will remain a carefree bachelor. At least for a year."

Carter stroked his chin thoughtfully as he pondered the idea. It was just ridiculous enough to work. If he was of a mind to avoid marriage. Which he was not. Perhaps he should tell his friends of his change of heart? No, hearing Benton's scheme was much too entertaining. "I have no interest in pursuing this rather outrageous course, yet I feel compelled to ask, where does one find an inappropriate female? A brothel, perchance?"

Dawson snickered. Viscount Benton threw the towel back at Carter. The marquess ducked and it flew passed his ear.

"I said make your father livid, Atwood," the viscount huffed. "Not give the man a heart seizure."

Dawson topped off his glass of ale from the pitcher on the table. "Benton is right. You cannot be boorish. The duke needs to believe you will go through with the marriage."

"Exactly." Benton's lips curved in an amused smile. "The duke knows you would never marry a lightskirt. Hell, even I wouldn't marry a soiled dove, and there's not much I won't do."

The three friends laughed in agreement.

"A daughter of a merchant might do nicely," Dawson suggested excitedly. He took a sip of his drink, grimaced, then set it on the table.

"Capital idea," Benton acknowledged. "Nothing will boil the duke's blood faster than the notion of having a chit, reeking with the smell of trade, for a daughter-in-law."

Carter was at a loss for words. Everything they said was true. The duke would be appalled at the notion of his only son marrying a woman of inferior breeding. Thankfully it was unnecessary to entertain the notion.

"Who's ready for another round of swordplay?" the marquess asked, determined to change the subject. "Dawson?"

"No thanks." Dawson gingerly placed the foil he held on the bench beside him. "You nearly skewered Benton with that last lunge. I have no interest in being sliced to ribbons in the name of good sport. If I am going to die with a sword in my hand, I want it to be for a good and noble cause."

A loud clash of steel, accompanied by the murmur of several male voices, suddenly drew their attention. A considerable crowd of men had gathered in a circle. Within the cleared space in the center of the crowd, two men were engaged in swift, intense swordplay.

"Hmm, that appears a bit personal," Benton observed.

Carter nodded his head in agreement. Judging by the reaction of the crowd, this was not an ordinary match. The men so eagerly observing it all wore that avid interest men often display at the prospect of bloodshed.

Their curiosity piqued, the three friends moved closer to the action. The younger man of the dueling pair was thinner and shorter. He wore a crisp, white linen shirt, and a gold satin waistcoat adorned with intricate silver embroidery. He moved with elegance and grace, never seeming to break from the proper form or stance.

His opponent was a taller, solidly built man, dressed in a simple black waistcoat and a white linen shirt that had obviously seen many washings. His style of swordplay was not nearly as polished. It was more determined, more deliberate. More accurate, Carter conceded as with a glinting flurry of moves, the taller man shredded his opponent's right sleeve.

"Impressive," Benton muttered, when the man next blocked the attack from his opponent and then quickly put him on the defensive. "He moves as though the sword were a part of his arm."

"Who is he? A new instructor?" Carter asked.

"He certainly possesses the skill," Dawson replied. "Though I don't believe he is employed here. I met him last week. His name is Gregory Roddington. Major Gregory

Roddington, actually. From what I gather, he's some sort of war hero. He was the youngest officer attached to Wellington's staff and appointed himself admirably on the battlefield, especially at Waterloo. Rumors abound that Wellington himself is trying to secure a knighthood for him as recognition of his exemplary service to the crown."

"Apparently they'll allow anyone admittance to the club these days," the viscount scoffed, but Carter could see his friend's eyes light with respect.

As far as Carter knew, Benton had never done anything even remotely honorable, yet he had a keen respect for those who did, even though he tried to hide it.

"'Tis hard to believe he is only six and twenty," Dawson commented.

"War ages a man," Carter said wryly, agreeing the major looked older, more hardened than his years would indicate.

"Still, he's a capital fellow. Good for a laugh."

At that moment, the major attacked with a flurry of ferocious strikes. Off balance, his opponent fell back, then desperately brought his sword up to defend his face. Pressing his advantage, the major circled under the weapon, then with the tip of his blade neatly dislodged the sword from the other man's hand.

It fell to the floor with a loud clatter. Moving so fast it was barely seen, the major then pressed the end of his blade into the base of his opponent's throat.

"My match, I believe," he muttered.

Panting hard, the younger man nodded. He seemed dazed, uncertain of exactly how he had been beaten. The major saluted his vanquished opponent, then looked up and seemed to notice the audience for the first time.

"Introduce us, Dawson," Carter demanded as the crowd began to disperse.

"Major," Dawson called out. "May I beg a moment of your time?"

The man turned, his expression startled. "Sorry, Mr. Dawson. Since resigning my commission I am trying very hard to distance myself from my former rank. To no avail." Ironic amusement tempered his voice. "My friends call me Roddy. I would be honored if you would do the same."

"Thank you, Roddy. May I present Carter Grayson, Marquess of Atwood and Sebastian Dodd, Viscount Benton."

"My lords." The major executed a bow. "A pleasure to make your acquaintance."

"We enjoyed your little show, Roddington," the viscount replied. "Though it appeared somewhat more than a friendly match."

"Did it?" The major shrugged, seemingly unconcerned with the observation. "Strange, I hardly know the man."

The crowd made a wide berth as the men walked toward the door. Carter caught the edges of several conversations as they pushed through the crowd, making little sense of the comments he overheard.

"What is this all about?" he asked Dawson. The two of them had dropped back while the major and Benton led the way out of the club.

Dawson's eyes widened and Carter wondered at his friend's sudden anxiety. "Apparently the swordplay we just witnessed was a point of honor," Dawson whispered to Carter.

"Whose honor?"

"The major's." Dawson craned his neck forward, as if needing to confirm the major and the viscount were still engaged in conversation before speaking. "There's a bit of a mysterious cloud regarding Roddington's background. Rumors, I'm sure."

Carter was intrigued. "What sort of rumors?"

"It seems he is illegitimate. There are some who say he was fathered by a nobleman. And others who say he is of royal birth."

Carter could not hold back the laugh that rumbled up from his chest. "If Prinny were in truth the father of only half the offspring that are attributed to him, he wouldn't be able to stand."

"The Regent isn't the only royal in England," Dawson replied with mild indignity.

Benton glanced over his shoulder at them. "We are going to the Bull and Finch for some food and drink. In exchange for buying him supper, the major has graciously agreed to teach me how he disarmed his opponent so thoroughly."

"Sounds as if you are on the better end of that bargain, Benton," Carter called out.

"You have not seen me eat or drink, my lord," the major readily replied.

When the four men reached the tavern, they discovered a brawl underway, blocking the entrance. Fists were flying, limbs were flailing, bodies were being flung through the air.

"I don't fancy wading into the middle of all that mess," Dawson said cautiously, backing up.

"I've seen worse," the major replied. "And I'm hungry. I'll meet you inside."

They watched as Roddington pushed himself into the chaos of brawling men, stepping around and over bodies, ducking and dodging to avoid any stray blows aimed his way. When he was safely through the doorway, he waved to them, then disappeared inside.

"Damn!" Benton broke into a grin. "Gentlemen, shall we?"

The viscount followed the major's lead. Swallowing hard, Dawson kept close to the viscount's coattails, while Carter brought up the rear. They had just crossed over the threshold when one of the brawlers lost his balance and careened into Carter.

"Watch it!" Carter yelled sharply, swinging his closed fist upward. His blow landed directly on the culprit's jaw. He staggered back, arms flailing, then fell awkwardly to the ground, swearing loudly.

Carter's hand stung, yet he felt vitally alive. Grinning, he began to follow his friends toward the taproom when suddenly he heard a loud shout.

"He's got a knife!" Dawson cried.

Carter turned, saw the flash of steel, and scrambled to get out of the way. There were several shouts and then another body suddenly appeared, stepping between the marquess and his would-be assailant.

"Halt!" The command was quickly followed by the unmistakable sound of a pistol being cocked.

Carter whirled his head. The major stood tall, his feet braced apart, the pistol in his right hand calmly pointed at the man's chest. "Now, lads, a bit of fisticuffs we can understand, but knives take all the fun out of it, don't you agree?"

One of the man's companions came forward to help him, eyeing the major, and his pistol, most warily. "We don't want no trouble," he grumbled.

"Fine. Then off with the lot of you."

The man on the ground flinched violently as he regained his feet. One of the other brawlers took the knife away and handed it to Carter. The marquess fingered it thoughtfully, surprised at how calm he felt in the midst of such obvious danger.

Gradually, the crowd shuffled away. "You are a handy individual to have around," Carter finally said, breaking through the silent tension. He brushed the dirt from his coat and smiled at the major. "How would you like to accompany us to a society ball this evening?"

"It's bound to be rather dull compared to the afternoon you've just had, but we can promise there will be a few laughs," Benton added.

The major slowly eased back the hammer on his pistol and returned it to his coat pocket. "Sounds delightful. I can hardly wait."

Five hours later, fresh from a lukewarm bath, Major Gregory Roddington began to shave. His former batman, now his personal servant, Julius Parker, had somehow managed to keep the shaving water hot, which was more than could be said for the bathwater. But Roddy didn't mind. He had lived in far worse conditions than these shabby London accommodations.

"There's a man at the door asking to see you," Parker said. "He refused to give his name."

Roddy nodded. He had been waiting, wondering why the man was so late. "Send him in."

Ignoring Parker's clear disapproval, Roddy shrugged into a robe, cinching the belt tightly around his waist. Then he resumed his shaving.

"I've come for my money," the visitor declared the moment he entered the room.

"It's on the table," Roddy replied. His back was toward the visitor, but the mirror propped in front of him allowed his eyes to follow the man's every move.

"I should charge you more," the man grumbled as he slid the two gold coins off the table and thrust them into his pocket. "I didn't know the bloke was going to sucker punch me."

The major smiled grimly. "It looked like a clean blow to me."

"Yeah, well, he punches damn hard for a toff." The

man rubbed his hand gingerly along his jawline, wincing several times. Roddy could see the shadow of a bruise had already begun to form. "I thought them aristocrats were a bunch of limp-wristed dandies."

"Apparently not all of them."

"Humph." The man grunted, but didn't seem convinced. "I'm telling you right now, there'll be an extra charge the next time."

Roddy rinsed off his shaving blade, placed it on the rim of his bowl, then pressed a towel to his face. Finally turning, he faced the man who had so recently been staring down the barrel of his finest pistol. "Though it did not go specifically as I had planned, the outcome is satisfactory," he said confidently. "There will be no need for a next time."

Chapter Four

The Duke of Warwick's London townhome was a rather overwhelming place, Dorothea thought as she slowly circled around the outer edges of the ballroom. Antique mirrors lined the walls, rich gold satin drapes were pulled back to reveal the long windows leading out to the terraced gardens, six enormous crystal chandeliers hung from the gilded ceiling. She had heard that the room had been designed in a similar style as Versailles, yet with the memories of the vanquished Napoleon so fresh in everyone's mind, no one dared to make any references to the French.

She reached the end of the room, turned, and could not contain her gasp of delight. The room was magnificent, decked out in the finest accompaniments. No expense had been spared for the ball, and Dorothea still had difficulty believing it had all been done for her. The innumerable porcelain vases were overflowing with white lilies, the ten-piece orchestra placed in the balcony above the dance floor, the hundreds of lit beeswax candles shimmered and glittered off the mirrored surfaces.

Dozens of rooms beyond the main ballroom were also set up, awaiting the pleasure of the many guests. This would not, she was pleased to note, be an overcrowded, stuffy affair. The Duke of Warwick, or rather his daughter-in-law, Lady Meredith, had the sense to ensure there would be ample room for all of the four hundred or so guests that had been invited. And from the looks of things, not one person had refused the invitation.

The generosity of her temporary chaperones was humbling and Dorothea silently scolded herself for not enjoying the affair more. As a girl growing up in Yorkshire, she had dreamt of such a moment, though even her fertile imagination had not included cases of chilled French champagne being so casually served to the guests by white-gloved footmen dressed formally in blue and gold livery.

While standing in the receiving line earlier, she thought it might be necessary to pinch her arm to truly believe it was all real. If only her sisters were here to share in this moment! But Gwendolyn was nearing the end of her confinement and naturally not participating in any society events. And Emma, at sixteen, was too young to be included. She was languishing at home in Yorkshire with uncle Fletcher and aunt Mildred, no doubt bored to tears.

Dorothea promised herself she would write Emma a long, detailed letter tomorrow afternoon. At least that way she could share some of the excitement of the evening with her sister.

Dorothea's thoughts were interrupted as a hush fell over the crowd. She turned and saw the Duke of Warwick was leading Lady Meredith onto the dance floor. Dorothea moved herself toward the center of the room, searching for the Marquess of Dardington. He had explained to her earlier in the day that his father, the Duke of Warwick, would insist on opening the dancing at the ball himself.

The idea of dancing with the duke had put a flutter of butterfly nerves in Dorothea's stomach, but Lord Dardington had quickly explained that the only woman the Duke of Warwick danced with in public anymore was his daughter-in-law, Lady Meredith.

And since his wife would be dancing with his father, Lord Dardington thought it appropriate that he be the one to dance with Dorothea. It was a better choice, yet not all that much of a reprieve, for she found her temporary guardian at times an equally intimidating man.

"Smile," Lord Dardington commanded as they made their first circuit around the floor.

"I am," she muttered beneath her breath, girding herself to endure the scrutiny as all eyes in the room swung toward her. "Smiling so broadly I fear my face will split in two."

"Now that would be something of extreme interest to all those meddlesome gossips," he replied. "To see your face break in half."

His lighthearted teasing eased her nerves. Normally Dorothea enjoyed being the center of attention, but she had been long enough in society to learn that along with scrutiny came the criticism. Occasionally warranted, but more often than not petty and mean spirited.

The two couples made a second, slow circuit of the dance floor and then finally the other guests joined them. Dorothea's breathing gradually returned to a steady cadence as the polished ballroom floor quickly became crowded with additional couples.

After a few minutes, the music ended. Lord Dardington steered Dorothea toward his wife and father, and the four of them left the dance floor together.

"Ah, now you shall have an opportunity to practice your skill at coquetry," the duke observed dryly as a gaggle of gentlemen eagerly converged on them. "Meredith tells me she is impressed with your approach when it comes to capturing their attention."

Dorothea blushed and lowered her chin. In Yorkshire, she had considered herself something of an expert in the fine art of flirting, but here in Town the level of pretense that men and women engaged in was far beyond her talents. "I fear I have much to learn," she whispered.

"I believe you are a quick study," Lord Dardington interjected. "However, if you encounter any problems, I am here to assist."

Dorothea could not help the skeptical look she gave Lord Dardington, uncertain how much help he could offer. More than likely, he would scare off a large number of her potential suitors, and that would not be much help when her intent was to find a husband. Then again, would she truly wish to marry a man who could not hold his own against an intimidating opponent?

She smiled coyly as the gentlemen clamored around her, trying not to be obvious as her eyes searched the group for one man in particular. One man she feared was not in attendance.

Carter Grayson, Marquess of Atwood. He had remained in her thoughts these six days since the Earl of Wessex's ball. Lady Meredith had expressed mild surprise when there had been no note, no flowers, no call from the handsome marquess, but Dorothea knew this would be the outcome. She had no expectation of being pursued by a man of his stature.

Still, it had been disappointing to be proven correct.

"Miss Ellingham, I simply must insist that you allow me a dance."

Dorothea turned and her eyes fell on the impressive girth of Sir Perry. His florid face flushed, he bowed as low as his corseted chest would allow. When he straightened, the tuff of pale blond hair that grew on the crown of his head remained over his eyes. Hastily he pushed it back over his scalp.

"Of course I shall reserve a dance for you," she answered, hoping Sir Perry was not going to make a nuisance of himself. "A quadrille would be perfect."

"I am honored." He poked at the strands of hair that had again fallen over his eyes. "And for the second dance, perhaps a waltz?"

Dorothea inwardly groaned. She had been introduced to Sir Perry the second week she arrived in Town and during that initial conversation had ruled him out as a possible husband. He was too old, too self-important, and much too boring.

Still, she thought it cruel to cut him directly. He was harmless and it never hurt to have a circle of admirers. A waltz, however, was far too intimate a dance to consider engaging in with him. It would most certainly give him the wrong impression of her feelings.

She smiled vaguely in response to his request, but Sir Perry did not seem to notice. The sound of his own voice was the only thing he preferred to his meals, and he soon dominated the conversation. The other gentlemen appeared to be waiting for him to catch his breath so they could get in a word.

Dorothea's smile widened as she appreciated the ironic humor of the situation. Tuning out Sir Perry's prattle, she began to look about the ballroom.

Her gaze halted on one gentleman in particular and a shiver of awareness went down her spine. *Atwood!* She recognized him instantly. His broad shoulders were unmistakable, his dark hair brushed and gleaming in the candlelight. He was tall and athletically built; his midnight blue eyes clear, intelligent, and assessing.

Dorothea could not contain the sigh that fell from her

lips. The marquess was what her younger sister Emma would call dangerously handsome.

Unexpectedly he turned and looked directly at Dorothea. Their eyes met and her breath hitched. He was standing on the opposite side of the room, and yet she felt the full force of his regard. His expression never altered; it remained calm, open, and pleasant. Yet she read within it an unspoken challenge.

A ripple of nervous energy went through her, along with an unfamiliar flush of heat. It was as if her entire body was blushing.

Against her better judgment, Dorothea commanded herself to stare at him directly. He was dressed in formal evening clothes, as he had been the other night. They were luxurious and expertly tailored and she wondered briefly what he would look like in more casual attire, or even more shocking, what he would look like wearing no clothing at all.

The image brought another flush to her face. Dorothea nearly groaned out loud. Drat! She had wanted to remain poised and inscrutable when she next faced the marquess. Instead, she appeared gauche and naïve.

She took a deliberate breath and waited for her wits to stop spinning. Really. He was just a man. No different certainly from most of his gender.

Yet for all his refined looks and manners, he had a rugged appeal that she found alarmingly attractive. And the glimpse she had been given of his humorous side had only whetted her appetite for more.

He slipped into the crowd. Dorothea's eyes searched frantically for his whereabouts, darting to and fro before she suddenly caught herself. What was she doing? Making a complete and utter ninny of herself, that was certain. How truly mortifying.

Scolding herself for squandering the opportunity to bask in the attention of the numerous gentlemen standing right in front of her, Dorothea blinked hard.

Sir Perry was still droning on about something. No matter.

"Gentlemen, my dance card looks woefully bare." Her unexpected interruption startled Sir Perry into silence. Seizing the moment, Dorothea smiled flirtatiously at her circle of admirers. "Pray tell, whose name shall I write in for the first waltz?"

"Looking for anyone in particular?"

The male voice at Carter's ear startled him, but he managed not to jump. "Not so much looking as avoiding," he said drolly.

"Hmm, let me guess," Viscount Benton said. His eyes swept the room and his expression grew puzzled. "Hell, there are almost too many unmarried ladies here to select just one that you need to avoid."

"Yes," Carter agreed grimly. "And nearly half of these females are on my father's infernal list."

The viscount's brow rose. "I thought you were going to burn that damn list."

The marquess shrugged. "I was, but then I reasoned it would be far wiser to memorize the names, so I know which females I must ignore."

"And how is that going?" Benton asked, amusement edging his tone.

"Not well."

"Perhaps we should retreat to the card room," the viscount suggested. "Unmarried females generally refrain from sitting at the tables."

"I think it is safer if we leave the ball," Carter replied, wishing again that he had sent his regrets. He could hardly try to court a woman with his father here. Besides, the one female who most captured his attention was tonight's honored guest, and she was already taken. By Arthur Pengrove, of all people. "There is a new girl working at Raven's Paradise. Madame Angelina assures me she is supremely talented."

The viscount cleared his throat. Confused, Carter looked closely at his friend. "Are you blushing, Benton?"

"Don't be an idiot, Atwood," the viscount scoffed. "I would be more than happy to accompany you to the brothel and I shall even wager that I will be the first to have a go at the new girl."

"Then what is the problem?"

Benton looked away. He almost seemed . . . embarrassed. But that was impossible. Carter had known the viscount for years. And in all that time he had never once seen him as discomforted as he now appeared.

"I can't leave yet," Benton finally admitted. "I promised my grandmother I would do her a great favor and dance with the niece of her dearest friend. By any chance, are you acquainted with Miss Phoebe Garret?"

Carter started laughing. For all his swagger and bravado, his scandalous and outrageous behavior, at his core Benton had an honorable streak he could not eradicate. Though he certainly tried his damndest.

A favor for his grandmother. How priceless! Carter could hardly wait to tell Dawson, knowing their friend would appreciate the utter irony of it all. "Miss Garret is on my list," he said. "The first name, actually."

Benton grinned. "Then I am safe. If the duke has earmarked her as one of your potential brides, she will no doubt be very unimpressed with my lesser title and wealth. I can fulfill my duty to my grandmother without fear of giving Miss Garret the wrong impression of any interest in her."

Carter tugged at the cuffs of his shirt. "That is assuming Miss Garret will grant you a dance. She is a somewhat timid creature who will more than likely be frightened speechless when a rogue with your reputation approaches her."

"What a perfectly delectable thought." The viscount's lips rose in a wider smile. "I had forgotten a blackened reputation can be a most useful tool when it comes to the marriage mart. It scares many a scheming mother away. You should consider acquiring one yourself."

"God forbid. My reputation is already dark enough. Besides, a rake merely scares off one sort of female and attracts another." Carter barely kept himself from shuddering. "No, thank you."

"Tell me, which one of these simpering ladies is Phoebe Garret?"

Carter searched the room. He had only met Miss Garret a few times, but he well remembered her dark hair and full figure. "She is currently at the back of the ballroom, partially hidden by a massive potted palm."

"Naturally. I am not surprised that she demonstrates the prerequisite characteristic of cowering that your father finds so endlessly appealing." The viscount craned his neck in the direction Carter indicated. "Egad, she's a bit long in the tooth," he remarked. "No wonder her relatives are cornering men to partner her for dances."

"She isn't that old." Carter shrugged. "Nearly four and twenty, I believe, which is younger than you or I."

"She's practically in her dotage."

"That's most unkind," Carter replied.

"It's just an observation. I don't make these ridiculous rules. Nor do I follow them."

The two men stared at Miss Garret. As if somehow sensing she was being observed, she slowly sank farther behind the palm fronds. Benton sighed.

"Age can add an interesting bit of maturity and depth to a woman's countenance," Carter remarked. "Alas, that is not the case with Miss Garret. I think she is simply too shy for her own good, and her natural hesitation coupled with her age and her anxious mother's proclivity to rush her into a match unfortunately leaves the woman with a desperate air."

The viscount's eyes widened with concern. "Desperation in a female can be most unnerving."

"And dangerous. Be sure to remember that, Benton."

"Ah, there you are." Peter Dawson's voice broke into the conversation. "I told Roddy we'd find you two eventually."

Carter smiled, pleased to see a few more friendly male faces. "Major, I'm so glad you could make it tonight," he said sincerely.

"I assumed I had you to thank for the invitation, Atwood," Roddington replied. "The Duke of Warwick is hardly within the circle of my acquaintances."

"I had a feeling you might enjoy yourself this evening." Carter looked around the room. "Most men of Warwick's rank know how to throw an exceptional party."

"Aren't you the son of a duke?" Roddington asked.

Carter turned in surprise. It was hardly a secret, but he was startled that the major would be aware of the connection. "Yes, my father is the Duke of Hansborough."

"Yet we try not to hold it against him," Benton interjected in a dry tone.

"Is the duke here?" Roddy inquired casually.

"Somewhere." Carter's mouth twisted. "We are not much in agreement these days, my father and I. Especially when it comes to the subject of finding a marriageable young lady."

The major's eyes widened slightly. "For you or for him?"

For him? Carter nearly choked on his tongue. The idea

of his widowed father taking a bride was something that had never once entered his mind. Though he supposed it was a reasonable question. Carter's mother had been dead for many years. And his father was not yet an old man. In fact, men older than the duke had successfully married and even fathered additional children.

Dawson picked up the thread of the conversation. "That's a rather intriguing suggestion. If the duke was saddled with a young bride to chase around, he wouldn't be half as interested in what you were doing. What do you think, Atwood?"

Carter stared at Dawson dumbly. What did he think of the idea? It was bullshit, pure and simple. His father had deeply loved his wife and was devoted to honoring her memory. He would never, nor should he, consider replacing her.

"I think marriage is far too much on everyone's minds these days," Carter said sharply, refusing to examine his feelings on the matter too closely. "Come, gentlemen, let's engage in a few obligatory dances and then leave the ball to find some true entertainment."

Dorothea absently fingered the white satin ribbon on the skirt of her gown and drew herself farther into the corner. She had deliberately left the next few dances unclaimed on her card, leaving herself the option of resting or perhaps partnering with someone who had not presented himself to her. Like the Marquess of Atwood?

"Miss Ellingham?"

Trying to hide her yelp of shock, Dorothea nearly bit through her tongue. *Gracious, he's here!* She offered him a polite curtsy. "Good evening, my lord." She kept her expression cool, fearing she would be unable to smile without looking and feeling like a total ninny. "How good of you to attend my ball."

"I would not have missed it for anything. Please, allow me to introduce a friend, Major Gregory Roddington, a recent hero of the war."

Distractedly, Dorothea turned her attention to the handsome man beside the marquess. He bowed to her and smiled.

"A pleasure to make your acquaintance, Miss Ellingham. They are playing a quadrille. Would you do me the honor of standing up with me?" the major asked. "Though I'm afraid I can claim no great skill on the dance floor, I promise to try and execute the steps in the correct order."

"Ah, but can you avoid crushing my toes, Major Roddington?" she asked with a flirtatious tilt of her chin.

"I can try," he answered with a twinkling grin.

Dorothea swallowed a small sigh of disappointment. The major seemed to be a very pleasant, affable man, but it was Atwood's attention she craved, not his friend's. How marvelous it would be to dance, and flirt, with the marquess. But he had not asked her.

"I shall be delighted to dance with you, sir." Pasting a bright smile on her face, Dorothea allowed the major to lead her onto the dance floor.

They assumed their places. Major Roddington initially set himself on the wrong side. The gentleman on his left gave him a sharp poke, pointing out the error. Hastily changing positions, the major favored her with a sheepish grin.

Dorothea's answering smile held true warmth. Perhaps it was better to be paired with the major. He seemed a kind man. He was handsome in an unpolished, rugged way, with a trim, fit physique. She liked how he smiled at his ineptitude, for it was a rare treat indeed to encounter a man who did not take himself so seriously.

The music began and each couple bowed elegantly. Hands held, they came together in the pattern of the dance. They crossed next to each other, took a few steps forward, then back.

Dorothea pivoted gracefully on the ball of her foot, turned to the man on her right, and came face-to-face with the Marquess of Atwood. She sucked in a sharp breath. He appeared not to notice as he took her hand.

And squeezed it playfully. *Good heavens!* She gazed intently at the marquess, certain she must be mistaken at what had happened. Or wistful?

Regaining her composure, Dorothea repeated the dance pattern. She waited breathlessly as her hand once again was clasped within the palm of the marquess's large one. And then . . . another squeeze, followed by a gentle caress.

Dorothea's feet stumbled as she missed a step. The major sent her a sympathetic glance. Had he seen what happened? No, that was unlikely. He was concentrating too hard on where to place his feet and when to turn. She swallowed. Why did Lord Atwood keep touching her in such a manner? Was he flirting? Teasing? But if he was interested in her, then why hadn't he asked her to dance?

Deciding the only way to complete the dance successfully, Dorothea concluded she must ignore Atwood and focus her attention exclusively on the major. When the steps next brought them close, she smiled charmingly at Major Roddington, tilting her head deliberately to one side. Her best side. The side that she always thought showcased her features to their fullest advantage.

"How are your toes faring, Miss Ellingham?" the major whispered.

"They are quite safe at the moment," she whispered back. "I think you are far too modest in your assessment of your dancing skills."

He laughed, and she caught a quick glimpse of a most appealing dimple in his cheek. "You are very well-mannered, young lady."

"Nonsense. I applaud your effort."

"You must forgive my lack of entertaining conversation." The major smiled as he turned to face her again. "I confess, I am counting the steps. Which I know is terribly gauche."

They twirled, then met again. "At least you are counting silently in your head," Dorothea quipped. "I know of at least two gentlemen who mutter the numbers under their breath as they dance. 'Tis most distracting."

"Are you insulting the major?" Lord Atwood interjected.

The unexpected question seemed to startle Roddington as much as Dorothea. He missed his footing and did indeed step on her toe. Dorothea skillfully hid her wince.

She was forced to wait until the figures drew them together before she could answer the marquess. "Stop being such a pest, my lord, and pay attention to your own partner."

The marquess abruptly ceased dancing, causing the other two couples in their set to bump into each other. One of the gentlemen coughed deferentially to gain the marquess's attention. Atwood immediately inclined his head in apology and took up where he had left off, though Dorothea noted gleefully that he was no longer in time to the music.

She raised her brow challengingly at Lord Atwood as they came together for a final time. He gazed into her eyes with an intense stare, but did nothing improper. She inhaled, feeling jittery and oddly disappointed.

The major escorted her from the dance floor. Lord Atwood retreated in the opposite direction. Dorothea smiled routinely, expressing her thanks, trying to settle her nerves. It had been fun dancing with the major, yet it was the moments when she met and sparred with the marquess that stuck in her mind.

There was a brief pause as the musicians set themselves for the next dance.

"I believe you have promised the waltz to me, Miss Ellingham," a deep voice proclaimed.

"Did I?" she remarked airily. Dorothea consulted the dance card that hung from her wrist on a white satin ribbon, not especially caring for the possessive tone in Lord Rosen's voice.

Previously he had treated her with a formal reserve she initially found intimidating and later decided was more amusing than anything else. He had been among the first to notice her when she came to Town, monopolizing her shamefully at her first society outing. A meeting with the Marquess of Dardington quickly changed that circumstance, but a few weeks ago Lord Rosen had made a second appearance as a potential suitor.

Dorothea had dismissed him from her thoughts because she had been pursuing Arthur Pengrove. And, she also admitted, because Lord Rosen was a bit daunting. He was older, nearly forty, a gentleman with sophisticated tastes and libertarian ways. He was, by many accounts, an accomplished rake. What then could he possibly see in her? She vacillated wildly between feeling flattered and puzzled by his attention.

"There, see my name." Lord Rosen pointed to her dance card. "'Tis written in such a fine, feminine hand. It appears that everything you do is close to perfection."

Heavens above, was he teasing? She glanced up at him. He sent her a provocative glance and she wondered what he really thought. Did he in truth hold her in any esteem? Or was this part of an elaborate game, a carefully orchestrated seduction?

Resolving not to let herself be provoked, Dorothea repressed a waspish retort and composed her features into blandness. Surely nothing would scare the handsome, dashing Lord Rosen away faster than a limp, placid female.

He appraised her with a measuring gaze and Dorothea realized her ploy had not worked. In fact, it seemed to have the opposite result. Instead of becoming bored and disinterested in her, Lord Rosen seemed keener than ever to spend time in her company.

"The waltz is the most intimate of dances, is it not?" he whispered.

"It can be," she replied, her voice thin and fragile. Oh, dear this would not do. Not at all. Dorothea cleared her throat. "With the right partner," she added in a far stronger tone.

"Yes, the choice of a partner can make the difference in so many of life's experiences," he said smoothly.

Dorothea felt the color rush to her cheeks. There were those who said a reformed rake made the best husband. Her own brother-in-law, Jason Barrington, was living proof of the truth in that statement. Still, Dorothea was not convinced of the universal application of that theory and wondered again if it was wise to test it personally.

On the other hand, Arthur Pengrove was no longer a possible matrimonial candidate. Perhaps she had been too hasty in her assessment of Lord Rosen's character. A more mature, worldly gentleman like Lord Rosen might make the ideal husband for her.

Besides, her own requirement that she kiss any gentleman whom she considered to be a potential husband before agreeing to marriage would be an easy feat to accomplish. Given his reputation and experience, it was safe to say that Lord Rosen would not object nor censure what others might label as forward behavior when she encouraged a kiss.

Dorothea offered him a warm smile. "The music is about to begin, my lord. Shall we?"

She put her hand on his outstretched arm. He instantly covered it with his own, squeezing it with an intimate familiarity that pushed at the boundaries of propriety. Dorothea ignored the jolt of warning that rushed to her head. They would be dancing in a crowded ballroom, in plain view of hundreds of guests, including Lord Dardington, her self-appointed protector.

What possible harm could occur?

Chapter Five

Thirty minutes later, Dorothea pulled away from Lord Rosen's embrace and gazed at him distractedly, wondering how she had managed to find herself alone in the garden with him. She had been amenable when at the end of their dance he had suggested they stroll outside for some fresh air. He had been charming and urbane, flattering, yet not too obvious in his remarks. She had enjoyed his wit, but even more, she had been impressed with the gentlemanly reverence he displayed toward her.

Caught in the romance of the moment, Dorothea wondered if he could possibly be the right man for her. There in the moonlight, with the stars twinkling brightly and the sweet smell of the spring flowers perfuming the air, she decided to find out.

She leaned forward, allowing him to kiss her. Lord Rosen's lips pressed forcefully against hers and in that instant Dorothea knew she had made a dreadful mistake. A foolish mistake.

There was danger in Lord Rosen's kiss, possession in his embrace. He was not subtle or gentle; rather, he was conquering and almost brutal. He felt large, ruthless, and powerful as he held her tightly against his chest. Though it was executed with great skill, and no doubt endless experience, Dorothea found something indefinably unpleasant in his kiss. It left her feeling uncomfortable, uneasy.

"We need to return to the ball," she said breathlessly

"Relax," he cooed at her, his voice a harsh rasp on her nerves. "There is plenty of time before we are missed."

Instinctively, Dorothea put up her arm, bracing it against his chest to hold him at bay. He smiled indolently at her and lunged forward. Dorothea stood fast, stiffening her elbow, keeping her arm firmly in place. His expression became perturbed as he realized she was serious.

"We need to return to the ball," she repeated.

"Come now, my pet. There's no need to be coy. We both know what we want."

Oh, Lord, now she was in serious trouble. Her left hand, so firmly planted in the center of Lord Rosen's chest, began to tremble. The idea of wrestling with him was too undignified to be borne, but if necessary, Dorothea would fight with every ounce of her strength.

She raised her chin and met his eyes squarely. Speaking in a normal, quiet tone was an effort. "I really must insist."

His eyebrow lifted. "I cannot believe you would be so cruel as to deny us both such untold pleasure. You see before you a man at the mercy of your beauty."

She sent a frosty glare in his direction. "At my mercy? I believe you to be more attuned with your base appetites, my lord."

Appreciative laughter fell from his lips. "And yours."

"Hardly!"

He drew back slightly, his gaze openly skeptical. "You came out here willingly. You kissed me willingly."

Dorothea swallowed past the lump that was lodged in her throat. She had come outside of her own accord. But surely he could not think she was going to bestow upon him more than a single kiss?

"One kiss is all that I allow, my lord. At least to a man who is not my husband or my betrothed. Lest you forget, I am a lady. An innocent, unmarried lady."

Lord Rosen must have seen her temper flair, for he paused. His dark eyes surveyed her critically. "Do you believe yourself worthy of becoming my wife?"

Dorothea winced. That was rather blunt. What did he expect now, that she plead her cause? Enumerate her finer qualities, expound on her many virtues, show him her teeth? What nerve! Beneath her escalating fear, Dorothea grew angry. But she held her temper.

"That is not for me to decide, my lord," she replied, keeping her voice cool. "Only you can determine who is worthy to be your wife."

He smiled, seemingly pleased at her response, yet his heightened color indicated he had not fully regained his temper.

"Perhaps that is what I am attempting to do right now. Determine your worth."

Shock forced a nervous giggle from her. She should have been prepared for this nonsense. Or better still, she should have been smart enough to avoid it altogether. The good Lord help her if by some miracle Lord Rosen did propose. He possessed in abundance that superior smugness prevalent in men who felt they needed to prove themselves with women. He would not take kindly to being rejected.

Somehow, Dorothea managed a strained smile. "This seems a rather awkward time and place to make such an important decision about your future."

"It could very well be your future also," he insisted.

If you please me. He did not say the words aloud, but his intent was obvious with every sultry, proud look. Pointedly,

Lord Rosen glanced down at her arm, the physical barrier she held between them. His smug expression told her he expected her to lower it.

Dorothea stiffened. "I think not, my lord," she proclaimed.

His expression of disbelief was comical, and unfortunately short-lived. Lord Rosen glared at her, clearly annoyed. Dorothea's fear returned. *If I survive this incident without harm, I vow I shall be more diligent in the future,* she promised herself silently.

Dorothea dipped a quick curtsy and turned away, scolding herself not to scurry so fast, yet she could feel Lord Rosen's penetrating gaze boring into her back.

"Miss Ellingham!" he shouted.

Her discomfort heightened. Her pace quickened. She was supremely conscious of how wildly her heart was thudding. It was undignified and a bit lowering to scuttle away like a frightened child, yet Dorothea reasoned it was far better to be a coward than a fool.

There was a sound behind her. His footsteps? *Dear God!* No longer giving any thought to how she appeared, Dorothea lifted her skirt above her ankles and broke into a run. Her feet crunched noisily on the gravel path, the stones cutting through the soft leather soles of her elegant dancing slippers.

Ignoring the pain, Dorothea kept running. Her shoulder brushed the side of a lush hedge as she turned the corner, but she dared not slow her speed. She was concentrating so intently on the sounds behind her that she paid little attention to what was directly in front.

It was like hitting a brick wall. A wall with powerful arms. Dorothea screeched as those masculine arms encircled her, imprisoned her. Twisting from the hold, she backed away on unsteady legs, trying to prepare herself to meet her attacker. Lifting her head, she met his eyes fully.

Lord Atwood! Dorothea's mouth dropped open, aghast. Feeling off balance, she caught his arm and tried to steady herself, physically and emotionally.

"Gracious, woman, what is the matter?"

Shocked speechless, Dorothea stared at him. The moonlight reflected off his face, giving his features an almost angelic glow. Normally, physical beauty did not overwhelm her so intently. It had taken several years for her to come to the realization, but she did know that physical appearance did not directly correlate to a person's character.

Lord Rosen being an excellent example of that fact. His very appealing face and form hid a darkness in his personality, a sharpness of temperament that was at odds with his outer beauty.

Something about the marquess's looks . . . or maybe it was his bearing, drew her near. A kind of magnetic virility that made her take notice. Even when she did not want to be looking.

"Are you in distress, Miss Ellingham?" the marquess asked in a gentle tone. "Can I be of assistance?"

"No." She shook her head vehemently. "I'm perfectly fine."

The lift of his brow told her of his skepticism at her response, but thankfully he did not press her. There was a strained silence, broken only by her harsh, labored breaths. Mortified, Dorothea attempted to stifle the noise, which made matters worse.

"I was unaware that Mr. Pengrove was in attendance this evening," Lord Atwood commented.

"He is here?" Dorothea gazed wildly about the garden.

"Wasn't that him in the lower garden with you?"

"No, that was Lord Rosen." Dorothea, still feeling

terribly rattled, replied without thinking. Then nearly groaned at her answer.

"Lord Rosen?" Ill-concealed surprise shadowed the marquess's moonlit features. "I thought you had an understanding with Mr. Pengrove."

"An understanding of what?"

"Marriage."

Oh, dear. Embarrassment and mortification fought for domination in Dorothea's heart. How *did* he know about Arthur's proposal? And why did he know only half the story, for clearly he believed she had accepted Arthur's suit?

"Mr. Pengrove and I are merely friends. We have no plans to marry."

She nearly laughed at Lord Atwood's blank look of amazement and might have, if she had not been so stunned herself.

"Forgive my mistake," he said, eyeing her with puzzlement. "Then you will gladly accept the title of Lady Rosen?"

"No." Dorothea looked away, then sighed. "I must say, my lord, you appear to have far too keen an interest in my marital status."

"Do I? I beg your pardon. Marriage is too much on my mind these days."

"On mine, too, I confess." Her heart skipped. Was Lord Atwood in the market for a bride?

"Did you not mean to say love and marriage are too much on your mind?" he asked, his voice lilting with humor.

"Love and marriage?" Dorothea took a moment to consider her reply. "Marriage is an act of combining family, fortune, and convenience."

"It is, but I thought most young women strive to fall in love before they marry."

"Do they? I'm not certain. I only know I wish very

much to marry, and love is not a major factor under my consideration when searching for a husband."

His mouth curled. "You surprise me, Miss Ellingham. I would have wagered anything that you were a starry-eyed romantic."

Dorothea gave him a faint smile. "I have grown beyond that stage. I know that genuine love can exist between couples, but it is rare to find and even harder to hold."

"I can agree with that sentiment."

"From personal experience?"

He winced. "Heavens, no. I myself have never been in love. But I have borne witness to couples who profess themselves madly in love when they marry and within the year their relationship has fallen to apathy or boredom or worse."

"I too have seen the same." Her mouth twisted wryly. "That is why I am resolved to control my own fate when I marry and leave love out of the decision."

He cocked his head to one side and studied her. "Are they mutually exclusive?" he asked. "Love and marriage?"

"For some. For too many." She couldn't help but smile. This was the most unusual conversation she had ever had with a man, but the most honest. "I think in the very best circumstances, love comes after marriage."

"Between a man and his wife?"

"Sometimes. If they are very fortunate." She studied her dancing slippers with a great intensity, then suddenly lifted her head. "And if not, then the world will not end. One can learn to be content with whatever parts another person is willing to share."

He tilted his head curiously. "Does that not make for a very cold marriage bed?"

"I know very little of either love or passion yet I cannot fathom that love is necessary in order to achieve fulfillment when sharing a bed with your spouse. Is it?"

Her question seemed to surprise him. "Not from a man's point of view. Yet I always believed a gently bred lady would feel differently."

"Yes, some might." Dorothea could not hold her tongue. "I am not one of them."

His face registered shock, but that quickly turned to curiosity. "You are not horrified at the notion of being labeled a wanton?"

"Ah, so a woman is wanton if she enjoys the pleasures of the flesh and the joys of her marriage bed without a full commitment of her heart, and a man is not?"

That comment had him nearly gaping with astonishment.

Dorothea faltered, realizing she had spoken far too boldly and honestly and quite possibly offended him with her outrageous comments.

His features softened as his eyes glinted with keen interest. "So, you will offer passion instead of love to your future husband, Miss Ellingham?"

She gave him a sharp, direct look. "I will offer both, my lord, in equal measure. But I will make my choice of that husband based on passion."

Her final remark rendered him speechless. Dorothea shifted from one foot to the other, becoming suddenly uncomfortable. There was no room for that sort of bare truth in a polite conversation between a man and a woman, at least not that degree of truth. She knew that, and yet something about Lord Atwood had compelled her to ignore her inner voice and say it anyway.

"Goodness, 'tis getting late," she said in a constrained voice. "You must excuse me, Lord Atwood. It would be rude to remain so long away from the ball."

He gave her a small, mysterious smile. "Of course, Miss Ellingham. I thank you for a most enlightening conversation."

Dorothea's heart began to pound and she quickly glanced away. She executed a low, graceful curtsy, then turned and walked away, her head held high.

Carter's eyes narrowed as he watched Miss Ellingham stalk away, her skirt billowing out in her haste to leave. As she disappeared through the French doors, he was struck by a sharp feeling of being intrigued. By her beauty, of course, her lovely figure, her witty personality.

But also by her woman's mind, something he rarely considered until that moment. She saw marriage in a very different way, and not, he greatly suspected, as other females did.

He had seen Arthur Pengrove kiss her and then sink down on one knee to propose. Therefore, when he again saw her kissing someone in the garden tonight, he assumed it was Pengrove, yet instead it was Lord Rosen, a reprobate and a womanizer, though a man astute enough to realize it would be suicide to play false with the affections of a woman under the protection of the Marquess of Dardington.

As difficult as it was to believe, Lord Rosen's intentions must have been honorable. Yet she was not engaged to him either. Perhaps she just enjoyed kissing gentlemen?

It would be easy to label her a woman of loose morals, but somehow that did not ring true. She claimed no knowledge of either love or passion, and he believed her. She spoke of wanting to find the passion in her marriage before the love, a notion more aligned with a man's thinking than a woman's.

Her words made him think, made him realize that perhaps all those young, innocent females his father insisted he consider for his bride had caused Carter's view of marriage to be too narrow and rigid. One could marry for duty alone, using common sense when selecting a mate. Or one could succumb to the sort of all-consuming romantic love that poets wrote about and women craved. Well, some women.

Frankly, neither of those approaches held much appeal, which most likely explained why he was having such difficulty setting his mind on a particular woman to take as his wife. Perhaps it was time to examine marriage in a different light entirely.

With Dorothea Ellingham? Carter smiled. She was a different sort of female and he had always been attracted to the unconventional. How else would one explain his close, long-standing friendship with Benton and Dawson, two men nearly diametrically opposed in everything from attitude to temperament?

Miss Ellingham's idea of a passionate marriage without the complications of love made the wedded state a very enticing arrangement. Pleased at the discovery of this revelation, Carter turned from the garden path and began walking back to the ballroom.

Yes, an adjustment to his attitude and thinking about marriage could very well be the answer he needed. His mind examined and expanded the idea over and over in his head, and Carter became convinced that a union with the lovely Dorothea could be a most agreeable one indeed.

Dorothea slipped into the ballroom unnoticed, dreading the continuation of the ball. She had succeeded in making a perfect ninny of herself this evening, first with Lord Rosen and then with the marquess. And now she would be forced to paste on a delighted smile for the guests and pretend that everything was as it should be and she was having a wonderful time.

Fortunately the next dance was promised to Mr. Browning. He was a pleasant man of modest property and spare conversation. He was also a confident, skillful dancer, which allowed Dorothea to forgo the necessity of establishing a polite dialogue. All she need do was follow his lead and let her mind wander back to the conversation with the marquess.

She had been brutally honest when she told Lord Atwood she was not searching for a man to fall in love with or trying to make one fall in love with her. Marriage was too serious a business, too important a decision to be trusted to a fickle heart.

Years ago she had decided how she would approach this most momentous, pivotal moment in her life. To select a husband, she would use her head, her common sense, and as her final test, a kiss. With those factors neatly aligned, Dorothea firmly believed the possibility of love between her and her future husband would exist.

For her, the mere possibility of love would be enough to enter into the marriage. And if love did not materialize, she would survive. She would not become bitter, or angry or resentful. She would make the most of her life, no matter what the circumstances.

"Punch, Miss Ellingham?"

Startled out of her reflections, Dorothea blinked up at Mr. Browning. "That would be lovely," she answered with a guilty smile.

He scuttled off to retrieve her punch. But solitude was denied her. Mere seconds after Mr. Browning disappeared, Sir Perry arrived at her side. Dorothea took a deep breath, willing herself to endure his painful conversation with a pleasant expression.

Mr. Browning returned. Dorothea sipped her punch, nodded with feigned interest at Sir Perry's prattle, then gratefully escaped when the next gentleman presented himself to claim his dance.

And so it went for the next few hours.

Though she tried to control the impulse, Dorothea found herself searching the room for Lord Atwood at the end of each dance. And each time she found him, their eyes met, for he made no effort to conceal the fact that he was watching for her as well.

Why then did he not approach her and ask for a dance? Surely her eclectic circle of admirers did not intimidate him. Lord Atwood hardly seemed the type of man who worried about competition. No, he was a bold man, who more than likely took what he wanted.

Pity he did not want her. Or her wanton inclinations. Dorothea groaned, still not believing she had been so idiotic as to reveal them. He no doubt thought her a female of loose morals, unfit to one day be a duchess.

"Goodness, I hope that frown on your face is not from displeasure," Lady Meredith said, catching Dorothea in a rare moment alone. She put her arm through Dorothea's and the two women began a circle of the ballroom.

Dorothea tried to smile. Lady Meredith had worked very hard to ensure the success of the ball. Dorothea would not have her believe her efforts were not appreciated.

"I'm just tired," Dorothea answered. "And a bit overwhelmed by all this grandeur."

Lady Meredith patted Dorothea's hand. "Naturally you are feeling fatigued. I think you've danced with nearly every bachelor here."

"Almost every one," Dorothea answered. She spied Lord Atwood across the room. He was speaking with Major Roddington and another gentleman whose name she could not remember. The trio turned and greeted a fourth man and then the group started toward the open doorway. Obviously, they were leaving. Dorothea sighed.

Lady Meredith glanced at Dorothea, then her eyes

quickly traveled to where Dorothea was so boldly staring. "Hmm, I cannot even begin to speculate as to which of those four gentlemen brought about that weary reaction," Lady Meredith whispered.

Dorothea shook her head, not even trying to disguise her interest. It hardly mattered if Lady Meredith knew of her infatuation with Lord Atwood. It would come to naught.

"Before you married Lord Dardington, did you ever say something to a gentleman that you regretted?" Dorothea asked.

"All the time." Lady Meredith's blue eyes sparkled. "Though truthfully, there were not an overabundance of opportunities for me to converse with gentlemen. You see, I was something of a social misfit."

"You?" Dorothea could not believe such a poised, confident woman like Lady Meredith had ever stumbled in society.

"Oh, yes. I was quite the disaster. My family being known for its eccentricities was not much of a help either. I had no particular interest in marriage and made no bones about it. I was too concerned with keeping my wild twin brothers out of harm's way and indulging my secret passion."

"You had a secret passion?" Dorothea glanced over her shoulder to ensure that no one was close enough to eavesdrop on their conversation. "Does Lord Dardington know of it?"

"He does. And while he does not strictly approve of it, he knows he cannot stop me, and thus I still indulge in it today."

Dorothea's mouth gaped open and her gaze slid away. "I would not have expected Lord Dardington to be so tolerant."

Lady Meredith ceased walking and cocked her head, visibly surprised. "Why, Dorothea Ellingham, you have a sinful mind!"

"Please, I meant no offense."

"None was taken." Lady Meredith tapped her fan against Dorothea's wrist and smiled. "My secret passion has nothing to do with a lover, so turn that thought right out of your head. Trevor is the only man who shares my heart, and my bed."

"I did not mean to imply . . . that is to say, I was not seeking to judge you, Lady Meredith." Dorothea's cheeks flushed with color. Lord, what was wrong with her tonight? It seemed that every innocent conversation she began quickly turned scandalous.

"I assure you there is no need to look so stricken. I suppose it was a natural assumption to conclude my secret passion includes a man. That is true, to a small extent, for a man is involved. A man of business." Lady Meredith smiled with amusement. "My secret passion is finance, Dorothea. I have a talent and an ambition for making money."

"Oh." Dorothea slowly let out the breath she had been holding. Despite her skepticism regarding love and marriage, she did appreciate the unique relations that certain couples shared. It was therefore an odd relief to be able to once again believe in the genuine love that Lady Meredith shared with her husband.

"It's no small skill and, if you will allow me to be boastful for a moment, making money through investments is something that I am very good at doing," Lady Meredith said. "But my talents are neither understood nor welcomed by those in society. 'Tis bad enough when a gentleman shows too must interest in his affairs of business, but a woman with financial intellect and insight." Lady Meredith shuddered. "'Tis thought to be unnatural."

Dorothea huffed with indignity. "We have brains, why must we hide them?"

Lady Meredith shrugged. "I believe that the majority of gentlemen are made very uneasy at the thought of a woman's intellect. Why else are those women who enjoy an intellectual discourse mockingly labeled as bluestockings?"

Dorothea nodded. It was true. Girls were taught from an early age not to appear too clever or bookish in front of a gentleman. "Did you conceal your interest in business from Lord Dardington before you married?"

"No."

"Did he object to it at all?"

"Initially, he ignored it. Then again, he also ignored me. Entirely."

Dorothea's eyes widened. "I always thought yours was a love match?"

"Hardly. When we first married, there were numerous difficulties that kept us apart and unhappy. Thankfully, those were eventually resolved and we discovered the love we shared for each other." Lady Meredith gestured politely to an elderly couple they passed, then smiled with kindness at a young man with shirt collar points so high he could barely move his head from side to side.

"Once our marriage became a happy one, I think Trevor might have wanted me to forgo my financial activities, but he soon realized it gave me a sense of fulfillment and accomplishment," she continued. "'Tis only because of him that those in society who are aware of my activities say very little about it. At least in public. Plus my father-in-law has long been my champion in society. One can never underestimate the power and influence of a duke."

Dorothea took a moment to ponder Lady Meredith's words. "You said that you had no interest in marriage. But if you did not marry, what did you plan to do? How did you plan to live?"

"However I wished. Thanks to my solid investments, having enough funds at my disposal gave me a degree of independence, a rare freedom. That is why I have insisted on very specific financial arrangements for each of my daughters. When they have reached their maturity, they are to be given an independent income that cannot be touched by any male relations, including their husbands."

"So you want your daughters to marry?" Dorothea asked, doubting she would take the independent road, even if it were offered. To her, marriage seemed a more natural, protective state for a woman.

"If my daughters find men who they care for and are worthy of them, naturally I would like them to marry. Though according to their father, as of yet, no men exist with the qualities that would deem them acceptable."

Dorothea joined Lady Meredith's laughter. "Lord Dardington has been excessively critical of my potential suitors and he is not even a blood relation. I cannot begin to imagine his reaction when a gentleman comes to call for one of his girls."

"I know one thing with certainty," Lady Meredith said, with a twisted smile. "Those young gentlemen will not be faint of heart. I may even have to remove Trevor from England for a while, just to give my daughters some peace."

Having completed the circuit of the ballroom, the two women returned to their original spot. Dorothea's nerves had settled. She felt calmer, more in control. "I suppose for some, married life will never be dull," she remarked.

"Oh, my, yes." Lady Meredith squeezed her arm in encouragement. "I know you are feeling anxious about finding a husband and I agree 'tis a most important decision. But your situation is not so dire that you must rush it. Take your time, be sure of whom you choose."

Dorothea smiled wanly. She knew Lady Meredith believed she was imparting sound advice, but Dorothea had to disagree. Her situation was dire. If she did not find a husband by the end of this Season, she would be relegated to life back in Yorkshire, where the pool of potential husbands was much smaller, and lacked the inclusion of a certain devilish marquess.

"I shall endeavor to do my best," Dorothea said with a small sigh.

"That is all anyone can ask of you," Lady Meredith replied. "You must remember, Dorothea, that marriage, like most everything in life, is what you make of it."

Chapter Six

"Several bouquets have been delivered for you, Miss Ellingham," the butler said to Dorothea as she joined Lord and Lady Dardington the next morning at the breakfast table. "Shall I leave them in the yellow salon so you may look at them after your meal?"

"Nonsense, Phillips. Bring them in here immediately," Lady Meredith said with a smile of enthusiasm. "I vow I am as curious as Dorothea to see what's been sent."

Dorothea settled herself in the chair opposite Lady Meredith's. She accepted a cup of hot chocolate from a footman but declined anything more than toast, forgoing the array of hot items in silver chafing dishes set on the sideboard.

As ordered, Phillips returned to the dining room with two footmen trailing on his heels, each carrying an assortment of flowers in their arms.

"How beautiful," Lady Meredith declared as she hastily pushed her empty plate away to make room on the table for the numerous bouquets.

Dorothea smiled and reached first for a lovely bouquet of pink and white primroses. The stems were all cut to the same

length and wound with white and pink striped satin ribbon.
"Oh, smell these," she said, holding them out toward Lady
Meredith.

"Delicious," Lady Meredith declared. "Who are they
from?"

Anxiously, Dorothea tore open the card. "Major Roddington," she answered with surprise. How sweet. Apparently he had enjoyed their dance together last night. "He's
asked to take me out for a drive this afternoon and hopes
I will consent to enjoying a quiet picnic lunch with him in
Banberry Park."

"A picnic. That sounds charming." Lady Meredith reached
for a nosegay of yellow peonies. "I bet I know who sent
these."

Dorothea and Lady Meredith glanced at each other,
smiled, then both pronounced at the same time, "Sir Perry!"

"Poor man, he suffers from an extreme lack of imagination," Lady Meredith commented. "He sends the exact same
bouquet every time. Twelve yellow peonies, tied with a satin
ribbon in a paler shade of yellow. Is there a poem today?"

Dorothea met Lady Meredith's amused gaze across the
table as she unsealed the card that accompanied the flowers.
She quickly scanned the contents. "Yes, unfortunately Sir
Perry has seen fit to regale me with another of his original
sonnets. It is written in his customary flowery, overblown
style and pays homage to my—" Dorothea sputtered,
blinked, then finally managed to choke out, "wrists."

The marquess, sitting at his usual place at the head of
the table, slowly lowered the newspaper he had been reading and peered at Dorothea over the top of the page. "Your
wrists? Sir Perry wrote a poem praising your wrists?
Surely, I misheard."

Dorothea giggled and Lady Meredith joined her. "Oh,
no, my lord, this epic poem is most assuredly an ode to my

delicate, fragile, beauteous wrists, dainty and pretty and lovelier than fists."

"The man's mad as a March hare," Lord Dardington pronounced. "I ask you, what sane person would single out that particular part of a woman's anatomy for praise?"

"Not so much mad as desperate, I believe," Dorothea said before she burst into another round of giggles. "Poor Sir Perry has written me no fewer than a dozen poems. Obviously, he is beginning to run out of body parts to extol."

Dorothea's comments sent Lady Meredith into another fit of laughter. When the older woman finally regained her composure, she once again turned her attention to Dorothea's flowers.

"Who sent this exquisite orchid?" Lady Meredith asked.

Dorothea thoughtfully fingered the delicate bloom before reaching for the card, but her momentary blush of anticipation soon turned to disappointment when she read the signature.

"It's from Lord Rosen. I remember he once told me that he cultivates them in his hothouse," Dorothea said with a casual air she was far from feeling. Turning to one of the footmen, she added, "Please give the orchid to Cook, with my compliments. I remember that she has a fondness for them."

Lady Meredith's brow lifted fractionally. Dorothea glanced away, then hastily broke off a piece of toast and began to eat. She had not told her guardians about her encounter with Lord Rosen and she had every intention of keeping them in the dark over what had occurred in the garden last night.

The orchid was removed and the tightness in Dorothea's chest eased. If only it were as easy to remove the memory of the time she spent in Lord Rosen's company.

Dorothea took a fortifying sip of her now lukewarm

chocolate and reached for another bouquet. Soon the remainder of the flowers and cards were sorted through. Vases were fetched and, with Dorothea's permission, Lady Meredith instructed which bouquets were to be placed in which rooms.

Dorothea requested that the primroses from Major Roddington be placed in her bedchamber. She saved Sir Perry's latest poem also, intending to enclose it along with the next letter she sent her sister Emma. She suspected the younger girl would find it similarly absurd and amusing.

"That felt a bit like Christmas morning, did it not?" Lady Meredith asked after the table had been cleared of all the foliage. "So many delightful surprises."

"It was fun," Dorothea agreed, though her heart harbored a beat of disappointment. There had been nothing from Lord Atwood.

"I received three invitations requesting my company on a carriage ride this afternoon, but I would like to go on the picnic with Major Roddington," Dorothea said. "May I, Lord Dardington?"

Once again, the marquess slowly lowered the newspaper he was holding. "I am not acquainted with a Major Roddington."

"I met him last night at the ball," Dorothea replied hastily. "He was most charming."

"Humph." The paper rattled as it was snapped back into place, once more concealing Lord Dardington's features.

"The weather seems ideal for an outing in the park," Lady Meredith said. "I believe it would be a splendid day for Dorothea to have her picnic with the major."

Lord Dardington dropped his paper onto the table and glared at his wife. "We know nothing about him. Who is he? Who are his people? How did he even get an invitation to the ball if we are not acquainted with him?"

Dorothea shook her head and shrugged helplessly. "Lord Atwood introduced us, therefore I assume they are friends. As for the rest, I don't really know."

The marquess gestured toward both women with a wave of his hand. "Honestly! You cannot possibly expect me to give you permission to drive out with this man when you know so little about him."

Lady Meredith pinched the bridge of her nose with her thumb and forefinger. "That is the point of the outing, Trevor, to give Dorothea and the major an opportunity to become better acquainted."

"They can do that in our drawing room," the marquess grumbled. "Surrounded by a proper group of chaperones and other callers."

Lady Meredith muttered something under her breath. Dorothea's stomach dipped with disappointment. It would have been lovely to get away from the house for part of the afternoon. Plus the outing would provide the perfect distraction from her brooding over Lord Atwood.

"A picnic in a public park in the middle of the afternoon is a perfectly respectable outing and a very reasonable request." Lady Meredith eyed her husband shrewdly. "And as I recall, just last night you promised me that you would strive to be fair and reasonable regarding Dorothea's gentlemen callers."

A muscle clenched in Lord Dardington's jaw. He lifted his coffee cup, took a long sip, then replaced the delicate china cup back in the saucer. Lady Meredith smiled at him serenely.

"If she goes with him, she will need a far more substantial chaperone than her maid," the marquess finally said.

Dorothea's stomach tumbled again. Oh, dear. Was the marquess going to assign himself to the task of chaperoning her? If that were the case, she might as well stay home.

"I will gladly undertake that duty and our daughters will accompany me," Lady Meredith answered. "You know how much they enjoy going on picnics."

"You and the girls?" Lord Dardington drummed his fingers on the table. "How will you all fit in his carriage?"

Dorothea was thinking the exact same thing. Though she appreciated Lady Meredith's efforts to assist her, this was not the result she had hoped to achieve. Major Roddington had struck her as an even-tempered, pleasant man, but she worried at his reaction when he discovered their picnic would now include four additional people. Three of them little girls.

"I would never dream of being so rude as to foist myself and our daughters upon the poor man." Lady Meredith cleared her throat. "Dorothea will ride out with the major when he comes to call. The girls and I will either follow behind them or perhaps arrive beforehand at the park at an agreed-upon location.

"Riding in our own carriage is a necessity, since the girls will insist upon bringing along their favorite books and dolls and Cook will no doubt pack a lunch with all their favorite foods in quantities far more appropriate to feeding Wellington's army than three youngsters."

It was a reasonable compromise. One that Lord Dardington should not find objectionable, but Dorothea knew that he might. She held her breath tensely as she awaited his answer.

"You may send word to Roddington that you would be delighted to accept his invitation," Lord Dardington finally said. "Though be certain to include the new details required for you to participate in the outing. I vow, only a man with honorable intentions would agree to have Lady Meredith and my darling daughters so near."

Dorothea felt the smile well up from her heart. "Thank you, my lord. If you will excuse me, I shall write to him immediately."

"Don't forget about the other gentlemen," Lady Meredith chided gently.

Other gentlemen? Dorothea stared blankly at Lady Meredith.

"Major Roddington was not the only man who sent you flowers and invitations," Lady Meredith added.

Of course. Dorothea blushed. Her head was truly fuzzy this morning. A combination of a late night and . . . well, it didn't bear too close thinking as to what else had her rattled.

"You are right, Lady Meredith. This will be the perfect time to also compose notes of acknowledgment and thanks to the others who were so kind to me."

With a final smile, Dorothea quit the room. The remainder of the morning passed swiftly, and at the appointed hour Major Roddington promptly presented himself. He smiled with genuine warmth when she greeted him, and she noted with a sense of satisfaction how his eyes lit up with appreciation as he took in her fashionable ensemble.

"You look lovely, Miss Ellingham."

"Thank you."

Dorothea lowered her chin and smiled, glad that she had taken the extra time to make a special effort with her appearance. The deep blue shade of her muslin gown set off the blue in her eyes, and the matching hat she wore looked best with a section of her blond curls trailing down to her shoulders.

The major held his own against Lord Dardington as the marquess quizzed him sharply about the planned outing. After what seemed like an eternity to Dorothea, they were finally able to escape from the house. Her eyes lightened with interest when she caught sight of the handsome phaeton waiting at the curb.

"No need to look so impressed, Miss Ellingham," the major said with a grin. "The carriage is on loan."

"You must be a very good friend if you were allowed to borrow such prime equipment," Dorothea replied, knowing such a fine rig and impressive cattle could not be rented from a stable.

"Though I have not known him long, the Marquess of Atwood has proven to be an amiable and generous man."

Dorothea's foot stumbled as she lifted it onto the carriage step and she nearly lost her balance. Had she heard correctly? Had he really said the Marquess of Atwood?

"My, yes, Lord Atwood is generous," she said, her face warming with embarrassment. Good heavens, who would have ever thought the marquess and the major would be such close friends. It was surprising, for they seemed very different in personality and circumstance.

As usual, the London streets were crowded and the carriage horses, though well trained, were eager to run. It was necessary for the major to keep his concentration on the spirited horses, but Dorothea did not mind the lack of conversation. She spent the time enjoying the view and the fresh air and admiring his skill as he tightly held the reins and expertly negotiated them through the streets.

Within the hour they safely arrived at Banberry Park, a charming enclave on the outskirts of Town. There were a small number of people strolling on the marked paths, enjoying the pleasant spring weather. Dorothea turned her head and immediately she spied a most familiar group.

"I see Lady Meredith and her daughters have arrived," Dorothea said, answering Lady Meredith's wave with one of her own.

"Shall we join them?" the major asked.

"As long as we remain in view, we can set our picnic in a separate location," Dorothea replied.

The major glanced at the chaos surrounding the marchioness, with the many blankets, toys, servants, and boisterous children, and turned the carriage in the opposite direction.

Dorothea smiled prettily at him as he assisted her down from the vehicle. They chose a shady spot beneath a majestic chestnut tree. With great aplomb, the major spread a blanket on the grass, then settled her comfortably upon it.

He opened the straw basket and began rooting around inside. "I asked my batman to procure our lunch from the tavern down the street from my lodgings. I hope you find it to your liking, Miss Ellingham."

"Your batman," Dorothea teased. "Do you not employ a proper valet?"

The major's brows knit together. "You're right, since I am no longer in the military, I should now call him my valet. Though honestly, he is more a jack-of-all-trades and in truth a loyal friend. Parker served with me in the Peninsula and later fought by my side at Waterloo. 'Tis difficult to relegate a man to an inferior position after he has saved your life."

"Were you in the army a long time?"

"Since I was fifteen. I joined as a regular foot soldier. It took many years and a minor bequest from a distant relation before I was able to purchase my commission."

"Ah, so there was no rich father to smooth the way?" she asked with a grin.

He looked momentarily startled, then suddenly grew very still. "No father at all, actually. At least not one who would claim me."

"Oh." Dorothea had no idea what to say. She had never before met anyone who was so open and honest about such a sordid, personal fact.

"I've shocked you," he said gravely. "Forgive me."

Lowering his gaze, the major turned from her and hastily began to unpack the contents of the picnic basket.

He placed a wedge of cheese, a crust of bread, and several red, ripe strawberries on a plate, then held it out to her.

"'Tis I who should apologize," Dorothea said quietly, ashamed it had taken her so long to respond. The poor man. She had not meant to add to his discomfort by remaining silent for so long. She had simply not known what to say. Dorothea took the plate he offered and tried to smile.

He shrugged his shoulders, as though it did not matter, but Dorothea was not fooled. His base birth had obviously had a profound impact on his life, as one would expect.

"Many individuals crumble under adversity," she continued in a soft voice. "Yet you have obviously thrived. I find that most commendable."

The major gazed off in the distance. "You are a very kind woman, Miss Ellingham, but there is no need to pretend. I know my limitations are not merely due to the circumstances of my birth. I am not elegant or polished like these other fine London gentlemen. I'm a soldier, far better suited to lead a cavalry charge against the French than conversing in polite company."

"For a man who claims to have no social graces, you are doing a superb job of charming me, sir." He turned to face her and Dorothea's gaze locked with his. "And I freely confess to being a woman who prefers a natural, not a practiced, charm."

His rough laugh was deep and filled with humor. "Your efforts to appease me are appreciated, yet I refuse to hide from the truth."

"That you are charming? I agree it is foolish to try and hide that fact."

"You are running circles around me, Miss Ellingham," he replied with an easy grin.

"I believe you can hold your own very well, sir." She

took a bite of a strawberry, licking away a drop of the sweet juice from her lips. "Very well, indeed."

The major leaned forward, his eyes warm with amusement. It was far too soon to even think about kissing him, yet she found herself wondering what it would be like. Pleasant, she was fairly certain, and perhaps something more?

A loud shout of laughter followed by a chorus of girlish giggles abruptly shattered the mood. Remembering they were out in a very public place, Dorothea shifted her position. Demurely, she set her back against the sturdy trunk of the tree, tucking the skirt of her blue muslin gown around her legs and ankles. The major stretched out on his side, his head propped on one elbow.

"It's shocking to find such peace and tranquility so close to the center of London," he said.

"You were not raised here?"

"No. I grew up in the north of England, near Wales."

"Alone? With only your mother?" She lowered her chin as a hot blush rose to her cheeks. Curse her wicked, curious tongue. "I'm so sorry. I do not mean to pry."

"It's all right, Miss Ellingham. Truly." He fiddled with the stem of a small wildflower growing near the trunk of the tree. "I never knew my father. My mother was governess to a wealthy, titled family. She fell in love with a neighboring nobleman. When she found herself carrying his child, he refused her any aid. Having no other choice, she returned home, where some of her relations still lived."

"They took her into their home?" Dorothea asked, relieved to hear this poor woman had not been totally abandoned.

"In a manner of speaking. They gave her, and later me, a place to sleep, food to eat. Her family always thought her a disgrace and treated her accordingly. They tried to convince her to give me away, but she refused. Not surprisingly, they ignored me. But at least they were not so heartless as to throw us out on the street."

"It must have been very difficult for you."

"It was lonely, isolating," the major admitted. "Not many families in the village encouraged an acquaintance with Emily Roddington's baseborn son."

Dorothea tried to imagine him as a young boy, enduring the taunts and isolation. "I am sorry."

"There's no need." His eyes burned into her and she felt the intensity of his emotions. "It's who I am, it's what made me strong. Strong enough to survive the army. And Napoleon's soldiers."

Dorothea leaned harder against the tree trunk, ignoring the rough bark digging into her back. "I'm very glad that you survived. All of it."

He tilted his head and she could see the muscle in his cheek working as he struggled to contain himself. An unexpected pressure on the side of her fingers caused her to look down. The major's ungloved hand was resting close to hers on the picnic blanket.

A swirl of compassion invaded her heart. Carefully, casually, Dorothea inched her fingers closer. One more slow, deliberate move and they would be touching. She pushed her hand over the smooth surface of the blanket and then suddenly—

"I hope you have some saved food for us, Roddy," a deep baritone voice implored. "I'm starved."

"Atwood! Benton! What are you doing here?" The major snatched his hand away, leapt to his feet, and walked toward the approaching men.

Startled, Dorothea swung her head around and caught sight of two elegantly garbed gentlemen on horseback. Good heavens, she had heard correctly. It was the marquess. Fighting the edgy quiver of nerves the sight of Lord

Atwood produced in her chest, Dorothea concentrated her attention on the other gentleman. The one who had spoken.

She recognized him from last night's ball, though she could not recall his name.

"Ah, Miss Ellingham, I presume?" The stranger dismounted, then bowed. "I am Viscount Benton. I must say, it is a pure delight to at last meet the woman who has so thoroughly captured my friend's attention."

Dorothea's head turned sharply toward Lord Atwood, fearing what he might have been saying about her. Yet Lord Atwood's expression remained open, innocent. Lud, what a ninny she was being! The viscount had meant Major Roddington, not the marquess.

Rattled, Dorothea struggled to regain her composure. She lifted her head and stared in frustration at Lord Atwood and the viscount, wishing they would get back on their horses and ride on. She felt awkward and unsettled. The major, however, appeared to be pleased at their unexpected arrival.

Dorothea blew out a sigh and told herself all would be well the moment the two uninvited guests departed.

She forced herself to smile at the viscount. He was a handsome devil, with dark, daring looks. He returned her smile with a devastating one of his own. Oh, dear. The very last thing she needed in her life was another handsome rogue flirting with her.

She very deliberately lowered her chin and turned her head away. Benton did not appear to be a fool. He would easily understand her message.

Dorothea's gaze was now fixed in the distance, centered upon Lady Meredith and the girls. She watched with curiosity as Lady Meredith settled the three girls in a rowboat that was nestled on the shore. With the help of the girl's governess, Lady Meredith pushed the small boat off the bank, then hopped inside. Taking up the oars, she began to row in an uneven line toward the other side of the lake.

Dorothea could see the girls smiling and giggling at their mother's antics. She smiled, too. It looked like they were having a grand time.

"I see that Lady Meredith has taken the girls for a boat ride. Perhaps we can go next, Major Roddington?" Dorothea asked, deciding that if the viscount and marquess wouldn't leave, then she must find a way to escape. There would only be room in the boat for her and the major.

"What?" The major jerked his head toward the small lake, his eyes widened.

"I heard Dardington's wife was a plucky kind of woman," Lord Atwood said with admiration. "I'm sure she knows what she is doing."

The words had no sooner left the marquess's mouth when a sharp, splintering sound echoed up from the lake, followed immediately by a chorus of female screams and loud splashes.

"Oh, my goodness, they've all fallen into the lake!" Dorothea shouted.

All three men turned, then started sprinting down the hill, pulling off their coats as they ran. Hastily, Dorothea grabbed the reins of Lord Atwood's and Viscount Benton's horses before the animals could bolt. Tugging on the reins, she too ran down the hill, the horses obediently following.

Lord Atwood hit the water first, with the major a few seconds behind. There was so much splashing in the middle of the lake, Dorothea could barely distinguish Lady Meredith's adult form. She appeared to be holding at least one, perhaps two of her daughters as she struggled to stay afloat. There was no sign of the boat. It must have sunk to the bottom after taking on too much water.

"Hurry, hurry," Dorothea whispered frantically.

It was quickly apparent that Lord Atwood was by far the strongest swimmer. He reached the center of the lake well ahead of the viscount and the major. It was then Dorothea saw two female heads bobbing distinctly above the surface—Lady Meredith and Stephanie, her oldest daughter. The two younger ones were missing.

Without hesitation, Lord Atwood dove under the water. He quickly resurfaced, a child in his arms. He passed the little girl to Viscount Benton, then dove under again. This time he resurfaced alone.

Dorothea tensed, fear pressing heavily on her chest. Her lips began moving in silent prayer. *Oh, please, dear God, let the child be found.* The marquess dove under a third time. Everyone seemed to be holding their collective breath as they waited for him to emerge, and then finally he broke through the water.

There was a sputtering sound and then a lusty cry as the child he held began to shriek. Dorothea, along with the servants and bystanders who had gathered on the shore, let out a loud cheer. Slowly, they all began to swim toward shore, the men assisting the children and Lady Meredith.

It was a tearful, relieved reunion as Dorothea and the servants gathered around the drenched group. Dorothea snatched a picnic blanket from the ground and wrapped it around Lady Meredith's shoulders, giving her a fierce hug. She then hugged each of the girls, who were also wrapped in blankets, huddled close to their mother.

"Gracious, we shall have quite a tale to tell Papa, won't we, girls?" Lady Meredith smiled shakily down at her daughters, who regarded her with wide, solemn eyes.

"I think he shall be very angry with us," Stephanie replied as her teeth began to chatter.

"Perhaps." Lady Meredith vigorously rubbed her daughter's arm. "That's why we must smile and laugh when we tell him of our adventure, to let him know that we were not afraid. All right, girls?"

Three soggy heads nodded in unison. Dorothea lifted her gaze from Lady Meredith and the children and turned to regard the three men who had risked their lives to save the females.

They were equally wet, though seemingly unconcerned as murky water steadily dripped from their hair and clothing. Caught in the jubilation of the moment, they were joking and laughing with each other, a trait Dorothea had observed was common among men after victoriously escaping peril.

"Christ, Roddy, it seems as if danger likes to follow you around," Viscount Benton declared.

"Truly," Lord Atwood agreed. "'Tis hard to believe you survived the war."

Major Roddington grinned sheepishly, then pushed a lock of wet hair off his forehead. "It must be this English soil. I too am starting to feel as though it is safer for me to be battling the French."

After taking Miss Ellingham home, a still damp Major Roddington entered his bachelor apartment. His servant, Parker, emerged from the small sitting room, took one look at his master, and smiled.

"By the looks of you, it seems that things went as planned," Parker said, his grin widening.

"Hardly." The major gritted his teeth in frustration. He shrugged out of his damp coat and flung it on the floor, then nearly groaned when he caught a glimpse of his best boots. They were stiff and waterlogged, ruined, most likely beyond salvation, and he certainly did not have the necessary funds to replace them. "What the hell did you do to that damn boat, Parker?"

The servant's face turned ashen at the major's rare show of temper. "Exactly what you asked, sir."

"I think not," Roddy snapped. "The boat was supposed to spring a sizable leak almost immediately when it was put in the water, so it would not be taken too far from shore. Instead, it was rowed to nearly the center of the lake before it splintered into dozens of pieces."

Parker's brow knit together with worry. "Was Miss Ellingham injured?"

Roddy slapped his hand down on the table. Hard. "No, you bloody idiot, she wasn't injured. She wasn't even in the damn boat."

"What happened?"

"Lady Meredith and her daughters took the boat out on the lake. I was too far away to even notice. It broke apart when they were far from shore." Roddy raked his fingers through his hair. "Christ Almighty, they could have easily drowned. The girls are so young, I swear the oldest can't be more than nine or ten."

Parker's face lost any remaining bits of color. "Were they badly hurt?" he asked.

Roddy let out a ragged breath. "Not really. More frightened, I think. The two younger ones were wailing something awful when they were pulled from the water, but their mother managed to calm them down."

"You were able to save them." Parker's tense face collapsed with relief. "Then you're still a hero."

"Atwood saved them," he replied with great resentment, antagonism flowing through his veins. Truly, could it have been any worse? All this careful planning and in the end it was Atwood who garnered all the glory. Fate really was a harsh, unkind master.

I will make my own fate, Roddy vowed to himself. *I will not allow myself to be pushed away from everything that should be mine by rights. Especially by Atwood, of all people.*

"The marquess pulled all four females from the water?" Parker asked.

The edge of admiration in Parker's voice made Roddy want to scream in frustration. "No. He rescued the two youngest girls, the ones who actually needed the most help. The older daughter managed to keep her head above the water and while frightened, was not in any real danger. Benton assisted her."

"And the marchioness?"

Roddy grunted. "She swims like a fish. I made a grand show of lending her assistance, but clearly it was unnecessary."

Roddy pulled out a chair from his small dining table and sat as a sudden exhaustion overtook his agitation. In his mind he could hear the frightened cries of those innocent young girls, could see the panic and terror on their mother's face. Maybe he should just give up and walk away. Before some other innocent bystanders were truly injured.

But how could he? This was the closest he had ever come to his prey. If he did not strike now, the opportunity would be lost, possibly forever. 'Twould be foolish indeed to back off when victory was within his grasp.

"I'm sorry, sir," Parker said contritely. "I did my best. I bored holes in several places on the bottom and sides of the rowboat, just as you told me. I assumed the vessel would start taking on water immediately. I never expected the wood to be so weak that it would splinter."

Roddy drew in a steadying breath. There was no cause to blame Parker. "Serves us right for trying to stage a rescue on the water. We are cavalry men, Parker, not sailors."

"Yes, sir."

Roddy sighed. It was not Parker's fault that things had gone awry. He, and he alone, must bear the burden of this afternoon's near disaster. Once again, he thought of abandoning his mission. He was young, capable, and now, thanks to his war record, a man with a few influential friends.

Opportunities for financial gain abounded in India. Even in the American colonies. Perhaps it was time for him to make a move, to go somewhere far away, where he could have a fresh start, a new beginning. Yet as tempting as it seemed, Roddy knew himself too well. He was not ready. There was more to be done, more to accomplish. He could not look toward his future until he settled his past. Here, in England.

"From now on we must be especially diligent and careful," Roddy told his servant. "We cannot afford any more mistakes. The stakes are simply too high, Parker. Too damn high."

Chapter Seven

The dinner invitation from the Marquess and Marchioness of Dardington arrived later that evening, a few moments before Carter was set to leave for the Lancasters' musical soiree. Written in Lady Dardington's own hand, it was graciously and informally worded. Carter thought it totally unnecessary, but he understood the Dardingtons' desire to tangibly express their gratitude for his assistance at the lake this afternoon. His only hope was that it would be, as the invitation promised, a small, family affair.

"The footman is waiting for an answer, my lord," his valet, Dunsford, said.

"Tell him to inform Lady Dardington that I shall be delighted to attend," Carter instructed.

The valet bowed and exited, but returned a few minutes later.

"Is there a problem, Dunsford?" he asked as the servant held out Carter's evening jacket. "Does the footman require a written reply instead of a verbal one?"

"No, my lord. Lord Dardington's servant has gone." The valet adjusted the collar on the jacket, then stepped away, lifted his chin, and thrust his shoulders back. "His Grace, the Duke of Hansborough, has arrived. He wishes to speak with you."

"My father is here?" Carter's amusement at his valet's stiff formality disappeared. His father never came to his bachelor apartments. Something must be wrong. "Does he appear upset?"

The valet shook his head. "His Grace maintained a proper, even temperament upon arrival and while being shown to the sitting room. He expressed no urgency in seeing you, but did however insist upon it."

Of course. His father rarely displayed any sort of emotions in public, saving his anger and displeasure for those private moments between himself and his son.

"Very good, Dunsford. Please inform the duke that I shall be with him shortly."

Carter picked up a brush and slowly applied it to his already groomed hair. He waited until he was sure his valet had enough time to deliver the message before striding across his bedchamber, through his dressing room, and into the spacious sitting area of his home.

His foot had barely stepped onto the Aubusson rug when a figure moved forward from the corner of the room. "Good evening, Carter."

"Hello, sir." Carter struggled to hide his surprise. The duke never came toward anyone. Much like a king with his subjects, the duke always waited for people to approach him. "To what do I owe this unexpected visit?"

"Can't a man stop in and say hello to his son?" the duke asked gruffly. "Does there have to be a reason?"

"When the two individuals in question are you and I, sir, there almost always is a specific reason."

The duke cleared his throat and took another step closer. For an instant, Carter had the strangest sensation that the duke meant to embrace him, something he seldom did when Carter was a boy and never once after he had reached his tenth birthday.

Seeking to defuse the odd tension swirling about the room, Carter headed for the crystal decanters of spirits on the credenza. He poured them both a glass of whiskey, then slowly crossed back to his father, taking note of the older man's appearance.

The duke was dressed formally for an evening out, confirming that nothing initially seemed amiss. Yet as Carter looked closer, something did seem different about his father. His hair appeared to have several additional gray streaks, his broad shoulders were slightly stooped. It must be a trick of the light, Carter decided. The duke was never anything but invincible.

The duke accepted the glass, then pulled himself up to his usual rigid stance. "A salute to your good health. May you never take it for granted."

"To your good health, sir," Carter replied automatically, and then he stopped short, his whiskey glass not yet at his lips.

Was his father ill? Was this the real reason for this unexpected visit? Carter's stomach turned to lead. He took but a small sip of his whiskey.

"I can see that you are dressed to go out for the evening, so I shall be direct," the duke began as he sat down. "I heard there was a bit of a commotion at Banberry Park today. Something about you taking a dunk in the lake?"

Carter waved his hand dismissively. "It was nothing."

"There was also talk of an incident in front of the Bull and Finch tavern last week where some thug pulled a knife on you and nearly succeeding in burying it in your chest." The duke took another swallow of his drink. "In light of this troubling information, I feel compelled to ask, is this merely a string of bad luck or are you deliberately courting danger?"

"To spite you?" Carter laughed at the ridiculous question, feeling almost giddy with relief. His father's health was not in jeopardy. This time when he tipped the glass to his lips, he was able to take a long, enjoyable swallow.

"I asked you a question," the duke said, his voice sharp.

Carter's smile faded. The duke was serious. "It was too outrageous for a response," he countered. "If I wanted to injure myself, there are far easier and less painful methods than drowning or getting knifed."

"I'm serious."

"So am I." Carter downed his whiskey in two swallows. "These were two unrelated, random events in which I was an unwitting participant. Nothing more."

The duke sat up, adjusting his lean frame in the elegant chair. "I am relieved to hear this is not a deliberate pattern of behavior. Yet these harrowing experiences serve to further illustrate my position. Time is of the essence. If anything fatal had occurred, you would have left this world without an heir."

Ah, so now they came to the heart of the matter, the reason for the visit. His father was concerned about the continuation of the family line. "If I promise that I shall endeavor to keep myself alive long enough to father a legitimate heir, will that set your mind at rest, sir?"

The duke slammed his half-full whiskey glass on the nearby side table. "God Almighty, Carter, you are my only child. Do you not think I would be devastated at your loss, out of my mind with grief and pain?"

Carter simply stared at his father, too stunned to think of a response.

"I was at my club this afternoon when I heard that you had been in the lake and nearly drowned trying to rescue Dardington's girls," the duke continued. "I assumed there was some exaggeration to the tale, but it sounded dire. Most dire."

"Of course I dove in to save the children. I daresay you would have done the same, had you been there, sir." Carter rubbed his forehead. His father was clearly distressed, obviously concerned. It was completely . . . unexpected. "I was never in any great peril. I am a strong swimmer."

"And the knife incident?"

"A tavern brawl that I happened upon. But I was not alone. Benton, Dawson, and the major were there, too. They had my back."

"I suppose that is some consolation." The duke picked up his glass, drained it, then leaned back in his chair. "The Marchioness of Dardington has sent me an invitation to a private dinner party she is having in your honor tomorrow evening. I am unable to attend. I must leave for Shrewsbury in the morning and will be gone for the remainder of the week. I have important estate business that requires my immediate attention. I wanted you to know I would have been there, if it were possible."

Carter could barely hide his shock. "I understand. Thank you for telling me."

The corner of the duke's mouth trembled slightly. "Well, I wanted you to know." Then, as though he felt guilty for revealing the depth of his concern and emotions, he added, "And I wanted to know how you were coming with your marriage plans. How many of the young ladies on my list have you spoken with recently?"

Carter felt a stab of emotion, akin to relief. The duke's odd behavior had been surprising and unsettling. It felt better to be back on familiar ground. "May we drop the list for tonight, sir? In light of the trauma of this afternoon."

"Neatly put." The duke scoffed. "You were always one to press the advantage at any opportunity."

"It happens so rarely when dealing with you, sir. I'd be a fool not to act when the chance presents itself."

The duke allowed the remark to pass and even managed a tight smile. They continued a civil dialogue as they waited for the duke's carriage to be summoned and parted with a firm handshake.

Yet when he took to his bed in the early morning hours, Carter was still trying to puzzle out the true reason for his father's visit.

Carter was the first guest of honor to arrive at the Dardingtons' elegant London townhome the following evening. He felt slightly uncomfortable at the effervescent praise he received the moment he crossed the threshold. Lady Dardington, who insisted he address her as Meredith, clung to his arm tightly, exalting his quick thinking and unselfish sacrifice and repeatedly expressed her thanks for his heroic efforts on behalf of herself and her daughters.

Yet her gratitude paled in comparison to her husband's. It was somewhat shocking to see the normally stoic Lord Dardington in such an emotional state. There was a suspicious trace of moisture in his eyes when he shook Carter's hand and echoed his wife's thanks. The extent of his love and devotion to his wife and children was almost humbling to witness.

Thankfully, Benton and Roddington soon made their appearance, thus spreading the gratitude among the three gentlemen. The major took it all in stride, while Benton eagerly lapped up the endless praise and Carter tried to downplay his own heroics.

"I feel like a conquering Roman general victoriously returning from the wars," the viscount confided to Carter with a lopsided grin.

"Don't mention that to Dardington or else he'll arrange for a bevy of Egyptian slave girls to entertain us," Carter said ruefully. "I swear the man is so grateful he would give us the deeds to his estates if we even hinted that we were interested in acquiring them."

"It never hurts to have a man of the marquess's stature in our debt," Benton observed wryly.

The two men abruptly ceased trading quips when the three Dardington daughters, along with their governess, entered the drawing room. The girls filed in front of their rescuers in a single line. Then, without prompting, each child executed a passable curtsy.

Carter stood uneasily beside Benton and Roddington, uncertain how to react. He was not much around children and knew next to nothing of them. Fortunately, little was required except to appear interested in the apparently rehearsed proceedings.

Dry, quiet, and up close, they were a remarkable pretty trio, inheriting the finest points of their very attractive parents. The eldest read a note of thanks she had composed before presenting a copy to each of them, along with a picture her two younger sisters had drawn.

The presentation concluded, the girls were quickly hustled off to the nursery. Carter seized the opportunity to let his eyes wander toward Miss Ellingham. She was dressed in a shimmering gown of pale lavender that made her hair appear golden and her skin creamy and delectable. He had always thought her a pretty woman, but tonight she looked positively beautiful.

The gown's narrow bodice offered a delightful view of her perfectly rounded breasts, displaying her overabundant charms in an odd combination of virginity and sensuality that had him thinking the most inappropriate thoughts.

As if somehow sensing his randy thoughts, she suddenly

looked away from the Countess of Marchdale, Benton's paternal grandmother, with whom she was conversing, and caught his gaze. He inclined his head, captivated by the brightness of her smile and the sparkle in her eyes.

The way she returned his stare let him know she recognized his admiration. But did she appreciate it? Of that, Carter was far less certain.

Dinner was announced and the small party of guests entered the dining room. Carter was seated next to Lady Meredith on his left and the Countess of Marchdale on his right. Miss Ellingham was on the opposite side of the table, sandwiched between Benton and Roddington.

It was easy to be entertained by Lady Marchdale's lively conversation and wicked sense of humor, yet throughout the meal, Carter remained very much aware of Miss Ellingham. He tried to distract his thoughts and concentrate on the delicious food, but then Miss Ellingham's fingers glided over the stem of her crystal wine goblet, unwittingly drawing Carter's gaze.

She had slender, elegant fingers. He imagined them moving across his body in a sensual, teasing stroke. The resulting fantasy made him hot and embarrassingly hard. Letting out a low, strangled sigh, Carter took a large bite of his sole in cream sauce.

Miss Ellingham smiled at something the major said to her, then turned in his direction and caught Carter's stare. There was no lowering of her lashes, no maidenly blush. Instead her blue eyes met his with an unspoken challenge, as if daring him to intercede.

Damn. It was that challenge that intrigued him most of all.

"I applaud your taste in females," the Countess of Marchdale remarked. "Miss Ellingham is a lovely girl. She has that elusive, alluring type of beauty that men find so irresistible. Her character appears solid also, a rarity among females with such prime looks. I think she could make any one of you a good wife." Lady Marchdale waved her fork around the table, to include the major and the viscount, as well as himself.

"I shall be certain to mention that to your grandson," Carter replied, not bothering to hide his smile. "No doubt he will want to act on it immediately."

"We both know that is a bald-faced lie." Lady Marchdale rested her fork on the edge of her plate, then with her free hand swatted his forearm with her fingertips. Carter nearly yelped in surprise. She had a strong slap for an elderly woman. "Sebastian will never seriously consider a girl once I give my approval of her. 'Tis like stamping the poor creature with the plague."

Carter silently agreed. He and Benton were very much alike in this regard—they readily closed their minds to any female recommended by an elderly relation. "Perhaps on this occasion Benton will appreciate your advice?"

"When pigs fly," Lady Marchdale scoffed. She signaled to the footman to refill her wineglass before continuing. "On second thought, Miss Ellingham is probably best suited as a wife for the major, given her family background and fortune." She lowered her voice and leaned close to Carter's ear. "Did you know he was a bastard?"

Carter nearly sprayed his mouthful of wine across the table. "You must not say such harsh, unfair things about a man's character, Lady Marchdale. Major Roddington is a good and decent man, one I am proud to call my friend."

Lady Marchdale let out a rather unladylike snort. "That is not what I meant, as you very well know. I was referring to his lack of a father, not impugning his character. Oh, I do wish I had my fan, young man, so I could rap your knuckles properly."

Carter's mouth twitched. It was no wonder Benton despaired at his grandmother's outspoken opinions. "I don't think that Major Roddington has any interest in marriage at this time."

"No man wants to get married," the countess declared. "Except those poor fools who are bewitched by a pretty face or desperate to escape debtors' prison."

"Well, since I am blessed with a considerable fortune and an immunity to bewitching females, does that mean I shall never be ready to take on a wife?"

She laughed heartily. "Men can be so infernally irrational. They feel they need to prepare for everything, as if that would make one whit of a difference when it comes to living with a woman. Marriage can be either heaven or hell. 'Tis up to you to decide which one you'd rather endure and then make it happen. I should know. I buried three husbands and they all went to meet their Maker with a smile upon their lips."

Three? Carter had forgotten. But why did they die happy men? Because they had lived contented lives or because they were finally able to escape Lady Marchdale? Carter absently rubbed the sore spot on his hand and decided it would be prudent not to inquire too closely.

Disciplining his errant thoughts, he smiled at the countess. Her confident tone had piqued his curiosity. "Tell me, my lady, if a man can never truly be ready for marriage, how does he overcome his reluctance?"

"You like to gamble, do you not? Then find a lovely young woman who fires your blood and roll the dice. You might find yourself delighted with the outcome."

She was right. Marriage was a step he knew he must take and it was far better to find a way to embrace his fate rather than fight it. His eyes naturally pulled themselves across the table toward Miss Ellingham. Was she his fate?

When dinner concluded, the ladies left the gentlemen to their port and cigars, as was the custom during more formal affairs. After a pleasant interlude, the men rejoined the women in the drawing room.

As he entered the room, Carter's eyes sought out Miss Ellingham. She was standing near the French doors on the opposite side of the room. Roddington immediately joined her.

She smiled in greeting, her face showing true delight. The sight left Carter feeling oddly deflated. He turned to answer a question posed to him by Lord Dardington. Once finished, he returned his gaze to the French doors. Miss Ellingham was gone. So was Roddington.

"Dorothea is showing the major my prize-winning rose garden," Lady Meredith informed him as she glided to Carter's side. "Why don't you join them?"

Carter lifted an eyebrow in feigned surprise, but the denial that he was eager for Miss Ellingham's company died on his lips. It would be rude to lie when Lady Meredith's perceptive eyes had clearly observed the truth of the matter.

"I believe I would enjoy some fresh air," he replied. "Excuse me."

It was a clear, cool evening. Carter walked with purpose through the large garden, following one, then another path of paving stones, his gaze darting to the many secluded alcoves artfully incorporated into the garden's design. A design clearly done by a man with romance and privacy on his mind.

His diligence was eventually rewarded when he spied his prey in a cozy alcove bounded on three sides by boxwood hedges. The major appeared to have his arms around Miss Ellingham. Carter stepped closer, never moving his eyes from the pair. When he saw Roddington start to dip his head forward, Carter coughed. Loudly.

The pair instantly sprang apart. Looking guilty? Carter was unsure.

"Atwood." Roddington smiled.

Carter return the grin, ignoring the flash of jealousy that drummed through his head. Poor sod. The major was no doubt relieved it was not Lord Dardington who had discovered them. "Enjoying the night air?"

"Yes, but there's a bit of a chill out here. I was just going to fetch a shawl for Miss Ellingham. Will you keep her company while I'm gone?"

"My pleasure."

Carter deliberately held his position on the pathway, waiting until the major drew near. "About Miss Ellingham," he whispered as the major walked past. "Are your affections in any way engaged?'

Roddington stopped. "Not romantically."

"A favor then, Roddington, if you please."

"Anything."

"Step away from her."

The major's brow rose. "For you?"

Carter nodded. "If you don't mind?"

Roddington barely hesitated. "Not at all. Anything for a friend."

Carter smiled inwardly, his spirits buoyed. This was all falling into place rather neatly. He waited another moment, gazing quietly in the distance before approaching her. She angled her head sharply in greeting, then twirled on her heel, presenting him with her back, a gesture that spoke volumes. A gesture he could not resist.

"Why is it, Miss Ellingham, that nearly every time I see you out of doors you are with a different gentleman? Locked in an embrace."

Her shoulders stiffened, but she did not take the bait. "You exaggerate, my lord."

"Not really. First it was Pengrove, then Rosen, and now Roddington. Is this some sort of contest? Do you hope to kiss every unwed man in London this Season?"

That remark got her attention. She turned toward him, her eyes blazing with emotion. "Do not presume to judge me, my lord," she said hotly. "You know nothing about me."

"I know that you have a fondness for kissing," he replied, with a subtle challenge in his voice that practically dared her to refute him. "And an interest in passion."

"Who I kiss and where I kiss them is none of your concern."

"What if I decided that it should be?"

"Ha!" She tossed her head, revealing the slender column of her throat. Lord, what he wouldn't do for the right to nibble at that delicate nape.

Carter reached out and placed his palm beneath her chin, bringing her face around so their eyes met. Then he slowly, gently brushed his thumb across her lips.

"You overstep your bounds, my lord," she said with a small shiver. From the cold or from his touch? Carter was uncertain.

He repeated the motion and she tried to back away, but her legs bumped into a garden bench. Her eyes blazed with frustration. Carter stared down at her, sucking in a sharp breath. He took note of the rapid rise of her breath as she fought to calm her temper, saw the pulse quicken in the hollow of her throat.

She truly was a tasty morsel, never more appealing than when she was in high emotions. No wonder so many men longed to kiss her. She had a mouth that begged to be tasted.

As if reading his thoughts, she suddenly moistened her lips with the tip of her tongue. They glistened in the moonlight, so soft, so plump, so tempting.

"Ah, to hell with it," Carter muttered as he reached for

her. He was not a man accustomed to denying himself. When he wanted something, he took it, and that especially included the woman he intended to make his wife.

Their mouths melded together as he boldly captured her lips. She acquiesced with a sigh, her entire body softening against him. He tightened his embrace, running his tongue along the line of her pressed lips. She trembled, parting them. His tongue found hers and he stroked it boldly, eliciting a sharp response of delight.

The pounding of emotions coursing through his body shocked him. It was more complex than the painfully hard erection in his breeches. That was familiar, understandable when kissing a beautiful woman. But the primitive feelings of possession, the erotic need to conquer and then comfort was unmistakable and entirely new.

It felt as if her body was coming alive in his arms, responding instinctively to his desire. It was an exquisite sensation, building the fever within him to a nearly uncontrollable pitch. He felt a stab of something deep in his chest. Puzzlement? Frustration? He couldn't define or understand it.

With a cry deep in his throat, Carter broke off the kiss, breathing hard, as if he'd just run a long race. A tangible desire filled the air between them. It was remarkable, unusual, and completely unexpected.

Dorothea was stunned. She fought to remain on her feet, feeling decidedly weak-kneed. A chill skittered across her skin and she tingled all over. There was a passion, a spark, an energy that she had never felt before in any other kiss.

For the first time in her life, she understood the real power of sexual attraction. It took every measure of her self-control to keep from throwing herself forward into his embrace and begging for more.

Speaking was difficult, maintaining a normal tone fairly

impossible. Yet somehow, Dorothea managed. "I did not give you permission to kiss me, my lord."

"Permission? Truly, Miss Ellingham, that would have taken all the fun out of it, don't you think?"

"Hardly."

A devastatingly handsome smile flooded his features, heightening his appeal even more. As if that were even possible, Dorothea thought grimly to herself.

"So, where do I rank among those kisses?" he asked with an impish gleam in his eye.

At the very top. Dorothea's hand flew to cover her mouth and then thankfully she realized she had possessed the presence of mind to keep that particular thought to herself. "This is not a contest, my lord," she said primly. "I do not rate the content or quality of a gentleman's kiss."

"I thought that was the more polite way to phrase it."

Dorothea's body went still as heated embarrassment flooded her cheeks. He said that deliberately, to taunt her. Annoyed, she pulled a leaf from a nearby plant and crumbled it in her fingers.

"If you must know, I only kiss a man I am strongly considering for marriage."

His gaze remained puzzled and then his eyes lit as the revelation struck. "After you kiss him, you decide if you will marry?"

"'Tis not as ridiculous as you are making it sound," Dorothea insisted. "Many other factors about the gentleman have been carefully considered before that point."

"The kiss is the final test?"

"In a manner of speaking, though I would hardly phrase it in that particular way," she remarked in rising embarrassment, for it was precisely as the marquess described it. "I think a kiss says a great deal about the potential success of a marriage."

"Spoken like a starry-eyed virgin." Lord Atwood's handsome face brimmed with knowing superiority. "A passionate kiss will not ensure a happy marriage. Over time, lust fades. Sometimes quickly, other times gradually, but it does eventually disappear."

"Spoken like an experienced rake," Dorothea countered. "I am not a green girl from the country, my lord. I know something of love and lust and the lack of it in marriage."

"From experience?" he mocked.

"From observation."

"And yet you are still eager to embrace marriage?"

"I am," she replied. "I am willing to make sacrifices, to do my part to make my marriage a success. When necessary, I can put all my efforts into making my husband's life easier. I will run his household efficiently, plan his social life accordingly, and be an asset in any and every way. I will not, however, be referred to as the burdensome wife by a husband who is dutifully and miserably tied to me."

He offered her a sly smile. "How can you avoid it?"

"By ensuring there is passion in the beginning. By marrying a man whose kiss excites me beyond measure."

He made a clucking sound with his tongue. "And you claimed not to be a romantic, Miss Ellingham."

"That is true. I am not. I do not pine to find my soul mate, my one true love. What I require in a mate goes beyond the basics of good character, sensible temperament, and compatibility. I know I must marry a man I find attractive, exciting. Equally, he should feel an attraction for me. With that firmly in place, I believe anything is possible."

"What happens if it does not go beyond that stage? If you and your husband never fall in love?"

"I will be content. 'Tis far more than many other couples achieve." Dorothea glanced up at him, her face open and honest. "I do not have an overly inflated expectation of marriage. I expect my opinion to be respected, my feelings considered, my worth to be appreciated by my husband."

"Passion will fade, and if love does not exist, why would you remain faithful?"

"A vow is a vow, Lord Atwood. There are no exceptions or codicils."

"Even under the most trying of circumstances?"

Dorothea bit back a grimace. "I will honor the fidelity of my marriage vows and expect my husband to do the same, even though some might consider that naïve and unfashionable."

He nodded as if he understood, even agreed with her answer. That was unexpected. Many wealthy aristocrats kept mistresses while their wives kept silent.

Dorothea's heart started beating hard. She caught the scent of his warm skin mingled with the sweet aroma of the spring blooms. It was erotic, intoxicating. His handsome face was contemplative as he stared intently down at her. What was he thinking? Feeling?

"You know, Miss Ellingham, you never did answer my question. About my kiss?" Reaching out, he lifted a stray wisp of hair and brushed it behind her ear.

Dorothea's eyes widened. She held herself very still, concentrating on retaining her composure and ignoring the riot of emotions that claimed her at his touch. "On the contrary, my lord, I have answered a great many of your questions. Far too many questions that were far too personal."

His eyes narrowed as he smiled. "What about my kiss, Miss Ellingham? Do you decree it worthy enough to be your husband? Or do you require a second sample?"

Dorothea swallowed the squeak that rose in her throat. He could not possibly be serious. Marriage between them? She did not dare to believe it could really happen. Lord

Atwood was a man who liked to flirt and tease. Surely he was teasing her now. Still, she could not deny the thrill she felt at the thought of actually winning his regard, of becoming his wife now that she had experienced his kiss.

"A second kiss?" She tossed her head, striving to look offended. "Impossible."

"Afraid?" he taunted in a soft voice.

"Not at all." She lifted her chin and attempted to look calm. Yet deep inside, she feared if he kissed her again, she might very well swoon. "I am merely being practical, my lord. I have never kissed a gentleman a second time and I vowed the only occasion I ever would do so was after I agreed to be his wife."

Chapter Eight

Carter smiled. It was precisely the type of challenging remark he had hoped she would make. Hearing it solidified in his mind the thought that had been swirling in his head ever since he had spoken with her at the Duke of Warwick's ball and learned her progressive ideas about marriage. She would be an excellent wife. For him.

Oh, his father would not be entirely thrilled with her, given her lack of fortune and family prestige, and her limited connections. Not to mention the fact that she was not on the duke's infernal list of potential daughters-in-law.

But those objections would soon disappear when Carter made plain his determination to take her for his wife. His lips curled in an ironic line as he realized selecting Miss Ellingham as his bride was eerily close to Benton's idiotic plan to thwart the duke by finding an unsuitable woman and insisting she was the only one he would marry.

But Miss Ellingham was not unsuitable. She was a genteel woman, a gentleman's daughter, raised as a lady. This was the obvious answer. He needed to take a wife. Sooner, rather than later. And thus he was perfectly sincere in his offer, in fact pleased with himself at finding such a brilliant solution.

This was no sham. They would marry. She would belong to him.

"Since it appears the only way I can procure that most desired second kiss, then obviously we must marry. My dear, won't you say yes to my proposal so that we may kiss again?" He leaned closer, his eyes darkening with purpose. "Kiss and perhaps a bit more."

It took a few moments for his words to register in her mind. Carter fancied he knew precisely when she had digested them fully, for she pursed her lips, shook her head, then drew a deep breath. "I fear you have drunk too much wine with dinner, my lord."

"Only two glasses."

"Then your head must have hit a branch or something when you jumped in the lake yesterday afternoon, for clearly your brain is addled."

"I am serious."

"About marrying me? We barely know each other."

His smile broadened. The more she objected, the more the correctness of his decision was confirmed in his mind. "I have it on very good authority that knowing someone well and planning too much is not a requirement for a successful marriage."

She was staring up at him with astonishment. No, it was more than astonishment. Disbelief and open skepticism were present, too. "And you dared to disparage my method of engaging in a single kiss to aid in the final choice? For shame, my lord."

"On the contrary. I applaud your rather, hmm, unique ideas of choosing a husband. 'Tis progressive and most effective." He eyed her from head to toe with deliberate slowness. "And thoroughly enjoyable."

She rolled her eyes and attempted to step around him. He blocked the way effortlessly. For several seconds they simply stared at each other. The more he gazed into her lovely face, the more aroused he became. Yes, this was the right decision. He would no have difficulties providing the heir his father so keenly craved. No difficulty at all.

"Your proposal is so completely unexpected," she finally muttered, still unconvinced and distrustful. "I need time to consider my answer."

"Why?"

"Why?" she sputtered, crossing her arms under her breasts. "Unlike you, my lord, I take the idea of marriage most seriously."

"But the kiss . . ." He let his voice trail off suggestively.

Cheeks blushing, she shifted from one foot to the other. "The kiss is but one part of my decision. There are other, equally important considerations."

"I have taken those into account. My wealth, my lineage, my age, all make me an excellent candidate. My wife will not want for anything. She will eventually take her place among the highest ranks of society when I inherit the dukedom. Most women would be honored at the proposal."

Her mouth quirked. "I am not most women," she declared ruefully. "And while I certainly agree that you are considered by many to be the prize of the matrimonial Season, my requirements in a husband extend beyond his wealth and position. Temperament and compatibility are also key elements to be considered, not to mention character."

"I will gladly compare my character to that of Lord Rosen," he replied with confidence.

"That is hardly a testimonial. Napoleon would rank higher in character when compared to Lord Rosen," she said. "Besides, I rejected him."

Carter scratched his head, mystified by her reaction. This was not precisely how he envisioned his proposal being received. Though honestly, he had not spent much time planning it. Maybe that was the reason it was going so poorly?

"My dear, we both know very well that you have been actively seeking a husband. I, in turn, require a wife and have decided you would make me an excellent one. Even more beneficial, the spark of passion you require is very evident between us."

The sound of her laughter carried no humor. "Is it really that simple, my lord?"

"It can be." Carter creased his brow. Perhaps he had miscalculated with his impromptu proposal. Perhaps she wanted, needed more. "Unless you require a more chivalrous, romantic gesture?"

Her face alighted with interest. "If I did, would you provide it?"

"Reluctantly."

He was surprised to see the flash of disappointment on her lovely face. Carter frowned. Maybe this was not the brilliant idea he thought, proposing so hastily. Perhaps Miss Ellingham was more of a romantic than she knew.

For a moment her expression turned wistful. Then she shook her head, blinked her eyes, and lifted her chin. "You are right, my lord. I deplore pretense, especially between a man and a woman. I would not appreciate any false show of regard or affection from you unless it was sincerely and honestly given."

Damn! Carter surveyed her silently. While not enamored with the idea, he certainly felt enough genuine passion and regard for her that he could have enacted a more memorable marriage proposal. He simply had not realized it would be necessary.

He glanced at the nearest rose bush, his eyes resting on a single, perfectly formed bloom. It would take little effort to pluck the rose, brush it across his lips, gallantly present it to her and ask again if she would be his bride. Yet instinctively he knew that could be a fatal move. Surely she would regard the gesture as pure artifice.

For a long time she did not move, did not speak. Her lovely blue eyes remained clouded with confusion and mistrust. Carter began to pace about in the small space, the restless movement helping to contain his frustration. He was racking his brain, trying to formulate his next argument, when she let out a long sigh.

The sound of it hurt him somewhere deep inside and a swell of disappointment filled his throat. The emotions caught him completely by surprise. *She is going to refuse!* Without thinking, Carter abruptly went down on one knee and took her hand in his. "Please, Miss Ellingham, accept my offer of marriage. I vow you shall never regret becoming my wife."

She considered him in silence, her breasts rising and falling rapidly. Then, at long last, her eyes softened and she slowly nodded. "I grant you my permission to speak with Lord Dardington. If he agrees, we shall marry."

Carter's heart leapt. Reacting purely on emotion, he stood up, grabbed her forcefully around the waist, and brought his mouth down upon hers.

It happened so quickly, Dorothea had no time to resist. Stunned, she languished in his strong, powerful arms, her body pressed intimately against his heated strength. There were times when she had not liked the press of a man's lips against hers, had not liked feeling so dominated by a large, powerful male. But this was different. This was magical.

He angled his head to deepen the kiss, then flicked his tongue inside, coaxing her, daring her to respond. Dorothea's hands tightened into fists on the front of his evening coat as she leaned into him, her emotions rioting.

She needed, wanted, craved. Dorothea rose up on her

toes, returning the kiss, her tongue darting and teasing and tasting. Desire, bold and unexpected, roared through her veins. Opening her hands, she released his coat and twined her arms around his strong neck. He made a low noise deep in his throat and the sound seemed to vibrate through her.

It was a soul-searing kiss, a promise of passion and delight that left her body feeling weak, her mind numb. His hands felt strong and warm as they wandered over her back, then lower. Cupping her bottom, he pulled her closer to his hardness.

It was madness. It was passion. It was irresistible. Her body seemed to melt into his, tightening with longing at each kiss, each caress. He kissed her throat, pressing his lips against a sensitive spot right below her ear, and Dorothea forgot everything but the feelings exploding inside her.

"You are so sweet," he whispered. "So incredibly delightful."

Dorothea couldn't catch her breath. She arched forward, kissing him back in growing abandonment. His hand moved from her backside up to her shoulder, then down across her chest. She felt her dress loosen, enough to allow his hand access. His fingers slid inside the garment, moving lightly across the curves of her breasts, caressing the bare flesh.

"Atwood . . ." she breathed shakily.

"Carter. My name is Carter. Say it."

"Carter," she whispered, hardly believing how wildly excited she could become by merely saying his name.

He inhaled sharply. With his fingertips he circled and teased her nipples until they hardened. Dorothea moaned. The shocking pleasure of his touch sent a bolt of passion spiraling through her. Moaning again, she arched herself forward until her breasts were even deeper into his large hands, her body quivering with want and longing.

"Exquisite," he whispered, lowering his head.

He placed a trail of kisses down her neck and across her bare shoulder, then shockingly put his mouth on her breast. Dorothea cried out. He pulled the nipple fully into his mouth and pleasure shook her with such force she thought she might faint. Her pulse quickened and she wondered whose heart was thundering louder, hers or his.

Awash in a sea of pleasure, Dorothea felt the desire race through every part of her body. All of her awareness and concentration was centered on him and the fire he was creating deep inside her. His kisses, his touch, his strength. Yet when she felt his questing fingers sliding along the inside of her thigh, Dorothea's addled brain awoke.

"Enough!" With strength she never knew she possessed, she pulled away.

Carter immediately moved toward her, his face dark with passion. "It's all right. There's no need to be afraid. I'm not going to hurt you."

"I am not afraid," she lied. Her breath was billowing out in alarming gasps, her chest heaving. She felt raw and restless and so completely unlike herself it was damn near terrifying.

He reached out to brush an errant curl from her cheek. The graze of his knuckle made her skin tingle. "Your passion excites me," he confessed in a husky voice.

And me. Shivering with yearning, Dorothea closed her eyes. Her complete abandon and lack of control was a startling discovery.

"We are not yet engaged, my lord, much less married," she declared, opening her eyes and staring into his, wanting to impress upon him her genuine concern.

A slow, sensual smile spread across his face. "I was hoping you would be bold enough to anticipate those vows."

Hot color washed into her cheeks. How mortifying! Even more so because it was true. With the right approach, Dorothea feared he could get her to do just about anything.

"I will pretend that I did not hear that insulting remark," she bristled, inhaling deeply to control her mixed emotions. She needed to gain control of the situation, but that was somewhat difficult given her heightened emotions. And her loosened clothing.

Turning away, she began to hastily adjust the front of her gown, tugging her bodice into place. She felt him move closer and her body instinctively went rigid, but the hands at her back merely fastened the hooks of her gown. Which was only fair, she decided, since he had been the one to open them.

"There, all safely covered again," he announced.

"Thank you." Gathering up her courage, she turned to face him.

His eyes ran over her in a slow, sensual caress, sending a curl of heat into her midsection. "I will speak with Lord Dardington tomorrow," he announced.

"Tomorrow," Dorothea echoed. Her pulse began to thump as the full implication of his words registered in her brain. This was real, this was happening.

She had done it. She had secured a husband, had wrangled a proposal from one of society's most eligible gentleman. Not only wrangled the proposal, but for all intents and purposes accepted it.

Saints above, I am going to be a marchioness. And someday, a duchess!

There was, of course, a very slight chance that Lord Dardington would refuse Lord Atwood's offer. Yet given his current state of mind and excessive gratitude for Atwood's rescue of his daughters, that seemed highly unlikely.

Besides, Carter clearly would not take no for an answer. Dorothea firmly believed if there were any objections put forth by Lord Dardington, they would be summarily disarmed.

She would marry him and in doing so achieve a noble and social status far higher than she had ever dared aspire. Yet shockingly, a sense of victory and accomplishment was not foremost in her heart.

"We should return to the drawing room, before someone is sent to fetch us," Dorothea suggested.

"In a moment." His hand caught hers, fingers entwined. She stiffened, but then he surprised her utterly by slowly raising her arm and tenderly kissing her palm. A gasp of pleasure escaped her lips. Temptation to once again melt into his arms reared at his gallant, lover's gesture, but Dorothea strengthened her resolve. She would not succumb so easily, so predictably.

She had wanted a man whose kisses excited her, and Carter's certainly did. Yet there was an edge to his passion she did not understand, an intensity that left her feeling vulnerable and exposed. It was equally intoxicating and troubling.

In addition to passion, Dorothea also wanted a man she understood, a man she could exert some control over. Carter was neither of those things. He was a puzzle she did not comprehend, an unmovable force she could not manipulate. Well, at least not easily.

She initially thought him to be a provocative, yet guarded man, but his kisses disproved her opinion. There was far more to the Marquess of Atwood than she originally believed.

If only she could decide if that was a good thing.

Frustrated at her mixed emotions, Dorothea tried to control another burst of excitement as it fluttered through her. There was still time to change her mind. No one would force her to go through with the marriage.

But honestly, she'd be a fool to turn him down. He was handsome, titled, and rich. Without question this was the best offer she would ever receive. Yet, as they rejoined everyone in the drawing room, Dorothea continued to wonder, if this was such a wonderful, extraordinary match, why was there a nagging dose of doubt crowding into her mind?

"Well?" Dorothea prompted anxiously. "What do you think of Lord Atwood?"

She lowered herself into a dainty, gilded chair and stared across the room at her older sister. Gwendolyn creased her brow thoughtfully, then firmly declared, "You don't love him."

"Thank God." Dorothea did not bother hiding her shudder. Falling in love with Carter at this stage in their relationship would put her at a great disadvantage.

"Then why marry him?"

Dorothea groaned. "Surely your eyes cannot be so blinded by your adoration of your husband that you cannot appreciate the finer qualities of another man, sister."

Gwendolyn folded her hands and rested them across her large, pregnant belly. "Lord Atwood is very handsome."

"And rich, and titled, and a physically appealing specimen," Dorothea added pertly.

"Hmm." Gwendolyn seemed to ponder that remark for a moment. "So tell me, how does he kiss?"

Dorothea smiled mischievously. Ah, her sister had remembered. "Divinely. He kisses like a man who has not eaten for weeks and I am a feast he has stumbled upon."

"Passing your ridiculous kissing test does not make him a good choice for a husband." Gwendolyn's voice grew stronger, more commanding, as she took on the role of protective older sister. "Especially since his reputation would imply that he has a great deal of experience kissing women. Naturally, he has some skill."

Dorothea swallowed. Gwen was right. To a point. But Carter's experience with other women was not something Dorothea wanted to focus upon. "That is hardly a fair statement. You married a man with a far worse reputation, a man many labeled a rake of the highest order."

"True, but I loved him. As he loved me," Gwendolyn answered. "Jason wanted me as his wife, knowing full well he would have to reform. I am proud to say he has succeeded beyond anyone's expectations, though I never doubted him for a moment."

Reform? Dorothea wondered if that was a word in Lord Atwood's vocabulary. Her chair creaked as she readjusted her position. Silently, she looked around her sister's finely appointed private sitting room, a recent gift from her husband. He had commissioned the room as a surprise when they discovered she was to have a child.

The pale greens and warm amber tones, inviting atmosphere, and comfortable furnishings captured Gwendolyn's personality with alarming accuracy, but the costly furniture, rugs, and paintings reflected Jason's exquisite taste in expensive furnishings. The home he provided for his wife was a testament to his determination to give her everything she could possibly desire.

Not that Gwen especially cared about material items. She had always been the more practical, down-to-earth sister, but love had mellowed her personality, had softened away any of her sharp edges.

Dorothea took a deep breath, trying to hide her

annoyance. She had made a special effort to journey out from London for an afternoon to visit her sister, wanting very much for Gwendolyn to meet her future husband. Meet and approve of him, she silently admitted. Not question the choice.

"Love aside, I daresay you would not have married Jason if his kisses had not thrilled you," Dorothea insisted.

Gwen snorted. "There is more to marriage than compatibility between the sheets."

Dorothea's head snapped up. "What?"

"Sex, Dorothea. I'm talking about the intimacy which occurs between a man and a woman."

"I know to what you are referring, Gwendolyn," Dorothea huffed.

"Yes, of course you believe you know, but you only understand the mechanics of the act. The biology behind it. The reality is far different." Gwendolyn pursed her lips. "Without a deep emotional bond, a man of Atwood's jaded tastes and experience will not be easy to keep entertained in the bedroom."

Flustered, Dorothea squirmed on her chair. It had to be Gwendolyn's advanced stage of pregnancy that brought on such frank talk. That, and Gwendolyn's genuine concern for her happiness. Dorothea struggled to keep that in the forefront of her mind, hoping it would help her retain her equilibrium.

"Lord Atwood is a man of character," she insisted. "He will treat me with respect and dignity. I cannot believe you don't see it."

"I can hardly form a judgment of his character after a ten-minute conversation in which we discussed your drive from Town and the unseasonably warm weather."

"You may interrogate him over tea," Dorothea decided.

"We have several hours before we must begin our journey back."

Gwendolyn leaned forward, then shifted back, obviously searching for a more comfortable position. Dorothea winced. Her sister's distended belly was enormous. Though she was a tall woman, the baby she carried distorted her figure grotesquely. It hurt Dorothea's back just to look at her.

"I cannot sit in a drawing room with a strange man and take tea in my condition," Gwendolyn declared. "'Tis highly improper."

"I assure you Lord Atwood is not especially strange," Dorothea responded with a smile. "A bit odd at times and exceedingly vexing, but not that peculiar."

"Brat," Gwendolyn replied with affection. "If my back were not aching so horribly, I'd throw this pillow at you."

"Enceinte or not, you would most certainly miss me by a mile." Dorothea's grin widened. "Well, at least I've finally coaxed a smile from you."

"I warn you, it won't last. My mood changes quicker than the weather these days," Gwendolyn grumbled.

"It's to be expected," Dorothea said, though in truth she had no idea if that was the case. She had never before been around a woman so advanced in pregnancy, and frankly, the change in her sister was rather frightening.

Knowing it might take ten minutes for Gwendolyn to rise from her chair and pull the rope to summon a servant, Dorothea took the initiative to arrange for tea. The stately butler appeared in a moment, his expression blank as he averted his gaze from his employer's expanded belly.

"Have tea brought in here," Gwendolyn commanded. "There is sufficient room for the four of us to be comfortably seated if Mr. Barrington and Lord Atwood decide to join us."

"Very good, madam." The butler bowed stiffly. "Is there

anything specific you would like Cook to include on the tea tray?"

"Whatever is freshly baked will be sufficient, but be sure there are a variety and quantity of sandwiches. I'm certain the men will be hungry."

"I am sure Cook will not disappoint," the butler declared, bowing a final time before leaving.

Dorothea watched him soundlessly exit the room, her mind turning. This was a far cry from the simple way they had been raised, with a handful of servants in a quiet, rural community. Yet Dorothea was heartened to see that her sister had adjusted well to a more formal atmosphere. She only hoped she too would adapt quickly, for she suspected her life with Lord Atwood would be even more structured.

"The men will be hungry?" Dorothea questioned.

"Well, if pressed I suppose I might be tempted to nibble on a sandwich or two," Gwendolyn replied innocently.

"Only two?"

"Yes, yes, I know I look as though I have done nothing but stuff my face morning, noon, and night for the past few months, but there is a reason for my exceptionally large belly." Gwendolyn bit her bottom lip. "I have not said a word about this to Jason, but the physician thinks I might be carrying twins."

Dorothea managed to stifle her gasp of alarm, but was not as quick to conceal her expression of shock.

"Good Lord, Dorothea, must you look so terrified? I'm frightened enough at the notion of birthing two babies without having you scare me to pieces." Gwendolyn inhaled a deep breath, then slowly released it. "My husband is a twin, therefore it was certainly within the realm of possibilities that I too would be so blessed."

Dorothea blanched. Was it a blessing? Childbirth was dangerous business for a woman under the best of circumstances. Birthing twins would be a far greater risk for Gwendolyn and the unborn babes.

Their conversation was abruptly interrupted by the arrival of the gentlemen. Gwendolyn glared at her and Dorothea silently acknowledged the request. She would keep her sister's counsel and not reveal what she had been told to her brother-in-law. In truth, he could do nothing to alter the situation and if it kept Gwendolyn's nerves steadier having her husband in the dark for the time being, then so be it.

The presence of the two men seemed to dwarf the small, feminine room. Dorothea stared at the pair, unable to stop herself from making a comparison. They were both of a similar age and physical stature. Jason was fair in coloring, Atwood dark. Lord Atwood was slightly taller, while Jason was broader in the shoulders. Each man was appealing in his own way, though Dorothea thought Lord Atwood by far the more handsome of the duo.

He came to her side, unexpectedly grasped her hand firmly in his own, and brought it to his lips. Dorothea felt her body heat and her skin flush with color. Embarrassed, she glanced over to see if her sister or brother-in-law had noticed, but they were too preoccupied with each other to pay attention to much else.

"Jason, cease hovering," Gwendolyn exclaimed in a strong whisper as her husband attempted to place another pillow behind her back. "Please."

"Of course, my love," he answered in a soothing tone. "Shall I ask Dorothea to pour our tea?"

"I am perfectly capable of lifting a teapot," Gwendolyn grumbled in a petulant tone.

"I know, I only thought it might be easier if Dorothea did the honors."

"Well, I would prefer to act as the hostess in my own

home. I don't know why you think that I would want to willingly shirk my duties when—".

Gwendolyn abruptly halted her tirade and stared at Lord Atwood, as though suddenly remembering his presence in the room.

"Please, there is no need for you to go to any additional fuss on my account," he said congenially. "The last thing I would want is for our visit to place an added strain on you, Mrs. Barrington."

"It hasn't." Gwendolyn's eyes welled with tears. "I would never forgive Dorothea if she married someone before I had met him. I wanted so much to be with her during the Season, but my pregnancy prevented it. I had hoped I would be able to attend a few quiet affairs early in the social calendar, before my predicament became too noticeable. But it seemed as though my stomach popped out within a month of discovering I was with child and my belly has not ceased expanding."

Gwendolyn lowered her head into her open palms and sighed heavily. "And now I have mentioned my condition openly in mixed company. How impossibly rude. Pray, forgive me, my lord."

Carter's face contorted with kindness. "I do not mean to cause you greater distress, Mrs. Barrington, but anyone with two functioning eyes is aware of your condition."

Gwen let out a small laugh, but then her face crumpled. "I must look a fright," she sniffed. "Bloated like a great cow, waddling about like a fat Christmas goose."

"You are as beautiful as ever," Jason cooed gently. "Even more so with our child growing inside you."

"Oh, shut up, Jason," Gwendolyn snapped, giving her husband a murderous look. "I'm not a simpleton. I can see my reflection in a mirror."

"Yes, and it makes you more womanly, more enchanting," Jason insisted.

"It most certainly does not," Gwendolyn barked. "Does it, Dorothea?"

Dorothea wanted to sink through the floor. Her desire to make a favorable impression on Lord Atwood was going severely awry. Was it possible that they were now all openly discussing Gwendolyn's pregnancy? How mortifyingly inappropriate.

Gwendolyn had always been the steady one, the one she could count upon to hold everything together. For years Gwendolyn had been ostracized by the social community of their Yorkshire village and she had borne the unfair censure with grace and dignity.

That, apparently, was no longer the case. Carrying a child, or God help them all, perhaps two, made her sister irrational, and weepy and weak. Dorothea shuddered. If Gwendolyn could not be counted upon to retain her good sense and equilibrium while pregnant, what chance would Dorothea have if she ever carried a child?

"You look lovely, Gwen," Dorothea replied. "Entrancing in an entirely different way."

They all seemed to hold their breaths as they collectively waited for Gwendolyn's reaction to her sister's remark.

"I vow I am not such a disagreeable harpy under normal circumstances, Lord Atwood," Gwendolyn said wistfully.

Carter smiled kindly. "How very disappointing. I was hoping this marriage would bring me some lively, entertaining relations. Alas, my own are rather, staid, proper, and on occasion deadly boring."

For a moment Gwendolyn looked as if she would burst into tears, then she started laughing. "Thank you, my lord. For treating me like a person and not a porcelain doll that would break if you came too near."

"If I may be so indelicate, a woman in your condition should be allowed to do and say anything that she wishes."

"Do you hear that, Jason?"

"Yes, I did, my love. Sound advice that I fully intend upon taking."

Dorothea stole a glimpse of her sister as Gwendolyn poured the tea. She offered Lord Atwood the first cup, then poured a second for Dorothea. As she drank her hot tea, the sour feeling in the pit of Dorothea's stomach slowly eased. Carter went out of his way to be charming and amusing, treading carefully around Gwendolyn's unpredictable emotions. By the time they took their leave, Gwen was smiling and giggling.

Jason walked them out to the carriage. Carter tactfully pulled ahead to check on the horses, allowing her a moment of privacy.

"Atwood seems like a fine man, Dorothea," Jason said. "You've done well."

"So everyone keeps saying." She tugged on the bonnet ribbon tied under her chin, making certain it was secure for the open carriage ride back to London. "It's all happening so quickly, I feel that I've had no time to think."

Jason laughed. "Trust me, that's the best way to approach marriage. Let your feelings and emotions guide you. Love is never wrong."

Dorothea lowered her head. Oh, dear, Jason had misinterpreted things completely. Feeling too embarrassed to correct the mistaken notion that she and Lord Atwood were in love, Dorothea hugged her brother-in-law good-bye.

"Take good care of Gwen and my future niece or nephew," she admonished.

"I shall endeavor to do my best, no matter how ill-tempered she becomes."

Dorothea spied Gwendolyn standing at the window and

she waved until the carriage brought them down the drive and well out of sight of the house. Only then did she glance up at Carter.

He had his eyes firmly on the road, his hands tightly gripping the reins. She settled herself more comfortably beside him, enjoying the stillness, not at all minding the silence. It was a good silence, a comfortable quiet.

All things being equal, the visit had gone well. Carter had not been overly shocked at the unusual situation, although it might just be good manners that prevented him from being too critical.

But more importantly, Gwendolyn and Jason had liked Lord Atwood and approved of the match. Jason had even gone so far as to say he believed she had made a good choice.

They made a sharp turn and Carter's left hand instinctively reached out to ensure she was safely seated. Dorothea smiled her thanks and her heart lightened. She fervently hoped that Jason was right.

Chapter Nine

The announcement of the impending marriage of Miss Dorothea Ellingham to Carter Grayson, Marquess of Atwood, appeared in *The Times* the morning the Duke of Hansborough returned to London. To say he was angry when he read the paper was an understatement of mythic proportions. The dishes in the kitchen rattled, the horses stabled in the mews reared, and a flustered upstairs maid dropped a priceless antique vase as the duke repeatedly bellowed his outrage.

In his more optimistic moments Carter had told himself the duke's anger would be swift, sharp, and short-lived. Yet as he stood before his father in the duke's private study, he grudgingly acknowledged that was not proving to be the case.

"I had to read the announcement in the newspaper," the duke roared, tossing the offending item on his desk, where it scattered across the dark mahogany. "The newspaper! Was I not owed the common courtesy of being told beforehand, *in person?*"

"You were not in Town," Carter answered, raising his voice to be heard above his father's disapproving bellows. "There was no opportunity."

"You could have waited. You should have waited." The duke paused, his eyes narrowing with alarm. "Unless there is a specific need for the marriage to occur with undue haste?"

A chill of anger swept through Carter at the inference. "You dishonor me, sir, by asking such a callous, inappropriate question." He cared little for his own reputation, for it was hardly stellar. However, he would not allow his future wife's honor and integrity to be impugned, even by his own father. "The time frame is perfectly acceptable, and I will insist to you that there is no need for a hasty wedding. We are not running off to Gretna Green nor arranging for a ceremony by special license. The banns shall be dutifully read and we will marry in three weeks' time."

"Three weeks?" The duke rubbed his hands together. "Hmm, then there is still time for you to reconsider."

"Sir, you have continually badgered me to get married and now that I have chosen a bride, you wish me to call off the wedding?" Carter's jaw clenched in anger. He paced off the carpet and onto the intricate parquet floor, his boot heels clicking loudly.

The duke leaned forward, closing his hands on the newspaper spread on his desk. "I want you to call off *this* wedding, to this particular female. After a reasonable amount of time has passed, I then want you to select a bride from the women on my list. You still have it, don't you?"

"I do not!" Though in that moment Carter desperately wished he did have the list on his person, just so he could crumple it in his father's face before tossing it into the fireplace. "I swear, I shall not be held accountable for my actions if you mention that damn list once more, sir. I shall choose my bride, not you."

The duke's hand balled into a tight fist. He stood, paced,

turned, then banged his closed fist on his desktop. "Why must you be so infernally stubborn?"

"I am your son," Carter blurted out, not bothering to hide his irritation. "I come by my stubbornness naturally."

"You get it from your mother's side of the family," the duke grumbled. He took a long, deep breath, then slowly sank down into his chair. His face was as dark as a thundercloud until suddenly he smiled. "If you insist upon this course of action, then I insist upon meeting Miss Ellingham immediately."

Ah, so that's how he was going to play it. Denied his way, the duke now planned to intimidate and essentially frighten off Miss Ellingham. As if that could ever work! Carter forced an answering smile. "If you cannot control your temper any better than you are, sir, you will meet my fiancée at the church on the morning of our wedding."

The duke looked at him cautiously, and Carter had the distinct impression his father was weighing the threat in his mind.

"I view your Miss Ellingham as a social upstart and a fortune hunter," the duke replied. "And I'll make no bones about the matter. Mark my words, she's after your title and your money."

"Perhaps she has fallen in love with me," Carter suggested casually.

"Fallen in love with your money, you mean."

Carter squared his shoulders. "Your flattering assessment of my personal charm aside, I firmly believe Miss Ellingham is not a fortune hunter. She is a very comely female, genteel in her upbringing. True, she has no great family connections or wealth, but I have enough of that for the both of us. We will suit, Father. That's all that matters."

The duke's eyes narrowed into sharp points. "You're damn quick to defend her."

"She will be my wife and as such deserves every courtesy."

Gradually the duke's hard expression faded. "I can see I am wasting my breath arguing the point with you."

"You are, indeed."

"All right, then. I will withhold my final judgment until I meet the girl." The duke took on a serious expression. "You will bring her to dinner this evening."

"I have plans."

"Break them."

Carter gulped, his sense of victory short-lived. He had confidence that his future bride could cope with his father, but she would need time to prepare herself. "I am certain Miss Ellingham is also engaged for the evening."

The duke waved his hand dismissively. "'Tis far more important for her to meet me and gain my approval of this match. She can be late to whatever event she had planned to attend."

Carter turned his head and cursed under his breath.

"I heard that," the duke muttered.

"You were meant to," Carter countered. He took a deep breath, allowing his anger to cool. Eyeing his father thoughtfully, Carter realized he might as well get the meeting between the duke and Miss Ellingham over with. A day or two would not make that much difference. Either she had the backbone to stomach the duke or else she would have to try to avoid him for a good part of their marriage. "We will be here at eight."

"Sharp," the duke commanded, his brows tightly pinched.

Carter flinched, but did not answer. He would need to send an urgent note to his fiancée and beg her indulgence to change her plans. And to sweeten the last-minute request, he would wisely add an expensive bauble as further enticement.

* * *

The tersely worded note from Lord Atwood arrived when Dorothea rose from an afternoon nap. She had not been sleeping well at night, making the occasional afternoon rest a necessity if she was to keep her eyes open and her conversation coherent during these late-night social events. Her initial delight at hearing from her fiancé was quickly dispelled when she learned the reason for the message was a request to dine with his father. That very evening.

She had heard the gossip about her future father-in-law and none of it had instilled a great desire to meet him. He was said to be a harsh man, a stickler for propriety, a man much enamored of his own rank and position. Even Lord Dardington had once referred to him as a horror, and he feared no one.

Dorothea highly doubted the meeting was intended to welcome her into the family. Oh, no, she felt certain the duke desired just the opposite.

"Please, Lady Meredith, help me decide what I should wear," Dorothea pleaded as the two women stood together in front of her open wardrobe. "I do not want to give the duke any reason to find fault with me."

"If he judges you solely on your appearance, he is even more of a fool than I thought," Lady Meredith quipped.

Dorothea blanched. "Maybe I should decline the invitation. I could beg off, telling Lord Atwood I was feeling ill." She cast a hopeful look at Lady Meredith, then belatedly realized there was far too much truth in the statement. She had been feeling decidedly queasy ever since the note arrived.

"You shall never best the duke if you avoid him." Lady Meredith's grim expression softened. "You need to let him know that you are serious about your marriage and your new position in society."

Dorothea nodded and stared at the floor as she considered her options. She needed to be reasonable, even if the duke was not, given the very late hour the invitation was issued. She needed also to remember that she was doing this to accommodate her future husband. It was important that Carter realize she was willing to make sacrifices when necessary. Of course, it was equally important that he understand there were limits to her patience and affability.

"White can give my complexion a dull, washed-out look at times," Dorothea remarked, questioning the choice of the gown Lady Meredith had selected from the bulging wardrobe. "I think the red silk gown would be better."

"There are many shades of white," Lady Meredith protested, holding the gown against Dorothea's chest. "This one in particular sets off your hair and eyes. The satin sheen is delicate and flattering. Plus, white should effectively complement whatever Lord Atwood has sent you."

Lady Meredith motioned to the maid, who held out a small black velvet pouch. Hastily untying the gold cord, Dorothea pulled out a pair of teardrop-shaped earrings and a matching emerald pendant. She gasped. The brilliant green of the many-faceted stones shimmered in the fading daylight, dazzling in their sparkle.

"They are magnificent," Dorothea exclaimed.

"What does the note say?" Lady Meredith asked.

"Beautiful jewels are meant for a beautiful woman. I hope you will favor my request and wear them tonight." Dorothea sighed. It was a romantic gesture that stirred a variety of complex emotions inside her. Was he wooing her? Trying to please or impress her? Or was he arming her for this meeting with his father? Thinking the latter might be his prime motivation left Dorothea with a vaguely dissatisfied feeling.

"It's settled. You will wear them tonight with your white gown," Lady Meredith insisted. "They will give you a regal air and display most effectively to the duke that you are a worthy bride for his son."

Dubiously, Dorothea accepted the magnificent jewelry, concerned that Lady Meredith had hit upon the most unsettling reason the jewels might have been gifted to her. Yet later that evening, as Dorothea surveyed herself in the cheval glass, her reflection gave her pause. Lady Meredith was right. The gown and jewels gave her a noble, mature look, boosting her flagging confidence. Perhaps the exact reason for the gift was not as important as the result.

Carter's approving smile when she entered the front hall also gave her a lift. She thanked him prettily for the jewelry and would have even ventured a kiss, had not Lord and Lady Dardington, along with half a dozen servants, been watching.

Carter distracted her with amusing small talk on the carriage ride and she felt herself start to relax. The even mood stayed with her until they divested themselves of their outer garments and passed them to two silent, formally attired footmen.

With Carter by her side, Dorothea followed the butler across the cold marble foyer and willed herself not to shudder. The interior furnishings were even more impressive than the massive, stately exterior of the duke's mansion, but the overall effect left her feeling cold. They conveyed an impersonal grandeur that money and good taste could not eliminate, a gloominess that made all the inherent beauty of these priceless furnishings seem forbidding.

Her steps faltered and then she felt Carter's strong hand at her elbow. "Try not to worry. You'll do fine."

Dorothea glanced frantically over her shoulder, worried one of the servants who stood like sentry guards every few feet could hear her. "What if the duke doesn't like me?" she asked, rising high on her toes to whisper in Carter's ear.

"Then he is an ass."

The glib statement did not ease her nerves. As if she would ever dare to dismiss a man of rank and privilege so boldly, a man who could create such an opulent environment and live comfortably within it. "I suppose I should have inquired before now, but do you have any sage advice to impart on how best to handle things this evening?"

"You must be yourself, my dear. No need to posture and put on airs. And no false flattery. The duke abhors it."

Wonderful. Flattery and feigning interest in the other person's conversation was a social skill Dorothea relied on heavily.

The sound of approaching footsteps brought her thoughts abruptly to the present. With chilled fingers, Dorothea smoothed the white satin of her gown and prepared herself to meet the duke.

He was clad entirely in black, the only exception his white shirt and cravat. The formality of such attire was common among gentlemen, but the duke wore his elegant clothing in a manner that was more somber than most. She could see very little resemblance between father and son and decided Carter must have taken after his mother.

In looks and apparently temperament, thank heavens, for Lord Atwood did not have the brooding, almost morose demeanor his father sported so naturally. Or perhaps he did? With a start, Dorothea realized she had not been around him enough to know how much like his formidable father he truly could be.

Carter introduced her. For a long moment the duke did not acknowledge her, but instead glared sourly at his son. When he at last turned his attention in her direction, Dorothea's heart lurched. The duke seemed to delight in looking down his aristocratic nose at her, his expression dark and foreboding. .

"You're late," he said gruffly.

Were they? Dorothea's mind went blank and her tongue went numb. Flustered, she swooped into a deep, elegant curtsy. The duke's expression did not alter. As she rose, Dorothea felt a flush of embarrassment. Clearly, the duke was not impressed. This was even more ghastly than she had feared.

"We are not late, sir," Carter replied. "Given the very short length at which the invitation was extended, I would venture to say we were right on time."

"Humph."

"Actually, you are fortunate indeed that we are even here."

The duke's eyes flashed with anger. Most people would have been warned to tread carefully, but apparently Carter had a differing view when it came to his father.

"And if we are discontented at any time, we will have to depart early," Carter added.

Dorothea blinked. Had he lost his mind? He was taunting his father, almost daring him to give them a reason to storm off.

They retired to a drawing room that featured two enormous marble fireplaces evenly spaced along one very long wall. Dorothea kept her eyes on the ornately carved mantel of the one nearest her as she tried to settle her nerves.

The duke engaged his son in conversation, yet while he spoke, he stared at Dorothea. Though it was difficult, Dorothea refused to squirm, vowing she would ignore his impolite glare. His manners were an abomination. Even her uncle Fletcher would not be so rude as to deliberately put a guest ill at ease.

She decided it must be some sort of test. And while she did not understand precisely what was required, she was determined to pass it.

After what felt like an eternity, they were called for

dinner. They entered another cavernous room, which boasted a massive dining table that had been polished to a mirror finish. Dorothea counted no fewer than twenty-four chairs as she was escorted down the length of the table.

Her momentary relief at spying three elaborate place settings clustered at one end of the table was dashed when she realized they would now be close enough to converse through the *entire* meal.

Once they were all settled, the first course was served. It was lobster bisque, her favorite. Yet Dorothea honestly feared if she tried to swallow a spoonful it would not rest quietly in her stomach.

Utilizing a trick Gwendolyn had taught her, she slowly glided her spoon through the hot liquid, then lifted a nearly empty spoon to her lips. The duke and his son appeared to be doing something similar, though they occasionally ate some of the delicate broth. But not much, from what Dorothea could tell.

The plates were cleared and the next course was served. The silence in the room became increasingly unbearable.

Dorothea wished she had the courage to introduce a topic upon which they could all pleasantly converse, but her mind blanked completely. It would be just her luck that she would innocently select something that would enrage the duke, which in turn would cause Carter to explode in a temper and stomp from the room.

She glanced beneath her lashes at Lord Atwood, hoping he would rescue them all by saying something appropriate, but all she received was a brief smile of reassurance before he returned his attention to his dinner plate.

Dorothea felt like screaming.

"I did not attend the Aldertons' ball last week but I heard his corset snapped in the middle of the ballroom floor and he literally burst out of his clothes," the duke said. "That must have been a sight to behold."

"It happened on the receiving line," Dorothea interjected softly.

"Hmm, what did you say? Speak up, girl."

"I said it happened on the receiving line, Your Grace."

"And how would you know that tidbit?"

"Because I was there, standing directly in front of him when the strings of his corset broke."

"It certainly must have caused a racket." The duke feigned a casual indifference to her remark, but Dorothea could see the true interest glistening in his eyes.

"Actually, the corset strings did not make a sound, but as I curtsied in greeting I could not help but notice Lord Alderton's girth expanding before my very eyes. In mere seconds, the silver buttons on his waistcoat broke free and shot across the room as if they had been fired from a pistol. There were shrieks of horror from several directions."

"Ha!" The duke grinned, then leaned forward in his chair. "Did the buttons strike anyone?"

"I don't believe so, for they could have caused significant hurt, and I saw no blood."

"Hornsby told me that one nearly shot out his eye," Carter added, his face also sporting a grin.

"I'm not surprised," Dorothea muttered.

"What did you do when Alderton started, hmm, expanding?" the duke asked.

"I pretended that nothing at all was amiss. I averted my eyes from the split seams of Lord Alderton's jacket, commented on the lovely weather and my delight at attending his ball. I even promised him a dance before moving on to greet Lady Alderton, who was completely oblivious to the mishap."

"She always was a simpleton," the duke grumbled. "And

he is a pompous ass. They are an ideal match in so many ways, each deserving such an irritating spouse."

Dorothea glanced curiously at the duke. His remarks suggested there might be some sort of history between him and the Aldertons, but Dorothea was not about to ask any questions.

"I think Miss Ellingham should be commended for coping with the disaster in such a skillful, refined manner," Carter remarked.

"And you think gracefully handling a single society mishap qualifies her to become a duchess?" the duke challenged.

"No, Your Grace," Dorothea interrupted. "I think the incident demonstrates how very essential it is to not overestimate one's own importance." She took a small sip of water from the lovely crystal goblet to clear the dryness from her throat. "If Lord Alderton had not been so concerned about his appearance, he would have allowed his tailor to make a garment that fit him properly, rather than trying to stuff himself into an outfit two sizes too small."

The duke stared at her so long Dorothea felt the hairs on the back of her neck starting to rise in alarm. Yet she refused to lower her gaze or defend her comments. Then, unexpectedly, miraculously, the older man offered her the barest hint of a smile.

"You have a great deal to learn about London society," he said.

"I know. I'm sure I shall make many mistakes." She lifted the white linen napkin from her lap and dabbed at the corner of her mouth. "Though I promise I shall never burst out of my clothing at a society affair."

"Bravo," Carter commented with a grin.

"And I know there would be far fewer blunders if I had

someone to guide me, to assist me in the murky society waters," she added pointedly, her eyes on the duke.

"That is women's domain," the duke declared dismissively.

"Not entirely." Dorothea forced a smile. "You gravely underestimate the male influence, especially among the bullying society matrons. I know they would defer to the opinion of a man they respected."

"You mean someone like me." The duke flicked his gaze over her, his expression cagey. "I see what you are trying to do, Miss Ellingham. Buttering me up in order to gain my approval and support."

"Is it working?"

Lord Atwood coughed. Dorothea turned her head, pleading with her eyes for him not to intervene. This was between her and the duke.

"I'll have to let you know."

"Fair enough, Your Grace." Dorothea glanced down at her plate and realized she had eaten almost half her creamed fillet of halibut. And she didn't even like fish. With a crooked smile she forked up another mouthful.

To her vast relief, the duke decided to drop the brunt of his disapproving manner as the roast beef course was served. An undercurrent of tension lingered, but it was not as all-encompassing and oppressive as when they first arrived.

Despite the recovery of the evening, Dorothea's head was plagued with a dull ache by the time they departed. When Carter handed her into his carriage, she gratefully sank back against the velvet squabs and closed her eyes, willing the tension to ease from her mind.

Seeming to understand and respect her need for solitude, her fiancé allowed them to sit in silence until they were nearly halfway to the Smith-Johnsons' ball.

"About my father—"

"There is no need to apologize," Dorothea interrupted. "You were not responsible for his behavior. Though I feel I need to ask. Does the duke improve upon further acquaintance?"

"Honestly?"

"Please."

"Not really." A glimmer of amusement flickered in Carter's eyes as he appraised her with a measuring gaze. "Well, you did ask for honesty."

"I did. And I appreciate the truth." Her chin jutted out determinedly. "Never fear. I will learn to handle him."

"Or avoid him."

Dorothea's eyes widened. It was a telling comment. One that explained a good deal about the animosity that swirled beneath the surface between father and son. Avoidance had apparently been the method that Carter had decided to enact when coping with his father. And clearly that tactic had been employed with limited success.

"Thank you for the warning," she said quietly.

"I will protect you as much as I can," he promised. "And once you have given birth to an heir, I feel certain his criticism will ebb."

Dorothea wasn't sure she could wait that long. "I have been surrounded by women for most of my life, with the exception of my uncle Fletcher, a gentleman who keeps his thoughts and opinions to himself. These many females are a strong-willed, opinionated group. In order to survive, I have learned how to deflect an argument, ignore most criticism, and hide as many of my missteps as possible."

"I am heartened to learn of it."

"I do, however, have one request."

Carter's eyes lit with a momentary start of suspicion, but then it vanished, replaced by a cautious curiosity. "After you endured this evening with such grace and dignity, I feel I owe you anything."

Dorothea smiled. She very much liked the idea of having him in her debt.

"Kiss me," she whispered.

Punctuating her request with a likewise action, Dorothea lunged forward and wrapped her arms around a very startled marquess. He felt strong and solid and smelled divine. Bringing her mouth to his, she slowly skimmed her lips back and forth across his. He smiled faintly and allowed her teasing, doing nothing to either encourage or reject her advances.

Charmed at the notion that she was in control, Dorothea cupped his face in her hands. She would not be satisfied with merely pressing their mouths together. She wanted the passion and excitement she knew he could arouse in her. Boldly, she nibbled his lower lip, seeking entrance, and slowly, tantalizingly, he opened to her. Her tongue curled against his, tasting and teasing, and he responded by kissing her back with total abandon.

Dorothea instinctively began to move her body, amazed at the intense jolt of desire she felt, captivated by the tumbling sensations. He heated her blood in a way that no one else had ever done, in a way she did not fully understand. She only knew it intrigued and excited her and she wanted more. Much more.

His mouth was magical, enthralling her utterly. His hands moved on her throat, down the column of her neck, across her shoulders, then lower, his fingers lightly stroking her skin as he discovered the roundness of her breasts.

Dorothea found herself arching forward into his hot touch, blindly seeking the pleasure he was arousing so effortlessly in her. All too soon, he broke off the kiss, even as she felt her entire body growing restless and edgy.

She leaned against him, gulping air in deep, uneven breaths, frantically trying to figure out how she could get him to start kissing her again.

He exhaled raggedly. She lifted her head. His eyes were closed, his thumb and forefinger clenching the bridge of his nose as he struggled to rein in his passion.

"We are to be married," she purred, in her best seductive voice. "Sharing a kiss or two is perfectly acceptable."

He wiped a palm down his face and stared at her, his expression unreadable. "It is quickly progressing beyond a kiss. And as much as I want you, my dear, I will not take my future wife's virginity in the back of a carriage."

The flat, blunt statement washed over Dorothea like a bucket of ice water. She sucked in a breath through clenched teeth and pulled away as a wave of deep embarrassment heated her cheeks.

"I hardly meant for things to go that far," she muttered, her voice displaying only a partial tremor of mortification. She felt hot all over, certain her face was turning an unattractive shade of red. She desperately needed a draft of cool air to embrace her, but she dared not reach out to lower the window and draw even more attention to her plight.

Was it not a few days ago he had wickedly whispered his hope that she would be amenable to anticipating their marriage vows? Had he not tried to seduce her in the moonlight, to encourage a wanton and uninhibited response? What had changed so suddenly? Did he no longer feel a passion for her?

She tensed, yet dared to risk another glance at his face. The spark of heated desire revealed in his gaze soothed her wounded vanity. He was not unaffected by their embrace. He was merely able to control it better. The realization made Dorothea feel exposed, vulnerable.

There was no opportunity to ponder those feelings, for

the coach rambled to a full stop. A footman opened the carriage door and lowered the step. Routinely, Dorothea extended her hand and allowed herself to be helped out. She turned, waiting for Carter to descend, but he remained seated, leaning his upper torso forward to speak with her.

"I bid you good evening, my dear. I do hope you will enjoy the party."

"You aren't coming inside?"

"Alas, I have other plans."

"Oh." Dorothea struggled to stretch her mouth into a strained smile. The sting of disappointment she felt was swift and sharp.

"You will, however, need an escort to take you inside." He turned his head and scanned the few carriages that were arriving at the front gate.

Dorothea straightened, her pride bristling at being passed over to another man as if she were a burdensome old maid. "There is no need to fret on my account. Lord and Lady Dardington have most likely arrived. I should not have too much difficulty locating them once I am inside."

She pivoted on her heel, but he was at her side before she had taken her first step. "Don't be ridiculous. Naturally I shall escort you safely inside."

He was all elegance and good manners, and that angered Dorothea even more. She wanted him to stay with her because he desired it, not because he felt it was the proper thing to do.

Nevertheless, she allowed him to take her arm and walk her into the party. It was the typical crush, with people everywhere, but somehow Carter found Lord Dardington among the masses.

He greeted the older man cordially, then bowed over her hand and bid her a crisp good night. As she watched his broad back fade from view, Dorothea felt a sharp pang of loss. Inexplicably she found herself fighting back a brace of tears.

She could feel Lord Dardington's cool gaze upon her. Dorothea glanced down at her hands, then lifted her chin, doing her best to appear unconcerned. The wedding announcement had been made, the agreement struck. She would marry the marquess and make the best of the situation. Surprisingly, that knowledge and resolve brought a flood of relief to her confused emotions.

She *had* chosen the right man. Now all she needed to do was to wait until he realized it.

Carter did not want to leave the ball, or more specifically, he did not want to leave Dorothea. But he had made plans to spend the evening with Benton, Dawson, and the major, and Carter felt he must stick with those arrangements. Acquiring a fiancée, and soon a wife, was going to alter his life but his friendship with these men would remain strong.

"I read the most appalling bit of news in *The Times* today, Atwood," Viscount Benton said as he discarded one of his playing cards and reached for another. "There was an announcement of your marriage. Surely that was some sort of ghastly error?"

Carter blinked through the smoke-filled air and smiled cagily at the men seated around the table. They had been drinking, smoking, and gambling for nearly five hours and not a word had been said concerning his upcoming nuptials. He wondered briefly why Benton sought to introduce the topic now, but concluded his friend had most likely just remembered. After all, the viscount had been on a winning streak for most of the night.

"'Tis true, Benton," he answered. "Miss Ellingham and I are to be married."

Benton shot a wicked smile in Carter's direction. "Dorothea Ellingham, the very same female under Dardington's protection? Then I know it must be true. Only a simpleton would cross Dardington. Unless your brains have gone missing?"

The viscount looked so hopeful that Carter burst out laughing. "I am merely following your advice, Benton. I tossed out my father's list of potential brides and found a woman on my own to marry."

"Ah, so this is my plan in action?" The viscount squinted down at his cards for a long moment, then tilted his head to one side. "But you were supposed to find someone unsuitable and then pretend to want to take her as your bride. That would have bought you more time as a bachelor. Miss Ellingham is a perfectly acceptable female, therefore you will have to go through with it."

"I am very aware of that fact," Carter answered as he slid the last card across the table to Dawson.

Dawson accepted it with a smile, then frowned when he turned it over. The man really did have the worst face for cards, far too open and honest. "I confess I was also surprised to read the announcement," Dawson added. "I thought it was Roddy who had Miss Ellingham in his sights."

The three men turned toward the major. He abruptly ceased shuffling the cards in his hands when he realized they were staring at him. "I took her on a single picnic," he declared, straightening in his chair.

"Ah, well, I for one wish you great happiness, Atwood," Dawson said sincerely. "She is a lovely woman."

"And I wish you a return to your senses before the date," Benton quipped. "There is still time to escape. I hear the hunting in Scotland can be prime this time of year."

Carter smiled. "I have no desire to escape. The marriage is on my terms and I'm pleased with this decision. Won't you be happy for me?"

Benton shook his head violently. "I would be happier if I did not believe you had lost your mind."

"To Atwood's marriage," Dawson said, lifting his glass.

Roddy followed suit, but Benton slumped forward, propped his elbow on the table, and rested his chin in his hand. "I cannot condone this decision, however lovely the future bride. You will not be able to exchange her for a new one, you know. She will be a part of your life forever. Perhaps, if the vicar is to be believed, into eternity." The viscount shuddered visibly at the notion.

"You're drunk," Carter declared.

"Damn right. You should be, too. No sane, sober man would take this step unless he was under the hatches."

"But it's what I want," Carter replied mildly.

"And you always get whatever you desire, don't you, Atwood?" Roddy declared before lifting his glass and draining it in one long gulp.

Carter narrowed his eyes at the major's venomous tone. "You told me you had no interest in the lady. Were you lying?"

"I'm not a liar!" Roddy snarled.

He lunged toward Carter. Despite his minor inebriation, Carter managed to tilt himself out of the way. Before the major could regroup, Dawson jumped between the two men.

"Calm down, Roddy!" Dawson shouted. "There's no need for any of this nonsense."

The major shrugged off Dawson's hand and stood on his feet. "He called me a liar."

"Oh, do shut up," Benton moaned. "That racket is playing havoc inside my head. Atwood meant no insult, did you?"

"I'm sure he did not," Dawson interjected. "Nor did the major. I fear we've all had too much good brandy tonight."

"Hell, Dawson, there is no such thing as too much brandy," Benton insisted. He refilled each glass before casting a stern glance at Carter and the major. "To friendship."

Carter waited expectantly for Roddy to make the first conciliatory move. With a sheepish grin, the major raised his glass in salute. Carter accepted the unspoken apology and did the same, but he was not entirely certain that too much brandy was the true reason for the major's tirade. And the thought left him very unsettled.

Chapter Ten

The wedding ceremony between Carter Grayson, Marquess of Atwood and Miss Dorothea Ellingham took place promptly at ten o'clock on a Wednesday morning the third week of May. St. George's Church at Hanover Square was near bursting at the corners as gentry and common folk alike crowded inside the stately building, craning their necks for a glimpse of the bride and groom.

Dorothea wore a lovely gown of pale blue satin trimmed with exquisite lace and a small matching bonnet. The ride from Lord and Lady Dardington's home was brief, and she was grateful, for it left no time for her nerves to flutter and catch hold.

Lord Atwood was waiting on the church steps when she arrived. Dressed in a blue superfine coat with a gold embroidered waistcoat and a fall of elegant Belgium lace on his cravat, he looked devilishly handsome and noble. Dorothea nearly felt the need to pinch herself, scarcely believing she was about to marry such an elegant, aristocratic man.

He sauntered down the church steps the moment the coach halted and insisted on helping her himself. She shifted the prayer book that had once belonged to her mother to her left hand, placed her right in his, and stepped down to stand beside him.

"You look lovely," he said.

"Thank you."

Lady Meredith bustled behind her, adjusting the lace on the short train of Dorothea's gown. When she was satisfied with the result, Lady Meredith bent toward her and kissed her cheek.

Dorothea gulped back the emotions rising in her throat. Lady Meredith had been so much more than a social sponsor. She had been a kind, loyal friend and Dorothea knew she would very much miss being an everyday part of the Dardington household.

Lord Dardington embraced her next, paying careful attention to his wife's admonishment not to muss her hair or bonnet. Then he turned to take Lady Meredith's arm and escort her inside the church.

Dorothea's heart lurched as she watched them leave. But she was saved from an embarrassing display of emotions by a rustling noise. She lifted her head and for the first time noticed Viscount Benton was also on the church steps, looking utterly ridiculous holding a dainty, feminine bouquet of white roses tied with white satin ribbon.

"Benton is standing up with me," Carter explained.

"He hardly looks pleased at the idea," Dorothea blurted out, apparently loud enough for the viscount to hear, for he stepped forward and bowed gracefully.

"I beg of you not to take my opinion personally. 'Tis an inbred abhorrence of marriage that facilitates my dour mood, not a particular prejudice against you. I further confess that I advised my good friend Atwood not to get into the carriage that brought us here this morning, but instead to mount his fastest horse and head in the opposite direction.

"When he failed to heed my warning, I knew there was

no help for it, so I begged the honor of having your bridal bouquet crafted from the humble blooms in my hothouse." The viscount presented the flowers to her with an elegant flourish. "They pale in comparison to your beauty, but I do hope they bring you some small measure of happiness on this most important and joyous occasion."

Dorothea lifted the flowers to her face and took a deep breath. It was a stunning bouquet that smelled delicious. Yet finding no words to appropriately reply to such an odd statement, she answered Lord Benton with a wry smile of thanks. The viscount promptly withdrew and entered the church, leaving the bride and groom alone.

Dorothea felt calm and in control as she placed her hand on the arm Lord Atwood offered. The moment their feet landed on the marble-floored church vestibule, the sound of trumpets and an organ heralding their arrival filled the air.

Dorothea swallowed hard. She could see her sister, Emma, in the front pew, with aunt Mildred beside her and uncle Fletcher next to his wife. Naturally, Gwendolyn was not there, and the lack of seeing her older sister brought a well of tears to Dorothea's eyes. How could she possibly get married without her beloved Gwen in attendance?

Hoping to distract her sudden distress, she clenched her fingers tightly around her bouquet. Carter must have sensed her nerves, or felt her trembling, for he abruptly ceased walking.

"Second thoughts?" he asked casually.

His question sent a shiver down Dorothea's spine and made her feel a flush of panic. "Hell, no," she whispered furiously. "Are you having second thoughts?"

He seemed startled by her question. Or maybe it was her answer? "I feel ready," he said, and he smiled at her. "And flattered to hear you are so firmly set on this course. *Hell, no,* indeed."

She laughed, the flutter of nerves draining away. "Perhaps that was not the best choice of words, considering the circumstances," she said hastily. "And where we are standing."

"Better to curse before the ceremony than after, don't you think?"

"I will make no promises on that score, my lord," she replied primly.

He smiled again and squeezed her hand. A swirl of calm surrounded her heart. This was the right decision; he was the right choice to be her husband. Had his kiss not told her so? Dorothea focused her eyes on the front of the church where her family was seated. Their encouraging expressions, coupled with Lord Atwood's rock-steady arm, allowed her to gracefully glide down the aisle, her face open and smiling.

But her nerves returned the moment the vicar asked her to recite her marriage vows. She struggled to concentrate on every word, to keep her voice steady and strong as she repeated the vows that would bind her to this man for all eternity.

"Wilt thou have this woman as thy wedded wife?"

There was only an instant of silence before Carter answered, but Dorothea held her breath until he spoke the words, "I will."

Dorothea's voice was not as loud as she would have liked when she repeated her vows, but it was steady. At the conclusion of the ceremony, the vicar offered the suggestion that the groom seal the union with a kiss. There were a few mumblings of interest at this very progressive notion.

Puzzled, Dorothea turned her face toward her new husband. Carter smiled mischievously, put his arms around her waist, and kissed her possessively, full on the lips. The mumblings of the congregations rose in volume, followed by several gasps.

As the marquess escorted his new wife back down the aisle, Dorothea caught a glimpse of her father-in-law. The duke was sitting in the front pew, still as a stone. His expression was guarded, his eyes focused forward. He did not turn or glance in their direction as they walked past him.

A prick of unease skittered down Dorothea's back. She probably should not have allowed the kiss, even though it was meant in good humor and sanctioned by the vicar. Which left her to wonder, was the duke most distressed over the kiss or the marriage itself?

Fortunately, there was no time to dwell on the duke's ill mood. When the newly wed couple reached the end of the aisle, they were crowded with well-wishers. The gentlemen shook Atwood's hand and slapped him on the back, then waited eagerly for their chance to embrace the bride.

Dorothea noticed several younger women dab at their eyes with lace handkerchiefs as they offered her congratulations. She idly wondered if they had been sincerely moved by the service or were expressing regret that Lord Atwood was now a married man.

As Dorothea embraced her sister, Emma, a tear trickled down Dorothea's cheek. She couldn't help it. This was such an emotional day.

"I never would have figured you to be a watering pot," Emma teased, her own eyes suspiciously bright.

"I fear I may be more like Aunt Mildred than any of us suspected." Dorothea laughed. It felt wonderful to share this private moment with her younger sister. It almost, though not quite, made up for the fact that Gwen was missing.

It seemed a bit surprising that she would miss her sisters so much, for Dorothea had always prided herself on her sense of independence. Growing up, the trio had clashed on various occasions, as sisters were wont to do. But the deep abiding love and strong sense of loyalty they shared was as impermeable as ever. On a day when so much had drastically changed in Dorothea's life, this constant was a great comfort.

She would bring Emma to London the minute she turned seventeen and host the most sensational coming-out the *ton* had ever seen. It would be a delight to watch her lovely, artistically talented sister shine amongst the highest echelon of society. Now that she had successfully elevated her status as the Marquess of Atwood's wife, it would be foolish not to take full advantage of the situation.

Aunt Mildred embraced her next. She was weepy and sniffly and could barely speak. Uncle Fletcher gave her a quick, awkward hug and Dorothea could tell from his eyes that he still felt a measure of guilt for pilfering and then spending her dowry several years prior. If not for the generosity of Gwen and Jason, Dorothea would be entering this marriage with nothing, though Lord Atwood had expressed very little interest in her modest dowry.

But this was not a day to dwell on the mistakes and hurts of the past. Dorothea bore no grudge toward her uncle, who seemed to genuinely repent for his transgressions.

There was a great deal of laughter and gaiety at the wedding breakfast that followed, hosted at the home of Lord and Lady Dardington. The chilled champagne flowed freely during the lavish celebration and the numerous guests imbibed with obvious relish. There were toasts to the bride and groom, which became progressively sillier as the party wore on, and lively music to enhance the festive atmosphere.

The three Dardington girls had attended the ceremony with their governess, sitting quiet and unnoticed at the back of the church. But they were in the thick of the celebration at the wedding breakfast, and Dorothea was glad to hear their happy, excited squeals.

Even the Duke of Hansborough seemed to be enjoying himself. He sat among a circle of older gentlemen, eating and drinking with gusto, his face breaking into a smile every now and again.

Dorothea was pleased. She wanted to be surrounded by happiness today. With a broad smile, she circulated among the many guests, basking in the attention. Separated from her groom, she chatted with several matrons, one of whom pointed out a small tear in the lace of her train. A few skillfully applied stitches by Lady Meredith's maid in the privacy of her bedchamber soon repaired the damage.

On her way to rejoin the festivities, Dorothea turned the corner of the long gallery hallway and found herself face-to-face with Major Roddington. She quickly hid her surprise. She had seen very little of the major since her engagement to Carter had been decided.

Major Roddington was handsome as ever, yet up close she could see the telltale signs of little sleep. For a split second she worried that she was the cause, but then he smiled with genuine warmth and Dorothea felt a great rush of relief.

"I wish you joy in your marriage," he said quietly, breaking the long silence.

"Thank you, Major."

Dorothea smiled a bit shyly, wondering how different things might have turned out if Carter had not interrupted them in the garden that night at the Dardingtons' dinner party. The soft expression in his eyes seemed to indicate he was thinking the very same thing, but of course he made no mention of his thoughts. After all, it was her wedding day.

"Will you be taking an extended wedding trip, Lady Atwood?" the major inquired.

"Not at this time. We will spend a week or two at the family estate and then return to London for the remainder of the Season."

"May I call on you when you are back in London?"

"I would like that very much. I have a feeling I shall need the support of all of my friends as I assume my new duties."

"You may count on me."

Dorothea's smile widened. She reached out to take his hand in gratitude, but a female voice interrupted.

"Ah, there you are," Emma called out. "Lord Atwood asked me to help him find you. 'Tis nearly time for the two of you to depart."

The major glanced down the hallway. At the sight of Emma he bowed toward Dorothea and quickly retreated, almost as if he were avoiding an encounter with her youngest sister. Which was ridiculous, since they were not acquainted.

"I just repaired my wedding dress and now need to change into my traveling costume," Dorothea told Emma with a sigh. "If I had realized the lateness of the hour I would have not wasted the time having the repair made."

"I'll come with you while you change," Emma offered. "It will give us a few minutes for some private conversation."

The two sisters hurried to Dorothea's bedchamber, where a maid was waiting.

"I won't have to return to Yorkshire after the wedding," Emma confided as the maid helped Dorothea remove her lovely gown. "Aunt Mildred and Uncle Fletcher are allowing me to stay with Gwen and Jason. I'm planning to be there when Gwen's baby is born."

Baby? Dorothea frowned. Apparently Gwen was still keeping her suspicions that she was carrying twins to herself. "I know Gwen will be glad of your comforting presence when her time comes," Dorothea answered. "And Jason, too."

"Actually, he was the one who extended the invitation," Emma said. She placed Dorothea's blue bonnet on the top of her traveling case and handed the maid the elegant white one. "He thought it would help ease Gwen's mind if I were with her during the final weeks of her confinement."

"I'm sure it will help. I shall visit too before the baby arrives," Dorothea declared, hoping Emma would be able to find a way to cope with their emotional, unpredictable eldest sister.

Emma knit her brow in puzzlement. "You will be rather busy, Dorothea. I doubt your new husband will grant you permission to be away from him so soon after your wedding."

"I am a married woman, not a slave. Atwood will not object to my being with my sister," Dorothea said confidently, though in truth she wondered if he would allow it.

How strange to think that the restrictions on her life were still as strong, still as confining. She somehow hoped that being married would afford her more choices, more chances to make her own decisions about her life. Yet in some ways so little was different. She had merely exchanged the dictates of a male guardian for the dictates of a husband.

Ah, but one can learn to manage a husband. The thought popped into her mind and Dorothea smiled. Therein lay the great difference. A final pinch on her cheeks to restore their color and she was once again ready to greet her new husband.

Carter was waiting for her in the gravel drive, surrounded by most of the guests. Dorothea took her time saying goodbye to everyone, saving Lord and Lady Dardington for last.

"Be happy," Lady Meredith whispered in her ear as she gripped Dorothea in a tight hug.

Lord Dardington took her hands in his. "Atwood seems like a fine man. Yet if you should ever find yourself in need of help, know that you can come to me."

Dorothea squeezed his hand, smiling through the tears that suddenly welled in her eyes. "Thank you. For everything."

With a final sniff, Dorothea put her hand on Carter's forearm and allowed him to escort her to the carriage. She climbed the two steps, but before settling herself inside the elegant coach, Dorothea turned and tossed her bridal bouquet. Directly at Viscount Benton. He caught it automatically, his expression puzzled.

"'Tis said that the individual who catches the bride's bouquet will be the next one married," Dorothea announced with a smile.

There was a great roar of laughter from the crowd, most of whom were very aware of Benton's view of the subject. He gazed down at the bouquet with obvious distaste, looking for all the world as if he held a nest of vipers. Then wrinkling his brow, the viscount surveyed the throng surrounding him.

Bypassing several pretty, eager young misses casting him coy glances, he handed the flowers to the Dardingtons' eldest daughter. Stephanie's face broke into a happy grin as she held the prize reverently in front of her.

"Well done, Benton," Carter joked, before he entered the carriage and sat beside his bride.

The newlyweds turned toward the window and waved as the coach pulled out of the drive. There were shouts and cheers that could be heard until the carriage turned onto the busy street. And then a hushed silence filled the coach.

"I'm glad that's over," Atwood remarked.

"I thought it went rather well," Dorothea replied, deciding she was not going to be sensitive over his obvious relief. Most men did not enjoy weddings, especially their own.

Summoning a pleasant expression, Dorothea turned to her husband. A lock of his dark hair had fallen over his left brow. Captivated by the teasing eyes, she drew closer, close enough to feel the warmth radiating from his lean, powerful body. His clean, masculine scent seemed to surround her, intoxicate her.

Carter's gaze lowered to Dorothea's mouth. His eyes darkened, his breath hitched. She leaned in a little closer . . .

The carriage hit a deep rut and they were thrown apart. The spell was immediately broken. A sigh whooshed out of her lungs as Carter leaned back in his seat, turning away from her. Dorothea felt a keen rush of disappointment that she immediately struggled to conceal. A bride should be happy and smiling on her wedding day.

She mentioned the food at the wedding breakfast, inquiring as to which dishes were his favorites. He responded in kind and they spoke of inconsequential matters for the next few miles. Upon reaching the outskirts of Town they made a brief stop at a posting inn.

Atwood left the coach and to Dorothea's great surprise did not return. Instead, he mounted a spirited gray stallion and continued the journey on horseback, leaving his bride to her own company.

As she sat alone in the coach, Dorothea caught an occasional glimpse of her groom riding past her. She wondered constantly what thoughts were crowded into his head. Was he happy? Pleased he had chosen her for his wife?

These worries were her only companion for the remainder of the journey. After what felt like an eternity, the carriage came to a stop at the top of a hill. Dorothea gazed out her window to the valley below. Nestled in the center was a magnificent stone mansion, surrounded by parklands and intricately designed gardens, and beyond that thick woods.

Even at this distance, Dorothea could see sprays of water shooting high in the air from the marble fountains, spotted also the diminutive figures of several gardeners as they toiled in the many-colored flower beds. Normally she would have been entranced by the sight of such a beautiful place, but her nerves had started to fray with each mile they drove.

"Ravenswood Manor," Carter proclaimed, drawing his horse beside the carriage window.

"'Tis magnificent," Dorothea responded.

"Oh, hell, I was afraid of this," Atwood muttered beneath his breath. "It appears we have a welcoming committee."

Stupefied, Dorothea peered closely at the house, noticing the two rows of staff neatly lined in front of the main entrance. Oh, dear, this was the very last thing she needed. She was tired, out of sorts, and trying to cope with a brand-new husband. Now there would be servants to gawk at her.

When they reached the manor, Atwood himself assisted her down from the carriage. He introduced her to the upper house servants, the butler, housekeeper, cook, and head footman, then turned to lead her away. But Dorothea tugged gently on his arm. "I should like to meet all the staff, if you please."

A corner of his mouth edged upward and his eyes glittered with an emotion she could not identify. It might have been an annoyance, but frankly Dorothea didn't care. No doubt the staff had been standing outside for at least an hour, perhaps longer. She felt it was her duty to acknowledge them with a personal greeting and a smile.

Dorothea fully expected the butler, or housekeeper, to take over at that point, but again she was surprised. Carter continued down one row and up the next, calling each servant by name. Dorothea was vastly relieved to find so many kind eyes and shy smiles as the staff bowed or bobbed a curtsy.

"It has been a long journey and a most tiring day," Carter said as the staff began to file inside the manor. "I'll have Mrs. Simpson show you to your rooms. I'm sure you would like to rest before supper."

Dorothea struggled to contain her shock. They had just arrived and once again he was planning to leave her on her own?

"Naturally I should like to freshen up, but I doubt I will nap," she answered.

He smiled charmingly. "Nevertheless, I'm certain the rest will do you good. Mrs. Simpson." He made a motion with his left hand and the housekeeper materialized at Dorothea's side. She had not even realized the woman was so near. "Please show Lady Atwood to her chambers. I will see you at dinner."

And with that settled, he left. Dorothea felt almost too shocked to have a reaction. It had been such an extraordinary day, fraught with excessive emotions. Exhaustion lay just beneath the surface, yet Dorothea knew that sleep was an impossibility. So what precisely was she going to do for the remainder of the afternoon?

She turned to the waiting Mrs. Simpson and gave her a brave smile. "Could I possibly impose upon you for a tour of the house?"

"'Tis a very large residence, my lady. Seeing everything will take hours."

"Well, perhaps just the first floor today," Dorothea countered, starting to feel an edge of desperation.

Mrs. Simpson arched her brow, hesitated, then answered, "I shall be honored, my lady."

They started with the numerous formal rooms, all grandly and expensively furnished. After seeing the duke's London home, Dorothea expected nothing less, but there was a comforting quality to these quarters that was lacking in London. Ravenswood felt more like a home and less like a showpiece, though it was grand enough to qualify as one. The clear difference buoyed Dorothea's spirits.

All it took was a few words of praise at the excellent condition in which she found everything and Mrs. Simpson's formal attitude faded. Dorothea was vastly relieved. They concluded the tour in Dorothea's rooms, a pleasant, large suite that included a well-furnished sitting room and a spectacular view of the gardens.

As predicted, once she was alone, Dorothea was unable to sleep. Instead, she lay on her back beneath the soft sheets that smelled pleasantly of fresh lavender, staring at the elaborate silk bed hangings, wondering when it would be time to dress for dinner.

When someone finally arrived at her suite, Dorothea was delighted to see it was Mrs. Simpson.

"I thought it might be best if I assist you this evening, since your maid hasn't yet arrived," the housekeeper said. "I have some skill with arranging hair."

"I've yet to hire a personal maid and would very much appreciate your advice. By any chance is there a local girl who might suit?"

Mrs. Simpson bit her lower lip thoughtfully. "Sarah Mallory has a bit of experience and I know her family would be grateful for the income. She was widowed last year and forced to return home. I don't think she wants to remarry and there are nine other siblings in the household to feed."

"She sounds perfect. Can you arrange an interview later this week?"

"I'd be delighted."

Grinning with satisfaction at making her first decision as mistress of her own home, Dorothea felt herself relax. Mrs. Simpson had not exaggerated her expertise with hair. She pinned Dorothea's blonde curls in an elegant upsweep that showcased the long line of her throat and the creamy perfection of her chest, so elegantly exposed by her daring décolletage.

"You look stunning, my lady." Mrs. Simpson smiled. "Lord Atwood won't be able to keep his eyes off you."

Or his hands. The raucous thought popped unbidden into Dorothea's head. But wasn't that what she wanted? To beguile and bewitch her husband?

On less than steady legs, Dorothea followed the housekeeper downstairs to the drawing room, still pondering that thought.

Carter was waiting for her. He had changed from his wedding finery into more casual attire. His hair was still damp from a recent bath and his jaw was freshly shaved. They walked into the dining room and took their seats and again spoke of their wedding and the festivities that followed.

"At least my father did not make a scene," Carter said as the second course was served.

"The duke is not the most congenial of men, yet I find myself respecting him for his honesty," Dorothea replied. "He did not approve of our marriage initially but seems to have accepted it. I felt when he wished us well, he truly meant it."

Carter's mouth drew tight for a moment. "You seemed pleased to have your younger sister attend the ceremony."

Dorothea felt her face warm. "Yes. It was delightful to be with Emma again. I had not realized how much I missed her."

"Ah, is that not so often the case? We rarely appreciate

the real blessings in our life until they are gone." He took a sip of wine and stared at her over the rim. "After we are settled back in Town, you must invite Emma to visit."

"Nothing would please me more. She is entertaining company, well, that is, when one can drag her away from her easel."

His brow rose in confusion. Dorothea explained. "Emma paints. She is extremely talented. Jason has arranged for a private instructor, and her progress under his able tutelage is nothing short of remarkable."

"If you wish, we can commission her to do your portrait."

"Honestly? 'Tis a very generous offer. I would be delighted."

He shrugged. "Well, if it's dreadful, we can always hang it in the kitchen."

"You will do no such thing, sir. Emma will produce a beautiful portrait, one that you will be proud to display beside these ancestral portraits done by some of the art world's greatest masters," Dorothea insisted, fully believing in Emma's work.

"Her task shall be made far easier with such a beautiful female as her subject."

He regarded her through hooded eyes, saying nothing else. She took a bite of her chicken and slowly chewed, barely tasting it. "You're making me nervous," she finally blurted out.

"I am?" He began drumming his fingers on the arm of his chair. "How?"

"You are silent. And staring very intently."

"'Tis a husband's prerogative to appreciate his wife's beauty and grace."

A flood of deep color entered Dorothea's face. She did not like the way he said the word *wife*. As if she were his possession, his property. Flustered, she picked up her wine goblet and took a large gulp. The sharp, pungent, full-bodied flavor rolled over her tongue, warming her body as it glided down her throat.

"I find that I am quite full. Shall we ask for dessert to be served?" she inquired after setting her nearly empty goblet back on the white linen cloth.

He leaned in very close. "You are the only sweet I want on this night, my dear. Shall we?"

He extended his hand. Dorothea glanced down at it, for a moment feeling vaguely lost.

"I thought it might be easier if we started out together," he added. "Unless you prefer to go to your chambers and wait for me there?"

"Like some medieval sacrificial virgin awaiting her lord and master," Dorothea muttered.

"Lord and master?" Carter laughed. "Oh, my dear, 'tis comments like that which make me very glad we are married."

Still smiling, he stood, walked around to her chair, then leaned down and whispered in her ear, so none of the footmen could hear him. "I believe it is time for us to retire."

Obediently, Dorothea rose from her chair. He caught her hand and led her purposefully from the dining room. The blush that started in Dorothea's cheeks quickly spread to her neck as they casually sauntered past what seemed like an army of footmen, all completely aware of where Lord Atwood was taking his bride and what he planned to do with her.

She had never before felt so uncertain. If only she knew more about what was to come! Yes, she understood the biology of it all, but the particulars of how it was done, how it all felt, eluded her completely. Dorothea clasped her free hand to her stomach and glanced at the flickering wall sconces as if searching for answers in their glowing warmth.

Finally, Carter stopped in front of a solid oak door. She thought her chambers were also located in this section of the house, but her nerves had stolen her sense of direction and she realized she could be anywhere in the mansion.

With a mysterious smile, he opened the door, walked over the threshold, then gently tugged her inside.

It was the largest, most opulent bedchamber Dorothea had ever seen, dominated in the center by an enormous canopied bed. The four mahogany posters at the corners rose majestically skyward, yet barely reached the intricately painted ceiling. The bed was draped in royal blue velvet, with a matching brocade spread that was invitingly turned down.

The window drapes were the same shade of blue, embroidered with gold threads that gave them a shimmering, luxurious sheen. They were drawn shut to prevent the morning light from disturbing his lordship's slumber.

The furniture was a mix of dark and lighter woods, each design masculine and functional. She thought the room suited him with its mix of elegant strength and masculine beauty.

Her feet felt rooted to the floor, but she forced herself to turn and face him. Instantly she felt caught in his mesmerizing stare. She couldn't blink, was unable to look away, captured in his sensual spell.

He tipped her chin with one hand. There was a spark of intensity in his eyes that stole any words from Dorothea's mind. He was staring at her with the heat and desire of a man in need, his breathing harsh while hers bellowed in rapid response.

She waited almost breathlessly for the kiss that she knew would be forthcoming. Carter's lips sank into hers and a warm, liquid rush of pleasure cascaded over her entire body. Dorothea lifted her hand and closed it around his raised arm in an attempt to steady herself.

He ended the kiss and pulled away, bestowing upon her a grin so wicked, so sexy, her knees quivered. Then he reached behind his back with his free hand and Dorothea heard the lock click into place. A wicked sigh shivered through her.

They were completely alone.

Chapter Eleven

Dorothea tried not to look apprehensive. She took a few steps into the room, then paused. The large bed loomed directly in front, a stark reminder of what was to come, what she felt so suddenly unprepared to face.

Silently Carter pulled off his jacket, yanked his neck cloth free, unbuttoned his waistcoat, and tossed the garments haphazardly on a chair. He removed his clothes with an economy of motion and grace Dorothea envied, knowing she would look like a clumsy contortionist if she tried to struggle out of her gown herself.

He regarded her warily and she could only imagine how her odd thoughts appeared to him, reflected on her face. Annoyed with herself for showing so little fortitude, she glanced away. This was her wedding night, not a tooth extraction. She had wanted to experience this intimacy for a long time and had been privileged to choose this man as her partner. Such a skittish, hesitant reaction was ridiculous.

Tightening her jaw for strength, Dorothea lifted her chin. Wearing only an open shirt and black satin knee breeches, her bridegroom was a formidable figure. Dorothea could see the swirls of dark hair that covered the upper muscles of his chest peeking through the white linen. He was tall and powerful, broad and masculine, so incredibly . . . male. Her mouth went dry.

They stared at each other, exchanging thoughts and emotions without saying a word. Outwardly, she knew she looked calm and curious. Inside, Dorothea felt like screaming.

She forced herself to speak. "My lord."

"My lady?"

His expression alarmed her. He appeared to be exerting a tremendous amount of control, looking for all the world as if he wanted to pounce on her. And eat her alive. Dorothea shivered.

"Are you cold?" he asked.

"No."

"Afraid?"

"Nervous," she clarified. "I want very much to please you, my lord."

"Carter," he whispered. "I believe the intimacy that we are about to enjoy dictates more informal terms. Don't you agree, Dorothea?"

"Yes. Yes, I do."

"Now, the first thing we need to do is get you more comfortable."

Before she could question precisely what he meant, Carter reached out and began removing the pins from her hair. The silky tresses fell across her back and shoulders, a showering golden mane. He stroked it softly, almost reverently, as if he were fascinated by the texture of the silken threads.

His large hands were gentle, the rhythmic caresses hypnotic. Dorothea felt her eyes slowly close as her body began to relax. But the languid feeling abruptly disappeared when he moved his hand forward to cup her breast.

Her startled gasp echoed through the chamber as a bolt of sensation flashed between her legs.

"We'll go slowly," he promised. "'Tis better that way." She swayed into him and he laughed, a short bark of mirth. "That is to say, as slow as I can manage. You are an extraordinary temptation, my dear."

She felt her confidence soar, knowing he found her attractive, desirable. After his odd behavior this afternoon, it was the reaffirmation she needed, the assurance she craved. Dorothea reached up and ran the edge of her finger along his jaw. The surface was smooth, yet when she reversed the direction of her hand she could feel the rough edge of his whiskers. It was a strangely erotic sensation.

He put his mouth to hers, nibbling her lower lip until she willingly opened to him. Relaxing, Dorothea curled her tongue against his. She adored his kisses. Her hands came up to cling to his broad shoulders as the familiar excitement flared deep in her belly, making her feel hot all over.

His kisses moved from her mouth to her cheek, then drifted down the column of the neck. His light, teasing touch made her breath catch, her skin tingle.

He drew down her bodice, then tugged down the edge of her lace chemise to bare her breasts. Dorothea inhaled a sharp gasp, which Carter ignored.

She could feel his warm breath against her bare flesh. With light, soft flicks of his tongue, he headed toward her nipple. It tightened and rose to greet him as he drew closer, but he circled around it, nipping playfully with his teeth and lips.

Mindlessly, Dorothea reached up to clutch his head, lacing her fingers in his hair, pressing him closer.

"You are very sensitive, very responsive," he murmured just before he took the fullness of her breast into his mouth.

"Oh, my," she cried out in a shaky whimper.

Heat speared through her limbs and she moved her legs restlessly, urgently. His sharp tongue laved her nipple, then suckled deeply. Desire burned through her, shattering her thoughts, rendering her incapable of thinking or feeling anything but this extraordinary hunger.

"Too many clothes," he rasped.

His hands reached around her shoulders to the middle of her back, working furiously at the various fastenings. The gown gaped forward and he tugged on it, forcing it away from her body. She next felt his hand reach under her hem. He ran his fingers possessively over the top of her stocking, smoothing the skin of her bare thighs. He rolled the delicate silk downward, kneeling before her as he held her ankle and pulled the fabric free.

At his command, she stepped out of the gown. All that was left on her quivering body was her partially open chemise and drawers. Dorothea shivered. Her hands moved instinctively to cover herself, modesty momentarily overtaking her desire.

"No hiding," Carter insisted. Standing once again, his eyes locked on hers. "And no secrets."

Dorothea felt an unfamiliar jolt inside her chest. The idea of being that close, that honest with a man was terrifying yet amazingly appealing. Was it possible? Could they forge a bond so strong, so true that it could withstand the frailties of their natures, that it could endure the test of time?

"No secrets," she repeated, and to prove the sincerity of her words Dorothea reached down and untied the three remaining closed ribbons on her chemise. Forcing herself not to think about it, she lifted the garment over her head, then yanked off her drawers. She heard the swift intake of his breath as the last of the silk slid away, exposing her naked flesh to his eyes.

"Your beauty would unman a saint," he declared.

Kissing her mouth firmly, Carter swept Dorothea off her feet and carried her to his bed, depositing her in the center. She bounced once on the firm mattress as he quickly removed his remaining clothing, tossing his shirt, breeches, and smallclothes to the floor.

He soon joined her in the bed, his hard naked flesh sliding against her own. It was startling, vulnerable, to be touching her whole self to him without any barriers between them. Startling and delightful.

She could feel the hardness of him engulfing her; his oak-hard chest, the strength of his corded arm muscles, the flatness of his lean stomach. She liked the feel of his body, so different from her own.

Liked the feel and liked the sight. In the glow of the candlelight she could see that the hair on his chest followed a line down his flat stomach, growing thicker between his legs. Feeling shy, she merely glanced there, and got an eyeful of his engorged, jutting penis.

Oh, dear. He was going to put that inside her?

Her rising desire tempered considerably. But her fear was soon distracted by Carter's lips. He turned her on her side and seized her mouth in a fierce kiss. His hands were everywhere as they explored her body slowly, deliberately, thoroughly, arousing her with infinite skill.

A surge of embarrassment struck when he reached her womanhood and cupped the silken curls between her thighs. With incredible gentleness he drew his fingers over her. Barely touching, they traced a torturous line of excitement around the swollen, tender flesh, sending tremors of passion through her. Moaning as her head fell back, she started moving against his hand, following his rhythm and then creating one of her own.

He probed with his fingertips, parting her folds, sliding one finger up inside her. Dorothea lunged. There was moisture, a wetness that had come from her own body. It seemed to please him, for he growled in her ear and once again took her nipple into his mouth.

His mouth and fingers continued to work their magic on her untutored body. Dorothea could hear the small cries of pleasure coming from her own throat, a keening, almost animal sound of desperation and excitement. The feeling continued to build until she thought it would consume her. She couldn't seem to get close enough. She tightened her hold on his shoulders, urgently seeking more, her breath coming in short, rapid bursts.

"Easy, love," he coaxed, his voice a deep timbre. "Don't rush it, let it come naturally."

She tried to do as he asked. Honestly. The wetness flowed and her body turned to fire until at last the crest broke. Mindlessly, Dorothea arched her back as waves of sensation washed over her and a bolt of liquid hot pleasure shot through her entire being.

Eyes closed, she collapsed against the damp bedsheets, breathing hard, her body open and relaxed. Lost in a haze, she felt Carter smooth her hair back from her damp brow. She lifted her face toward his and he kissed her lips softly, gently.

"God Almighty, you are beautiful," he rasped.

"That was incredible." Dorothea smiled. A quiet, secretive, womanly smile. She did not know, had not realized it would be such a physical and emotional act, an intimate exploration of the secrets of the flesh between man and woman. A closeness that bordered on the spiritual.

But her languid pleasure was interrupted by a bold

caress. She opened her eyes and found Carter looming above her, pressing her shoulders against the soft mattress, pushing her legs open with his knees.

She reached up and splayed her hands against the hard muscles of his chest. He truly was a beautiful man. A rush of emotions invaded her heart as she prepared herself for this ultimate intimacy, an edge of nerves mingling with a knot of anticipation deep inside.

Dorothea felt his hardness pressing against her, probing for entrance. It startled her and she tensed, remembering how large he was, but he pushed her legs wider apart and pressed on.

"Relax," he murmured. His hands hooked her knees and he held her in place. "You are wet and open and ready for me. I will have you now."

She tried to do as he bid, but the tightness and discomfort as he pushed his penis inside her had her wriggling beneath him, searching desperately for a means of escape.

"Bloody hell, Dorothea. Stay still!"

His strangled voice startled her. His breathing was hard as he seemed to struggle to maintain control. Struggle and lose.

Her grip on his shoulders tightened at the same moment he lifted his hips and thrust forward. The sharpness of the pain took her breath away. She groaned, but he misunderstood the sound, for he thrust forward again, harder. Arching upward, Dorothea dug her fingers into his shoulders, trying to pull herself away, but that too was wrong, for it encouraged him even more.

Realizing the struggles were making it worse, Dorothea forced her body to relax. He pressed forward again, his huge, swollen penis stretching her flesh, filling her completely. The pain lessened as she gradually allowed herself to succumb to Carter's possession. But the joy, the excitement did not return. She felt disconnected from what was happening and she yearned to recapture the earlier, urgent emotion.

She wanted to somehow verbalize this dilemma to him, but everything was moving so fast, so intensely, it was impossible. Her brain seemed to have shut down, along with her voice and the confusion between her mind and body and heart jumbled together inside, paralyzing her.

When Dorothea thought she could stand it no longer, when the words inside her seemed to finally rise up and were ready to release themselves, she heard Carter's low, deep growl. He surged forward a final time, his body clenching and shuddering. She felt the warm rush of his seed spurt into her aching passage, then with a final groan he collapsed on top of her.

It seemed a long time before either of them could draw a calming breath. Strange, but the weight of him on top of her now, the weight that had felt so oppressive before was now a solid, warm comfort. Idly, Dorothea ran her fingers over his sweat-soaked back, listening to the sharp bellows of his breath tickle her ear.

She shifted her hips slightly and realized with a start that their flesh was still joined in the most intimate way.

Carter must have felt it too, for he laughed suddenly. "Jesus, I'm still hard." He reached over and tenderly stroked her hair. "Give me a few minutes to recover and we'll have another go at it, sweetheart."

His words froze her blood. *Oh, dear Lord! He wants to do it again?* Her heart clamored with panic, her sore body tensed at the notion of another invasion. She struggled to find the words to tell him that she needed more time to recover. He pressed a tender kiss to her brow and cheek. She tensed, but he only continued with these sweet kisses.

And then finally, thankfully, she heard the deep, steady rhythm of his breathing and realized he had fallen asleep.

Dorothea stared up at the ceiling, uncertain what she was feeling. Her body ached and tingled in various unmentionable places. Between her legs, she was sticky and wet with her husband's seed and the last remnants of her virginal blood. Beside her, Carter snored deeply and she hoped he would stay in that deep slumber for the remainder of the night.

It had all started so promisingly. She had been nervous, but Carter had calmed her nerves, distracted her fear with gentle caresses that had stirred her passion. He had been giving and generous, bringing her body skillfully to a crescendo of desire and then hurling her over the edge.

The sensations had been wondrous and all consuming. Yet as she drifted inside the joy and enormity of the moment, the pain had struck. Deep, sharp, and real. First physical, but next emotional. He had thrust himself inside her as though she was his possession, regardless of how she felt.

She had wanted to call out to him, to tell him to stop, to wait, but her voice had failed her. Instead, she lay pinioned beneath him as he plunged and withdrew. Thankfully, it did not take long for his control to break, for his body to jerk convulsively as his warm essence spurted into her tender body.

He had held her a long time after it was over, seeming to revel in the stillness. There were sweet, light kisses pressed on her neck, her cheeks, her lips. His tenderness and care had brought forth a rush of emotions she couldn't define. She snuggled into his hard warmth, craving the connection that had eluded her when their bodies had been joined.

His announcement that they would repeat the act had put her in a total panic. Thankfully, he had fallen asleep before he could make good on his promise, still holding her tightly in his arms. She too had tried to rest, but it was impossible. Cautiously she waited until she felt his possessive hold slacken. Seizing her chance, she uncurled herself from his grasp and scurried to the relative safety of her side of the bed.

She lay there for hours, practically memorizing each delicate fold in the opulent silk bed hangings above her. She tried to remain still and silent, yet could not prevent the sighs that continued to escape. Fortunately she mastered any tears that threatened, for she honestly knew not why she wanted to weep.

From disappointment? Pain? Or something even more profound? She believed they were forming a solid relationship yet when he possessed her body she had felt a distance from him that was as wide and vast as the ocean, a distance from herself that she could not identify or understand. It had been a strange, frightening feeling that effectively pushed all chance of pleasure aside.

A sudden movement in the bed froze her thoughts. Dorothea stiffened, holding herself perfectly still, fearing even to breathe. Finally Carter ceased his rustling, rolled closer to the center of the massive bed, and fell back to sleep with astonishing speed, his scent and warmth surrounding her.

Dorothea listened to his deep, steady breathing and tried to do the same, but sleep was impossible while her heart pounded with such confusion and self-doubt. Had she made a dreadful mistake? Had she chosen the wrong man to be her husband or was she simply not suited to be a wife? Perhaps if there was a deep abiding love between them she would have felt more of a connection. As it stood, they were practically strangers.

Strangers who were now married, bound to each other for life. Strangers who shared embarrassing physical intimacies, yet knew so little of each other. Blinking quickly to hold back any tears, Dorothea scolded herself for being so maudlin, so melodramatic.

She deliberately closed her eyes, but her body was so tense, her mind so full, the blessed escape of sleep would not come. After another hour, or maybe two, she gave up the pretense and crept from the bed. She suspected one of the several interior doors in this bedchamber led to her own rooms, but feared her clumsy rustling about the chamber would wake Carter.

And she had a fair suspicion of what would happen then. She believed if she told him no, he would respect her decision and not force her. But he would demand an explanation, and that she was not yet prepared to give. It was all still too new, too raw, too confusing.

In the dim candlelight, Dorothea found the washstand. She carefully poured some clean water into the porcelain basin. She wrung out a cloth and ran it over her body, then pressed it between her legs, washing away the remaining traces of semen and blood. The water was cool, but it helped ease the burning, the soreness.

Desperate for something to cover herself, she picked through the mountain of clothes strewn about the floor. She found her chemise, but several of the front ribbons were missing. Tossing it aside, she grabbed the marquess's wrinkled shirt and pulled it over her head. The long sleeves came down to her fingertips and the bottom fell to the tops of her knees. It was perfect.

Surprisingly, the soft, warm linen felt comforting as it

draped around her skin. Wrapping her arms around her waist, Dorothea hugged herself and breathed deeply. The garment smelled of Carter, which might have made it objectionable when in fact it did just the opposite.

The familiar scent brought a sense of comfort, a reaction she could not fully understand. *Like everything else about tonight,* she decided with a shrug.

Padding barefoot to the large wing chair in the corner, Dorothea curled herself into a comfortable position and forced her body, and her mind, to relax. She suspected she would stay there until dawn broke, yet amazingly she soon fell into a deep, dreamless sleep.

Carter heard the knock on his bedchamber door, but he did not want to acknowledge it. His head was hazy with the memory of an erotic dream of Dorothea and he wanted to savor the image as long as possible.

She was a Siren, his brand-new wife. A beautiful, passionate temptress with a body made for sex and a spirited temperament that fired a man's blood, assaulted his senses.

Deflowering a virgin was heady business, Carter decided. And unchartered territory for him. His previous lovers had always been experienced women. The novelty of tutoring a woman as passionate as Dorothea in the art of lovemaking had kept him painfully aroused for the majority of yesterday afternoon.

That was why he had left the carriage and ridden his horse when they stopped at the first posting inn yesterday, remembering well his vow not to take his wife's virginity in a coach. Likewise, he had taken himself away so soon after they arrived at Ravenswood Manor. He had not wanted to turn into an uncouth beast, ravaging his innocent bride in the middle of the day, consummating their union for the first time in a hasty, rushed manner.

It had been the correct decision. He had relished the opportunity to explore her lovely form, to tease and excite her, to watch her climax as he readied her body for his possession.

His arousal had been painful in its intensity when he bedded her last night, yet her untried body had satisfied him as no other woman had ever done. She had been so wet and warm, so impossibly tight. He had practically spilled himself the moment he became fully sheathed inside her. Miraculously, he had somehow managed to control himself long enough to seek a full and satisfying climax.

Remembering it now made him rock hard. Reflexively, his arm reached across the wide expanse of his bed. Perhaps it was time to awaken. Time to awaken and experience again this heady bliss.

But when he opened his eyes, the bed was empty. Only the faint scent of her lavender perfume lingered, mingling with the earthy, appealing smell of sex. Annoyed, Carter sat upright.

The knocking persisted. "Come in!" he barked, his mood worsening. Where was his wife?

His valet, Dunsford, stood in the doorway. "Shall I have hot water brought for you to shave, or would you prefer a bath this morning, my lord?"

"Where is Lady Atwood?" Carter demanded, ignoring the questions.

The valet was so startled he took a step backward. "I, um . . . am uncertain."

"Has she had her breakfast?"

"I regret to inform you that I am unaware of her ladyship's schedule, but will be happy to ask Mrs. Simpson," the valet offered in a voice laced with stiffness.

"Never mind," Carter replied, tossing back the covers. "Have Mrs. Simpson instruct Lady Atwood to meet me in the drawing room in an hour."

What Carter really wanted was to have his missing wife summoned to his bedchamber, but he would not embarrass her in front of the staff with such a blatant request.

After bathing and eating a hearty breakfast, Carter's mood was much improved. He arrived at the drawing room before his wife and settled in comfortably to await her arrival.

She came precisely at the appointed time. Her eyes widened slightly when she saw he was already inside. He smiled and stood on his feet. Dorothea shut the elaborate gilded doors behind her, yet took only two steps into the room. Her hands twisted together nervously at her waist.

Carter thought the gesture naively endearing.

"Good morning," she said softly. "Mrs. Simpson said that you wanted to see me."

"Good morning." He came forward and dipped his head, intending to kiss her lips. She turned as he drew near and he ended up kissing her cheek. "I missed you in my bed this morning."

"I thought it would be strange if I awakened there with you," she said quietly.

"I would hardly have minded," he replied, his eyes searching her face. "We could have once again recaptured the pleasure of last night."

"Ah, last night." She lifted her hand to her mouth and began to chew on her fingernail. "It was very . . . um, emotional, was it not?"

Emotional? He thought it a damn sight more than emotional. It was bloody fantastic.

"Will you wish to repeat it again this evening?" she inquired.

This evening? He wished to repeat it right now, this very minute. He was hardly sated. Their initial coupling had only whetted his appetite for more. Yet there would be no pleasure for him unless Dorothea also undertook this journey to ecstasy. Was it the daylight that made her so shy, so reticent?

"I doubt I can wait until this evening, sweetheart."

For several seconds, she said nothing. Then she gazed into his eyes, her features neutral. "Very well. What time shall I expect you in my bedchamber?"

Her stilted, formal reply was the first inkling that his bride had not enjoyed the delights of their nuptial bed to the same extent as he. Her small, nervous step away from him as he approached her was the second sign.

"Are you still very sore?"

"Carter, please. Must we discuss this?"

Irrationally, her quiet plea brought on his anger. "Yes. I will not have you cringing and cowering every time I approach you."

Her eyes flashed. "I hardly did that, sir," Dorothea said defensively. "Nor would I ever act in such a manner. I know and accept my duties as your wife. All my duties. And I should like to point out that I would not have said one word about last night unless you asked me."

Well, she had him there. He had been the one to bring up the topic. But only because he anticipated a completely different response.

"I know the initial bedding can be difficult for a woman, but I thought I prepared your body well. I don't understand what went wrong."

"Ah, so you speak from experience? You have deflowered a good many virgins over the years?"

Carter winced. That comment rankled. She made

him sound like a sexual deviant. Was that truly what she believed?

"You were my first, and last, virgin," he stated emphatically.

"A rare honor for me, then."

"Dorothea, what is wrong? Did I hurt you that badly?" He reached for her hand and held it between his palms, startled to feel its chill. He anxiously studied her face, but it was a mask of impassive stone. "We promised last night there would be no secrets between us."

She squeezed his hand, then slowly pulled it away. "It wasn't all horrid. It started out quite wonderfully actually, right until, well, you know."

"Until what? Until I penetrated you?"

Dorothea groaned. "I really cannot have this discussion with you."

"'Tis my fault. I should have taken you slow and easy, but you were so passionate, so giving. I lost my head." He accompanied his apology with a boyish grin, designed to melt even the coldest heart. But Dorothea did not smile. She averted her eyes.

"I know it is different for a man. I understand that you were only being true to your nature. Rest assured, I will fulfill my wifely duties with all the passion I can muster."

He made a gruff, impatient sound. "No matter how abhorrent they are to you?"

"I did not say that," she insisted, crossing her arms against her breasts.

The gesture called his attention to her ample bosom. He recalled the luscious shade of her dusty rose nipples contrasting with the milky smoothness of creamy round breasts. The sight and taste of them had driven him to near madness, and the memory was more than enough to bring him swiftly to arousal again.

With effort he lifted his gaze from her luscious body. And then he saw it. The vulnerability on her beautiful face, the uncertainty and wariness shadowed in her eyes. It made him feel like an utter cad.

She had trusted him to treat her gently and he had failed her. Unintentional, but that did not make it any better. His passion and desire had made him selfish. It was hardly the way to treat a wife, and certainly not what she deserved.

She appeared to recover her composure, then attempted a smile. It failed. "It wasn't that awful," she whispered. "That is to say, well, at least the most painful part ended quickly."

She released a long, slow breath, then straightened her shoulders, like a soldier determined to go into battle despite his fear.

Carter felt his gut clench. He had never been so wounded by a remark in his entire life. He knew how to pleasure a woman. How to make her pant with anticipation, move her entire body with restless desire, shout at the top of her lungs when she reached her climax.

"I can assure you, madam, that I have not taken you as my wife solely for the purpose of appeasing my rabid, unnatural hunger for sex."

"I assumed that was what a mistress was for, poor thing."

His head jerked up. His former mistresses were hardly poor things. Due to his generosity they were financially independent women, and he had never once heard a complaint from any of them regarding his sexual prowess. "We agreed before our marriage to honor our vows of fidelity. I will not take a mistress, nor do I want one. I want you."

Her breath hitched. "Truly?"

"Yes. As my wife, only you can produce an heir."

The hopeful expression faded from her lovely face at

his final words. Instantly he realized he should not have admitted the last. Telling a woman he wanted her to bear his children was not a helpful approach to this problem. Besides, he truly did not want another woman. He wanted Dorothea.

"I know my duty, sir," she said coldly. "I will not shirk it. There will be an heir, as you require."

Carter sighed loudly, raking his outstretched fingers through his hair. "Saints preserve us all, I will not have my wife consider bedding me a duty. It will be a joy and a pleasure for both of us."

She shrugged as if she had no earthly idea how to make that happen.

"You enjoy my kisses," he said, almost more to himself than her. "My touch does not appear to revolt you."

"I never said that it did. Carter, please, last night was not a complete disaster. I enjoyed it, well, all except for the very last bit. And I can school myself to endure that part of the act. It was over quickly enough." She tilted her head to one side, her expression thoughtful. "Though perhaps the problem has more to do with size. Apparently I am small and you are rather, um, rather large. Maybe if we joined our bodies while your . . . while you . . . while it was much smaller it would bring me less discomfort?"

Carter sputtered. Another man might have been angry. She had insulted his skills as a lover as well as his lack of endurance. Over quickly, indeed! The one thing she had accomplished was compliment the size of his equipment, but that was unintentional. Enter her while he was small? Surely he had not just heard her spew such nonsense.

Carter had always prided himself on being a considerate lover, patient and lustful. Not since he was an untried lad had it been necessary for him to exert a great deal of effort in seducing a female. A few charming words, a sultry smile, a passionate kiss and they were in his bed, eager and willing. And they left it satisfied, often purring their contentment.

It would be so with his wife. Carter's helplessness escalated, but he knew he could not unleash his frustration on her. She was blameless. He had misread the situation utterly, he had bungled it all badly and put a fear of copulation into Dorothea in the process. What an idiot. He knew he would have to dispense with the fear if he ever wanted an eager, passionate wife in his bed.

His path was clear. He would have to woo, to romance, to seduce his bride. He owed it to himself, but more importantly, he owed it to her.

Chapter Twelve

The day after her wedding was turning out to be far more complicated, and emotional, than Dorothea ever anticipated. After a thoroughly embarrassing conversation with her husband, which ended with his abrupt departure, Dorothea was once again left to her own devices.

She had offended him with her comments about their wedding night. Offended, angered, and possibly wounded him. Well, wounded his pride. His feelings she barely understood, but his pride was obvious.

The harmony of their relationship was now strained and she worried it would not be easily restored. Married but one day and already facing a crisis. This was not what she had imagined when she agreed to be his wife.

A shuffling noise at the drawing room doorway startled her, and Dorothea wondered if Carter had returned. She turned, struggling to swallow, half hoping, half dreading his appearance. But instead it was Mrs. Simpson who stood hesitantly in the doorway, inquiring if this was a good time to consult her ladyship on the daily menus for the rest of the week.

Thinking it terribly bad manners to take out her peculiar

mood on the hapless housekeeper, Dorothea dutifully agreed. She read through the splendid meals Cook had temptingly created for their pleasure, murmuring her approval in what she hoped was an authoritative manner. This was an unfamiliar task, made all the more challenging since she had no notion of what foods her husband preferred. But she trusted that his staff would be aware of his lordship's likes and dislikes.

Mrs. Simpson's grin of approval when she finished eased some of Dorothea's nerves. She might have gotten off on the wrong foot with her husband, yet miraculously she had managed to make a favorable impression on the staff.

"Please convey my thanks to Cook for devising such an ambitious menu," Dorothea told the housekeeper as Mrs. Simpson handed over the menus. "And compliment her on the lovely dinner she served us last evening. Lord Atwood and I enjoyed every bite."

Another nod and smile of approval was soon forthcoming. Mrs. Simpson turned to leave, but paused a moment before departing. "Would you like to see the rest of the house today, my lady? I am at your disposal."

"Why not?" Dorothea replied, decided it was as good a way as any to spend her day. Perhaps it might even distract her mind from her matrimonial dilemma and chase away some of her gloomy thoughts.

They started on the top floor of the mansion. The domestic quarters were clean, neat, and in good repair. Though they were simple and plain, Dorothea was impressed by the quality of furnishings, linen, and blankets given to the staff, along with the ample piles of fuel for their fireplaces.

The third floor contained two distinct wings of bedchambers. The east wing was reserved for family members, including the suites for the lord and lady of the manor. Thankfully Mrs. Simpson strolled by those closed doors and negligently waved her hand in their general direction, knowing full well that Dorothea had been inside both sets of rooms.

Dorothea clenched her thumb and forefinger on the bridge of her nose tightly to hold back her reaction as she scuttled past those doors. Highly doubting she could have entered Carter's rooms, seen that bed, and kept her emotions level, she asked several pointed questions about the furnishings in the opulent suite reserved for the duke as they entered those chambers.

"It has by far the prettiest view of the gardens," Mrs. Simpson declared. She pulled back the heavy gold velvet draperies to emphasize her point. "'Tis such a shame that the duke so seldom visits the estate. Why, it's going on five years since we have last seen him."

"I imagine he has other estates to attend," Dorothea replied.

"To be sure. But none so fine as Ravenswood," Mrs. Simpson said proudly.

They continued on to the west wing of the third floor, which also boasted an abundance of elegant, comfortable bedchambers. These were the rooms chosen for close friends and houseguests during house parties, Mrs. Simpson explained, and thus always kept at the ready.

"Is there a great deal of entertaining done here?" Dorothea asked.

"There was, back when the duchess was alive. We are all hoping with Lord Atwood married, the house will once again ring with laughter and good cheer. The staff does not mind the extra work involved and appreciates the opportunity to showcase their skills and dedication."

Dorothea silently wondered if the rest of the servants truly were as eager to tackle the heavy workload of keeping guests happy. Back home, their cook and two housemaids complained mightily on the rare occasions there was a dinner party. Dorothea could only imagine the tasks involved when a dwelling of this size was filled with spoiled aristocrats and their servants making demands of the staff.

She had already seen many of the manor's second- and first-floor rooms, but lacking anything specific to do with her day, Dorothea asked to see them again. The rooms were numerous and splendidly furnished, and Mrs. Simpson a knowledgeable guide. Dorothea's mind could barely absorb the details.

There were two drawing rooms, both cavernous, though one was larger than the other, a music room filled with all manner of instruments, the majority of which Dorothea could not, nor ever hope to, play with any level of proficiency. A formal ballroom, a library, a study, a den, a morning room, a breakfast parlor, a private salon designed exclusively for the lady of the house.

She could barely absorb all the layout, let alone all the details Mrs. Simpson so easily imparted, but somehow Dorothea made all the appropriate responses to the housekeeper's comments. Yet when they entered the long portrait gallery, Dorothea fell silent. Generations of noble ancestors seemed to stare down their noses as she paraded past them. Disapprovingly, Dorothea mused gloomily, glaring back up at the canvases.

How could she ever measure up to these proud, haughty aristocrats? What had she been thinking when she agreed to be Carter's marchioness and, someday, his duchess?

Dorothea paused and stared up into the stern countenance of a Tudor lord, the first Duke of Hansborough. Henry VIII used to chop off his wives' heads if they displeased him. Had that been the kinder decision? A swift end to the constant battle and bickering?

She let out a pathetic sigh. Preferring death to marriage? Oh dear, her gloomy mood truly had gone too far. Silently commanding herself to cease this foolishness immediately, Dorothea narrowed her eyes and glared at the portrait.

She was a resourceful woman. A determined female. This messy beginning to her marriage would work itself out. It simply had to, and she would accept nothing less than tranquility along with a dose of happiness in her life.

Bolstered by her determination not to be so easily discouraged, Dorothea invited Mrs. Simpson to take tea with her. They settled into the private salon reserved for the lady of the house, nibbling on crustless sandwiches and sipping strong, hot tea. It was the first meal since her wedding ceremony that Dorothea actually tasted.

"If I may be so bold as to ask, is there a Mr. Simpson?" Dorothea inquired, knowing the title of missus was often used as a courtesy with a housekeeper.

"Oh, yes, my lady. I was married for thirty years. Mr. Simpson died of the fever back in '07."

"I am sorry for your loss." Dorothea cleared her throat. "Though I confess to being interested in hearing any wisdom you would care to impart on coping with a husband."

The housekeeper looked startled and Dorothea knew she had blundered. Badly. The nobility did not share confidences with their servants. She tried a dismissing smile, hoping to drop the matter, but Mrs. Simpson surprised her by speaking.

"There is no simple answer when it comes to men. Husbands or otherwise." Mrs. Simpson smiled fondly. "But I can tell you a bit about Lord Atwood. I was here when he was growing up. You couldn't find a more thoughtful, considerate boy if you tried. He was always kind to everyone, even the servants, and there are not many aristocrats of any age who show consideration to those they deem inferior."

Dorothea knew that remark was aimed squarely at the duke, a proud and haughty man. Fortunately, his son had not taken on the same superior manner. Her heart gentled when she imagined Carter as a young boy. Mischievous and smiling, always ready for an adventure. "Lord Atwood was an only child?"

"Yes, to his regret. He often expressed the desire for siblings, but it was not to be." Mrs. Simpson took a dainty bite of her sandwich. "Though he would say he wanted a brother, not a sister. I believe having to endure the antics of the Alderton girls, who were spoiled rotten and always demanding the impossible, prompted that attitude. I daresay, one would need to search far and wide to find two bolder little girls. And they grew into a pair of high-spirited, forward-thinking young ladies," she added in a lowered, confiding tone.

"Alderton? As in Lord and Lady Alderton?"

"Yes. They are the estate's nearest neighbors. The families were close friends for many years. For a time there was even talk of Lord Atwood marrying the youngest daughter, but the two families had some sort of falling-out and ceased speaking to each other. They seldom meet now, and only if it is an event that involves the entire neighborhood."

"Hmm. I wonder what could have caused such a rift?"

Mrs. Simpson shrugged and shifted on her chair. "The gossips have speculated for years, but no firm truth has ever been revealed. Some say it was a dispute over the property lines, while others contend it was Lord Alderton's failure to honor a gambling debt."

Dorothea lifted the heavy porcelain teapot and poured them each a second cup of tea. She remembered the dinner when she had been introduced to the duke and his disdainful remarks about Lord Alderton along with his gleeful delight in hearing the story of Alderton's embarrassment when his corset strings had snapped during the ball. The reason for it might not been well known, but clearly bad blood between the two families existed. She tucked that piece of information in the back of her mind, theorizing it might come in handy someday.

"I suppose I shall learn how to manage my new husband on my own, but I know I will never master the running of this household without your able, expert assistance."

There was a sound of jingling keys as Mrs. Simpson leaned forward. Her smile was broad and genuine. "I am happy to serve. I know we shall get on famously together, my lady."

The footman arrived to clear their tea, and Mrs. Simpson left to attend to her duties. In quick succession, Dorothea reviewed and discarded what she would now do with herself. Writing letters to her sister, or even Lady Meredith, would be torturous, for she had no notion of what to say. A nap might be a good idea, since she had slept so poorly the previous night, but her mind and body were too restless for sleep.

She could not visit the neighbors, since she did not know them, nor pay a call on the vicar or the tenants without her husband accompanying her for the same reason. They had passed a prosperous-looking village on the way from Town yesterday, but Dorothea was not in the mood to shop. Nor did she have any coin on her person, though she imagined any purchases could easily be charged to her husband.

She settled on taking a leisurely stroll of the formal gardens. Only the early spring flowers had fully bloomed, but their fragrance and color were a soothing balm to Dorothea's mood. She noted with an amused smile that the flowers in one particular bed were the exact yellow shade of her muslin afternoon gown.

It was new, as were nearly all the clothes she had brought with her, a flattering design boasting a low bodice, high waist, and puff sleeves. She especially liked the embroidered detail of tiny leaves in a vibrant shade of green around the neckline and hem. When Dorothea stood in the dressmaker's shop having the garment fitted, Lady Meredith remarked that Lord Atwood would not be able to take his eyes off her when she was wearing the garment.

Yet that had hardly been the case when he had seen her in it earlier today. Carter had barely noticed the gown, except to imply how quickly he wanted it stripped from her body.

Dorothea turned a corner and there he stood, as if her thoughts had conjured him. He was dressed for riding, the polish on his knee-high leather boots gleaming in the sunshine. Her initial inclination was to turn and run the other way, but that smacked too much of cowardice. Instead, she plunged ahead, though she kept her gaze carefully focused on the gravel pathway.

"Lady Atwood." He bowed.

"My lord." She returned the formal greeting, punctuating it with a low, deep curtsy that brought a deep wrinkled frown to Carter's brow.

For some reason, that pleased her.

"Are you having a pleasant day?" he asked.

"Delightful. And you?"

"I've been riding, seeing to the condition of the larger planting fields and talking with some of my tenants."

She blinked in confusion. "I had no idea you took such an active role in the running of your estate."

"You never asked," he shot back.

She refused to take offense at his tone. No matter what, they would speak civilly to each other. "Mrs. Simpson has shown me the entire house, from the attic room to the cellar larder. It was all in first-rate order. I must commend you, my lord, on the dedication and diligence of your staff."

"Carter," he said forcefully.

Dorothea creased her forehead, hoping to appear deep in thought. Then she smiled. "And how did you find your lands? In as good repair as the house, I hope?"

One side of his lip twitched. "All is in excellent condition. My staff and tenants take pride in their work." He lowered his head. "And I do pay them well, too."

Dorothea grinned, the tension inside her easing at his lighthearted manner. "'Tis a very wise decision. I suggest you continue with the practice. From what I've heard, you can easily afford it."

He gave her a crooked smile in return. "In addition to my tenants, I also happened across a few of our neighbors. I was besieged by no less than five invitations from the local gentry. Everyone is very anxious to meet you."

Dorothea was surprised. "I thought everyone would be in Town at this time of year."

"Spending the Season in London is a costly venture, as you know. Only those with daughters to marry or sons looking for adventure or a bride make the journey into Town."

A few short months ago she was one of those searching females. Was that comment meant to be a jibe at her recent situation? No, she insisted silently, shaking her head. She would not read insult where none was given. Carter was not so petty.

"I would not want to shirk my obligations to the local society by avoiding them completely," she replied.

As you are shirking your duty to your husband? He did not speak the words, but Dorothea swore she could hear them loud and clear.

"We are newly wed," he said. "It should not cause great offense if we decline these social invitations."

"All of them?"

His expression became serious. "Perhaps it would be politic to accept one. Tea with Mrs. Snidely, I think. She is a born gossip who will delight in broadcasting her opinions about you to the neighborhood, along with everything she can learn about us."

Everything? Dorothea blanched. How amazingly humiliating. But their marital discord would be kept a secret. It was the way of the nobility. Dragging her eyes away from his, she said, "I'll leave it to your judgment to decide about the invitations."

"Very good."

She clasped her hands firmly in front of her. The silence between them hung heavy. Dorothea could see the muscle in his jaw flexing as he clenched and unclenched his teeth. Such a handsome, strong jaw.

"Since Mrs. Simpson has already shown you the house, I could take you on a tour of the estate." He hesitated. "I assume you ride?"

"Hmm." The noncommittal answer seemed safest. She did ride, though not very well and generally at a snail's pace. One glance at her husband's strong thighs had Dorothea assuming his skill far exceeded hers. He would not be impressed when he saw her on a horse.

"I need to change into my riding habit," she mentioned, hoping that would put him off the idea. Men hated to be kept waiting while a woman changed her clothing.

"I'll meet you in the stables when you are ready," he answered. "I need time to consult with my stable master on which mount will be yours when we are in residence."

Neatly trapped, Dorothea had no choice but to agree. She took as long a time as she dared to change, then presented herself at the stables. The pleasant scent of horses and leather surrounded her the moment she entered. Not surprisingly, the stables were kept in pristine condition. Carter introduced her to Jack Kenny, the stable master. Middle-aged, with a trim build and a weather-beaten complexion, he was a short man who smiled often.

At his command, one of the younger grooms led a horse from the stall to the mounting block. Dorothea's heart sank. The horse looked enormous. Tall, sleek, and prancing with energy. He seemed the kind of horse that would excel at leading a cavalry charge. She knew without a doubt if she tried riding him, she'd fall on her backside before they left the courtyard.

"What is his name?" she asked the groom as he put a sidesaddle on the horse's back and began to cinch the straps.

"El Diablo, my lady."

The devil? Carter had chosen a devil horse for her to ride? Obviously he expected her to be a dashing, hell-bent rider. He probably imagined them charging across the fields together, laughing, racing, jumping streams, fences, and hedges. Her spirits plummeted further. Was this yet another thing she would fail at so dismally as his wife?

"If you prefer, you can ride with me," Carter offered.

Dorothea's head snapped up, suspicions forming in her mind. One gaze at his face and she knew the truth. His innocent expression did not fool her for an instant. She would bet her last farthing that the stables were filled with much gentler, far more appropriate mounts for her to ride.

"Your horse hardly looks tame," she retorted, eyeing the great black beast as he snorted and pranced about the stable yard, presenting a great challenge to the strong groom who was holding his reins.

"Caesar is a well-trained brute," Carter responded with a fond tone. "Large enough to easily carry us both on a leisurely ride."

"He seems all spirit and temper," she said, unsure how

she felt at Carter's attempt to manipulate her. It was a relief not to have to try to prove her equestrian skills, since they were so limited, and yet she had some pride.

"Under the right conditions, Caesar is as gentle as a lamb." Carter's eyes measured her. "Come and say hello to him."

Dorothea approached the horse. He looked at her curiously, but stayed quietly in place. She reached out and slowly stroked his neck. He reared his head, swished his tail, and blew through his nose. She turned back to El Diablo. Pride or no pride, the choice was clear.

"I suppose I shall try my luck with you on Caesar."

The charming smile Carter bestowed upon her reached his eyes. She was still fighting to regain her breath when he put his hands on her waist and easily lifted her onto the front of his saddle. Then he swung up behind her and placed one arm tightly around her midriff. "Is this better?"

"It is, as you well know," she answered primly.

He bent his head and touched his lips to her ear. "At least give me credit for discovering a way to hold you in my arms."

She was trying to think of a snappy retort when he tightened the circle of his embrace, forcing her back against his front. She was now surrounded by his muscular arms, his strong, hard body at her back. A wave of pleasure washed over her, and Dorothea felt a sense of security unlike anything she had ever known. It warmed her body, but also her heart.

All thoughts of being prim and distant flew out of her head. She took a deep breath and sank deeper into the curve of his warm strength. She settled her shoulders against his chest and tucked her gloved hands around his forearm.

"Ready?"

She could hear the amusement in his voice. Turning, she glanced at him over her shoulder. "Not too fast, please. I should hate to topple off and drag you down with me."

A teasing light danced in the depths of his eyes. "I have not fallen off a horse since I was seven years old. But I assure you, dear wife, if something does go amiss, I will endeavor to make certain that I take the full brunt of the impact and have you land on top of me."

Dorothea squeezed the hard, solid strength of arm. "You are hardly a soft cushion, my lord."

He shifted behind her, adjusting his position so that her hips nestled tightly against his thighs. Dorothea stiffened, but then she forced herself to relax and let the sensations flow around her. They set off at a brisk pace.

The warmth and strength of Carter's body pressing against hers coupled with the undulating motion of the horse mimicked far too well the rhythm of making love. A memory that might have agitated and distressed her, but instead it slowly began to awaken her desire.

She heard Carter's breathing change, turning deep and quick. Wicked, sensual thoughts formed in her mind. For an instant she allowed herself to consider the ridiculous impulse that swirled in her head—was it possible to make love while riding on a horse?

"Pardon?"

His breathless voice startled her and her entire body went rigid. *Saints above, did I speak those thoughts aloud?*

"The lake," Dorothea squeaked, knowing she must sound like a half-wit. "'Tis very pretty."

"Not just pretty, but functional." She felt his breath caress her cheek. "It's stocked with fish."

Dorothea ran her hand self-consciously across the skirt of her riding habit. Her legs felt warm and heavy and she knew if she did not regain control of herself quickly, she was going to regret it.

"Do you like to fish?" It was hardly an interesting topic, but it provided a diversion from her physical dilemma.

"'Tis difficult to find the patience for it." He placed a tender kiss on her neck, in the sensitive spot directly behind her ear. "Regretfully, I was never disciplined enough to appreciate the concept of delayed gratification."

Carter lifted his arm and Dorothea panicked, wondering where he was going to place it. She scrambled to think, trying to decide how to react. The kiss had sent pleasant shivers down her spine. He was her husband and she needed to learn to accept his touch without reservation.

Determined to be cooperative, she let her head drop back against his shoulder. And waited, her breath held.

But instead of giving her a teasing caress, Carter waved at the workers in the field, who returned the greeting with enthusiasm. She felt her face heat with embarrassment, along with a flat, disappointed feeling that made no sense at all.

Recovering her emotions, Dorothea sought to concentrate on the surroundings and ignore the physical distraction of her handsome, muscular husband. They rode through fields of grazing cattle and sheep into the deep green meadow. Carter was congenial and charming, pointing out sights of interest, telling her a story or two from his childhood. By the time they returned to the stables a few hours later, Dorothea was smiling and relaxed.

Yet by evening, her fragile sensation of contentment had vanished. At dinner, she struggled to do justice to Cook's sumptuous meal, but her appetite, and nerve, completely deserted her. Carter, she noted with a tinge of annoyance, ate with obvious relish, complimenting each dish. At least she had been successful with the menu, though the lion's share of the credit belonged to Cook, since she had devised it. Dorothea had merely approved the selections.

"Shall we adjourn to the drawing room?"

Dorothea placed her dessert fork on the edge of the plate near her barely eaten slice of cake and gave her husband a weak smile. "If you wish."

He leaned close and his breath fell gently against her hair. "Unless you prefer to retire?"

"To my bedchamber?"

"I believe it is more comfortable than residing in the stables."

She could feel her forced smile begin to tremble. "Alone?"

There was surprise in his eyes at her direct challenge. Clearly he had not expected her to bring up the overshadowing topic that clouded their every interaction. Yet Dorothea simply had to know what was happening. Would he come to her chamber tonight?

"I assume you would prefer your privacy and therefore shall honor your wishes to wait before I return to your bed."

Carter put his arm around her waist, leaned down, and kissed her softly on the lips. Her mouth sagged open before she somehow managed to close it. Kisses were wonderful, marvelous, melting. But they led to other things she was not as eager to embrace. She pulled back, just a fraction, and he obediently released her lips.

"Sleep well, Dorothea. I will see you in the morning."

Then, with a cryptic smile, he turned and walked out of the room.

Carter regretted his words, and actions, the minute he exited the room, for it seemed as though he was leaving all the sparkle and life behind him. But it was better this way.

More than anything, Carter wanted Dorothea to find deep pleasure in their marital bed. He wanted her satisfied, replete, and contented. And he knew that would take time.

A single look at her tonight in her gauzy gold silk evening gown had left him breathless. The bodice was so low that one small tug would have exposed her nipples. Her glorious pink nipples that tasted like the sweetest nectar.

He had spent the majority of dinner with a rock-hard erection, shoveling food he barely tasted into his mouth as if that would somehow quench his hunger. Naturally it had not. The only thing that would appease his appetite was a naked, panting, eager wife, writhing in his bed.

He was terribly frustrated, in body as well as mind, but the commitment had been made, the course set. Carter cleared his throat, admonishing himself to stop this self-inflicted torture. Restraint was the order of the day. They had made progress today, and the last thing Carter wanted was to jeopardize this promising start. He could hardly credit that after their disastrous morning conversation they were able to banter and tease, even relax for a time together on their afternoon ride.

She was not a naturally cold woman; there was fire and passion inside her, and he was determined to have an ardent, receptive woman in his bed. Since she had already experienced intercourse, and been unimpressed with it, a slow seduction was needed.

He could see that limited physical contact was already heightening her interest. A stolen kiss, a single heated caress, an occasional brush of his fingertips on her exposed flesh left Dorothea breathless and intrigued. Soon her awareness of him would be so excruciating she would come apart at the very idea of being near him. And then they would both burst into flames.

* * *

Another restless night and Dorothea was up at dawn, an occurrence that would have shocked her sisters and anyone else who knew how she relished her morning sleep. She expected a solitary breakfast, but Carter surprised her by awaiting her in the morning room. He drank a second cup of coffee while she ate her toast.

They conversed pleasantly, discussing their plans for the day, and Dorothea agreed to another afternoon ride. When she was finished with her meal, he signaled one of the footmen, and the servant soon returned with a large basket. Placing it on the table, Carter slid it slowly in front of her.

"For you."

Feeling petty because her first reaction was suspicion, Dorothea carefully lifted the wicker lid. Two soulful brown eyes set into a ball of fluffy golden fur stared up at her. At her smile, the little creature began wagging his tail madly, along with the majority of his hindquarters.

"Oh, my!" Dorothea exclaimed, picking up the squirming puppy and tucking him beneath her chin. "He's adorable. Is he really meant for me?"

Carter smiled. "We have a great many dogs about the estate, but I thought you would enjoy having a companion that was exclusively your own."

"Oh, Carter, he is a delight. Thank you."

Carter reached over to stroke behind the dog's ears. "He should grow to a respectable size, as any worthwhile dog should. One thing I can't abide is a woman carrying a dog about and treating it like an infant."

"You mean like the Dowager Countess Hastings?" Dorothea held the puppy between her two outstretched hands, then brought him close enough so their noses were touching. The animal went into near spasms of joy as he began licking her face.

Carter released a sigh of annoyance. "I swear, the dowager stuffs her pet with treats until the poor creature is so fat he can barely stand."

"I suppose that is why her footman carries him about on a pillow."

"A red velvet pillow," Carter corrected with a snort of disgust. "I was at a picnic one afternoon and the dowager nearly swallowed her tongue in apoplexy when her servant brought the pug to her on a plain, ordinary white pillow."

"I vow I shall never do anything so ridiculous. Anyway, it looks as though my darling puppy will not fit on a pillow for more than a month or two at most."

"Especially if you keep feeding him."

Ignoring his words, Dorothea continued to offer the puppy the remaining scraps of egg from Carter's plate as she cuddled him. When the meal was finished, the animal licked her hand in gratitude. He next gave a huge yawn, curled himself in a tight ball against her chest, and promptly fell asleep. Smiling, Dorothea settled him back inside his cozy basket.

"I know what you are tying to do," she said to Carter as she nestled the blanket around the dog. "And in all fairness, I should tell you that it will not work."

"I'm sure I don't understand what you mean."

A faint smiled played on her lips. "You know perfectly well what I mean. My new puppy is a bribe. Creative and heartfelt, I'll grant you that, but a bribe nevertheless."

"A bribe for what? Your affection? Strange, I thought I already had your regard. Or was I mistaken?"

"Of course not. You know that I care for you. I would not have married you if it were otherwise."

"Then what do you mean?"

"He is a bribe to bring me into your bed."

Carter tossed a puzzled glance down at the basket. "Why would that be necessary? You are my wife, my property. You have already told me, in no uncertain terms, that you will do your wifely duty. Hence I have no need to waste my money on a sure thing."

His voice turned husky. "I can command you now to lie on your back and spread your legs. Or turn you onto your hands and knees so I may take you from behind, thrusting deep inside as your inner muscles cling to me, sheathe me in their warmth and wetness."

Dorothea stiffened at the image. She looked into his eyes, heavy-lidded and burning, and lost her ability to speak.

His voice deepened to a low, seductive tone. "Remember how it felt to have my hands on you? My mouth, my tongue? Your hips arching to meet my touch, your body trembling with release?"

Dorothea could feel the muscles in her throat contract, but she didn't speak, didn't utter a sound. The torrid images conjured in her mind by Carter's passionate words left her speechless. She feigned an indignant expression, yet doubted her husband was fooled.

"Lady Atwood, I was wondering—oh, I do beg your pardon." Mrs. Simpson's steady voice, tinged with embarrassment, came from the doorway. "I'll return later."

"There's no need, Mrs. Simpson," Dorothea said in a rush. "Lord Atwood was just leaving."

Carter's eyes flared a deep molten blue. Half expecting him to shout at Mrs. Simpson to disappear, Dorothea waited, unsure what she preferred—for him to respect her wishes and depart, or to get her alone and give in to the smoldering desire he was stirring between them.

"Yes, do come in," Carter finally intoned. "I want Lady

Atwood to complete all her household duties this morning so she may devote her undivided attention to me for the remainder of the day."

Then with an irresistible smile tugging at his lips, he favored Dorothea with an elegant bow and quit the room.

Chapter Thirteen

Carter knew he was making progress. Not as far nor as fast as he would have preferred, but progress nonetheless. He was starting to know his wife, beginning to learn her likes and dislikes, to understand how her mind worked. Well, as much as any man could understand the intricacies of a female mind.

Dorothea hadn't cringed at his intimate words yesterday morning. True, she had tightened her jaw and been resolute in her bearing, but she had stood and listened to every word. Stood and shivered and been intrigued by the erotic pictures he had painted in her mind. With time, with patience, with the right approach to seduction, Carter firmly believed he could turn Dorothea into a sensual, exciting woman, who would crave rather than cringe from his touch.

Sooner would be better than later, he acknowledged with a wry grin. The sexual ache that was curled so tightly inside his body was a constant companion, and not a welcome one. But it was necessary to undergo this torture to achieve the ultimate prize, and he was committed to making the sacrifice.

Today he was taking Dorothea into the village to visit the shops. He could tell she was surprised at the suggestion, but pleased, too. After all, what female did not noticeably brighten at the prospect of shopping?

It was a beautiful, sunny day. The sky was a deep azure blue; the few clouds that dared to appear on the horizon were puffy white balls that floated lazily across the sky. Forsaking the large, cumbersome coach, they drove alone into the village, cozily seated next to each other in Carter's open curricle.

He identified a few landmarks along the way, but for the majority of the journey they were silent. But it was a good silence, a comfortable silence. Carter's spirits lifted. Another sign of the progress they had achieved in their relationship.

Though it was not market day, the village streets were bustling with activity. They received many curious stares, and Carter smiled and doffed his hat to those souls brave enough to meet his gaze.

"Where shall we begin?" he asked Dorothea after he had secured the carriage horses and assisted her out.

"The millinery shop," she replied. "Mrs. Simpson told me that the widow Jenkins has been struggling lately to pay her bills. I'm sure our patronage will be appreciated."

The bell placed strategically on the door tinkled merrily as they went inside. A middle-aged woman hurried forward from the back of the shop, pulling up short when she caught sight of her patrons. Standing still as a post, her eyes bulging, her mouth open, the woman stared at them in a speechless trance.

"Mrs. Jenkins?" Dorothea said softly.

Visibly shaking off her stupor, the woman took a step toward them. "Yes? Hello. Or rather good afternoon."

"Good afternoon. I am Lord Atwood and this is Lady

Atwood." Carter smiled. The shopkeeper continued to stare. Well, it was no wonder the woman had trouble paying her bills. She had no skill at all in dealing with customers.

"Our housekeeper, Mrs. Simpson, told us about your lovely shop," Dorothea said as she slipped to Carter's side. "I can see she was not exaggerating the quality and selection of bonnets available."

"Oh, my lady." Mrs. Jenkins fairly gushed as she curtsied very grandly. "I am so honored to have you frequent my humble little establishment."

"We are most happy to be here, are we not, my lord?"

"Delighted."

Carter hardly knew where to look. There were hats and ribbons, gloves, and other feminine fripperies artfully displayed on and behind the counters. Far too much lace and feathers and silk for his tastes. Now, if there had been some sensual, female undergarments in view he might have taken more of an interest.

Dorothea, however, was clearly in her element. At Mrs. Jenkins's urging, she took a seat in front of a cheval mirror. The only other empty chair was a dainty, gilded piece. Carter eyed it with suspicion, doubting it would be comfortable and concerned it would not hold his weight. Wisely, he elected to stand.

"You have a most unusual selection of hats, Mrs. Jenkins," Dorothea proclaimed. "Do you design them all yourself?"

"I most certainly do. After consulting all the latest fashion plates, of course. If I may?"

Mrs. Jenkins turned to her right and lifted a concoction off the counter that resembled a fruit basket. Carter saw Dorothea's eyes widen momentarily in true alarm, but she quickly recovered. Casting a broad smile at the giddy Mrs. Jenkins, Dorothea obligingly removed the simple, elegant hat she wore and placed the fruit monstrosity on her head.

"Ahh." Mrs. Jenkins's sigh of excitement was so loud it could easily be heard the length and breadth of the street. "It looks perfect on you. Even more beautiful than I envisioned. Don't you agree, my lord?"

Carter managed to hold back his grunt of laughter. He was no expert of fashion, but even he knew the bonnet was a horror. "Everything my wife wears looks beautiful, Mrs. Jenkins."

"Oh, my." Mrs. Jenkins began fanning her hand in front of her face. "Never in my wildest dreams would I have believed that one of my modest creations would be worn by such an elegant, important lady. It fairly takes my breath away."

The stricken look returned to Dorothea's eyes. She swiveled around to face him. The color was high in her cheeks, matching the shade of a cluster of silk cherries that hung over her left brow. "Do you think I should purchase it, my lord?"

"I insist." He grinned devilishly. "That one and at least one more."

"I agree." Dorothea turned back toward the mirror, pressing her hand to her abdomen as if searching for strength. "However, I believe this bonnet will be the perfect gift for my sister, Gwendolyn."

Mrs. Jenkins's face fell. "Your sister?"

"She is married to Mr. Jason Barrington. Her father-in-law is the Earl of Stafford. Dear Gwen is not out in society these days because she is expecting a happy event at any time. But she will soon return to the social whirl of Town. I just know when she sees this hat her spirits will be greatly lifted."

Mrs. Jenkins's eyes warmed. "I am overwhelmed at

the thought of having another London lady of quality wearing my creations. But we now must find something extraordinary for you, Lady Atwood."

"This one matches your gown," Carter said, unable to resist an overwrought, fussy bonnet, which to his eye resembled an abandoned bird's nest.

"You are right, my lord. The colors are nearly the exact shade as the marchioness's walking dress!" Mrs. Jenkins exclaimed.

"Ah, true serendipity," he replied with a grin as the blush of color drained from Dorothea's cheeks.

Mrs. Jenkins arranged the hat on Dorothea's head. It was difficult to believe, but the bonnet looked even worse than when it was displayed on the counter.

"The colors do blend well with my ensemble," Dorothea said weakly.

Carter's mouth went slack. He had been joking, teasing her. From what he had noticed of her wardrobe, his wife preferred, simple, elegant lines on her clothing and a restrained hand on the extra ribbons, flounces, and embroidery. Was she truly going to forsake her own sense of style and good taste just to aid Mrs. Jenkins?

Carter received his answer ten minutes later as they left the shop and strolled down the street.

"I can feel your laughter, my lord," Dorothea said in a steady voice.

"I beg to differ, my dear. I am masterfully keeping my emotions under control, and given your current appearance that is a Herculean task."

Dorothea shrugged. "There are worse things in the world than walking down the street wearing a nest fit for birds on one's head."

"True," he replied, trying to bite back his grin without

much success. "You could be balancing a basket of fruit instead."

"With birds pecking at it." Dorothea giggled. She bent over slightly with laughter, then straightened as the concoction on her head began to shift. "I cannot wait to give Gwendolyn her gift. It truly will lift her spirits, of that I have no doubt."

Carter laughed again, but a sobering thought brought on a more serious concern. "Perhaps it is a greater cruelty to give Mrs. Jenkins false hope by purchasing and wearing her bonnets. Her talent for making hats seems limited at best."

Dorothea shook her head. Carter watched in amusement as the nest dipped to one side, then righted itself in the center of her head. "Mrs. Jenkins's bonnets are well constructed, fashioned from good quality materials. Unfortunately, she has a very heavy hand with the fripperies and a somewhat vivid imagination. It is certainly not to my taste, but I can think of several women in London who would find these hats divine, especially if they believed them to be the height of fashion."

"Even I know that fashion is not set in this sleepy little village."

She smiled, and Carter was struck by how truly beautiful she looked. Even wearing that ridiculous bonnet.

"All Mrs. Jenkins needs to succeed is for the women in the area to embrace her designs. I believe my patronage will go far in making that happen."

Quite the understatement, he was certain. But at what cost? "My dear, dare I point out that your slender neck will surely collapse if you continue to wear these monstrosities upon your head."

She arched a brow, but there was a twinkle in her eyes. "I can assure you this is the first and last time you will see me wearing such a voluminous hat. I have commissioned the making of another bonnet from Mrs. Jenkins and plan to gently guide her hand away from all the excessive ribbons, bows, feathers, and such. I feel confident that I can convince her to restrain her more exuberant designs in order to appeal to a broader base of customers, thus ensuring her financial success."

"And in the meantime?"

Dorothea sighed. "In the meantime, I shall wear this bonnet to advertise my support of her endeavors."

Carter leaned close and lowered his voice to a whisper. "I could easily contrive to have the hat blow off on the carriage ride home where it would forever be lost in the Ravenswood forest," he suggested.

"Don't tempt me," Dorothea responded with a wry grin. "Ah, now here is the confectioner's shop. I have a long list of sweets I wish to buy."

Mr. Harper was a pleasant man, with an easy smile. He enthusiastically welcomed them into the store, causing Carter a momentary flash of guilt. These were his lands, his people, his responsibility. Everyone's happy, surprised greeting brought home the fact that he visited the estate far too seldom.

Vowing that too would change now that he was married, Carter took his time examining Mr. Harper's wares, adding several of his own selections to Dorothea's long list. She was gracious and complimentary, and Mr. Harper beamed under the attention, though Carter was certain they had Mrs. Jenkins's appalling hat to thank for the extra ounces of sweets they were given. It was clear that poor Mr. Harper could not fully concentrate on the task of measuring as he was mesmerized by the bobbing, swaying contraption that was Dorothea's bonnet.

They visited several more shops, and in each Dorothea

displayed the same gracious demeanor, which soon endeared her to one and all. She was all smiles when they returned to Ravenswood, though she excused herself to attend to her correspondence and then confessed she might even indulge in a short nap before dinner.

Carter kissed her hand in what he believed to be a husbandly fashion as she left him. He watched her hungrily as she slipped away, climbing the stairs to her chambers, and looked forward to the day, very soon he hoped, when they would be taking that nap together.

"Fishing?" Dorothea glanced at the pole Carter carried with a dubious eye. "Actually, I've never been fishing."

"And you call yourself a country girl? For shame!"

"This country girl prefers indoor activities," she proclaimed.

"But it's a beautiful day. 'Tis a crime to waste the sunshine. Come, I'll teach you."

She could see the sparkle in his eyes, the challenge in his face. Goodness, his charm was nearly irresistible, as he damn well knew.

"Aren't there worms involved?" she asked with a shudder.

"Very small ones." She rolled her eyes, and he hastily added, "I will bait your hook and remove your fish when they are caught."

Hmm. Why was he so very keen on the outing? Normally, Dorothea would suspect an ulterior motive, specifically the opportunity for seduction, but honestly, how would that be possible with dirty worms and smelly fish?

She considered him for a long moment, trying in vain to decipher his reason. "I will join you, but only if we fish from shore," she finally said. "I don't particularly like small boats and I cannot swim."

"I know all the prime spots from shore."

"May my new puppy come along?"

Carter grimaced. "I worry he might wander off, or even worse, fall into the lake. There is nothing more unpleasant than the aroma of a wet dog."

"All right, he'll stay behind this time," Dorothea reluctantly agreed. "I just need to fetch my bonnet and we can be off."

He grabbed her hand before she could leave, his expression comically pained. "I beg of you to wear one from London, please. Mrs. Jenkins's hat will most assuredly scare away the fish."

"And attract the birds. Yes, I know. A London bonnet it will be."

She was fairly skipping by the time she joined him in the south garden as the prospect of spending time with him put her in a happy mood. It was a pleasant walk to the lake.

"Where do we sit?" Dorothea asked.

"Here, on the rocks." His arm swept outward to indicate the various boulders on one side of the lake.

"They are rather dirty," Dorothea remarked, glancing down at her lovely pale green day gown.

Carter released an exaggerated sigh. "If I knew you were going to be such a girl about this, madam, I would never have invited you along."

"Serves you right," she retorted with a teasing glance. "I should insist that you return to the manor and fetch a pillow for me to sit upon."

"A silk one?"

"A silk brocade pillow," she answered, trying to keep the humor from her face.

"I will not have my expensive pillows tossed about in the dirt, madam. Especially when you have sufficient natural padding." He grinned. "Instead, I will sacrifice my own clothing."

Carter gallantly removed his jacket and put it on the flattest section of a large rock. Dorothea daintily sat on it, modestly pulling her skirts down to cover her calf. Darn, he was fun to spar with, especially when he was relaxed and smiling.

It was a sunny afternoon. After a while, Carter rolled up his shirtsleeves. The sight of those tan, muscular arms did strange things to her stomach. Swallowing hard, she glanced outward, concentrating on her fishing line and pole.

Despite his claims that it was a well-stocked lake, they caught no fish. Dorothea presumed it was their quiet conversation that kept the fish at bay. He told her of his childhood and she shared a few stories about her sisters. Throughout the afternoon he was quick to smile and laugh, casual about keeping her physically close to him.

On the way back to the manor, Carter solicitously held her elbow or her gloved hand each time they came to a dip in the path. It was not an overtly sexual touch, but there was an edge of possession in the gesture that she found oddly thrilling.

It was obvious that he was allowing her the time to make the decision about their physical relationship and Dorothea was grateful. She was also practical. A man as virile as Carter would not wait forever for a reluctant wife to resume her marital duties.

It had been a good few days. They had spent considerable time together, and each day Carter could practically see another layer of his wife's resistance melt away. If he continued to play it right, it wouldn't be long before she was sharing his bed. And enjoying it.

In his quest to win Dorothea's trust and regard, Carter had sought to learn her daily routine. He knew that she took a long, leisurely bath nearly every evening before dinner, profusely thanking the staff for carrying up the many buckets of hot water necessary for her to enjoy this sensual indulgence.

He also knew she took her bath alone, without her maid in the room. It was here Carter prepared to make his next move, for the opportunity to continue his seduction was too good to miss.

He waited in his chambers until he heard her maid leave. Moving quietly through their shared private sitting room, he pressed his ear to Dorothea's bedchamber door. A smile lit his face at the sound of a splash. Slowly he turned the latch on the door.

The tub faced the fireplace, leaving her back toward him. She was humming, and the melodic noise, coupled with her attention to her bath, made it simple for him to enter the room undetected.

Tendrils of steam rose from the water, surrounding her in an exotic fog. From this angle he could see the slope of her elegant shoulders, the curve of her neck, the sweep of her naked arms as she lifted them from the water to wash herself.

She was so enticing, Carter had to swallow back a groan of appreciation. But he could not as easily control the other parts of his anatomy. Worried that he would distress her if she saw the obscene bulge in his breeches, he shifted his position and stood behind a padded chair, which shielded the lower half of his body.

Then he cleared his throat. Loudly.

Her head whipped around so fast he winced, fearing she might have injured herself.

"Carter! My goodness, what are you doing here?"

"You said to me the other day that you wanted to give me a small token. I have thought on it for some time and have at last decided what it will be."

"You want to take a bath with me?" Her voice was a squeak of feminine horror. Not a promising start.

"That would be a delight beyond measure, my dear. However, all I wish to do is watch you." He walked out from behind the chair and brought himself next to the tub. "And perhaps soap your back?"

"That's perverted."

"To be clean? I think not."

"You know very well what I mean, Carter."

He gazed at her. "My gift to you is the bath. Your gift to me is allowing me the pleasure of watching you in it."

"Do all your gifts come with conditions?"

"Invariably."

Her eyebrows drew together as she searched his face, watching closely as if weighing his words. They were a kind of truth. In his experience, gifts were rarely given without the expectation of some sort of return.

He knelt on the rug. Reaching for her hand so tightly gripping the edge of the tub, he lightly caressed her fingers. "You know very well that I shall leave if you insist, but I think it would better if I stayed."

"Better for whom?"

"Both of us. But mainly for you." He continued to gently rub her knuckles until he heard her exhale a long, slow breath.

"You may only stay a short time. The bath is supposed to help me relax."

"And so it will."

"Not with you standing there glowering at me," she grumbled.

He said nothing in response, merely sat back on his haunches and waited. She sat so motionless there was not a single ripple in the water. Then suddenly she moved, with vigor and purpose, as if she had firmly decided she would not allow him to ruin her bath.

Carter smiled at her tenacity. What made her different from other women? The newness of their relationship, the fact he had to work so hard to win her trust, to get his way? And she was his wife! The one female above all others he had a right to claim.

But Carter had discovered he did not want a woman who would merely perform her marital duty. He wanted an eager, willing, and passionate woman in his bed, and he knew Dorothea could be that woman.

A section of her golden hair had fallen from the pile atop her head. It waved around the side of her face, giving her a sexy, disheveled look. He longed to trail his fingers through it, but dared not be too forward lest she throw him out of the room.

In her agitation, she had forgotten to keep the washcloth plastered protectively across her breast. It bobbed and floated merrily in the center of the tub. Carter watched it for a moment before Dorothea swooped it up and wrung it out. There were now no coverings in her bath. The clear water gave him a delectable view of the honey-colored curls between her firm, long legs. He shifted against the tightening in his breeches. Perhaps this had not been such an inspired idea.

"May I beg a kiss?" he asked.

"A kiss?"

Still kneeling, he leaned forward and gently sucked the warm, moist skin on her neck. She lifted her head instinctively and he moved his lips up her throat to her ear-lobe. Her breathing quickened and then a low whimper escaped. He nearly climaxed at the sensual sound.

"Just one kiss, my sweet," he intoned hoarsely. "One small kiss."

She moaned and turned her lips toward his. He cradled her head in his hands as his lips playfully nipped over hers and then Carter dipped his tongue into Dorothea's mouth.

She moaned again, wrapping her fingers around his wrists, holding him close. Carter held her tightly, fighting for control, fighting to keep to his original plan of a slow seduction. A plan that seemed completely idiotic at the moment.

With great reluctance, Carter broke the kiss and stared down at his wife. Her eyes were closed, her chest rising and falling in a quick cadence. He could see the telltale flush of her arousal and then suddenly her eyes opened wide. She met his gaze and for a long moment considering him in silence, a silence that spoke to him, that let him know she was not yet ready.

Carter reached out and trailed a fingertip slowly along the tip of her nose. "I'll see you at dinner. Enjoy the remainder of your bath."

Shutting down his mind, ignoring the screaming demands of his overheated body, Carter swiftly left the room. The pace of his steps increased as he reached the end of the hallway and began trotting down the stairs, taking the treads two at a time. He hit the foyer and was nearly sprinting toward the front door when the butler called out.

"My lord, where are you going? Shall I call for your horse or a carriage?"

"It's not necessary, Cortland. I can reach the lake under my own power."

"The lake, my lord?"

"Yes. I wish to go swimming."

"But my lord, 'tis freezing this time of year."

"That's the point," Carter answered, his mouth twisting into a grim line.

A thick covering of clouds was fast approaching from the east. Dorothea's nose wrinkled with regret as she glanced up at the gray sky. She had planned what she thought was the perfect mid-morning outing, but it appeared the weather had other ideas. Drat!

"I fear my little surprise will be ruined, Cortland," she said as the butler stood beside her. "The rain seems imminent."

"So it does, my lady. But might I suggest an alternative?"

"Please do."

An hour later, Carter was summoned to the solarium. He stood taking in her surprise, his arms folded. She watched closely for his reaction, but could tell little of his feelings.

"Is it silly?" she asked.

"No, 'tis charming. An indoor picnic."

He moved closer and her pulses fluttered. The open space the servants had created among the tall trees and flowering pots suddenly seemed very small.

"You've done so many kind things for me, I wanted to do something to please you," she said. "Mrs. Simpson mentioned how much you enjoyed picnics when you were a lad."

"I did." He paused and looked around. "Though I remember none quite like this one."

"The rain decreed a change in my plans."

"I had no idea you were so clever."

"I'm not. It was really Cortland's idea. He arranged for

everything." She turned her head at the sudden noise by the potted ornamental palms. "I've invited someone else along. I hope you don't mind."

At the sound of her voice, the third member of their picnic scampered forward, a chubby, round bundle of fur. The puppy paused, nearly flipping himself over as he began eagerly sniffing the large basket covered with a linen cloth set in the center of their picnic blanket.

"I thought we agreed he was going to be an outside dog," Carter remarked wryly.

"He will be," Dorothea said confidently. "But he is far too young and small to be relegated to the kennels."

She scooped the puppy up in her arms and held him tightly to her breast. He squirmed in ecstasy, his entire body shaking with joy, his pink tongue darting out eagerly to lick her face.

"Have you chosen his name?" Carter asked.

They strolled over to the picnic blanket and sat down. Dorothea released the puppy, which instantly returned its attention to the wicker basket. "I've decided to call him Lancelot, after the legendary knight."

"A noble name."

"I have great hopes he will grow into it," Dorothea proclaimed.

She removed the cloth from the basket, pleased to hear Carter voice his delight as the contents were revealed. She piled his china plate high with cold roast beef, roasted chicken, crisp bread, sharp cheese, and fruit, then made a smaller serving of the same items for herself.

They ate heartily, with Dorothea tossing an occasional tidbit to the continually begging puppy. Finally realizing he would get no more treats, Lancelot began exploring his surroundings and was soon climbing over Carter's legs.

"Your dog is attempting to chew the leather tassels on my boots."

"Oh, gracious, isn't he a clever boy." Dorothea reached for the puppy, which instantly rolled onto its back. Unable to resist, she vigorously rubbed his plump, round tummy. Lancelot's pink tongue lolled to the side, and his breath exhaled in short, eager pants.

"You're spoiling him," Carter said mildly, as he took a sip of his wine.

"I'm just being affectionate. All animals deserve attention and love."

"As do all men?"

She observed her husband beneath lowered lashes, then favored him with a saucy wink. "Some more than others, I believe."

"He reminds me a great deal of a dog I had when I was younger. A faithful companion and a good friend."

"Were you a solitary boy?"

"Not especially. I had no siblings to play with, but there were many children on the estate, the son of our gamekeeper, the children of our stable master. My father was usually attending to business and social matters and was therefore unaware of my boyhood associations."

"Would he have disapproved?"

"Heartily." His expression unreadable, Carter took a bite of fruit. "I intend to be far more progressive with my own children."

A flood of warmth invaded Dorothea's stomach at the mention of children. Their children. Good God in heaven. There would be no little ones running about until she was ready and willing to accept him into her bed.

He reached for her, covering his hand over hers. "Children will come in due time."

She shut her eyes. Oh, dear Lord. It was not the children,

but the creating of them, as they both very well knew, that had thrown her into such a panic. "I don't know what you want me to say," she whispered.

"Look at me."

Startled, Dorothea opened her eyes. He rubbed his fingers up and down her arm gently as he lowered his voice. "I can wait. Moments like last night, when you were in the bath and we were both so aroused, so feverish, give me hope."

Her heart melted. He was a good man, a kind man. A devilishly attractive man. What was wrong with her? She should be counting her blessings and trying to figure out how to entice him into her bed, not deny him—and herself—the pleasure.

Nervously lifting her wineglass, she took another sip, only to find it empty. She hastily refilled it. They spoke of their visit with Mrs. Snidely the previous day, an event they both agreed was thoroughly annoying. Despite an underlying thread of sexual awareness, Dorothea was struck by their easy conversation and companionship.

"I must apologize again for my decision to take tea with Mrs. Snidely," Carter said before popping a strawberry into his mouth. "I honestly did not know she was so overbearing. I fear the social coup of being the first to host us went straight to her head and thus strengthened her sense of self-importance."

"An area in which no further encouragement was necessary," Dorothea agreed. "Though it wasn't entirely your fault. I was remiss in my social duties. I should have hosted a tea for all the local ladies, thus eliminating the problem."

"This is my estate. I'm the one who is supposed to know the inhabitants."

"Men are dismal failures in these sorts of matters. I

should have sought Mrs. Simpson's guidance. She is loyal and levelheaded and would have guided me on the correct path. A lesson learned. For both of us, my lord."

Dorothea reached for the wine bottle, surprised to discover the bottle was empty. With a puzzled shrug she reached for the second one that Cortland had prepared. Such a marvelous, clever butler. Dorothea chuckled to herself with appreciation.

The cork had been partially inserted back in the bottle to re-seal the wine, making it easy to remove. Well, relatively easy, for it did take her three tries to pull it out. She sipped her wine and asked Carter when he was going to take her fishing again. He smiled, that smile that always made her knees weaken, and teased her about her squeamish attitude.

They once again fell into an easy conversation, like two dear friends delighted to be in each other's company. Another hour passed. Lancelot woke up, ate a pile of chicken pieces Dorothea had carefully separated from the bone for him, made a game of tugging on the edge of the blanket for a time, then fell back to sleep. Reclining, Carter propped his back against the pillows and stretched his long, muscular legs beside hers.

Dorothea's breath caught in her chest. There was something so intimate, so relaxed about his pose. They were so close she could see the tiny lines at the corner of his eyes as he gazed lazily at her. A flutter of desire rose inside her. Pushing aside her misgivings, Dorothea answered the passion that was rising inside her, lifted her head, and kissed him full on the lips.

To have her initiate a kiss was heaven itself. Every inch of Carter's already aroused body tightened as their lips clung together. He had succeeded! She was relaxed and compliant, ready, nay eager, to make love.

His hands slid to the nape of her neck. He could feel her pulse beneath his fingers beating in a quick, rapid rhythm. She kissed him again, this time thrusting her tongue into his mouth. He could taste the wine on her breath, not an unpleasant sensation, but prevalent nonetheless.

Carter pulled back. Her eyes were slightly unfocused, misty with passion. Or something else? She cocked her head and smiled at him, then suddenly put one hand on the blanket as if she needed help keeping her balance. Carter groaned. If not for rotten luck, it seemed he would have no luck at all.

She was tipsy. No—foxed, and if he didn't miss his guess, close to passing out. He saw the nearly empty second bottle of wine and realized he had only drunk a few glasses from both bottles. His darling wife had consumed the rest. "Are you all right, Dorothea?"

"I feel rather giddy." She pressed the back of her hand over her eyes. "Which I have come to understand is normal when I am around you."

She started laughing, a tiny giggle that soon escalated into peals of laughter. Despite his massive disappointment, Carter managed to smile also. Then her laughter abruptly ceased and she launched herself at him, throwing her arms around his neck, kissing him feverishly on the cheek, neck, and throat.

Carter fell backward. His arms rose instinctively and he pulled her with him. She landed square on top of him, her legs between his. His cock rose stiffly in eager anticipation, but his mind knew the truth. Dorothea nuzzled her head against his shoulder, placing wet kisses along his neck. In a few minutes the kisses slowed, then stopped completely. Finally, there was only the sound of a soft, feminine snore.

He wanted to shout and scream in frustration, but that

would accomplish nothing except bring the servants running. Hell, the noise wouldn't even rouse his inebriated wife. Deciding this must be retribution for some of his prior sins, Carter shifted his back so he rested more comfortably against the cushions and gently stroked his sleeping wife's silken hair.

He waited in vain for a full hour, then finally admitted she was not going to awaken. Lifting her in his arms, Carter carried Dorothea up to her bedchamber. He jostled her deliberately as he set her on the bed, but she never even blinked.

After covering her with the soft blanket, he left to take another swim in the frigid lake.

Chapter Fourteen

Dorothea awoke in her bed, lying flat on her back, clad only in a light shift, her head pounding, her mouth parched. For a full minute she stared blankly at the ceiling, trying to recall how she got to her bedchamber and into her bed, but there were no memories of the event.

Wincing, she lifted her head from the pillow and stared out the window, trying to judge the time. Late afternoon? Early evening? There were only glimmers of dull gray light shining through the closed draperies, and she lacked the energy, and the strength, to walk across the room to open them.

Pressing the heel of her hand to her aching head, Dorothea struggled to recall the earlier events of the day. She had planned a picnic, but the rain had made it impossible. Carter had been pleased with her alternate plan of staying inside. They had enjoyed the food and the wine and the antics of her puppy, Lancelot, along with some congenial conversation.

They had laughed and flirted with each other. Carter had kissed her. Or did she kiss him? Either way, the velvety softness of his lips upon her skin had been a sensual delight. Dorothea vividly remembered responding to those kisses with her own passion and then . . . and then . . . ?

Had they made love? Drat, she couldn't remember. She moved her legs restlessly beneath the sheets, waiting to feel any physical evidence, but there was none. Sighing with relief, she rolled to her side. It would have been beyond awful to have made love with Carter for only the second time in their marriage and not remember a single detail.

There was a knock and then the bedchamber door opened. Dorothea sank beneath the sheets in total embarrassment. Yet through a wave of nausea she saw it was her maid, Sarah, who had entered the room. Not, thank the good Lord, Carter.

"Did you have a nice rest, my lady?" Sarah asked as she threw the draperies open wide.

Dorothea instantly shut her eyes as the light caused a dull pain to burn inside her head. "Is there any water?" she managed to croak.

It took but a moment for a large glass to be poured and brought to her. Grateful for Sarah's naturally quiet demeanor, Dorothea soaked in the silence and gulped down her water. The cool liquid calmed her rolling stomach and helped to keep the room from spinning. She accepted a second glass, finished that, and then tried to prepare herself to leave the bed.

Standing upright was challenging, but possible. Taking several deep breaths to steady herself, Dorothea managed to swing her legs toward the floor and then stand on them. Clutching the bedpost, she staggered a few steps, then swallowed again deeply.

Sarah, bless her heart, said not a word, acting as if seeing her mistress in such a pitiful state was nothing out of the ordinary.

"Is Lord Atwood about?" Dorothea asked.

"No, my lady. He's gone off with Mr. Higgins. He left right after you came upstairs to nap."

"I see." Dorothea tried to smile, but she was breathing too hard. Her efforts to stay upright and clearheaded were a great strain and a battle she feared she might be losing. She was fairly certain Mr. Higgins was the estate's steward, but her cloudy mind was unsure. Still, the effort to inquire seemed far too exhausting, so Dorothea kept silent.

"Shall I have a hot bath prepared?" Sarah suggested.

A bath! What a perfectly marvelous notion. Dorothea shook her head eagerly, then winced as the pain shot down to her teeth. My goodness, even her hair hurt. "A bath sounds like heaven."

With a knowing look, but a silent tongue, Sarah made the arrangements. Dorothea gratefully soaked in the hot water until it began to cool, then with the maid's assistance gingerly stepped from the tub. Feeling infinitely more human, she instructed Sarah to plait her hair. Dorothea paired her simple silk evening gown of bright blue with a filigree gold necklace and matching earbobs that had belonged to her mother, and at last felt ready to go down to dinner.

She arrived in the drawing room in a mild state of panic, concerned with how Carter would react. Would he pretend her drunken behavior earlier in the day had never occurred? Would he chastise her? Or be overtly disapproving?

Husbands unfairly had the right to dictate their wife's behavior and today's incident had the potential to bring on a lively discord. Dorothea was unsure if her nerves and recently sore head could tolerate a long lecture.

She asked the footman hovering outside the drawing room door to please refrain from announcing her and instead slipped quietly into the room. Carter was already there, dressed in formal black evening clothes, looking wildly handsome. Her heart did its customary jump.

"Ah, Dorothea, how nice to see you. I was unsure you would be coming to dinner tonight."

"Good evening, Carter." Dorothea swallowed down her nerves and told herself to act nonchalant. It seemed the best way to get her feet to move forward. "I apologize for being so late. I hope you aren't too famished."

"Actually, I ate dinner earlier with Mr. Higgins. We had a great deal of business to discuss. I hope you don't mind?"

"Not at all."

"I can join you at the table while you have your meal," he offered.

"Actually, I'd prefer to have a light respite served in here."

Carter nodded, then rang for a servant and relayed her request. "Oh, and be sure to bring tea with her ladyship's food. A large, hot pot of tea."

Dorothea stiffened her spine and told herself that was not the edges of a smile she saw on her husband's face when he requested her tea. Though in truth, strong black coffee might have been a better choice. They made polite conversation as her meal was brought and laid out and the awkward tension pervading the air soon lifted.

Feeling like one of the stray birds Gwendolyn used to eagerly collect and care for when they were children, Dorothea took very small, dainty bites of her dinner. She avoided anything that had a sauce, was laden with excess butter or heavily spiced, opting for the plainer fare.

Thankfully, it all settled well in her stomach. As she emptied her teacup for the third time, she realized her husband's gaze was intently fixed upon her. Lifting the linen napkin from her lap, Dorothea carefully dabbed at the corners of her mouth, then tilted her chin and met his eyes squarely.

"Better?" he asked with sympathy.

"Infinitely." Feeling she needed to say something more, she added quietly, "I don't normally drink that much wine. A glass usually, two at most."

"I'm pleased to hear that. For a moment I worried with you in my household the bills from the wine merchants might beggar me."

"Don't be cruel, my lord," she warned, though she smiled into her cup of tea.

He slid a look her way and winked. Oh, he was a sly one. A sly, sexy one. She shivered. "Shall we play some cards tonight?"

"Why not? Whist?"

She nodded. He produced a deck and beckoned her to the other side of the room. Dorothea waited as he opened the gaming table, then took the chair opposite his, reached for the cards, and idly shuffled the deck. "Shall we wager on the game or play for the fun of it?"

"Fun," he said deliberately. "Your fingers are far too nimble with those cards, my dear. I fear if we play for money I shall be fleeced."

Dorothea smiled. "Lord Dardington taught me."

"That explains a lot. I heard he was quite the shark in his day."

She nodded. "He is amazingly adept. When I first came to London he discouraged me from playing, declaring it a foolish waste of time and money."

Carter picked up the cards she dealt him and casually arranged them in his hand. "And yet he still taught you?"

"He insisted. There are card games at nearly every society function, well, except for when one attends the theatre, and Lord Dardington had the good sense to realize I was not always going to listen to his and Lady Meredith's advice. Therefore, if I was going to be exposed to card games, I should know how to play. And win."

"I thank you for the warning. I shall be on my guard tonight."

Dorothea laughed. She discarded two cards and drew two more. "I have a very strong suspicion that you are far from inexperienced in this area."

His lips curled into a smile. "My idle, misspent youth has come back to haunt me."

"I believe your card playing is far more recent than your long-ago misspent youth," Dorothea answered, her suspicions confirmed when he placed his cards face up on the table. Three kings. A winning hand.

Carter paused, his expression one of mocking horror. "Are you saying that I am old, Lady Atwood?"

"Well, not as old as some." She gave him a cocky grin, put the newly shuffled deck in the center of the table, and waited for him to cut the cards.

They played well into the night, nearly evenly matched in wins and losses. For a few moments Dorothea wondered if Carter was allowing her to win, but she soon rejected the idea. He was too competitive, but more important, too respectful of her to treat her like an inferior and contrive for her to win.

The clock chimed the midnight hour and they both looked at each other in surprise, startled to realize how quickly the time had gone. Carter suggested one final hand, which he won. They gathered the cards, folded the gaming table, and snuffed out the candles.

As she glided across the room, Dorothea realized her supper dishes had been cleared and the small table where she had eaten her meal returned to its rightful place in the room. Goodness, her attention had been so focused on the game, and her husband, she had neither seen nor heard the servants perform this task.

They started climbing the main staircase, and Dorothea searched for the words to tell him that she did not want tonight to be like all the others. She did not want to go to her bedchamber alone. She wanted him to come with her.

Yet when they reached the landing, her stomach tensed and her tongue failed. She pressed the heel of her hand to her chest and tried to ease the tightness, the panic. But it would not fade.

Seemingly unaware of her dilemma, Carter followed his usual nightly routine. With a pleasant smile, he lifted her hand to his lips and gently kissed the inside of her wrist. "Good night, Dorothea. Sleep well."

He turned away. Her heart leaped. *Say something!*

Letting out a small cry of distress, she reached out and caught him by the sleeve of his jacket. He looked down at her hand, then up to her face, his expression puzzled. It was now or never. "I would like a proper kiss, please," she said. "If you don't object?"

Dorothea's heart raced as she felt the tension in his body markedly increase. Lifting her other hand, she slowly traced the curve of his jaw with her fingertip, hoping to encourage him.

He cocked an eyebrow. "The hallway is a drafty place for a proper kiss."

There was an undercurrent in his voice that sent her pulse racing and her fear galloping. Dorothea's resolve began to unravel. *Stop thinking and start acting!*

She turned herself into him and slid her hands up the front of his jacket. "My maid always makes certain there is a warm fire in my bedchamber."

He tilted his head and considered her. She was struck by the force of his gaze and braced herself for his rejection.

He had been playing a sensual game of cat and mouse with her for the past five days. She knew he desired her. But she did not know the rules of his game. She did not know if part of their play involved him controlling the situation. It was therefore prudent to be prepared for any eventuality, though in truth Dorothea knew she would feel devastated if he walked away from her now.

"I am not a saint, Dorothea. If we retire to your bed-chamber, there will be more between us than a few heated kisses," he declared.

"I should hope so," she answered in a deliberately demure tone. "So, will you come with me?"

He slowly lowered his face to hers. The brush of his lips was whisper soft, yet filled with deep longing. The emotion behind it staggered her senses. "My God, Dorothea, I thought you would never ask."

She swayed into him as her knees suddenly gave way. He laughed, a deep, sensual sound that further weakened her legs. Holding her tightly against his strong body, Carter half carried, half dragged Dorothea to her bedchamber. He dismissed the curious-eyed Sarah with a curt nod, then closed and locked the door.

The air was charged. The room warm. The silence deafening. Dorothea felt aware of everything around her, yet was incapable of forming a coherent thought. But tonight was not for thinking. Tonight was for feeling.

She placed her arms around Carter's neck. Then, standing on her toes, she molded the curves of her body against his, lifted her chin, and kissed him full on the lips. The flame, now struck, quickly flared into a sensual fire.

Carter stroked his tongue slowly against her lower lip and she eagerly parted for him. As he deepened the kiss, he tugged at the pins in her hair. A cluster of her golden tresses tumbled down her back, and he searched for the remaining pins.

At the same time, Dorothea reached for the knot of his white cravat. Their arms bumped and tangled awkwardly. They stopped, regrouped, then tried again, achieving the same result.

"We seem to be working at cross-purposes," Carter grumbled. He took a step back. Smiling, he loosened the knot of his cravat, yanked the linen strip from his neck, and dropped it on the floor. "Your turn."

Dorothea's breath caught. Slowly she removed the remaining hairpins, tossing them on her dressing table. Carter's jacket went next, followed by her shoes. His waistcoat for her stockings. Her jewelry for his shoes. His shirt for her . . .

"Gown," he said softly. "Remove your gown. Please?"

She swallowed. Did she dare? "I can't release all the buttons down the back."

"Turn around."

His hoarse voice rasped along the edges of her nerves. Dorothea closed her eyes and did as he bade. His touch was gentle but the warmth and pressure of his hands weakened her knees even further. When the last button was free he stepped away. Slowly she pivoted around to face him.

His seductive eyes shimmered with something raw and brutal. They caught and captivated her. She could see how badly he wanted her, could almost feel the strain as he struggled to hold back his desire. Was she really going to do this? Her mind and pulse raced, knowing she was playing with fire.

Never one to give half-measures, Dorothea fought back her fear and lifted her chin boldly. She slid the sensual silk gown down one shoulder, then angled her body toward him as she did the same with the other. The garment fell off her upper torso, catching near her waist. Swaying her hips seductively, she encouraged the gown to fall further and it soon puddled at her feet.

Carter's breathing grew harsher, his eyes darker. Heat flooded her at his reaction, yet she shivered mightily at the evidence of his growing passion. Without saying a word, he unbuttoned the fall of his breeches, shoved them and his underclothes down his legs in one quick motion, and kicked them off.

Dorothea's teasing, playful attitude abruptly vanished as she caught sight of his lean muscles, broad shoulders, and full, jutting arousal. She peered under her lashes at him, her body flushing. His gaze roamed over her, lingering sensually on her breasts and at the shadow between her thighs, his mouth pressed in a hard, hungry line.

The scent of passion filled the air, crackling sensuously around them. Her fingers shook so badly she could barely untie the silk ribbon fastenings at the neckline of her chemise. Finally they gave way.

More silence. Dorothea's heart pounded against her throat. She could see his eyes staring at every inch of her flesh and she wanted to turn and hide. Never had she felt so emotionally and physically exposed. It was anguish. It was ecstasy.

Carter could see her struggle. He waited. If she turned from him he'd most likely lose his mind and smash the room to bits, but it had to be her decision. He would not make love to her unless she believed she was ready.

Her body was perfection. He stared at the curves of her breasts, so full and round, remembering how they had filled his hands. His body ached with desire and still he waited.

A step. Just one small step. That was all he needed, for her to take a step toward him. Carter smiled wolfishly and held out his hand. Her cheeks reddened and he realized she had glanced down at his erection. His penis rose with great interest at her curious perusal. Dorothea's eyes widened.

"You are even more beautiful than I recall," he rasped.

"You've thought of me?"

The laugh that bubbled from his chest was more of a groan. "You have haunted my dreams and most of my waking hours for days, my pretty little wife."

She moved her upper body forward, leaned only a fraction toward him, but it was enough. Enough to let him know she was ready. Carter scooped her into his embrace. He nuzzled her neck, kissed her throat, licked her earlobe. She let her head fall back, offering herself to him, and that simple act of surrender was his undoing.

The warm, womanly scent of her body filled his head as his mouth traveled lower. He licked her budding nipples with long strokes, then took the tips in his mouth and sucked. Dorothea moaned, then laced her fingers through his hair, pulling him closer.

He swept her in his arms and carried her to the bed. Dorothea felt the cool smoothness of the silk spread against her back. A sharp contrast to the hot, hard male body that covered her on top.

He looked deeply into her eyes as he caressed her body, running his hand smoothly down the flat of her belly, then settling between her thighs. His fingers coaxed and teased until she lifted herself toward him, begging for more. He answered her silent plea by pressing the heel of his hand against her core. She moaned and rocked against him, her breath coming loud and fast.

She ran her palms frantically over the strong muscles of his back. His skin was smooth and so hot it nearly burned. She felt her body lift itself toward him as she strained to bring herself closer. He kissed her lips hungrily, possessively, at the same time he slipped a finger between the damp folds of her womanhood.

"Carter," she moaned, tossing her head back against the pillows.

He trailed a line of kisses down her throat, across her breasts and belly, then settled his mouth against the honey curls that hid her womanly secrets.

Dorothea sat up in the bed. "Whatever are you doing?" she asked breathlessly.

"I'm kissing you."

Carter slowly pressed her shoulders back against the mattress. She reluctantly complied, but when he lowered his head again, her entire body contracted in shock.

It was too much! Too wicked, too intimate, too embarrassing. His breath touched her first and then she felt his fingers moving through her golden curls, opening the soft pink lips of her womanhood.

At the first wet stroke of his tongue she bit her lip to keep from screaming, but then he gently sucked the aching, sensitive bud of flesh where the most intense sensations were gathered. All thoughts of embarrassment fled.

She strained and quivered and arched herself off the mattress, feeling the tension build. Then suddenly, it was gone.

"Wait. No, don't stop," she cried between frantic pants for breath. "I'm nearly there."

"I think it will be better if you reach your climax with me inside you," he insisted, settling himself above her.

She shivered in heated anticipation as he lowered his hips. He rubbed his cock against her inner thigh, and her excitement spilled over the edge. She moaned and stretched her legs wider, encouraging his possession.

She could feel the thick, round head of his penis start to push inside her in a slow, patient rhythm. There was no pain this time, only a sense of fullness, a sense of completion.

Dorothea opened her eyes and was transfixed by the sight of him. His chest shiny with sweat, the muscles in his shoulders and arms flexed and bulging, the passion and intensity in his eyes all consuming. It was the most magnificent thing she had ever seen.

"Deeper," she moaned, locking her legs around him. "Faster."

He groaned and thrust forward, then drew back and shoved his entire length deep inside her. She rose to meet him, pushing her hips up off the mattress. The gesture seemed to make him lose control and he rode her harder and faster.

She felt her climax inching closer. He thrust once more, deep and hard, and her limbs stiffened as they started shaking with pleasure. Her inner muscles clenched as he continued to push her higher and higher, triggering his own peak. He shook and spasmed his release and she felt his warm, wet seed invade her welcoming body.

His head fell to the pillow beside hers. He was heavy and hard, but she didn't mind the crushing weight. She could hear his panting breath, as loud and rapid as her own. Then she felt the mattress dip and realized he had slid to her side, but was still close enough she could feel the heat and strength of his body.

"Are you all right?" he asked solemnly. "Was there any pain?"

She closed her eyes, hardly knowing what to say. Pain? Not a bit. She was floating, caught in a rapture of emotions she could not define or understand. She snaked her arm out until she found his hand. Gripping it tightly, she twined her fingers between his, never wanting to let go.

I love you. The words rose from her heart and hovered on her lips, the utter truth of them slamming into her with breath-stealing force. She loved him. The extraordinary certainty of it wrapped firmly around her heart. That was why their lovemaking had been so extraordinary tonight.

Partly Carter's skill, of course, and partly her determination to have this aspect of their life be a pleasant one, but mainly it was the engaging of her heart. That was the true difference between tonight and their wedding night.

She was attracted to him, trusted him, but most importantly, she loved him. Her love had allowed her to hold nothing back, to give of herself completely and with wanton abandonment.

"There was no pain," she finally answered.

"Good. Very good." He brushed the hair from her eyes, then gazed at her for a long moment, his expression tender.

"Is it always like this?" she whispered. "I mean, when one isn't a virgin?"

"No, hardly ever, really." Carter bent his arm, rested his elbow on the mattress, and propped his head on his open palm. "The attraction between us is strong, yet tonight it flared with an unexpected heat." He shook his head ruefully. "'Tis unlike anything I've ever experienced."

Dorothea's chest tightened with emotion. Unlike anything he had ever experienced. She liked the sound of that, liked it very much indeed.

The declaration of love hung on her lips, but she clamped them shut. She was not ready yet to speak of it. The emotions were too new, too intense, too profound to voice. It was too precious to reveal. The practical side of her nature, a small element at most times, was screaming at her loudly now, warning her to be cautious. It was too soon, too new to test this fragile love.

And greatly fearing to do anything else, Dorothea heeded that inner voice.

* * *

Over the next week, their relationship changed. It was as if a dam of sensuality and sexual freedom had burst and they were simply unable to keep their hands off each other. All it took was a look from Carter, a dark, sensual look, and Dorothea was on fire. She melted quickly at the caress of his hands; the pressure of his lips on any part of her body instantly filled her with longing. A longing for the physical fulfillment, but more desperately a longing for love. For Carter's love.

There were times when she felt on the verge of revealing her emotions, of proclaiming her love and devotion. Of shouting it out loudly when they rode together about the estate. Of whispering it softly in his ear when they reclined on the rocks at the lake, their fishing poles bobbing in the water.

Oddly, every moment seemed like the perfect time, but when the words bubbled to the surface, as they so often did, something held her back. Something in the depths of his eyes. A hesitation, a fear almost. As if he knew what she wanted to say and he was desperate to keep her from uttering those words. Because he feared them? Because he did not understand them? Because he did not return them?

She didn't know the reason, so she kept her love hidden, locked away. And though a joyous feeling, it also made her vulnerable, for it frightened her, knowing how her heart would shatter if Carter rejected her love.

Oh, what a foolish, naïve young woman she had been when she came to London, believing that a marriage without love was an acceptable, even preferable one. She knew better now.

But she stubbornly refused to think beyond that point. It stood to reason that if she could fall in love with Carter, than he could fall in love with her. In moments of weakness, she toyed with the idea of trying to force the issue, but a voice of reason always held her back.

True love, lasting love, required complete honesty. And the truth was that she wanted to be loved for herself, rather than what someone wanted her to be.

"We return to London tomorrow," Carter announced at breakfast.

There was quiet as Dorothea contemplated the slice of half-eaten toast on her dish. Why did they have to leave? Things were going so very well between them, weren't they? Was he growing bored with her? Tired of her exclusive company? "I shall instruct Sarah to pack my trunks."

"Excellent. I'd like to get an early start." Carter cleared his throat. "I think it would be best if Lancelot stays behind. A young dog of his breed needs a large area to run and play."

Dorothea sipped her hot chocolate. "There are plenty of parks in Town. I'm sure I can find a patch of green for him to frolic."

"And no doubt get trampled by a horse. Really, Dorothea, it's for his safety. We'll return in a few weeks, once the Season has officially ended."

Dorothea felt a lump of emotion clog her throat, but she swallowed it down. She was upset at having to leave the puppy behind, but she comforted herself with the knowledge that it would only be for a short time. "If you think it best, then he will stay here."

She could practically feel Carter's sigh of relief. *Marriage is about compromise,* she told herself sternly.

Leaving her darling Lancelot was difficult, but she was far more distressed at leaving Ravenswood, worried that once they left this idyllic place and returned to the distractions of society they would leave the best part of their relationship behind.

Was passion enough to keep their marriage close? Would she be able to hold her love inside herself, be content with having whatever part of himself Carter was willing to share, as she had so boastfully proclaimed before their wedding?

Secretly she feared she would not, for now that she had come to know him so well, she did not want a small part, she wanted all of him.

Chapter Fifteen

They arrived in London by late afternoon. Since Carter's bachelor apartments were hardly a suitable place to bring a young bride and it was too far into the Season to find a town house to rent in an appropriate neighborhood, they went directly to the duke's palatial mansion. It was not the arrangement that Dorothea would have preferred, but she was not consulted on the decision and it seemed waspish to complain.

The duke was not at home when they arrived, and they were informed by the very proper butler that he was not expected to return until very late that night. A circumstance that seemed to please rather than distress his son, which was understandable, given the strained relationship between the two.

And yet Dorothea could not imagine any members of her family acting in the same manner. If they were moving into one of her relatives' homes, they would have been welcomed with open arms. She supposed her genuine puzzlement over the difference was merely another example of her provincial upbringing.

Though he might not have made the effort to personally

greet them, the duke did not stint on their accommodations. They were given an entire wing of the house, which included separate apartments for each of them. There were two massive bedchambers, connected by a sitting room, separate dressing rooms, and a shared bathing room that contained the largest porcelain tub Dorothea had ever seen.

In addition, there was a study for Carter and a sunny private parlor for Dorothea, complete with upholstered furniture, two matching bookcases, and a desk. It was cozy and feminine, the perfect spot to entertain a few close female friends or write her letters.

Carter expressed regret that it was too late to begin a proper tour of the house, but Dorothea was relieved. She was tired from the journey, wound a bit tight with nerves, and feeling completely intimidated by the duke's housekeeper. Mrs. Simpson's London counterpart, the aptly named Mrs. Steele, possessed none of country housekeepers' warmth or kindness. Instead, she was a sharp-eyed, thin-lipped woman of indeterminate age who seemed to lack the ability to smile. Even partially. Dorothea was hardly anxious to be in her company.

After being shown to her rooms, Dorothea dismissed the housekeeper, removed her bonnet, and tossed it on the bed. Her maid, Sarah, was traveling in the servants' coach with their baggage and expected to arrive shortly. In the meantime, she would explore her immediate surroundings and hope that Carter would make an appearance soon. It all felt rather strange and lonely without him near.

She opened one of the several doors in her bedchamber and stepped into her private parlor. Shades of pink dominated the color scheme, which was unfortunate, since Dorothea was not particularly fond of pink. She made a mental note to see about having the draperies replaced at once, hoping that might be enough to change the overall atmosphere of the room. If not, the wallpaper would next fall victim to redecorating.

The antique furniture in the room was elegant and beautiful, but the arrangement of the pieces was awkward. Adding a second task in her mind, Dorothea squinted her eyes, trying to imagine how the writing desk would look near the windows and the upholstered chairs in front of the marble fireplace. That would be an easier fix than the draperies. All she would need was an hour or two and three strong, able-bodied footmen to get the room set to her preferences.

Leaving her private parlor, she threw open another door and walked into the sitting room adjoining her bedchamber with Carter's. It was done in various shades of green that conveyed a calm, cozy element Dorothea immediately liked.

She strode through the room, heading directly toward the door that led to Carter's chamber, and yanked it open. To her great disappointment, the room was empty.

Of course, this did make it the ideal opportunity to snoop about in private. The room was enormous, nearly twice the size of her own. Her bedchamber contained dainty furniture accented by soft feminine pastels with small floral patterns and stripes on the walls, curtains, bed linens, and rugs. Carter's bedchamber was done in subdued, masculine tones of dark green, taupe, and gold. The furnishings were solid and heavy, crafted from the finest woods. Idly she ran her open palm over the carved mahogany bedpost, marveling at the size and beauty of the piece.

Her children would be conceived in this bed. She shivered with delight at the notion, imagining her husband's strong, muscular, naked form, covered in a fine sheen of sweat as he labored to bring them both to climax. Finally sated, they would fall into a deep sleep, wrapped around each other, with Carter's naked chest pressing into her back.

The door from the hallway unexpectedly opened and Dorothea smiled with anticipation. Gracious, all she need do was think about making love with her husband and he magically appeared. How perfectly marvelous!

"Was there something you needed, my lady?"

The voice was alarmingly rough and unfamiliar. Dorothea tried not to openly frown as she stared at her husband's valet, a short, thin man with a decidedly nasal voice.

"I was looking for Lord Atwood."

"I believe he is in the library." The valet's face remained impassive as walked to the mahogany wardrobe, opened it, and began to fuss with Carter's clothing. After a long moment, the servant ceased his work and turned back to her. "Is there anything I can do for you, Lady Atwood?"

She compressed her lips into a tight line, wishing she had the nerve to tell the man to leave so she could be left in peace to continue her exploring. But her courage failed, for though his expression was blank, Dorothea felt certain the valet was silently smirking at her.

Gathering her dignity, and striving to look as much like a haughty noblewoman as possible, Dorothea turned, but a noise at the bedchamber door startled them both. Carter entered the room, then pulled up short, clearly confused to see his wife and valet in his bedchamber at the same time. "Is anything wrong?"

"Goodness, no," Dorothea answered with a forced smile. "I was just wondering where you were."

"Excuse me, my lord." The valet bowed and hastened from the room.

"I don't think he likes me very much," Dorothea mumbled.

"Dunsford?"

"Yes, your valet. Though he is only a servant, he does have opinions, you know," Dorothea muttered.

"Hmm. I've never actually thought much about it."

There was a knock at the door, and at Carter's command it opened. Dunsford reappeared with two footmen in tow, one carrying Carter's luggage and the other holding a pitcher of steaming water.

The valet seemed momentarily startled to find her still in the room, but he lowered his gaze and began instructing the other servants as to where things should be placed. When all was set to his satisfaction, Dunsford dismissed the footmen, yet remained in the chamber.

Ignoring them both, the valet opened Carter's wardrobe and began pulling out a selection of garments. It was at that moment that Dorothea realized the valet had chosen formal clothes more suitable for an evening away from home.

Dorothea's mouth fell open. "You're going out?"

The two men turned to stare at her, Carter's face hardening into a mask while the valet's frown was comically shocked. Apparently no one was supposed to have the audacity to question Lord Atwood about his comings and goings, even his wife.

"I will return at a more convenient time to finish my duties," Dunsford declared in a disapproving tone before once again scuttling from the chamber.

"I am meeting Benton at my club," Carter said when they were alone. He sat on one of the upholstered chairs near the fireplace and removed his boots. "We made these plans weeks ago."

Dorothea folded her arms, trying to contain her agitation. "Can't you break them?"

Carter leaned back in his chair and propped his feet on the ottoman. "It would be terribly rude."

Dorothea blinked and looked down at her slippers. "When will you return?" she inquired, hating herself for asking.

"Late, I expect. Or rather early morning." He crossed his feet at the ankles. "There's no need for you to wait up. I would hate to think I was disturbing your sleep."

Disturbing her sleep? Was he joking? Dorothea did not bother to hide her disappointment. She sank down on an open corner of the ottoman and expelled a long sigh. "'Tis our first night in London. I had hoped we would spend it together."

"Is there some place you specifically wish me to take you?"

"No," she answered honestly. "I was hoping for a quiet evening at home."

"Then you shall have your wish. I will instruct the staff to serve your dinner in your rooms."

The very brief stab of joy Dorothea felt when she thought he had relented immediately faded. "But you won't be joining me for that dinner," she said slowly.

"No. As I said, I'll be out with Benton," Carter replied calmly, the expression in his eyes impossible to penetrate. "I apologize for the misunderstanding, Dorothea, but I was unaware of your expectation when I made these plans."

Ah, polite to the end. He was sorry that she misunderstood, but not at all sorry that he was leaving her alone. Dorothea was unsure what distressed her more: his plans to leave her for the evening or the blank expression on his face, as if he had no earthly idea why that would bother her.

She felt like snatching up a pillow and hitting him over the head with it.

"Can't you see the viscount another night?"

He fixed her with a cool stare, and Dorothea knew she had crossed an invisible line. A spasm of disgust wrenched through her. Fearing she was close to losing her composure, she dug her fingernails bitingly into her palms and summoned every ounce of will she possessed to put a congenial expression on her face.

She was not going to be a martyr. She had entered this marriage without pretense or romantic expectations, as had Carter. It was not his fault that her feelings had so quickly and so deeply become engaged.

Though she supposed overall he could be less charming, less attractive, less appealing.

As if that would matter. The sad truth was that Dorothea knew she would love him no matter what the circumstances. Why, even at this moment, feeling hurt, angry, and frustrated, she still loved him. Though she didn't like him all that much.

"Please give my warmest regards to Viscount Benton," Dorothea said softly as she stood.

"I'm sure he will be delighted that you sought to remember him."

This time Carter spoke kindly, as if he were trying to soften the blow, but his abrupt dismissal of her stung.

Oh, my, how things had changed so quickly. The easy banter and camaraderie they had developed over the past few weeks had indeed been left behind in the country.

Yet knowing she had said all that she could on the matter, she turned and left, closing the sitting room door behind her. In a childish fit of temper, her hand fumbled to find a key, for she dearly would have enjoyed loudly locking the door. But alas, even that gesture was denied her, for none was to be found.

Despite her lonely night, Dorothea's optimistic spirit returned the following morning. Unfortunately, it did not last long. At breakfast she discovered her husband had already left the house and was not due to return until late afternoon.

He again abandoned her in the evening, but encouraged her to accept one of the many invitations that had been sent.

Not wanting to spend another lonely night in her rooms, Dorothea sent a message to Lord and Lady Dardington and asked to be included in their theatre party. A seat was easily found for her in the marquess's box. Though inwardly distressed, she spent the evening smiling so broadly that by the time she reached home her face hurt from the efforts.

By the third day in London she and her husband settled into a pattern that alternately frustrated and angered her.

The house was very large and she saw the duke infrequently, which pleased her. Alas, she also saw her husband infrequently, and that did not please her one bit. She understood that Carter had duties, responsibilities. She did not begrudge him those hours when he attended to matters of business, when he met with members of his political party, for he had begun to show a more active interest in the House of Lords. But she also knew he spent a great deal of time with his friends, engaging in the same pursuits he enjoyed before they had married. And that she did resent.

Her new status as the Marchioness of Atwood put her in great social demand. The invitations poured in, so many in fact that a secretary was hired to help her cope with the voluminous correspondence. Remembering well the lesson learned with Mrs. Snidely, Dorothea strove not to show favoritism to any one family or hostess. She therefore tried to accept as many invitations as possible, often attending three or even four events in one evening.

Regrettably, she did this for the most part without her husband. She knew it was the way of many society couples, but not all, and certainly not those that were newly married. On the rare occasion she accidentally encountered Carter at a ball or party, he would ask her to dance, make her smile with his witty observations, then graciously depart.

He always seemed pleased to see her, yet it was also apparent he had no qualms about leaving her. He did not deplore her company, nor did he seek it, even when he was at home. Worst of all, her courses had started, preventing them from engaging in a physical closeness.

Dorothea was frustrated with what she felt was the unnatural state of her marriage, especially at this early stage. She and Carter ran their lives on a parallel but separate course.

Within a few days, Dorothea grew tired of the endless social whirl. It was simply not as entertaining without Carter by her side. She toyed briefly with the idea of forsaking the parties and staying home at night, but feared she would become lonely shut away in her rooms with only a book or her embroidery to keep her company.

Unfortunately she was not even allowed to suffer this neglect in privacy, for these antics did not go unnoticed by the duke. Dorothea might have limited contact with her imposing father-in-law, yet it seemed every time she did see him he was quick to offer an unwanted comment.

Tonight was no exception. As she reached the landing on the center staircase, the duke appeared from the opposite wing. Dorothea blinked. Had he been lying in wait for her? It seemed so blatantly absurd, and yet his timing was too perfect for this to be mere happenstance.

"Where are you off to tonight?" the duke asked.

Dorothea tried to ignore his scrutinizing glare, but it was difficult. She always squirmed so desperately inside when he studied her, for it felt as if he was judging her, measuring her worth. Measuring and concluding she was worth very little.

"Lady Halifax is hosting a charity ball at Almack's."

"Will my son be there?"

"Probably not. He has no great affection for Lady Halifax or her charitable efforts."

One corner of the duke's mouth eased slightly upward. Most would consider it a hint of a smile. Dorothea knew better.

"Who is your escort?" he wanted to know.

"The major."

"Again? I vow you see more of him than your husband."

She snapped her gaze up to his, trembling, yet determined to hide the wound inflicted by the truth of his words. "That is hardly my choice."

The duke grunted with impatience. "A clever woman knows how to keep a man by her side. And in her bed. I want to hold my heir in my arms before I die, young lady."

"Then I advise you to watch your health most carefully, Your Grace, to ensure that you live for many, many years." Reaching down, Dorothea gathered the skirt of her gown by her fingertips and held it above her evening slippers to prevent herself from tripping. The gesture also helped conceal the trembling of her hands. "Now, if you will excuse me, I'm certain the major has arrived. I do not wish to be rude and keep him waiting."

Dismissing the duke, she moved past him, ignoring the prickling sensation she felt on the nape of her neck. She glided down the main staircase gracefully, her head high, her back straight. Roddy, bless his heart, was indeed waiting in the front foyer and she practically fell into his arms.

She heard the duke's deep, commanding voice call to her, but she kept moving, her mind focused on escaping. For a few hours at least, she was determined to forget the unhappy state of her circumstances.

* * *

Major Roddington's heels clicked on the polished marbled floor as he paced impatiently in the foyer. He had been told Lady Atwood would be down shortly and been asked to wait. Normally he wouldn't have minded, but being kept out of the private rooms of this particular house gnawed at his gut. It was a stark reminder of how he had failed to complete his task, of how the passing of time was only making this more difficult, more challenging.

Lady Atwood suddenly appeared, a tight smile of greeting on her face. Above her, Roddy could hear a voice of masculine discontent.

"Is that Lord Atwood shouting at you?" he asked.

"No, it's the duke."

She gestured toward a footman, who held out a silk evening cloak, but Roddy was no longer paying attention to her. At the sound of that same, low masculine voice, his head swung toward the landing and he felt a sudden, quick explosion of emotions. Close. He was so close.

He glanced up. At the sight of the elderly man clutching the banister with outstretched arms and frowning with such clear disapproval, a coldness like he had never felt seeped into Roddy's bones. Oh, he had seen the duke before, but always from a great distance or in a very crowded room. This was the first time since he was a lad of fifteen that he had been so near the all-powerful Duke of Hansborough.

The temptation was almost too great. Yet Roddy straightened, his inner discipline overtaking his impulsive inclination to rush up the staircase and have his say. Now was not the time for confrontation.

"He sounds angry," Roddy commented.

"I believe that is his normal tone." She tugged on her evening gloves and hastened toward the door. "Shall we?"

Roddy's eyes narrowed. He had come to know a bit about Dorothea over these last few days and he found her to be a pleasant, congenial woman. Her stiff, formal reticence was clearly out of character and obviously caused by the duke.

He escorted her silently from the house and assisted her into the carriage, then waited until the vehicle had rounded the corner before speaking. "Did you have a disagreement with the duke?"

She glanced over at him, her face pale in the moonlight. "His Grace finds much at fault with me. I fear the only way I shall ever gain his true approval is to present him with a grandson."

She blushed and Roddy realized she felt embarrassed at discussing something so intensely personal with a man who was not her husband. It made him feel like a real cad for even bringing the subject up.

"Well, I hope you present him with a whole pack of boys, each as sour-tempered as his grandfather."

She smiled, as he intended, and they let the matter drop. But the incident made Roddy start to wonder. Where was Atwood tonight? Why wasn't he there to defend his bride, to shelter her from the duke's barbs?

They were newly married, yet as far as Roddy could tell, Atwood spent most of his time away from his wife. He had seen him at Tattersall's yesterday, the boxing club the day before, and a local gaming hell last night.

He knew it was society's way for married couples to live separate lives, but this seemed to drift beyond acceptable standards. Roddy gritted his teeth and gazed out the window, deciding this was yet another prime example of how the wealthy, spoiled aristocracy did not appreciate the real treasures in their lives.

"I'm for home," Benton announced as he threw down his losing hand of cards.

Peter Dawson smiled in appreciation and raked in the substantial pile of coins. "Are you sure you won't play one more round?"

"No. I wish to leave before my pockets are totally empty." Benton turned to Carter. "And what of you, Atwood? Are you done for the night? Ready to go home at last to your lovely bride?"

Carter felt his jaw twitch. It was uttered in jest, but the barb struck at the heart. Though nothing directly had been said, Carter knew his friends wondered why he was not at home with his wife, but instead spending all of his evenings, and most of his days, out with them.

In fact, his life was going on exactly as it had before he had married. Actually, a bit better, since he was no longer plagued by the duke to find himself a wife. So why didn't he feel more content with the arrangement?

"Tell me, what is your opinion of love?" Carter asked.

The viscount paused in the act of putting on his coat, his expression curious. "Love of what? Drink? A new set of prime cattle? A pair of well-fitted, perfectly polished boots?"

"A woman," Carter snorted. Perfectly polished boots, indeed.

Benton fell silent. "Dear God, don't tell me you've fallen in love with your wife?" he finally asked.

Carter shook his head. "No, but I fear she might fancy herself in love with me."

Benton's brow lifted skeptically. "There is little to fear. She is a reasonably intelligent creature, well, for a woman. She will come to her senses soon enough and realize her mistake."

"Don't listen to Benton," Dawson interrupted. He stacked the deck of cards and left it in the center of the table. "I think it's bloody marvelous. Lady Atwood is a fine woman. You deserve the happiness her love and affection will bring you."

Was Dawson right? Should he just accept this gift of love and be content with it? But with love came the expectation of reciprocation, and therein lay the rub, for what Carter feared most was that he was incapable of loving her. Wholly, completely, the way she deserved.

She was his wife. He respected her. Adored her, really. They could build a solid, happy life together. It was what they agreed before they married, it was what they both wanted. And in his eyes, the volatile emotion of love seemed to threaten that stability.

Didn't love take time to develop, time to grow? How could Dorothea be so sure, when he was so conflicted?

It made him feel weak and foolish not to know his mind, not to understand his own emotions. It made him feel unsure, unsteady, inept. He reasoned by keeping his distance from Dorothea these past few days, the problem would somehow sort itself out, the solution would become clear.

Alas, he had been wrong. Just because he refused to confront the dilemma did not mean it did not exist.

The biggest irony of all was that he cared for her too much, respected her too much to declare an undying love until he was certain it was what he truly felt.

Carter jerked to his feet. He signaled for his coat to no one specifically and a servant raced off to fetch the garment. The three friends parted ways outside the gaming club, entering their respective carriages. Carter's mood was reflective on the ride back to the duke's mansion.

The hour was late when he arrived home. Carter dismissed his valet the moment he entered the bedchamber. Dunsford had a hovering, fussy air about him tonight that Carter found particularly annoying. The valet left in a snit, and a few moments later there was a soft knock.

Carter turned toward the door, ready to bellow at his servant to stay the hell away, when the interior door to the shared sitting room opened and Dorothea glided into the room.

She was dressed for bed in a long blue satin nightgown that dipped low in front, exposing the plump roundness of her lovely breasts. Her hair was unbound, floating around her shoulders in a shimmering golden wave.

Carter's groin tightened at the sight of her delicate, sensual beauty. He was hard before she made it halfway into the chamber.

"Forgive my intrusion." Her hand went to her throat and he could see the slight trembling of her hand. "I waited up to tell you that I will be leaving in the morning. I'm going to visit my sister Gwen and will most likely spend a day or two with her and Jason."

It took a moment for Carter to wrap his brain around her words. She was leaving him? No, that wasn't what she said. She was visiting her sister. Gwendolyn. The pretty woman with the very pregnant belly. He slowly regained his breath. "Is there any news of her child?"

Her eyes widened as though she was surprised he remembered. "The baby is due to arrive at any time. Emma writes that Gwen is very cross and weepy and Jason is nearly out of his mind trying to hide his worry and keep her distracted."

"It sounds as if you are needed."

"I am." She nodded her head. "Yet I confess it will also help me to feel useful."

Her comment rankled, for it implied she felt useless here. His fault? Probably. "I'll take you," he said gruffly.

"There is no need. The duke has put his carriage at my disposal. The journey takes no more than a few hours, so his coachman and equipment will return in the same day.

I can send word if I need transportation back to London, though I imagine my brother-in-law will be pleased to have me use his vehicle."

Her independent, self-sufficient attitude irritated Carter. Which was ridiculous, since he had been the one to foster it upon her by his neglect.

"Stay with me tonight," he said impulsively, fighting to keep his smile from turning predatory.

She lowered her gaze and her cheeks reddened. "My monthly courses are just ending."

Ah, so that question was answered. He had wondered, but didn't want to ask if she was carrying their child. The duke would be angry, but Carter didn't care. Dorothea wasn't breeding and he felt a rush of relief. Pregnancy was dangerous business for a woman.

"That doesn't matter, especially since you are at the end of your cycle. We can be inventive." He smiled coaxingly, but then noticed the shadows of exhaustion around her eyes, the fine lines of tension etched on her lovely face. Clearly she was tired, and here he was acting like a perfect ass. "Or we could just sleep together."

"You wouldn't mind having me in your bed just to sleep?"

His throat suddenly felt too tight to speak. Lord, he was a bounder if his wife believed he only wanted her around to satisfy his sexual urges.

"Come to bed, Dorothea." He held out his hand.

For an instant she didn't move. Then she drew in a long sigh and came close, stopping in front of him. "I have missed you, Carter."

Her simple truth cut him deep. He might not be capable of loving her with the devotion and intensity she deserved, but he could show her that he did care. He could be kinder, more considerate toward her. It was the very least she deserved.

He blew out the candles and helped her into his bed.

Tossing off his shirt and breeches, he climbed naked between the sheets and cradled her in his arms. Darkness surrounded them, forming a cocoon of peace. Carter kissed her temple and she snuggled close.

And in that moment, Carter knew a deep sense of peace. No matter what the state of their relationship, she belonged to him. She was his to hold and protect, to comfort and encourage. And that pleased him mightily.

Chapter Sixteen

Dorothea had not expected calm when they arrived at Jason and Gwendolyn's home, which lay on the outskirts of London, a four-hour drive from the center of the city. She knew from her sister Emma's letters that it had been tense and difficult as a moody, oftentimes weepy Gwendolyn neared the end of her confinement and the birth of her child.

Children, Dorothea corrected herself silently, for it was a real possibility that her sister would birth twins, a fact that she had shared with no one except Dorothea.

No, Dorothea had not expected calm to greet them, yet she was far from prepared to face the utter chaos that seemed to grip the house, and every person within it, as she and Carter stepped over the threshold.

They stood alone in the foyer, the young, confused underfootman who had answered the door by their side. Every few minutes, a servant would thunder up or down the staircase or dash in and out of a door, their expression serious and intent.

"The family is not receiving callers today," the underfootman said in a nervous voice. "You should probably come back another time."

"Mrs. Barrington is my sister," Dorothea repeated. "We have come today—"

"Dorothea!" Emma's shout from the top of the staircase was a trembling cry of relief. Wasting no time, the young woman rushed down the stairs and caught her older sister in a hug. "Thank God you are here. Gwen is in labor!"

Dorothea dredged up an overly bright smile. "Isn't that exciting news? Why, before too long you and I shall be aunts."

Emma drew back, her eyes wide. "You don't understand. It's been so long already and still the baby hasn't come."

Dorothea closed her eyes and swallowed hard. Oh, Lord, this was her greatest fear. That Gwen would not survive childbirth. It was an inconceivable horror that she had forced herself to disregard, yet the reality loomed before her now, stark and real.

A solid masculine hand landed on Dorothea's shoulder, the strong fingers stroking up and down her arm in a gesture of comfort. "When did her pains begin?" Carter asked.

"They started last night, right after dinner," Emma answered. "At first it wasn't too bad. Gwen was even laughing and joking for a time, but things changed dramatically with the dawn. She is in terrible pain. If you stand near her bedchamber door you can hear her scream."

A long, serious silence fell. "Take me to her," Dorothea insisted, as the tightness in her chest refused to ease. Arm in arm the two sisters began to climb the staircase, with Carter following close on their heels.

"What is the doctor saying about your sister's condition?" he asked.

Emma's brows drew together. "The midwife is with Gwen now."

"Where's the doctor?" Dorothea inquired.

"Gone." Emma stopped in mid-staircase and turned to

her. "He frightened Gwen and made her cry. So Jason threw him out of the house."

"Oh, dear." Dorothea put her arms around Emma and held her tightly.

Emma shuddered. "It wasn't pretty. The butler had to hold Jason back when he lunged toward the doctor, fists flying."

"What could the doctor have done to cause such a violent reaction?" Carter wanted to know.

"Jason wouldn't tell me. But he went pale as a ghost." Emma shuddered again and leaned into Dorothea. "I'm frightened. She's been in labor so long. Will the baby never arrive?"

Dorothea shook her head helplessly. She held Emma tightly, her gaze darting above her sister's bowed head to meet Carter's eyes.

"I'll speak with Barrington," he said, understanding her silent plea. "Where is he?"

"Outside Gwen's bedchamber," Emma mumbled, never lifting her head from Dorothea's comforting embrace.

Flashing Carter a look of earnest appreciation, Dorothea cradled Emma in her arms and pulled her up the remaining stairs.

"I sent word to Jason's brother, Lord Fairhurst, a few hours ago," Emma confided. "They won't let me see Gwen and I can offer no comfort to Jason, but I felt I had to do *something*."

"Hush, now, don't fret," Dorothea said soothingly. "You've done a fine job and I know Gwen is grateful you are here."

Seeing the fragile state of Emma's emotions brought a rush of tears to Dorothea's eyes. Goodness, she was only sixteen. Far too young to be coping with this crisis.

It seemed to take forever, but in truth Carter returned

after a few minutes. Not liking the frown of worry on her husband's face, Dorothea sent Emma off to the kitchen to ask for tea to be prepared so they could speak privately.

"Well?" Dorothea prompted.

Carter hesitated. "'Tis precisely as Emma said. Barrington is pacing the floorboards outside Gwen's chamber, nearly out of his mind with worry."

"Did you find out why he tried to punch the doctor?"

Carter's gaze slid evasively to the floor and her heart went along with it. *Oh, no.* Dorothea grasped his arm and squeezed tightly. "The truth. Please. I need to know."

"There appears to be some difficulty with the birth."

Dorothea held herself perfectly still. "Is Gwendolyn in grave danger?"

Carter pressed his fingertips to his temple. "There's always risk involved with childbirth."

"This sounds like more than the usual risk." Dorothea leaned forward intently. "Tell me."

Carter sighed, clearly unnerved. "The doctor feared that your sister would not be able to safely deliver the child and wanted to intervene. But he needed Barrington's permission. And he pressed him to make an impossible choice as to who would survive. His wife or his child."

For an instant Carter's handsome face blurred as a fresh wave of panic hit Dorothea. He reached out and caught her around the waist just before her wobbling legs threatened to give way. She clung to his neck, wishing it was all a horrible mistake, a bad dream from which she would soon awaken. But in her heart, she knew this was all too real.

"'Tis no wonder that Jason wanted to strike at the doctor." Dorothea convulsed softly with a sob. "What can we do?"

"We must not give in to despair," Carter insisted. "Gwen

is still fighting. We must hope and pray that she and her child come through this safely."

Dorothea nodded her head, wanting desperately to believe him. "Should we send for another doctor?"

"I suggested it, but Barrington said no. The midwife is experienced and your sister trusts her." Carter's voice was raw, but his expression was strong, comforting. "I believe it would aid Gwen greatly if you were with her. Do you think you can manage?"

Could she? Dorothea pressed a clenched fist to her stomach and choked back a sob. She had never been particularly helpful in a sickroom, having neither the temperament nor the constitution to aid her sisters or her aunt when they were feeling ill. But this was different. The stakes were dire. And if the worst, the unthinkable, were to happen . . . dear Lord, she could not allow Gwen to suffer alone.

Her stomach rioting with emotion, Dorothea released her grip from Carter's arm and drew herself up an inch. "I'll try."

"Good girl."

Carter's obvious approval gave her fledgling courage a much-needed boost. Hand in hand they walked down the long hallway, coming to a halt in front of her sister's bedchamber. Jason was huddled next to the closed door, his forehead pressed against the plaster wall. His jacket and cravat were missing, his waistcoat hung open, and the first three buttons of his shirt were undone.

It was nothing short of shocking to see her normally fastidious brother-in-law in such a disheveled state, but Dorothea barely spared him a glance, trusting Carter to see to him. All her strength and efforts had to be saved for Gwen.

Dorothea stood for a long moment in front of the door,

struggling to find the courage to enter Gwen's bedchamber, knowing she must appear calm and confident or else she would make matters worse. This was not the time to indulge in her fears and emotions; she had to be strong and positive. For Gwen. And Emma.

Somehow Dorothea managed to blink back her tears, straighten her spine, and reach for the doorknob. It was surprisingly calm and quiet as she entered the room. Two maids were stationed near the windows, speaking softly to each other. An older woman, who Dorothea assumed was the midwife, was standing at the foot of the four-poster bed, her hands on her hips.

There was no movement, no sounds from the figure swaddled beneath the blankets. A pain pressed against Dorothea's breastbone. It was too quiet, too still. On trembling legs she approached the bed. The sound alerted the midwife, for she quickly turned, her face defensive.

"Who are you?"

Resisting the instinct to cringe, Dorothea lifted her chin and spoke in her most regal tone, invoking a fair imitation of her father-in-law, the duke. "I am the Marchioness of Atwood, Mrs. Barrington's sister. I presume you are the midwife?"

"Yes, I'm Mrs. Johnson."

Dorothea cocked her brow and continued to stare until the older woman dipped a hasty curtsy. Then she sailed majestically past her, directly to Gwen's side. "How is my sister?"

"Tired," the midwife replied with an edge in her voice. "This is hardly an appropriate time for a visit."

"I am not here to socialize, I am here to help." As if proving her words, Dorothea sat gingerly on the edge of the mattress and stroked Gwen's cheek. Her sister did not move. "Why is she so still?"

"She's fallen into an exhausted sleep, but it won't last long."

Fearfully, Dorothea snatched her hand away. "Then I shall let her rest while she can. I heard that there were some difficulties with the birth."

"'Tis just taking a bit of time, that's all. A common occurrence with a first baby."

The midwife's words should have offered comfort, but they did not, for she refused to meet Dorothea's eyes when she spoke them.

"Kindly look at me, Mrs. Johnson," Dorothea commanded. After casting several worried glances her way, the midwife finally complied. Her blank expression offered no reassurance. "My sister will deliver her baby, her babies, safely and quickly, is that understood?"

Dorothea knew she must sound utterly ridiculous, but it seemed desperately important to use every ounce of her will and determination to influence the outcome. Gwen would not lose her life giving birth to her children. She would not!

"Yes, my lady."

"My brother-in-law believes you to be a highly qualified individual. Is he right, Mrs. Johnson?"

"Aye." The midwife's chest swelled with pride as she straightened her shoulders. "I've delivered more babes than I can count, and that's the God's honest truth."

"Then I expect you to use every ounce of that hard-earned skill to save my sister and her infants. She is more precious to me than I can adequately say."

The lingering resentment in Mrs. Johnson's eyes turned to sympathetic kindness. "I'll do all that I can, I promise you."

Dorothea smiled faintly. "Good. And I shall help."

At that moment, Gwen moaned. Her body restlessly twisted from side to side as though it were trying to avoid the pain and then suddenly she arched forward. The bedcovers flew off her body. Startled, Dorothea jumped from the bed.

"What's happening?" Gwen screeched.

Mrs. Johnson pushed past Dorothea to get to Gwen. She spoke to Gwen in a low, hushed voice, then motioned for Dorothea to come near.

"Is it really you, Dorothea?" Gwen asked in a reedy tone.

Dorothea swallowed hard, searching for a calm voice. Gwen's eyes were enormous in her pale face, which was etched with pain and fatigue. "Yes, it's me." She bent near the pillow and stroked Gwen's forehead.

The gesture appeared to calm the laboring woman. "I'm glad. It's hard being alone. I know that Jason is near to coming out of his skin because he wants to be with me, but truly, Dorothea, I cannot bear to have him here right now."

"Shh, don't worry about him. Jason understands. Birthing is women's business." Dorothea attempted a smile. "Carter came along, so I put him in charge of your husband. No doubt they are swilling brandy together at this very moment."

A tear slid down Gwendolyn's cheek. "I'm so tired, Dorothea. So very tired."

"I know, Gwen." She wrung the water from the cloth in the bedside basin and ran the damp linen over Gwen's brow. "I've just had a nice chat with Mrs. Johnson and we are in agreement. You will deliver these babies very soon. There are two?"

Gwen began nodding, then her head suddenly stilled and she gripped her belly with both hands. Dorothea felt a chill of pure fright wrap around her heart as the searing pain paralyzed her sister. Mrs. Johnson quickly appeared. She instructed Dorothea to prop several pillows behind Gwen's back and hold her hands tightly.

And thus the long vigil began. The minutes slid into hours. At one point the maids began lighting the candles and Dorothea realized night was approaching. And still Gwendolyn screamed and panted and labored to deliver her babies.

Knowing bravado was needed, Dorothea kept up a steady stream of encouragement. At times she doubted Gwen could even hear her, but she continued to speak, rattling off happy stories from their childhood, recalling fond memories of their parents.

It was loud and messy and monstrously frightening but the miracle of life would not be denied and, with her ebbing strength, Gwen at last pushed her children into the world.

"A boy and a girl. Fancy that," Mrs. Johnson muttered as she washed the afterbirth from the scrawny bodies of the protesting infants.

"Are they all right?" Gwen whispered.

Dorothea turned and craned her neck. "I can see their arms waving and their legs moving," she reported with a lopsided grin. Never had she felt such a giddy sense of relief.

The bedchamber door opened. Dorothea fully expected to see her brother-in-law, but instead Emma hovered hesitantly in the doorway, her eyes blinking uncertainly. "I thought I heard . . . oh, dear, the baby has arrived!" Emma's joyful expression quickly turned to puzzlement. "Two babies?"

Dorothea puffed out her cheeks. "You know our Gwen. She never does anything in half-measures."

The midwife and her assistant brought the babies to the bed. Dorothea and Emma eagerly crowded close to get a proper look.

"Would you like to hold them?" Mrs. Johnson asked Gwendolyn. "I need to go and find your husband and tell him the good news."

Gwen shook her head. "I fear my arms are too weak right now. Give them to my sisters instead."

Emma squealed with delight and reached out with both arms for the nearest babe, but Dorothea hesitated. Without waiting for her consent, Mrs. Johnson laid a swaddled bundle into Dorothea's arms. The infant nestled quietly for a few moments, then suddenly arched its back and turned its head in a frantic attempt to find her breast.

"Ah, this must be your son," Dorothea said with a smile. She placed the knuckle of her little finger near the babe's mouth and he greedily latched on, sucking furiously. Meanwhile, the baby girl in Emma's arms slept quietly and contentedly.

Jason entered the room, barreling past the maids clustered near the bed. Mrs. Johnson followed behind him. "Is she all right?" he asked the midwife. "Truly?"

"She is exhausted and jubilant, as only a new mother can be," Mrs. Johnson remarked as she gathered a pile of soiled linens and pressed them on one of the maids.

"But she will recover, will she not? You told me she would recover," Jason insisted, his voice rising.

"Do not carry on so, my love," Gwendolyn scolded in a tired voice. "You will frighten our children."

At the sound of Gwendolyn's voice, Jason froze. His eyes darted worriedly down to his wife. Dorothea could see his throat move as he swallowed, struggling to compose himself.

"Come, Jason, and greet your son and daughter," Dorothea said merrily, hoping to lighten the somber mood.

Her brother-in-law glanced toward the infants, his expression distracted. "In a moment." He sat on the edge of Gwendolyn's bed, then gently gathered her into his arms. He held her thus for a long time before Dorothea noticed his shoulders were shaking. With a start, she realized he was crying.

Turning away from the intimate moment, she walked near the window, the baby snuggled happily in her arms. Emma did the same. In unison, the new aunts began rocking to and fro, delighted to discover the babies liked it.

"Forgive the interruption."

Dorothea tore her gaze away from the baby and found Carter standing in front of her. "You are not interrupting," Dorothea bustled. "This is a family moment we are all thrilled to be sharing. Gwendolyn has safely delivered her babies. Look, this is her son."

She angled her arms and raised the baby so Carter could get a good view of the child. His expression turned curious. She smiled encouragingly and he inched forward, touching his finger to the baby's hand. At the contact, the infant's perfectly formed fingers curled around it.

"He's very small," Carter whispered.

"And red and wrinkled and sporting tufts of dark hair on his head," she whispered back before kissing the baby's forehead. "One would think with two such attractive parents he would look far less like a little troll."

Carter smiled. "An apt description, I'm afraid."

Dorothea nodded. "I vow our children will be much prettier, though I would never say so in front of my sisters."

It gave Dorothea a warm, tingly feeling to be speaking of children. After seeing the hell Gwendolyn had endured, she was hardly anxious to experience it herself, but holding the precious bundle of life was slowly changing her mind. Here was something filled with promise and possibilities. The reward was honestly worth the price.

Suddenly the baby stiffened his torso, screwed up his face, and let out a loud, lusty wail. The noise startled his sister and she joined in with a distinct squalling of her own.

"I think they want their mama," Emma said nervously. She scurried to the bed and handed the infant into Gwen's waiting arms.

"And their papa, too," Dorothea added. Before Jason had a chance to say anything, she tucked the noisy bundle into his arms.

His startled look of panic was comical. The bedchamber door opened again and Jason's brother, Lord Fairhurst, entered the room. His resemblance to Jason was nothing short of remarkable, for they too were twins.

"I thought I heard a familiar sound," Lord Fairhurst said as he drew near. His expression grew wistful when he saw the babies and Dorothea imagined he was thinking of his own child born earlier in the year.

"I'm a father," Jason announced in a slightly dazed voice.

"Two at once, heh." Lord Fairhurst chuckled. "Excellent job, Gwendolyn. My heartiest congratulations to you both."

They all spent a few more minutes fussing over the infants before the babies began crying again.

"I think it's best if we leave the new parents alone," Carter said. He set one hand on Dorothea's shoulder and the other on Emma's and urged them out of the room. "There will be plenty of time to admire the new arrivals in the morning."

Once in the hallway, Emma hugged Dorothea tightly, then declared she was off to bed. Lord Fairhurst announced he would wait to see his brother again before retiring. As they walked toward the bedchamber that had been hastily prepared for them, Carter and Dorothea were met by the butler, who inquired if they were in need of anything.

"Please have a tray of food sent to our room," Carter requested. "I've already eaten, but Lady Atwood has not."

The exhaustion hit Dorothea full force once they entered

the bedchamber. She dismissed the maid and allowed Carter to help her into a white linen nightgown packed in her trunk. By the time the food arrived, she was yawning repeatedly.

"I'm too exhausted to eat," Dorothea declared when Carter tried to tempt her with a piece of roasted chicken. "All I want is a warm, comfortable bed."

To prove her point, Dorothea climbed into the four-poster bed, snuggling beneath the blankets. She heard Carter rustle about the room as he disrobed. Then he slid beneath the covers and tucked himself close to her. Dorothea sighed with contentment and wrapped herself in his arms, settling into the perfect position. She closed her eyes, willing sleep to come, and then suddenly her stomach growled loudly.

She felt Carter's hand lightly stroke the lower half of her arm. "You should eat something," he said. "It will make you feel better."

Shaking her head, she turned and nibbled on his broad chest. "I'm too tired to eat."

"Hmm. I could say something appallingly crude, but I will restrain myself."

"I appreciate it."

She set her lips to the hollow of his throat and placed a warm, wet kiss in that delectable spot. "I thought you were exhausted," he whispered.

She silenced him with another kiss, this one on the lips. Pressing herself closer, Dorothea felt an aching twist of desire settle over her. Carter reached down and drew her knee up, then positioned her on her side, facing him.

She could see the raw desire in his eyes, but it was mixed with tenderness. Dorothea sighed. He *did* care for her. The knowledge gave her hope that one day his heart would open completely and he would come to love her as much as she loved him.

The thought fueled the excitement in her breast. Her exhaustion disappeared as passion curled and knotted within her. Dorothea could not keep still. Her hands roved sensually over Carter's naked shoulders and chest, his muscles rippling beneath her fingers.

Wantonly she molded herself closer, raising her nightgown so she could savor the hard, hot feel of his body against her flesh. Twining her arms around his neck, she leaned in and whispered, "May I have a kiss?"

She didn't need to ask twice. His mouth descended, his lips clinging to hers with frantic desire. It seemed as if all the passion he held within had finally burst and come flooding out.

She moaned in his mouth and leveraged herself up, brushing her breast against the edge of his jaw. Breaking their kiss, he impatiently shoved her nightgown out of the way, seizing the budding nipple between his lips. His tongue circled the delicate peak languidly, then he pulled it into his mouth, sucking hard.

Desire, hot and heavy, spiraled through her body. She reached down, fumbling between their bodies until she found her prize, the thick, stiff shaft of his penis. Lovingly she caressed the satiny hardness, then reached lower, delving into the springy tufts of hair covering his heavy testicles.

"I want you now," she whispered in his ear, rubbing herself suggestively against him. "Please?"

Dorothea rolled onto her back and drew up her knees. Carter grinned and crawled over her. Eyes locked, he entered her swiftly, forcefully. The room echoed with her sharp exhalation.

"Christ. Did I hurt you?"

"No, no," she choked. "It's fine. It's more than fine. It's wonderful."

To emphasize her point, Dorothea rocked herself forward. Carter sighed heavily and closed his eyes. Her hands slid down to the taut muscles of his buttocks and she pulled him closer. The heat of his body surrounded her and the longing deep inside her rose to meet it.

She heard the bed creak in a deliberate, steady rhythm as he thrust forward. At her urging, he increased the pace, working faster, cramming himself deep inside. She felt every thrust, every sensation. It was glorious. In this moment they were more than husband and wife. They were lovers, joined in body, in heart, in spirit.

She felt his hand slid down to her hip, twisting its way between their joined bodies, his long fingers searching until he found her core. He stroked her moist, sensitive folds while his penis continued to thrust deep and hard inside her.

Their mating took on a new urgency and the world around her disappeared as the tremors within her began. She tangled her hands in his hair and cried out, clinging to him as her body rode a wave of pure, intense ecstasy.

She reached completion first, but Carter soon followed. She let out a soft sob of emotion and wrapped herself even tighter around him as he shuddered violently, spilling his warm, wet seed deep inside her.

They lay entwined for a long time afterward, Dorothea curled on her side, her head nestled on Carter's shoulder, his arms wrapped around her. Her mind drifted on a pleasant, hopeful haze as she contemplated their future. Surely if she could cobble enough of these moments together the emotional intimacy she craved so desperately would develop?

"It's been a good day," he whispered.

"Indeed. A memorable one." She smiled. "Happiness may be ever fleeting, but at this precise moment in time, I feel it deeply."

"As do I."

And with those comforting words, Dorothea fell into a deep, dreamless sleep.

It was a festive atmosphere the following morning around the breakfast table. Emma had risen early and gotten a second look at the newborn twins. She reported that Gwendolyn had spent a peaceful night, while Jason had spent his time scuttling between his wife's chamber and the nursery. According to Emma, they were all planning on sleeping in, well, at least until the twins decided they were ready for their next feeding.

Lord Fairhurst had sent word to his wife and parents, as well as his sister, Lady Meredith, and they were expected to arrive after lunch. As Dorothea consulted with the cook over the menus for the next few days, a message arrived for Carter.

"It's from my father," Carter explained after he read the missive. "He requests my immediate presence in London on a matter of grave importance."

"Do you think he has taken sick?" Dorothea asked worriedly. Though she still had a somewhat adversarial relationship with her father-in-law, she did not wish him ill.

"He mentions nothing of his health," Carter answered. "This appears to be some sort of family emergency."

Dorothea hastily scribbled a few notes on the menu she was consulting. "I can be ready to leave within the hour."

Carter shook his head. "There is no need for you to rush away. I know you wish to spend more time with your family. I will ride to Town and see my father and then hopefully return before nightfall."

Dorothea caught his wrist and met his gaze. "Are you certain?"

"I am. Besides, it will be faster traveling on horseback than in the carriage."

"Then, may I beg a favor?"

His eyes brightened with interest and she found herself blushing. "In my haste to get here yesterday, I forgot to bring Gwendolyn's gift from Ravenswood. There is a hat box from Mrs. Jenkins's millinery in my room. Would you kindly bring it back with you when you return?"

Carter blinked. "You can't mean that overly decorated bonnet that resembled a bowl of fruit?"

"The very same. I believe my sister deserves a hearty laugh after all she has endured."

Carter laughingly agreed, then left to make the arrangements for his departure.

Though the mood of the household was jubilant, Dorothea felt an odd sense of melancholy once Carter had gone. Knowing Gwendolyn and the babies were sleeping, Dorothea decided to take a stroll outdoors and enjoy the morning sunshine.

She followed several marked paths through the formal section of the gardens, then ventured down to the parkland. It was cool and comforting. She emerged from a shaded section of hedgerows and squinted against the sudden brightness of sunlight. It was then she noticed a figure in the distance walking purposefully toward her. A male figure. Carter?

Her heart lifted at the notion and she quickened her step. "Major Roddington?" Dorothea questioned as she drew nearer and caught a glimpse of the gentleman's face. "Goodness, this is a surprise."

"A pleasant one, I hope."

"Yes, of course." She smiled in welcome, though her mind still registered shock. What in heaven's name was he doing here? "Is there something specific that brings you to this area?"

He smiled, a crooked, mirthless grin. "Why, I am here to see you."

"Oh?" His odd manner, as well as his words, brought a queasy sensation to her stomach. She did not remember ever telling him specifically where Gwendolyn and Jason lived, nor did she tell him that she was coming here to visit them. Obviously he had followed her. But why? "Shall we go up to the house and partake of some refreshments?" she suggested.

Her nerve endings tingling, Dorothea stepped forward, but the major swiftly moved to block her path. "There's no need to disturb your sister's household. We have sufficient privacy here."

"Nonsense. We shall be far more comfortable sitting in front of a warm fire."

All trace of the major's smile vanished. "I'm afraid I really must insist that we not go up to the house."

Dorothea's initial instinct was to turn around and flee, but astonishment held her paralyzed. He was not overtly threatening, yet his strange behavior seemed so out of character, so unlike the kind, even-tempered, gallant gentleman she knew. She shifted her puzzled gaze to his face and he quickly looked away, but not before she caught the expression of uncertainty in his eyes.

What was this all about? Dorothea scowled, trying to ignore the shiver of anxiety curling in her chest. They were alone, isolated. If things did become ugly or out of hand, there was no one in the vicinity who could come to her aid.

"You are scaring me, Roddy," she declared on a shaky

breath. With feigned calm she once again attempted to walk past him, but he would not allow her.

"I apologize. I never wanted to bring you into this mess, but things have gone badly, very badly, and I need your help." His features went taut and he appeared to be struggling with a difficult choice.

Dorothea shook her skepticism aside and tried to tamp down her fear. And then the major began to speak, to tell her a tale so incredible she was speechless. His voice was low, emotionless, but his words were powerful. She heard every word, but understanding them was a slow, confusing process.

A part of her could not credit what he was saying, could not believe such an absurd tale. Yet as she stared intently into his face she clearly saw depths of misery in his eyes. At that moment, her hesitation dissolved. There was too much passion and pain for this to be a lie. Her eyes misted in sympathy, and Dorothea reacted instinctively, from the heart.

She reached her arms around Roddy's broad shoulders and pulled him into a comforting hug. For a long moment the major's arms hung at his sides and then slowly he moved them around her.

"You believe me?" he whispered.

"Of course!"

"Thank you."

Dorothea closed her eyes and held tightly, but suddenly Roddy was harshly wrenched away. She heard a masculine grunt of surprise, followed by the distinct crack of a closed fist connecting with flesh and bone.

Horrified, she watched the major recover his balance and stare in shock at the man who had so unceremoniously assaulted him.

"Carter!" Dorothea's heart lurched. "What are you doing here? I thought you left for London hours ago."

"Was that the plan, Dorothea?" Carter barked, his voice

panting with anger. "Wait until I was gone before meeting with your lover?"

"Don't be ridiculous. Even if there were any truth to that absurd notion, how would I have known you were leaving this morning? 'Twas the note from your father that summoned you away."

Carter's eyes blazed with stormy, self-righteous indignation. "If Roddington was lurking nearby, it would be easy enough to send him a message when the opportunity presented itself. The beauty of it all is that I would have been none the wiser, but my horse threw a shoe a few miles into my journey and I had to walk him slowly back to the house."

Dorothea tried to ignore Carter's icy disdain, but his accusations hurt. How could he believe that she would turn to another man when she so clearly loved him?

"Do you trust me so little?" she asked in a burst of vexation.

He ignored her and turned to Roddy. "'Tis a bit of a cliché to ask what you are doing with my wife, when my eyes clearly tell me," Carter said, his expression closed and thunderous.

"Stop it!" Dorothea shouted. "You have it all wrong, Carter! Major Roddington came to speak with me on a matter of extreme importance."

"What matter?"

"A personal matter."

"Between lovers?" Carter mocked.

"Between friends," Dorothea insisted.

Now what? Would the major reveal the truth to Carter? She cast her eyes over at Roddy and they exchanged a silent look.

A look that Carter caught, and it further enraged his already escalating temper. "God help me, I shall not be made a fool," he cried, lunging forward, fists clenched.

Heedless of her own safety, Dorothea placed herself between the two combatants. Carter tried to move her out of the way, but she would not budge.

"Give me one good reason why I should not blacken both his eyes?" Carter bellowed in rage.

"He is not my lover," Dorothea declared in a desperate tone. "Major Roddington is your brother."

Chapter Seventeen

Carter felt his body sway. He lifted his face to the sun and fleetingly closed his eyes, searching for divine intervention. Surely he had not heard Dorothea correctly. *My brother? Impossible!*

A gust of wind rustled the leaves in the trees, but he barely felt the breeze, barely felt the sting on his knuckles from the blow he had landed on Roddington's jaw.

"Carter?" Dorothea's voice was soft, questioning. A moment of utter silence settled over the garden and then he tilted his head from the sun's glare and looked directly at his wife. "You are out of your mind!" Carter exclaimed breathlessly. "How can he possibly be my brother?"

"Your half-brother." An uneasy expression flitted over her face. "It's the truth, Carter. That's why the major is here, to tell me."

"And you believed him!" Carter shook his head vigorously. "'Tis a lie. A bald-faced lie."

Dorothea's eyes glistened with unshed tears. "Please, Carter, you must listen to him before you make such a hasty judgment."

Why was she crying? For him or for Roddington? Carter

held up a commanding hand, hoping to silence her. He needed time to think. "I refuse to listen to this rubbish," he said forcefully, directing his words at the major.

Roddington folded his arms and stared back at him arrogantly. "I told her this is how you would react," he said bitterly.

"No!" Dorothea exclaimed quickly. "Carter is not like the duke. He is a reasonable man. He will listen. Tell him, Roddy."

Her fingers gripped Carter's forearm, pleading with him to stay. He resisted shrugging her off, though every instinct screamed at him to turn and storm away. She was so intent, so emotional. He would listen, refute the lies, and then leave.

It took a moment for the major to find his voice. "My mother was a genteel woman, the daughter of a knight," the major began. "She was raised in comfort, as befitting a lady, but when her father died he left debts for his only child. Once they were paid, there was very little money. She had no dowry and no desire to be a burden on her relatives, so she was forced to earn her way in the world."

Carter snorted. God help him if Roddington said his mother had become the duke's mistress. He would smash his nose, no matter how emotional Dorothea became. It was a well-known fact that the Duke of Hansborough adored his wife and was a loyal and faithful husband.

As if reading the direction of Carter's thoughts, Roddington scowled. "She found employment as a governess," he said with emphasis.

"My governess was a woman I remember fondly," Carter replied. "She was a family retainer who had also taken charge of my father when he was a boy. A female far too old to have given birth to you."

"I never claimed my mother was hired to care for you,"

Roddington shot back. "It was not her employer who violated her trust, who took advantage of a young, pretty, helpless woman. It was the duke who resided on the neighboring estate who seduced her and then abandoned her to bear the child alone and in shame."

"Who was your mother's employer?" Dorothea asked.

"Lord and Lady Alderton."

"That proves nothing!" Carter shouted, though he was rattled to hear the name. The Aldertons' estate bordered on Ravenswood Manor and his father was the only duke in that county.

Dorothea looked stricken. "Your father has a great dislike of Lord and Lady Alderton. Perhaps the origin of the feud has something to do with this mess."

Carter shifted his weight uncomfortably. Snippets of conversation came to mind. Things he had overheard as a child, words spoken in anger between his parents, words that made no sense, had no meaning. Until now.

"I certainly require more proof than the odd happenstance of Roddington's mother once being employed by the Aldertons," Carter declared. "If that's even true."

"That is easy enough to verify," Roddington countered. "As for the rest, as far as I know, my mother never publicly stated who had fathered her child. She only revealed the truth to me as she lay dying."

Dorothea set her fingers against her temple. "There must be some record, some kind of documents?"

"There were letters," Roddington said.

"Letters can be forged." Carter replied.

Roddington lifted both eyebrows. "How like your father, you are, Atwood. When I presented myself to him, those were his exact words."

"You've spoken with the duke?"

"Yes. Twice, actually." The major lowered his head and

stared at his boots. "The first time I was fifteen. I started for London the day after I buried my mother. It took me a few weeks to arrive and several days before I managed to waylay the duke on the street outside of his club.

"There I was, a green, naïve lad, grieving the loss of the only person who had ever loved me, facing the man who had ruined her life, ruined both of our lives. Yet try as I might, I couldn't hate him."

"What happened?" Dorothea asked.

"He gave me his card and told me to call at his house later that day. And so I arrived, filled with false hope and armed with the letters he had written to my mother.

"The duke listened intently to every word I spoke. Then he had a footman toss me out on the street. But before I left, he threatened to have me arrested and thrown into prison if I ever dared to breathe a word of these filthy lies."

The suppressed anger and resentment simmering deep inside Roddington was visible now. The major's eyes had gone dark and fierce. His hands were fisted tightly as if he would strike out if given the chance.

"Where are the letters?" Carter asked, watching the stiff set of Roddington's posture, trying to ascertain if he was telling the truth.

"He took them. I have no doubt they were tossed in the fire before my backside hit the street outside his fancy London mansion." Though he tried to keep his tone emotionless, the pain in Roddington's voice was raw.

"You said you have spoken with the duke twice," Dorothea prompted.

"I saw him again this morning. It was rather simple gaining access to the house now that I am known to the household staff."

The major stared pointedly at Dorothea and Carter realized what he meant. Roddington was frequently escorting her to society events. The duke's household would not think anything amiss if the major came to call. This was troubling. Carter wondered how deep the wounds of rejection went, how bitter the resentment tasted. Enough to do harm? To the duke?

Carter quickly surmised the urgent note from the duke he received this morning must be about the situation with Roddington. "What have you done?" Carter asked, his nerves suddenly on edge.

"Worried?" the major whispered in a combative tone.

Carter reflexively closed his fist, longing to have it connect with Roddington's face. He'd have liked nothing more than to see the major's eyes widen, his head snap back, and his arms flail as he tried to keep his balance and stay on his feet.

Yet something held his temper in check, kept his fists at his sides. "If you are here, running to my wife with your sorrowful tales, then the duke must have thrown you out. Again."

"Oh, no." Roddington's voice iced over. "I left of my own accord. The decision of how we proceed is now in the hands of the duke."

"What do you want?" Carter asked crisply, inwardly flinching at the sudden flash of light in the major's eyes. That did not bode well.

"I want the duke to stand before me and admit what he did, acknowledge that he acted in a heartless, dishonorable manner, and then I want him to beg my forgiveness, on behalf of my mother, for his cruelty and neglect."

A startled female gasp echoed through the silence. Carter turned and saw Dorothea clutching the fabric of her skirt as she tried to stop her hands from shaking. "The duke is a proud man," Dorothea ventured. "Even if your claim were proven, I am uncertain he would be agreeable to such a request."

Roddington drew his brows together quickly. "Then he will have to suffer the consequences of the scandal that will ensue."

Carter remained impassive, but the barb struck home. Roddington had done his research, he knew where to strike to inflict the greatest pain. The duke's pride in their family name and legacy was legendary. If there was one thing above all others the duke wanted to avoid, it was a taint to that noble lineage.

"You have far underestimated the duke's influence," Carter proclaimed. "He is a man respected and admired by society, by the Prince Regent himself. No one will take your side against him, no one will believe such lies."

"I am not a lad of fifteen anymore, to be so easily intimidated by the high and mighty Duke of Hansborough," Roddington sneered. "But more importantly, this is not a lie. And I have the document to prove it."

Roddy jammed his hat down on his head and urged his horse to a faster pace. The breeze hit him full-on, whipping at his face, but he ignored the sharp bite and crouched lower. The faster he rode, the faster he would reach Town and the faster this would all be over. Or would it?

He scowled. Should he have gone to Dorothea? The doubt of his actions twisted inside him, further confusing his thoughts. The confrontation with the duke this morning had gotten him nowhere but frustrated. Stalking down the halls of that palatial mansion, Roddy had wanted to smash his fist into something, knowing that pounding on something, or someone, was likely the only way he would gain any relief.

Instead, he had sent a message to Dorothea and been informed by the butler that she had gone to visit her sister. Uncertain what else to do, he had followed her to her sister's home. Given the distant relationship she seemed to have with her husband, he did not know that Atwood would be with her.

Roddy's scowl deepened. Why could he not simply walk away and forget the matter, let it go once and for all? The duke was never going to acknowledge his paternity. And really, what else did he want from the man? Money? No! To form a relationship, some sort of bond? Hardly.

Yet ever since he had been tossed so unceremoniously from that mansion when he was a lad, he had been obsessed with seeking vindication, and he knew in his heart he could never truly be content until he received the justice he felt he deserved. Not so much for himself, but for his mother.

He turned his horse sharply at the bend in the road, the muscles in his legs trembling with anger and hurt at the memory of his mother's sad, dispirited face. She was a frail, gentle woman who had been dealt a cruel blow in life, and as soon as he was old enough to understand, Roddy had sought to protect his mother from the censure they had lived under.

He had been a well-behaved boy, a model pupil, never complaining, never causing her a moment's anguish. Yet still she had suffered, for bearing a child out of wedlock, for proving herself unworthy in the eyes of those who sought to judge her circumstances.

Roddy could feel the sorrow rising in him, pushing next to the regret. When he arrived in London, his initial plan had been simple. He reasoned if he could gain Atwood's friendship, if he could prove himself to be a worthy man, then the marquess might support his claim, would aid him in making the duke take responsibility. Likewise, he had ingratiated himself with Dorothea, thus strengthening his ties to the family.

Like any intelligent military officer, Roddy had never underestimated the enemy. He had not underestimated the duke, who was as cold and hard and autocratic as Roddy believed, as chillingly cruel as he remembered from their one brief encounter so long ago.

What he had underestimated were his own feelings. The emotions he would feel toward Atwood, his half-brother, a strange mix of admiration and jealousy, a basic desire to be liked but, more importantly, believed. For Dorothea, he felt the genuine affection of friendship and the protective instincts of an older brother.

He wondered what their next move would be, then laughed out loud, knowing he had no idea what direction his own actions would take. He did not have in his possession a document proving the duke's paternity, because one did not exist. He had lied to Atwood and Dorothea to gain some time, to give more credence to the question he hoped he planted in their minds.

The letters detailing the relationship between his mother and the duke had taken from him, though he acknowledged they were hardly definitive proof. As Atwood had said, papers could be forged. The one remaining letter he had in his possession had been written by his mother the morning before she died, but it was more a puzzlement than proof. For though she wrote about him, the child she and the duke had created together, on the final line she admitted that she had misled the duke and she asked his pardon.

Not understanding what that could mean, Roddy had attributed those words to her illness, putting no credence in them. When he had so innocently given the duke those letters all those years ago, he had held this one back. Though it proved nothing, he could not destroy it, for it was all he had left of his mother.

How would this all end? With each mile closer to Town, Roddy began to realize that if this final attempt failed, he must somehow find the strength to live in the shadow of rejection. For if he did not . . . Roddy shook his head. The consequences did not bear thinking.

Dark clouds glowered overhead, suddenly threatening rain. Dorothea looked at Carter. His face was stony. She tried to imagine what he was thinking, feeling, but it was impossible.

"Do you think it is true?"

His voice was flat, emotionless. She inhaled deeply to steady her own rioting emotions. "I think it could be true. There are too many pieces that fit so neatly together. But more importantly, the major emphatically believes that the duke is his father and he is hell-bent on hearing those words fall from the duke's lips."

Carter grimaced. "Unfortunately, I agree with you, though in my mind I cannot credit such a tale. My father has always been so straitlaced, so proper. Having an affair with a governess? It smacks far too much of melodrama to be believed."

"What shall we do?"

He slowly let out a breath. "Go to London and speak with the duke. And then . . ." His voice trailed off and he shrugged.

Dorothea's heart ached as she watched the shadows move and shift across his handsome face. "I'm coming with you."

Something in Carter's chest twisted. He knew he should tell her it wasn't necessary, that he would handle the problem on his own, as he always had done. She deserved to be here, with her sisters, sharing in the happiness at the birth of the new babies.

But the words wouldn't come. Carter swore. He needed her. At this moment in time, when his world was turning upside down, Dorothea was the one constant in his life he could rely upon, the one individual he could trust to be honest and forthright.

She loved him. And he was a heartless rogue for taking advantage of that love, but he couldn't help himself. It was the only thing keeping him sane and focused at the moment.

While Dorothea gathered her things and said goodbye to her sisters, Carter went to the stables to arrange for their carriage to be made ready. He snapped at the stable hand when the man helpfully suggested it might not be best to drive in an open carriage in this threatening weather, then scowled at the sky as the dark clouds thickened.

"I'm ready!"

He glanced over his shoulder. Dorothea came bounding down the steps, her smile bright and full. She was dressed in a deep-blue traveling gown with a matching pelisse a shade lighter than the skirt. The ribbons in her bonnet sported the same shade of blue. The ache in his heart eased slightly.

They had driven a little over an hour when the first fat raindrop splattered on his shoulder.

"We should turn back," he said, as the drops began to fall steadily. "Or stop at the nearest inn."

"Nonsense." Dorothea shook her head emphatically. "'Tis only rain and might yet let up."

"If you catch a chill, I'll never forgive myself."

She wrinkled her nose. "Goodness, Carter, I'm not that delicate. And although you deem me to be a sweet, fluffy female, I assure you I will not melt in the rain."

The carriage dipped into a puddle, spraying water everywhere. He tightened the reins, but did not slow the pace. More drops of rain began to fall. The brim of his hat kept the rain from obstructing his vision, but if it kept falling at this rate they would be forced to stop.

He heard not a word of complaint from Dorothea. Not when her pelisse was so wet it turned a darker shade of blue, not when the rain trickling off the edge of her bonnet fell onto her already sodden skirt. She merely clutched his arm and huddled closer, trying to conceal the chattering of her teeth.

He looked over at her. She smiled with encouragement, her eyes warm and comforting, her lashes spiky with rain. Cursing beneath his breath, Carter stopped the carriage in the middle of the road. He handed Dorothea the reins, then jumped down from the curricle. His boots sank in the mud as he walked to her side.

"Why have we stopped?" she asked. "Is something wrong?"

A muscle bunched in Carter's jaw as he swung his cloak off his shoulders. "Here, take this," he insisted, enveloping her in the damp garment. "Your gown is nearly soaked through."

She shivered and shook her head. "But you'll freeze without it."

"Better me than you."

He meant it. She was his to hold and keep, to protect and care for, and he would do that as best he was able, as long as he had breath. The encounter with Roddington had left him feeling confused, powerless, yet with Dorothea beside him the weight pressing down on his shoulders did not feel as heavy. The least he could do was to see to her comfort, since he'd been enough of a fool to bring her out in this weather.

The rain had ceased falling by the time they arrived at

the duke's London home. Soggy, tired, and cold, they trudged upstairs to their suite. Carter insisted that a hot bath be prepared for Dorothea, then he retired to his own bedchamber to change.

He untied and pulled off his cravat, tossed off his coat and waistcoat, then yanked his damp shirt over his head. Dunsford, hovering near, fetched clean, dry garments from the wardrobe even as he clucked his tongue and lamented the condition of Carter's ruined clothing.

The sound of a feminine giggle and splash coming from behind the closed connecting door captured Carter's attention. He smiled. Dorothea must be in the tub. He imagined her luscious body, naked beneath a mountain of frothy bubbles, her cheeks flushed and warm from the steaming water. The urge to join her in that tub was a powerful enticement, but instead he toweled himself dry and dressed to meet with the duke.

Carter felt drained as he walked into his father's study, rather as if he had reached London on foot instead of riding in the carriage. It was as if a strange lethargy had taken over his body, making it hard to think, hard to concentrate. Visibly shaking off the mood, Carter strode forward. The duke was reading some papers when he entered, which he promptly put aside when he saw Carter.

"Damn, it took you long enough to get here."

"My horse threw a shoe. It took a while to make other arrangements."

"No matter. You are here now."

"Yes, as you commanded." Carter cleared his throat. This was harder than he expected it would be. "Major Roddington came to the Barringtons'. He's told me everything. I assume that was the reason you summoned me home?"

The duke gasped, paled. "He repeated those filthy lies to

you? Damn it all to hell, I'll have him arrested for slander and thrown into jail!"

Carter felt impatience rising inside him. "Is Roddington lying?"

"Yes!"

"He seems very passionate, very certain," Carter replied, the emotions storming through his head. He should have felt relief at hearing his father's denial, but though it was said with great conviction, to Carter's ears it lacked a ring of truth, a ring of certainty.

"I cannot account for the man's delusions."

"But why you? There must be some reason Roddington has drawn this conclusion."

The duke flicked a nervous glance at Carter, then shot to his feet. "Apparently his mother was employed by Lord and Lady Alderton."

"Yes, as a governess. Do you recall ever meeting her?"

The duke crossed his arms and stared haughtily down at his son. "Why would I be introduced to a governess?"

Carter shrugged. An excellent point. If anyone would have met the woman, it might have been his mother, for this was a female's domain. "Shall I make inquiries to the Aldertons regarding her tenure in their employ?"

"Good God, no! Alderton is a buffoon with a taste for gossip. He would like nothing better than to spread these horrific lies about me."

"If you don't wish to investigate this woman's past, then we should investigate Roddington."

"I've already done so."

Carter's eyes jerked up to meet his father's. "So soon? He told me he spoke with you this morning."

"Yes, well, it actually wasn't the first time he has darkened my doorstep."

The duke walked to the sideboard, poured himself a

generous measure of brandy, and took a long swallow. When Carter declined a portion, the duke refilled his own glass and took another long drink.

"He first appeared about ten years ago," the duke continued. "A gangly lad with a fiery temper and an outrageous tale to tell. I hired a Bow Street Runner to try to learn what I could, but he turned up very little. By then the boy had disappeared, so I thought the matter closed."

"But Roddington has been back in London for weeks," Carter said. "He's been in this house, he's escorted Dorothea to various social events. Hell, he came to my wedding."

"I barely caught a glimpse of him, was never formally introduced. How could I make the connection between that boy and the man everyone simply referred to as *the major?*" The duke closed his eyes and scrubbed his hand over his face. "I am too weary for all of this, Carter."

Carter blinked in surprise, then took note of the deep lines around his father's mouth, the slight dishevelment of his hair. "I am here to help," he said quietly.

"Thank you." The duke lifted his head. "I want you to contact Roddington. Offer him a substantial bank draft and send him on his way."

Carter stared at his father, shocked by his words. "Why?"

"Because that is the easiest and surest way to be rid of him."

"It seems illogical to encourage a man to engage in what amounts to nothing more than blackmail," Carter said. "Especially if there is no merit to his claim."

The duke's nostrils flared as a flush spread over his cheekbones. "I'm not a fool. Clearly the major's motivation is money. And while it is personally distasteful to succumb to such tactics, it is also the quickest way to solve this problem."

"He told me he has in his possession a document that will prove his claim."

A powerful emotion flickered over the duke's face and for a moment Carter thought he would break down. "The major is an opportunist looking for an easy way to make some money. I'm a wealthy man. If this is what it takes to be rid of him, then it is well worth the price."

A sharp pain shot along Carter's temple. His father never backed away from a confrontation, especially when he believed he was right. So why was he so eager to let Roddington best him?

"Giving him money will lend credence to his claim," Carter insisted. "I think it is a grave mistake. If he senses a weakness he will exploit it."

"He wants a scandal. I will do anything necessary to prevent one."

"Let him have his scandal," Carter argued. "We can weather the storm, brazen out the gossip, the snide, telling glances. The Season has nearly ended. By the time it begins again next year, this will no longer be such a juicy tidbit. The matrons of the *ton* will have found something new to draw their censure and disapproval."

The duke's expression turned distant. "I need for this to end."

Carter could see a bead of sweat forming on his father's neck. His eyes seemed unusually bright. Tears? Impossible. Unless . . . ?

"I will go to Roddington today," Carter responded. "He claims not to want any money, but I think I will be able to persuade him to take it."

The duke looked at Carter, his steely gray eyes sad and unfathomable. "I'm sorry you had to be involved in this mess."

"It affects you, Father. Naturally it would also involve me."

* * *

Dorothea was waiting when Carter emerged from the duke's study. She took one look at his ashen face and wordlessly took his hand, leading him to the drawing room. He heard her shoo away the footmen and leave instructions that they were not to be disturbed.

"It's true, then." Her words were a statement, not a question.

"He denies it."

She grasped his arm. "Yet you don't completely believe him, do you?"

"I don't know what to believe." Carter rubbed his forehead. He found it difficult to think with his mind so full of contradictions.

She slid her hand comfortingly up his arm and onto his shoulder. "How does the duke plan to handle this . . . um . . . delicate matter?"

"He wants to pay him off. Or rather, he wants me to pay Roddington off."

"Will it work?"

"Put yourself in Roddington's place. If you believed the duke was your natural father, would you take his money?"

Dorothea gnawed on her lower lip. "What are you going to do?"

"I'll speak with Roddington, as my father requested."

"I'm coming with you."

"No!" He grabbed her hands. "I need to do this on my own."

"I'm scared, Carter." She tore her gaze from his, her expression strained. "I'm worried that things might escalate into violence if you two are alone. My presence should keep the conversation civil."

"No."

"Carter, please."

Carter squeezed her hands, not liking that stubborn

tone in her voice. "I promise I shall do nothing to incite Roddington's anger. And no matter how I am provoked, I will keep my own temper in check."

He could see she was not entirely convinced, so he kept his expression firm. Finally, she sighed and nodded. "As you wish, my lord." Then she hesitated, looking down at their clasped hands. "Though the major is only half the problem, as you very well know."

Two hours later, Carter found himself knocking on a door in a run-down London neighborhood. It had not been difficult to find Roddington's direction.

"Yes?" A stoic, unfamiliar face peered out of the half-opened door.

Carter gazed levelly into the face of a man whose direct stare and stout bearing suggested military service. A comrade or servant? Honestly, it didn't much matter. Carter presented his card.

"The Marquess of Atwood to see Major Roddington. Is he at home?"

Revealing his identity put the man on even higher alert. He straightened his already squared shoulders as his mouth crumbled down in a frown. "The major's not here."

"Is he expected back soon? My business is of a personal nature and rather urgent."

"Ah, so now after all these years, it's urgent, my lord?" He favored Carter with a cold, appraising stare that Carter returned with equal measure. The question hung in the air.

The man blinked. "I'll let him know you've been here," he said gruffly.

Carter gave him a curt nod and turned around. He ducked his head under the low doorway as he exited the building, his mind in turmoil. For a full minute he stood on the street, trying to decide his next move. It was not a particularly fashionable neighborhood, but he had seen worse. Perhaps the duke was right, though. Perhaps all Roddington did want was money.

"Out slumming, Atwood?"

Carter relaxed at the familiar male voice. "Benton, what brings you to this part of Town?"

The viscount grinned. "I'll agree there's not much to recommend the area, but there is a superior tobacconist a few blocks away that I frequent."

"By any chance is there a decent tavern nearby?"

"I might know of one or two."

Carter grimaced. "Well, lead on, my friend. I find I have a great need for some strong libation."

Chapter Eighteen

"Tell me, Benton, what would you do if you discovered you had fathered a child?" Carter asked.

The viscount's head whipped around. "Christ's blood, what have you heard?"

Benton's face was white as a sheet. It took a moment for Carter to realize his friend thought he was referring to a child Benton had sired. Damn, no wonder the man looked so pale.

"Calm down, my friend. It's a theoretical question."

The viscount exhaled and slowly unfisted his clenched hands. "Bloody hell, Atwood. Questions like that can give a fellow a heart seizure."

"Sorry. Given the life we have both led, I suppose it's more than a rhetorical possibility."

"Damn right." Benton lifted his glass with a none too steady hand and took a long drink. "One is careful, of course, and takes precautions, but there's no guarantee. As far as I know, I have never gotten any female with child. And you?"

"What? No!" Carter felt his own hand begin to shake and he regretted ever starting the conversation. Something he probably would not have done if he had been completely sober.

"Well, it can't be Dawson," Benton mused. "The man's proper enough to be a vicar. No, make that a Catholic priest. Don't they take a vow of celibacy?"

The viscount signaled for another bottle of brandy. The luscious barmaid who brought it to their table lingered longer than necessary, tossing her long red hair and flashing her breasts practically beneath Benton's nose. The normally flirtatious viscount barely glanced at her.

"It's Roddington," Carter announced, when they were once again alone.

"Ah, army men. They have a hard life. Stands to reason they live it to the fullest. I wouldn't be surprised to hear he's left a trail of little soldiers across the Peninsula."

Carter shook his head, trying to clear his foggy brain. No, that wasn't right. "Roddington's not the father," he declared. "Roddington's the bastard."

Benton smiled amicably. "So I've heard. Still, one can't help but admire the man. He made his own way in the world, despite the disadvantages of his birth. There's opportunity for advancement in the military, but war is messy business. Thundering cannons, smoke and ash, corpses strewn on the battlefields. I wonder if I'd have the courage to so bravely acquit myself in battle."

A wave of confusion swirled in Carter's head. What the hell was Benton prattling on about—war and courage and battlefields? That had nothing to do with this conversation. "No, listen to me. Roddington is the bastard who claims the duke is his father."

"The duke? Which duke?"

Carter shot Benton a bleary-eyed glare. Even half-sotted, Benton could usually hold his own. They both could. It was a source of pride among them that they could keep their steps steady, no matter how much they had to drink. Well, except for the time they tripped and fell into a fresh pile of horse dung in the road. But that happened years ago, when they were still at Oxford.

Carter took another swallow of his brandy and tried to remember what he wanted to say. Hell, he must be far drunker than he realized. "Roddington claims my father is his father," Carter finally declared.

"The duke is whose father?"

"Roddington's."

Benton glared at him over the rim of his glass. "Surely you are joking."

Carter slumped forward dejectedly. "He denies it."

"Roddington?"

"No, the duke." Honestly, how difficult was this to understand?

Benton's eyes widened. "Frankly, I didn't think the old boy had it in him."

"I don't either. And yet . . ." Carter's voice trailed off as he stared forlornly into his now empty glass.

"Well, if I discovered I had a baseborn child, especially a son, I'd do all that I could to assist the poor bugger." Benton poured himself another portion, spilling more on the table than in his glass. "And I believe the duke would have done the same, illegitimate or not."

Carter nodded his head. Though the idea of his father being unfaithful was a bitter pill to swallow, he did agree that the duke would never have shirked his responsibilities. If Roddington was his child, the duke would have provided for him.

"Roddington claims he has proof of his paternity," Carter said. He reached for his brandy and saw not one, but two fuzzy goblets in front of him. Jesus, he was drunk.

Benton cocked a brow and peered at him though nearly

closed lids. "What sort of document would prove such a thing?"

"I have no idea." Carter frowned deeply and abandoned his attempt to lift his glass, either glass. "Do you think Roddington's bluffing?"

"Has to be," Benton concluded, his slurry voice authoritative. "You need to confront the major."

"I tried. That's where I was when I ran into you. At Roddington's rooms." Carter closed his eyes. "But he wasn't there."

"Shall we go back now? I'll come with you."

Carter felt a surge of gratitude. Hell, Benton was a damn good friend. 'Twas a real pity they weren't brothers. "I'm too drunk. So are you."

Benton slumped forward, then he raised his arm and beckoned the barmaid. "Coffee, my good woman. Pots and pots of it."

Despite reaching a modest level of sobriety a few hours later, Carter wisely elected to forgo a meeting with Roddington. At the viscount's urging, he stumbled into Benton's coach. A very sleepy footman opened the front door, showing no reaction at Carter's very early morning arrival home. With an apologetic smile, Carter handed the young man his hat and greatcoat and ordered him off to bed.

In his bedchamber, Carter found his valet dozing in a chair. Refusing his assistance, Carter likewise sent the protesting Dunsford to bed. Once alone, he shed his garments, leaving only his shirt and breeches. Crossing to the nightstand, he filled the porcelain basin with cold water, then plunged his head inside. The water had a bracing effect, and by the time he toweled himself dry, Carter felt relatively sober.

Barefoot, he crossed his room, walked through the spacious dressing room, and entered Dorothea's bedchamber.

The even sound of her breathing let him know she was asleep. Quietly he neared the bed, driven by a helpless need to see her.

For a long moment Carter simply watched her. The light from his single candle cast a warm, amber hue on her ivory skin. A section of her golden hair had come loose from her braid and was spread across the pillow.

Tempted by the sight, he reached for a fistful. Gathering it in his palm, Carter raised the silken tresses to his face and rubbed its softness against his cheek. The scent that was so uniquely Dorothea's filled his nostrils, permeated his soul.

His heart suddenly clenched. He could not put a name to what he was feeling, did not completely comprehend what she had come to mean to him. She was his wife, yet she was so much more—she was his partner, his mate.

He depended on her, trusted her, adored her as no other individual. He thought back and tried to remember when this realization had taken hold in his mind and then decided it wasn't a specific moment, but rather a collection of many that solidified her place in his heart.

After their time together at Ravenswood, he had returned to London determined to resume his activities as if everything in his life were the same, as if taking a wife had made no significant difference. He consciously shut her out of his life because keeping a carefully cultivated distance seemed the correct approach to a successful marriage, especially because her feelings for him were so strong.

He did not want to be the one who held all the emotional power in their relationship. It made him feel like a tyrant, a bully, to witness her vulnerability. So he had kept himself apart from her.

But the truth was that his days were dull without Dorothea in them. Her brilliant smile, her sexy saunter, her teasing words. When he was with her, the mundane seemed special, the ordinary important. He, a man who had always secretly mocked sentimentality, found himself feeling a great desire to be with Dorothea both in and out of bed.

Was that love? Carter sighed heavily.

Dorothea's eyes fluttered open. For a moment she stared up at him blankly, then she smiled as she recovered her wits. "I received your message saying you would be out this evening. I tried to wait for you, but couldn't keep my eyes open. Is it very late?"

Carter shook his head. Leaning close, he planted a kiss on her lips, a light, fluttering, brush against her softness. Pulling back far enough to see into her eyes, he studied her in silence for a long moment, his heart and mind rioting with revelations.

"I love you."

He said it plainly, quietly. No flourishes, no long speeches, no fancy, florid rhetoric. Simply, sincerely, and from the heart.

Her brow furrowed in confusion and he panicked, worried that after all this time he had done it wrong, that she needed a more passionate declaration, a more romantic setting. Should he have brought flowers? Jewelry?

Lacking any sentimental gifts, and the opportunity to obtain them at this point, he repeated the words. "I love you, Dorothea. With all of my being and all of my heart."

Her eyes were fully open now, round and wide with wonder. Carter wasn't sure if he had ever seen them so hopeful, so filled with joy.

"Oh, goodness."

She lifted her face toward him and their lips met. Softly, slowly at first, but then with a growing urgency. She was so beautiful, fitting in his arms so perfectly, his heart so completely.

They made love slowly, reverently. Every touch, every kiss held greater emotion, more meaning. There was passion, tempting and exciting, but it was tempered with an aching sweetness, a tenderness that came from the heart. From both their hearts.

When it was time for their bodies to be joined, Carter rolled on his back and urged Dorothea to climb on top of him. He wanted to give her the power of control, he wanted her to know that he would surrender himself completely to her.

The tips of her luscious breasts brushed against his chest. The sensual abrasion made his cock stand up harder as he ached to possess her. Her eyes were wicked and sultry when she lowered herself, sheathing his hardness fully inside. Wrapping his arms around her waist, Carter encouraged her movements, urging her to ride him hard and fast.

She braced herself on her knees and followed his silent commands, sweeping them both in a mindless passion. He tried to hold back his climax, to prolong the moment so he could capture it and hold it in his heart forever, but she was a temptress, undulating her hips urgently, pushing them both toward an explosive end.

The world receded to the edge of consciousness, straining the limits of his self-control. And then she leaned forward and whispered in his ear.

"I love you, Carter."

Release pounded through him. His hands dropped to her hips and he held her in place as he ground himself against her. She cried out, and he realized she was climaxing, too. He did nothing to stifle the shout of pleasure that came from his throat, and she joined him with her own keening cry.

Afterward, she slumped forward, a faint, drowsy smile

on her lips. He rolled to his side, then turned and laid his head beside hers on the pillow.

"I never dared to imagine it could be like this between us," Dorothea whispered. She pulled her bottom lip between her teeth, suddenly looking embarrassed. "I was such a fool to think that passion was all one needed in a marriage."

"Well, it was your passion that first intrigued me," he admitted with a grin. "And that thoroughly delectable first kiss."

"Carter!"

He cupped her face in his hands so he could look deeply into her eyes. "But you also told me that in the very best of circumstances, love comes after marriage. How lucky we are, dearest, to now be in those circumstances."

Her eyes turned soft, almost dreamy. "Somehow we managed to find our way into each other's hearts."

"Rather miraculous, is it not?"

"Yes, all things considered."

Her arms closed around his neck and he shifted his position so her head fell easily against his shoulder. Carter felt an almost obscene degree of contentment as he drifted off to sleep, but his mind was not totally at peace. He knew that in the morning, the problem of Major Gregory Roddington would still be with him, haunting and complex. Along with a phenomenal hangover.

Something was wrong with the duke, Carter decided as he glanced at his father. He had come into the morning room after Carter and Dorothea made their way down for a late breakfast, and joined them at the table. Though they had been living under the same roof, it was the first time the three of them had taken a meal together.

Beyond inquiring if the nasty business with Roddington had been concluded, the duke contributed nothing to the conversation, despite Dorothea's attempts to engage him. Instead, he gazed off in the distance, occasionally lifting his silver spoon and stirring it absently in his cup of tea.

Tea he had requested, but didn't drink. Because the duke disliked tea.

His father's obvious unease could of course be attributed to his distress over the Roddington mess, but Carter felt there was more to this agitation. And it worried him.

Carter knew his eyes were a trifle bloodshot, in part due to his heavy drinking last night, and he lacked the proper amount of sleep, thanks to several bouts of robust lovemaking with his darling wife, the memory of which brought a genuine, tender smile to his face. But even in this less than stellar condition, Carter could see that something was amiss with his father.

He caught the eye of the lone footman standing near the sideboard and nodded dismissively. The servant bowed and departed. Free from any prying ears, Carter turned to his father.

"Was there something you wished to tell me, sir?"

That brought the duke's head up. His expression shifted from denial to something startlingly different as he searched his son's face. "Actually, Carter, there is something."

The sound of a chair scraping against the hardwood floor distracted both men.

"I believe I need to consult with Cook about the evening's menu," Dorothea interjected. She rose hastily from her seat, but Carter reached over and clasped her arm.

"No. I want you to stay. You are my wife. You have every right to hear what my father has to say."

For an instant there was a flash of defiance in the duke's

eyes, but it soon faded, dulled by a quiet acceptance. "Carter's right. Please stay, Dorothea."

Dorothea resumed her seat and the duke continued. "I've been pondering it all night, trying to determine what Roddington hopes to gain by this nonsense, and I've yet to arrive at a sensible conclusion. From all accounts he is an honorable soldier, a man admired by many."

"Roddy is doing this, Your Grace, because he believes that you are his father," Dorothea said softly.

The duke's fingers gripped the edge of the dining table. "And what do you believe?"

"That someone is misinformed as to the truth," she answered.

The duke glowered. "Me?"

Carter reached protectively toward his wife. "Dorothea is not accusing you of anything, sir." He cleared his throat. "But the question needs to be asked. Is there any possibility this could be true?"

The faraway look returned to the duke's eyes. For several ticks of the clock he stared at Carter without any discernable expression on his face.

"Actually, I did know Emily Roddington," the duke finally admitted, his voice tinged with its customary sharpness. "We had a very complicated, unique relationship. It began as a friendship. An unlikely one, I'll grant you, but we were both lonely and unhappy, and misery does love company.

"She was a sweet woman, well, a girl really. Kind, thoughtful, compassionate." The edge was gone now, replaced by a wistful tone. "I was going through a difficult time in my life. Your mother and I were at odds over everything, the estates were in poor financial condition, the crops had failed for several years, and there were problems with the investments my father had made. There were days when I felt as though I were drowning beneath all that responsibility. Emily would listen to my difficulties without censure or criticism, would encourage me in my attempts to solve them. She was a good listener, someone who never sought to judge me."

"Did you love her?" Dorothea asked.

The duke's expression grew serious. "In a way. As a trusted friend and confidante. It was never a romantic relationship. I loved my wife, even though at the time we could barely be in the same room together without getting into some kind of ridiculous argument. I vowed to remain true to her, in the tradition of all Dukes of Hansborough."

"But you failed," Carter croaked.

The duke looked from him to Dorothea, then back again. "Once," he insisted, his voice straining with emotion. "It only happened once. It started from an embrace, a gesture of comfort, but somehow . . ." The duke's voice trailed off in confusion, as if he still did not understand how it had happened. "Emily's guilt was nearly as strong as my own. She resigned her position at the Aldertons, which greatly annoyed them, and left the county by the end of the week.

"I heard nothing of her until a year later, when a letter arrived. She told me that she had given birth to a child, our child. Her family had taken her in and she was being well treated, well cared for by them. She asked for a small stipend to be sent through my lawyer so she could be assured the child would have some financial security. I made arrangements for the funds to be deposited at once, providing considerably more than requested.

"I wanted to do more for Emily, much more, but she would not allow it. In that letter, she begged me to let the matter drop, to leave her in peace, and as much as I wanted to protest, I felt I had no right to deny her wishes."

A chill swept Carter as he struggled to accept the truth of his father's words. "Then Roddington is your son."

"No." The duke shifted his eyes toward him. "He is not mine."

Fury flashed through Carter, burning away his shock. He understood how Roddington must have felt when he confronted the duke, wanting only to hear the truth. "How can you possibly deny it?"

"Because Emily wrote that the child she gave birth to was a girl."

The silence in the room was all-consuming. Dorothea drew an audible breath as time slowed to a crawl. She wrapped her hand around Carter's, trying to offer some degree of comfort, for she knew his heart must be filled with anguish and uncertainty.

The silence of the room was finally broken by the sound of a door slamming, followed by an oath. There was a raised, angry voice and the sound of footsteps charging through the lower rooms of the house. Startled, they all turned to the door as a tall, muscular man crashed through it, dragging two young footmen with him.

Dorothea screamed and Carter leapt protectively in front of her. The two servants tried to wrestle the intruder to the ground, with little success. One footman's powdered white wig had been knocked askew, and there was a thin trickle of blood running down the nose of the other.

"What is the meaning of this?" the duke snapped.

No one answered. A third footman joined in the efforts, and they managed to contain the man's forward momentum. They dragged him, kicking and bucking, to his feet and were attempting to hustle him from the room when Carter yelled. "Wait! I know this man. He's Roddington's servant."

"Julius Parker, my lord," the man acknowledged, his eyes glittering with desperation. "I'm here about the major."

"Release him," Carter commanded, and the three servants reluctantly let go.

Parker tugged down his jacket and straightened his shoulders. "There's been trouble and I've got nowhere else to turn. The major's gone missing. I went to the pub looking for him earlier, and one of the barmaids told me there'd been a fight. A nasty group of blokes started brawling, and the major landed in the thick of it. Four men against one."

"Was Roddy the one?" Dorothea asked with dread.

"Aye. But that's not the worst of it. They dragged him out of the tavern after they knocked him out, and the barmaid said she heard them laughing about the money they would earn when they turned him over to the navy."

"Impressment?" Carter frowned. "That's been outlawed for several years."

Parker's nostrils flared. "When the need is there, laws mean nothing to some, even those in His Majesty's Navy."

"Perhaps the woman was mistaken," Dorothea suggested. "Perhaps the major has gone somewhere of his own accord."

Parker shook his head adamantly. "He's never been gone this long without telling me. And anyway, if he had left Town of his own free will, he would have taken this with him."

The servant reached into his pocket and pulled out a piece of parchment. It was worn and faded, the ink smudged. Since she was the nearest, Dorothea gingerly accepted the missive. Squinting hard, she read the salutation. "'Tis written to you, Your Grace."

With a snort of annoyance, the duke glanced down at the letter, but his eyes soon grew wide. "It's penned in Emily's hand."

No one stirred as the duke read the short note. When he finished, he lifted his head. Dorothea swore her heart skipped a beat, for the duke looked as if he had just taken a sharp blow to the gut.

"She begs my understanding and forgiveness for her lie," the duke whispered, despair on his face. "She thought it best to keep it from me, but as she neared her death, she reconsidered and wanted me to know the truth. The child she bore was not a girl, it was a boy."

"Roddy?" Dorothea choked out.

"Yes. The major is my son."

The duke's words hung in the air, and then the realization seemed to hit Carter full force. He sprang toward his father, his expression urgent. "We must help him." Carter turned to Parker. "Do you have any idea where Roddington was taken?"

"There's only one naval ship in port. I tried to talk my way on board, but got nowhere. That's why I'm here. I figured a man with a title would have a better chance."

All eyes turned to the duke.

He shook himself visibly out of his stupor. "Have the coach brought around immediately," he commanded, motioning for Carter to follow. "We're going to the docks."

Curses and shouts followed in the wake of the duke's carriage as it was driven through the London streets at a reckless speed. Pedestrians and vehicles alike scrambled to avoid getting run down, for it was obvious the large black coach would give no quarter. The three male passengers inside careened from side to side, yet miraculously kept their seats.

The duke periodically thrust his head out of the window,

demanding that the coachman drive faster, agreeing to a safer pace only when the pungent, briny odor of the sea assaulted their nostrils.

If the circumstances had not been so grave, Carter might have broken into a grin. His father was in prime ducal form as he led the charge up the gangplank and onto the deck of the ship, eyes blazing. The young sailor standing watch flushed a molten, blotchy red as he tried in vain to stop them.

The officer who was called to assist was soon reduced to a similar state, visibly wilting under the duke's verbal assault. It began with a threat to have him stripped of his rank and dismissed in disgrace from His Majesty's Navy and ended with a promise to have the poor fellow transported to a penal colony. Clapped in irons.

Roddy appeared on deck two minutes later.

Carter's stomach rolled with concern when he first saw him. The major's left eye was swollen and his bottom lip split, but he was able to stand on his own and walk without any visible effects.

Roddington's face registered surprise when he saw who had secured his release. For an instant he looked as if he might reject the help, but the alternative was obviously unthinkable.

"My coach is waiting," the duke announced.

If not for the presence of his servant, Carter doubted that Roddington would have gotten into the coach. Whatever Parker said tipped the scales, and as the servant climbed up on top of the box next to the driver, the major placed himself on the seat beside Carter. The duke was already regally situated on the opposite seat.

Roddington said nothing on the ride back. But he listened.

* * *

Dorothea had practically worn a path down the center of the drawing room carpet by the time she heard the front door open. Forgoing any attempt at dignity, she fairly flew down the staircase just in time to catch the sight of the duke and another man disappearing into his private study.

"Carter?"

The marquess turned and smiled at his wife, his face weary, yet pleased. "Everything is fine, my love."

"Was that Roddy? Did you find him?"

"Yes, thank God. I vow the duke would have torn the ship apart plank by plank if they had not produced him when they did."

"And now?"

Carter shrugged. "It wasn't easy, but the duke persuaded Roddington to come here."

"Is he staying?" Dorothea asked hopefully.

Before Carter could voice his opinion, the study door opened and the major strode out. He halted in mid-step when he saw them, his eyes lowering a fraction.

"I believe I owe you both an apology," the major said sheepishly. "I was far from honest when we first met, and that I truly regret."

"No matter," Carter replied. "We understand the circumstances were difficult for you."

Dorothea moved forward and hugged him. "Will you stay for a while? As you may have noticed, we have plenty of room. I vow there are more bedchambers in this house than I can count."

The major slowly shook his head. "I can't. But I thank you for the offer."

Dorothea gave him another hug, wishing there was something she could do or say to change his mind. It seemed so very sad to be losing him now that they knew the truth.

Carter extended his hand. After a moment's hesitation, Roddy took it. Dorothea's eyes welled with tears. How very different both their lives would have been if Emily had not lied. Carter would have had the brother he always craved and Roddy the family he needed.

"Do you have any idea where you are headed?" Dorothea questioned as they walked to the front door.

"None at all."

Roddy smiled, and she could see that a weight had been lifted, a burden destroyed. For that at least, she was grateful.

"Will you at least write to us?" Carter asked.

"I'll try."

And with that, Roddy turned and walked away.

"We'll be arriving at Ravenswood shortly, my dear. Turn around so I can fasten the back of your gown properly."

Dorothea shifted her head lazily and glanced at her husband. He sat beside her in the coach, not a hair out of place, not a wrinkle in sight, every button neatly and properly fastened while she was sprawled next to him, her garments in complete disarray.

How did he manage it?

Not ten minutes earlier they had been locked in a carnal embrace, with Dorothea's skirts bunched up around her waist and Carter's coat, waistcoat, cravat, and shirt tossed on the floor. They had been greedy for each other, straining and quivering, a tangle of devouring kisses, sensual caresses, and exploding passions.

Their bodies had swayed with the movement of the carriage, heightening the intensity of their lovemaking, but it had been the tender words of love Carter whispered in her ear that made the experience truly remarkable for Dorothea.

"If I had known that being ravaged inside a moving coach was so incredibly satisfying, I would have insisted that we do this the first time we journeyed to Ravenswood," she said, trailing her finger over the sculpted planes of her husband's cheek and jaw. Goodness, he was a handsome man.

"That was my fault," Carter replied with an easy grin. "I misjudged you, something I vow to never do again."

She smiled, a deep sense of happiness rippling through her. She presented Carter her back and he deftly buttoned her gown. The carriage slowed, turned, and bounced over a rut. The movement brought Dorothea's attention to the window.

The manor house came into view and she felt a jolt of excitement. By the time the carriage rumbled to a halt at the front door she was nearly bouncing in her seat.

"We're home," she announced.

Carter descended from the carriage first, then turned and lifted her out. Dorothea took a deep breath and savored it all. The warmth of the sun, the welcome in the servants' smiles, the joyful barks of her darling puppy—oh, my, he had grown.

But what she cherished most of all was the love in Carter's eyes.

Epilogue

A year later

The celebration for the Duke of Hansborough's sixtieth birthday started the London social Season with a bang. It was by far the most sought-after invitation in anyone's recent memory. Favors were called in, alliances forged, and begging of proportions heretofore unheard of were employed as people jockeyed to have their names included among the guests. Those lucky enough to receive one of the exclusive invitations crowed about it for weeks, knowing they had secured their position as one of the *ton's* elite.

A dinner party hosted by the duke's son and daughter-in-law, in their new London townhome, preceded the dazzling ball. Only family and close friends were included, and many of those excluded expressed true regret at being denied the opportunity to view the interior of the house, which was reported to be the most tastefully decorated home in London.

When it was confirmed that Major Gregory Roddington was indeed among those guests, the rumor mill began turning with an almost unstoppable force. Most declared the major's return to England and his appearance at the dinner was tantamount to proof that he was in truth the duke's natural son.

In the opinion of many, the fact that none of the duke's family would either confirm or deny those rumors lent further credence to its truth, making it an even juicier tidbit for the gossip-loving matrons.

"How ironic that Roddy chose to make a lengthy sea voyage after you saved him from being impressed into the navy," Dorothea joked to Carter when the gentlemen rejoined the ladies in the drawing room once they had finished with their port and cigars.

Carter laughed. "I can assure you, it was a far more pleasant adventure for him to travel in the comfort of a well-appointed cabin than swabbing the deck of a ship."

"I'm just so happy that he is back. He seems content, more settled," Dorothea observed. "We spoke at length the other day about the shipping business he plans to start."

"Father and I have both encouraged him to pursue the venture, though he will accept no financial support," Carter said in a frustrated tone.

Dorothea shrugged. "Then you must offer to be his partner."

The marquess lowered his chin and raised his eyebrow. "A nobleman in trade? Shocking."

"You could be a silent partner."

"*I* could manage it. However, my father would find the arrangement impossible. The duke silent? Highly unlikely."

Dorothea giggled, knowing her husband was right. Though he had softened some of his harsher edges, it was impossible for the duke to keep his opinions to himself, especially when it came to his family. She was just so very pleased that the duke considered her, and now Roddy, a member of that family.

"I think Roddy is at last becoming comfortable with this relationship," Dorothea observed. "Though he again said he does not want the duke to publicly acknowledge him."

"I know, and it frustrates the hell out of Father."

The couple exchanged a look, each knowing the other believed the major was doing this to purposely thwart the duke.

"Turnabout is fair play, is it not?" Dorothea said with a smile.

Eyes twinkling in agreement, the marquess took his wife's hand. They made their way to a cluster of guests seated comfortably before the drawing room windows and joined the lively conversation.

Gwen sat on an elegantly upholstered chair, with Jason lounging on the arm. The twins were sleeping soundly upstairs, two happy, healthy cherubs, loved and spoiled by all. Emma was standing by a cluster of guests, the traces of paint beneath her fingernails only slightly visible. She waved them energetically as she spoke with Lord and Lady Dardington. Every few moments, Viscount Benton would interrupt, adding a comment, and the volume of laughter increased.

"Benton seems in fine form tonight," Dorothea remarked to her husband.

"Yes, and speaking of Benton, I don't like how much attention he is paying to Emma," Carter grumbled as he put his hand on her shoulder.

Dorothea looked at him in surprise. "She is painting his portrait. Naturally they are together often."

"But is she always properly chaperoned?"

Dorothea hesitated. "I'm at most of the sessions."

"Most, but not all." Carter surveyed her levelly. "And I

caught you napping at the last one. You can hardly be an effective chaperone if you are asleep."

Heat flooded her cheeks. Dorothea dipped her head. "I cannot help my sudden tiredness."

"I know." His gaze drifted down to the slight swell of her belly before possessively settling his hand over her burgeoning womb. "This child will put gray in my hair long before it arrives," he declared, tempering his words with a loving smile.

Dorothea sighed happily, basking in Carter's love and affection. "I think you shall look very distinguished with silver at your temples."

"Hmm. Between the baby and Emma, my hair will be stark white within the year."

"Oh, stop being so vain." Dorothea's mouth quirked. "Our child will be a perfect angel, the envy of every parent in England. And Emma has no serious interest in Benton, beyond putting his likeness on canvas. She told me that his classic looks combined with his brooding charm are an irresistible lure to her creative muse. She is striving to capture the essence and energy of his masculinity in a way that no other artist had ever attempted."

"Good Lord, if she weren't so talented, I would refute that statement as a bunch of pure rot," Carter muttered.

"I repeat, there is no cause for worry. Benton is far too old for her."

"In my experience, any female between the ages of eighteen and eighty is a prime target for Benton's charms."

"He would not dare try to seduce Emma," Dorothea declared. "He has too much respect for you."

"Well, he does appreciate my skill with a sword and pistol. Perhaps it would be a good idea to remind him of that next week. I'll arrange for an afternoon of sport and bring Roddy along, too. His prowess with a sword is near legend."

Dorothea rolled her eyes. This protective streak of Carter's was normally very charming, but he could carry it a bit far. "Being around Benton is good practice for Emma. She has just turned seventeen and this will be her first Season. If she can learn to handle a rake of Benton's caliber, then she'll easily deal with any other handsome rogue. Now, enough about Emma. We have guests."

Carter groaned. "I finally understand what Dardington meant about having daughters. Promise me you shall only give birth to sons, my dear."

"Ah, that would be a birthday gift your father would long cherish."

They both laughed. Carter dipped his head and Dorothea curved herself into him. Heedless of their guests, the marquess lowered his face and pressed a lingering kiss on his wife's tender lips.

"I told you, Benton." Emma's voice rang out in triumph. "It's a love match!"

Dorothea's eyes flew open. Embarrassed, she tried to pull away, but Carter's arm was holding her firmly in place. He finished the kiss at leisure, his eyes smiling down at her, radiant with love.

The sight brought an incandescent flash of joy through Dorothea's entire body. Emma was right. Dorothea hadn't been looking for love in marriage, but oh, my, she had certainly found it.

ABOUT THE AUTHOR

Adrienne Basso lives with her family in New Jersey. She is the author of ten Zebra historical romances and is currently working on her next, to be published in 2011. Adrienne loves to hear from readers and you may write to her c/o Zebra Books. Please include a self-addressed stamped envelope if you wish a response.

Romantic Suspense from
Lisa Jackson

See How She Dies	0-8217-7605-3	$6.99US/$9.99CAN
Final Scream	0-8217-7712-2	$7.99US/$10.99CAN
Wishes	0-8217-6309-1	$5.99US/$7.99CAN
Whispers	0-8217-7603-7	$6.99US/$9.99CAN
Twice Kissed	0-8217-6038-6	$5.99US/$7.99CAN
Unspoken	0-8217-6402-0	$6.50US/$8.50CAN
If She Only Knew	0-8217-6708-9	$6.50US/$8.50CAN
Hot Blooded	0-8217-6841-7	$6.99US/$9.99CAN
Cold Blooded	0-8217-6934-0	$6.99US/$9.99CAN
The Night Before	0-8217-6936-7	$6.99US/$9.99CAN
The Morning After	0-8217-7295-3	$6.99US/$9.99CAN
Deep Freeze	0-8217-7296-1	$7.99US/$10.99CAN
Fatal Burn	0-8217-7577-4	$7.99US/$10.99CAN
Shiver	0-8217-7578-2	$7.99US/$10.99CAN
Most Likely to Die	0-8217-7576-6	$7.99US/$10.99CAN
Absolute Fear	0-8217-7936-2	$7.99US/$9.49CAN
Almost Dead	0-8217-7579-0	$7.99US/$10.99CAN
Lost Souls	0-8217-7938-9	$7.99US/$10.99CAN
Left to Die	1-4201-0276-1	$7.99US/$10.99CAN
Wicked Game	1-4201-0338-5	$7.99US/$9.99CAN
Malice	0-8217-7940-0	$7.99US/$9.49CAN

Available Wherever Books Are Sold!
Visit our website at **www.kensingtonbooks.com**